Sweet Dreams

Sweet Dreams

In the Mind of a Serial Killer

A Thriller by

January Valentine

Printed in the United States of America

ISBN 10: 0984957359
ISBN 13: 978-0-9849573-5-4
ISBN 13: 978-0-9849573-6-1 EBOOK

Library of Congress Control Number 2012947903

Book Design by Victoria Valentine
Edited by Susan Sabia
Proofreading by Phaedra Valentine
Song Lyrics by Victoria Valentine, *The Next Life (2002)*
Cover Art by Amanda R. Tucker
Sweet Dreams is available in Kindle version and as an audiobook on
Amazon and Audible. http://amzn.to/1uIvlXK

Water Forest Press Books
PO Box 295, Stormville, NY 12582
waterforestpress.com

"We serial killers are your sons, we are your husbands, we are everywhere. And there will be more of your children dead tomorrow."
—Ted Bundy

What makes a man? What makes a monster?

— Life

is this how you found me
crawled deep down inside me
dragged me thru this place
no chance to escape

PROLOGUE

SLEEPING PRETTY

She sat before her dressing table, smooth legs tucked beneath a padded bench, toes curled into the carpet. Her finely tapered fingers guided soft bristles through her hair. In a satin storm her tresses rained down, shimmering like moonlit waves in the glow of a table lamp.

"Enough grooming for one night." She sighed.

Patting a yawn she rose, shrugged a shoulder at a time, letting her floral robe pool onto a chair. She slathered hand cream from elbows to fingertips, taking care to saturate her perfect cuticles, then stepped across the room where she dropped onto her bed.

Beneath only a sheet, taut and sleek she stretched, her full lips arcing into a wider yawn, then tapped on the sound machine beside her. Almost every night, nature lulled her to sleep. Tonight she needed no lulling. A grueling shift at the salon had worn her out, both physically and emotionally. Bitching clients. Groping manager. . . he has to stop. . . talk to him tomorrow. . . Before she could envision a kick to his groin, which she would have loved to have done, which she should have done, her eyelids sealed shut and her chest pulsed in gentle rhythm.

In slumber so deep, pounding surf, thundering winds, went peacefully undetected. She didn't hear the footsteps either, as heavy boots met the rungs of the ladder. Slowly, one boot, then another, until both surfaced on the rickety fire escape, two stories high and rusted to the weathered brick outside her one bedroom apartment.

A window crept open. Like a phantom, dark and fluid, the figure poured over the ledge, seeped into the room, ambled to the bed. A knee dug into the mattress. One glove balanced beside her while the other waited for her eyes to bulge, to water, to plead. A scream stalled in her throat, and when she stopped breathing, the killer held a wilting red rose to her parted lips, dropped a note on her blood soaked pillowcase.

She lay in silence, but the ocean beside her body raged as if its own fury had been defiled. Before leaving the bedroom, and the slaughtered woman, the killer was drawn to the elemental sounds. Mouth slack, the head angled. Wide and dry, the eyes stared. The gloves snatched up the machine emitting melodic chaos, shook it to death, brought it to an ear, and when static roared, the killer flung it against the wall, where it also lay in silence.

There are Seasons and There are Reasons ...
and then there is, The Inevitable,
Troy Norton

put your lips on mine
sigh to my soul
send me your pain
breathe all the love you know

ATLANTA

When Leo left the coroner's office, his eyes stung with gathering tears sharper than the shafts of afternoon sun bouncing off the sidewalk. Squinting, he popped on a pair of Ray-Bans and crossed the four-lane street, dodging heavy traffic. He'd catch a cab, make it to the airport by five, and be back in Baltimore in time to watch a game before collapsing into bed. He needed something to take his mind off what he'd just seen.

It was autumn. Lazy clouds dotted a bright blue sky, and within an hour dusk would creep across the horizon. The city was a picture postcard, but a beautiful woman wasn't enjoying the day, or the scenery. She was stretched out on a slab in the building behind him, stiffer than the knot inside his chest.

When the file crossed his desk back in the Baltimore Prosecutor's office, Leo couldn't believe his eyes. Rather, Leo didn't *want* to believe the girl in the photo was Gina. So he had flown to Atlanta to convince himself the familiar name on the manila folder was actually the Gina he knew — had lusted for — but had never made love to.

The coroner who led him into the morgue was a middle-aged schlep, bushy-haired, prematurely gray with overworked eyes and matching green scrubs.

"She's in the cooler. And we have a full house right now. Hope you're not squeamish," he apologized. "The city keeps promising to hire help. But that's been going on for years now." The coroner shrugged. "Still not enough of us. For the traffic going in and outta this place, we need a dozen more." He stuck out a hand streaked with veins, "I'm Andy, by the way. Forensic Pathologist."

With a firm shake, Leo nodded. "Hell of a job. I'm Leo."

"Yeah. I know who you are. We don't usually get visits from district attorneys. Especially from outta state."

"Hmm." Leo grunted, shrugged his brows and bobbed his head once.

Leo felt for the man. He was obviously under a lot of stress. Leo also felt for Gina, and braced himself for the viewing of her body. However, nothing could have prepared him for what he would encounter during his twenty minute visit. The most gruesome twenty minutes of his life — so far. . .

After passing through two sets of swinging doors, Andy ushered Leo down a long, hospital-like corridor to the threshold of the autopsy suite where Andy nudged a floor pedal with his gray running shoe and a brutish door automatically slid to the right, baring the chilling interior.

They entered the spacious cooler, or as Andy proclaimed, "This is the crypt."

The morgue was one big refrigerator. Bodies littered the room, resting on gurneys shoved flush against two side walls. A narrow pathway in the center offered just enough space for an average sized adult to shimmy through without colliding with the gurneys, or their wrapped contents.

Leo wasn't expecting a grand tour of the place, but he got one. "See those wall shelves?" Andy stopped walking and pointed with a steady hand, exposing a slice of bulging gut when his scrub shirt strained. "Extra storage." He motioned to steel-braced metal racks suspended five feet above the floor, ascending almost as high as the ceiling.

"The ones piled with plastic bundles." Leo's comment

sounded droll. His hands were planted in his trouser pockets, and as he pivoted, his eyes narrowed. "Christ. It's like an industrial warehouse."

"Wall to wall," Andy said. "When we run out of room — well that's what happens when funds aren't allocated." His thin mouth drew into a scowl, tugging at the corners of his already drooping eyes. "Politics. Money for everything except where it's really needed."

"Tell me about it." Leo shook his head. "We go through the same shit. Not with morgues, per se, but the city in general. Too much skimming and waste. Nothing left for community." Thinking of local politics, Leo soured. The citizens he worked hard for always seemed to get the shaft.

Leo swore the stale air inside the crypt was tainted, and found it difficult to inhale rhythmic breaths. "Full house." He couldn't seem to clear his mind of sarcasm. "Damn. Doesn't seem to be much respect in packing them like bundles onto storage shelves." His mouth felt dry. He thought of the glass of scotch he'd grab as soon as he left.

"Not usually referred to that way, but yeah, I guess you could call them bundles. Those are the postmortems. They're waiting for a funeral director to pick them up," Andy explained as he once again began to make his way down the path. "The ones on the gurneys are scheduled for autopsies." As he walked, Andy's fingers fidgeted almost constantly, either rubbing his nose, scratching an ear, smoothing his hair, or pointing out the dead.

It was then that Leo's gaze, and mind, absorbed the morgue's layout, and silent occupants. From beneath form-fitting sheets, a variety of feet in an assortment of colors ranging from white, brown, purple, to gray, protruded deliberately; toe tags their only identifiable labels of death.

Leo focused on the mounded gurneys. *Like a crowded airport*, he mocked the morbid scene. The feet didn't point to the ceiling, but in death eased east and west, and a taunting juxtaposition crossed his mind. *Idling jets, stuck on a runway, waiting their turn to take off for the friendly skies . . . more like the unknown.*

"Feel the cold?" Andy asked. "Goes right through you. We keep the refrigeration set at thirty-five degrees."

Beads of perspiration formed along Leo's hairline. "You okay?" Andy asked.

With a rapid heart rate, and expanding lump in his throat, Leo nodded. Although the epitome of macho, he was human, and certain things still had the ability to penetrate his tough outer layer. "I have to admit. This place is creepy. Makes my job look a hell of a lot better."

Andy chuckled. "Eh. You get used to it. This place is like a conveyor belt. They come in. They go out. There's no focus on who they are, who they were. They're just part of a job that somebody has to do. We try for a twenty-four hour turnaround time. But it doesn't always happen," Andy explained while pulling on the lobe of his ear. "If they're here too long, or arrive too decomposed, we need to store them in the freezers." He motioned to a freestanding unit in the corner. "Even at this temp, decomposition's quick, you know?"

"Rich. Poor. Doesn't matter. I guess in here, all men are equal, huh?" Leo's stomach began to unwind as the initial shock wore off.

"That's right. This is one of the few places where money doesn't matter. No preferential treatment here. No politics." Andy smirked, then his face went blank. "You know. I can't seem to locate your friend." His eyes searched the ceiling tiles; his mouth sagged at the corners. "I've been checking tags, and I don't see her in here. She's not shelved, because my assistant just finished stitching her. . ."

Leo paled. "What?" He sucked in an involuntary gulp of nauseating air that coated his throat with a taste of death.

THE VIEWING OF THE BODY

Leo had almost forgotten the reason he was here. Gina. And with relaxation came apprehension. Enough of the tour and lecture. Leo didn't need to know about the system, frozen bodies, or processing time. And he certainly wasn't interested in a crash course on how to perform an autopsy. This was taking too long. He was growing anxious. He was here to see Gina, and then get the hell back out into life. "What are you talking about, you can't find her —" Maybe it *had* been a mistake. His mind reeled. *Maybe Gina isn't here after all. . .* Leo wanted to believe, but reasoning held him back from rejoicing. Reasoning and questions. If she wasn't here, then where the hell was she?

Andy let out a sigh and shook his head. One of his hands rested on a hip, while the other raked his hair. "Don't mind me. The brain's slipping." He continued to squint at the high ceiling, a confused look on his face. "Ah, right." He nodded his head enthusiastically. "The body's still in my office." He shot Leo a sheepish glance. "Sorry. Hope I didn't scare you."

Leo rolled his eyes. "Can we get on with this?"

From the crypt they entered a smaller room, similar to a doctor's office, but instead of a comfortably padded examination bench, an aluminum autopsy table was bolted to the floor. A side table held trays of medical instruments. The room also held cabinets and a desk. "This is my office. She's in here," Andy said. "In her own private refrigerator." He offered Leo a compassionate look, then stared soberly. "One thing I *did* give your friend is respect."

"I appreciate that," Leo replied. "She was a cool girl. She didn't deserve this."

"No one does."

"I know. But when it's your own. . . I guess it seems to matter more. Although it shouldn't."

Andy nodded and stood before the refrigerator. "Ready?"

Leo's eyes searched the room. It was cleaner, fresher than the rest of the place, but still unsettling. He noted there were no detectable organic odors, only chemicals, bleach and strong antiseptic. He was thankful he didn't find Gina's body in the mass cooler, with the others. Privacy seemed kinder. "As ready as I'll ever be."

Andy pulled out a metal drawer, and Gina's shrouded body. It was worse than Leo had imagined. He stood on legs he couldn't feel. And as a sheet was pulled down to just below the body's clavicle, Leo sucked in a sharp breath to stop the room from spinning. For a moment, he closed his eyes to escape a bout of de-realization — holding the gulp of air in his lungs for as long as he could to avoid inhaling another whiff of the indescribable smell of decomposition. Something like rotting garbage — worse than decaying carcasses in damp woodlands. *Was there an odor?* Maybe it was just his imagination. . . He patted the pocket of his jacket, feeling for the bottle of Xanax. If things got much worse, he'd have to take one.

It was Gina alright. Even in death she was a knockout. Clotted blood had been rinsed from her hair that now looked soft, and although her skin was white marble, she looked peacefully asleep. Her brows and lashes appeared groomed, but her mouth was a different story. The plump, laughing lips he had years before kissed, were coiled into two swollen rows of pinpricks from where a fine wire, attached to a long-stemmed rose, had sewn her mouth shut. *Like an orifice on a Thanksgiving turkey.* Leo cringed. He'd have to free himself of gruesome analogies if he didn't want to lose his breakfast right on the spot.

Voodoo then flashed across Leo's mind. But Gina wasn't a zombie. Still, could this be a crucial factor in the case? Was the killer some kind of voodoo freak? Leo would have to mention this to Cassidy, one of Baltimore's detectives, a good friend, and the guy who had clued him in on Gina's death. Cassidy knew Leo well — and was certain he would want to know everything about the murder. Even if it hadn't occurred in Baltimore, it was still big news — and Cassidy already had his hands on all the facts, and was methodically sorting through files. Just in case. . .

The voodoo analogy was inescapable as Leo's eyes then stumbled across the bold Y shaped cords of stitched skin that crept to Gina's shoulders. *Laced up like cowhide on a baseball.* Leo knew the incision ran straight down to her groin, covered by the sheet. He envisioned it, then forced his mind to roam elsewhere. Leo remembered the shell of the woman who had been gorgeous in life. Then he looked over at the man, who had hours earlier, seen Gina from the inside.

Shock that had dissipated to sorrow, now welled up into rage. Leo's face flushed. He rolled his hands into white-knuckled fists as he stared at her remains. Gina's throat had been slit; her gaping wounds were obvious. From a puncture beneath her left ear, a gash crossed her neck, ending at her severed right carotid. A blue tint around the cleaved edges, and pallor of the skin, were telltale signs of massive blood loss. Other slashes bit into sections of her shoulders and chest, as if someone had tried to hack her into pieces.

The wounds glared up at him. None had been stitched like the coroner's incision. They would be closed and packed by a mortician whose expertise would camouflage the violence her body had endured. But the lips. The lips would be a challenge for even the finest makeup artist.

Gina's body was a symbol of hatred, anger, insanity — all things evil and demonic that would plague Leo's mind for as long as he lived.

Leo knew there was even more butchery hidden by the sheet. For as much as he wanted to turn away, he stood his ground, unable to resist a sudden urge to reach for Gina's hand. He wanted to take her in his arms, to comfort her, to let her know he was with her, standing at her side, ready to break down and cry, and that he would never forget her. That he would find and punish the bastard that had done this to her. This he vowed.

Gina's skin felt like ice. Leo sifted her fingers with his. Her once impeccably manicured fingernails were ragged where they had been clipped by investigators searching for traces of DNA. Leo held Gina's hand, remembering the girl he had known, had touched, had cared for. He grimaced, tucked her lifeless hand back beneath the sheet. Eyes filled with grief, he stroked her hair.

"Are you done?" Andy asked.

Leo nodded.

"I just finished up a short time ago. Had you arrived an hour earlier, you could have been in on the post mortem. CSI was here. You could have talked to them."

"Thanks, but that wouldn't have worked." With a choked voice, Leo was forthcoming. "I'm out of my jurisdiction. No one knows I'm here."

"It's okay with me. I understand. I'd probably do the same thing myself. But I think they'd have spoken to you as a courtesy. And watching the procedure might have been beneficial —"

"That's okay, Andy. I appreciate your concern, and your time."

Andy was apparently trying to be helpful by involving him with details, but Leo needed to turn off realization, images of Gina's autopsy, thoughts that raked a sickening chill down his spine. He was relieved he'd taken a later flight out of Baltimore that morning, but swore, if he kept feeling this bad, and if Andy didn't stop treating him like a forensic colleague, he'd lose it before he could make it to the exit door.

As he re-draped Gina's body, Andy said inside a sigh, "Young ones still get to me."

Especially this one, Leo thought, with a fixed stare at the

nearby autopsy table upon which Gina had been studied like a specimen. A macabre comparison struck Leo's mind. In just about every TV crime drama he'd seen, the character performing the autopsy seemed to conveniently have a bloody burger plopped on a table beside him, chewing on bites as he analyzed the corpse, inside and out. But in this case, only an extra large bottle of Tums sat on Andy's desk; no sign of food, other than the dried ring of a dripping coffee cup. Andy was human. Leo patted his jacket pocket again . . . so was he.

Once outside, fresh air helped Leo digest what the coroner had said. Preliminary cause of death: Severed carotid artery causing extensive blood loss. "Unofficially," the coroner confided, "any of the stab wounds could have been fatal." The weapon was a razor sharp knife, long and serrated. The coroner had explained in greater detail than Leo needed to hear.

Gina Bellamy was twenty eight, three years younger than Leo, and believed to be the third victim of the killer law enforcement had coined *The Sweet Dreams Psycho* — because he left behind more than dead bodies, he left roses and ridiculous prose. He always struck at night, when his victims had apparently just settled into bed, ready for a good night's rest from which they'd never awaken.

The papers kept calling the murderer *he,* but since the killer's identity was still unknown, in reality, it could be a woman, a determined woman. Leo didn't care if it was a he or a she — he just wanted the bastard secured behind bars, strapped to a hard cot on death row. Better yet, on the way out, fried killer on a gurney.

The window that faced the back alley made Gina an easy target. The killer had used a crowbar to gain access. He could have known his victims; but he *had* to have known their routines. So far there were no witnesses, only corpses, and the killer hadn't left any prints or clues behind. Just badly written rhyme and sickly sweet roses, the stems of which had been imbedded into a variety of body parts coinciding with the verse in each sweet dreams note placed on the pillow, beside each victim's head.

Leo would never forget the death photo of the rosebud dangling morbidly from Gina's sealed and puckered mouth. Was that what he'd smelled inside the coroner's office? *Roses? Jesus.* Leo would never think of roses the same way again.

Gina's love note finished with the words: *Mommy's here to tuck you in slut - and to help you keep your big mouth shut. I'm holding the scissors now. Sweet Dreams, Sleeping Pretty.*

Leo tried to decipher the meaning of the note. If it meant anything at all. Gina Bellamy had been anything *but* a slut. Grief turned into anger. He began to boil.

If Leo had the opportunity, he'd show the bastard exactly what a long-stemmed rose could do — internally. Although Leo would have loved to get his hands on the guy, he knew his only realistic option would be to tear him apart in court and hope the state executed him. A rogue bullet and quick death would be too easy. Leo wanted the murderer to suffer, then be put to death.

AMBER HAWKE

"Mr. Gibraldi!" The female voice carried easily across the street; she made his name sound like an opera. The girl in the red, thigh-skimming skirt waved her arms frantically as if flagging a cab to escape a thunderstorm, or a dark night when a killer was on the loose. "Mr. Gibraldi!" she yelled again. "Your phone!"

Leo strained to see what the girl had in her hand. *My BlackBerry?* He patted his jacket pocket. After reporting in to Ginger at his Baltimore office, he'd been so upset, he must have left the phone on the crowded desk of the coroner's assistant.

"Hold on—" Her voice was closer now. Through her white silk blouse, Leo couldn't help but notice how the girl's breasts heaved and jiggled as she ran across the street to meet him.

Breathless, "So glad I caught you," she said in a gasp. "Saves me the trouble of mailing this to you." The girl with the beautiful voice held up the phone, then shoved it into Leo's chest.

The fluorescents in the coroner's office hadn't done this redhead justice. In sunlight, her eyes were turquoise and translucent. Leo felt as if he was staring into the Caribbean. He cocked his head, furrowed his chestnut brows. "You're the coroner's assistant." With a smooth voice, he reminded the girl who she was.

When he first entered the medical examiner's main office, he'd passed her desk, but hadn't noticed her in detail. The lab coat she'd worn, and her head-down position, masked her identity, and her body. Standing before him without the coat, with that beautiful chest heaving, made her much more interesting.

"And you're the absentminded assistant prosecutor from Baltimore," she said, then frowned. "Tell me if I have this right. Leonardo Gibraldi?" Her lips pouted appealingly when she enunciated *Gibraldi*.

"You've got it right. And you are?"

"Amber Hawke. Amber like that traffic light over there. Hawke like the bird but with an *e* on the end."

Was she coming on to him? Or was she always this flippant. From one glance Leo figured the name, and color, were an appropriate match for this woman's personality: *caution*. Amber didn't need to wear a sign. Leo would find out for himself.

"So, Amber Hawke with an *e*. How about a drink?"

If she accepted, Leo had a feeling she could easily relieve him of his grief.

She openly stared, as if deciding whether or not there was more than curiosity in his steady, hazel eyes.

Thirty and single, with nothing more in her life than sewing up corpses from eight to five, Monday through Friday, and on weekends when necessary, was getting old and cold. Leo was new, and hot — and while he and Andy viewed the dead girl's body, Amber was tiptoeing through Leo's personal files, with the help of a friend who had connections in Baltimore. Along with being mysterious cop-sexy, Leo Gibraldi was single. And in the opinion of some, a provocative state prosecutor was every bit as appealing as any detective.

"Well?" After a moment of watching electricity light up her eyes, Leo reminded, "What's the verdict on that drink?"

"I know a nice place. We can walk there." After a side-glance, she laced her arm through his. "Come on. It's right down the street."

The Corky Screw was spacious but intimately dimmed,

smelled like good food, had creaking wood floors, a dining loft, and a bar that stretched the length of the entire back wall. Just like the dressed-up dives Leo liked to inhabit, where one could grab lunch or dinner, then get sloshed in peace — he felt right at home.

Amber led him to a round corner table for four. Without waiting for Leo to pull out a chair she chose her seat, settled like a feather in a waning breeze, crossed one shapely leg over the other, and plopped her handbag onto the chair beside her. Leo sat across from her, with elbows resting on the tabletop. Chins in palms, they stared at each other.

"So what brings a prosecutor from Baltimore down to an Atlanta morgue?" Amber asked with a sharp brow. "You knew her?"

"I did," Leo answered, although he wished she hadn't brought up the subject of Gina, because he was just beginning to set it aside and sink into the tempting ocean eyes that were openly trying to pry into his head. "I knew her from high school. She was a sweet kid." He sighed. "After five years on the job, I thought I'd seen it all. But that photo. Man, saying a picture is worth a thousand words. . . Not for me. It left me speechless."

"Sorry about that," Amber said with a straight face, although Leo wondered if she really meant it. His intuition told him this woman could be cold as ice if she wanted to be.

"And by the way, my official title is Pathologist Assistant." She lifted her chin dramatically. "PA. Something like Physician's Assistant, only my patients are deceased."

Her words sounded coarse. Leo couldn't help but wonder. "Does that job harden you?"

Do I harden you? spread across her face as a slow grin curled her succulent lips. "After a while you get used to it. But to answer your question, *life* hardens people. Creation and destruction. That's about the size of it." After shrugging both brows, she looked across the room, raised a hand and called out, "Waitress," in a voice that surprised Leo. This woman, although sexy as hell, had some of the characteristics of a man. More than likely sensual, but charming? No.

"What can I get you?" A male waiter appeared, covering for the waitress Amber had flagged — an older woman whose workhorse arms lugged a tray filled with soiled glasses past their table. Capturing Amber's gaze, the waitress smiled an apology.

"Brandy, over lots of ice for me," Amber said, her eyes sweeping Leo's profile.

"Scotch, any kind," Leo told the waiter, "no ice."

After the waiter left . . . "I have to watch my booze intake," Amber said. "Any alcohol I ingest needs to be watered down."

Leo appeared puzzled. Did she have some sort of health issue?

"I have this problem." She lowered her eyes.

Leo cocked his head and frowned. "Nothing serious, I hope."

"Alcohol makes me horny." With that sharp brow she confronted him head-on, then grinned.

Amber's chameleon eyes had a voice of their own. As the color morphed, so did their expression. Leo felt he could easily read her emotions that cruised from interest, to curiosity, to indifference, shifting to wicked as they appeared now.

Bingo. Leo's first impression was right. She *had* been coming on to him. He smiled his first sincere smile since arriving in Atlanta at noon. "You had me scared there for a minute." He removed his hands from the table to let the waiter set down coasters and their drinks. "I'd hate to think you had some crazy illness that denied you the pleasure." He lifted his glass in a toast. "To Atlanta, and to health."

Amber raised her snifter filled more with ice than brandy. "To Baltimore — and to pleasure."

Leo grunted and looked into his glass. "So you come here often." He didn't ask, but stated as he raised his eyes and stared into hers.

"This place is a tradition. It's a professional hangout. You know, for big shots. Attorneys, coroners." Amber winked. "I've even seen a judge or two drop by after court. Oh, and cops. These walls attract quite a crowd."

"Hmm. Interesting."

Her gaze said: *Yes you are.* "When are you going back to Baltimore?"

"Today. Flight at five."

"It's six. You missed your flight."

"Damn. Guess Baltimore will have to wait till tomorrow." Leo's eyes began to catch her fire. "So what do people in Atlanta do on a Thursday evening?"

"They have a nice dinner, a few more drinks, and get invited to somebody's apartment for a nightcap."

"So where's your apartment?"

Amber's apartment wasn't far from The Corky Screw, sharing the same side of the street as the coroner's office, only it was in a cheerful new high-rise standing at the edge of the business district. There wasn't much of a view other than cars and pedestrians, but it was a calmer atmosphere than the downtown area they departed after three hours of drinks, dinner and more drinks. And from what Leo gathered, Amber didn't spend too much time in her apartment anyway, so the location of her apartment was a matter of semantics.

Amber's fourth floor rental was classy and modern, with stark white walls and high ceilings, polished hardwood floors, and galley kitchen with stainless steel appliances. From the moment Leo set foot in the door he noticed it was immaculate. Before leaving the entrance foyer, he slipped off his shoes, then shrugged out of his lightweight jacket and hung it on a hook behind the door.

After kicking off her heels, Amber took his hand and pulled him to the sofa. "A drink?"

"Sure. Why not." If this was going to be a memorable evening, he might as well include one of his memorable morning-after hangovers.

Amber left the room, returning with a tall glass of ice water for herself, a bottle of scotch and a squat glass for Leo. After pouring his drink, she set the bottle onto an ebony table beside the nappy cream-colored sofa.

Leo sank back into the cushions, unwinding from the day.

A few times over dinner, when he looked at Amber, Gina's face had appeared. It had been unsettling. And now, as Leo studied his right hand, splayed out on the thigh of his khaki trousers, he saw ten fingers rather than five.

"I think I've had enough," he said after he noticed the bottle of scotch had dropped several inches since Amber first brought it into the living room.

Amber's legs were curled beneath her as she sat sideways, facing him. She watched him intently, then reached out with a light touch, returning loose strands of chestnut hair to behind his ear. Her gaze clung to his profile. If his hair had been cropped any shorter, coarse and thick, it would have stood at attention. But it was a perfect length for a woman's taste, and for her fingers to twirl and thread, which was what Amber did as Leo began to doze beside her.

"Hey sleepyhead. Don't crap out on me. We only have tonight." Her eyes glistened in lamplight. "I'm glad I didn't stop you before you left my office."

Leo jerked awake, twisted in his seat to face her. He touched her cheek, then sifted a lock of her hair between his fingers. "Is this why they named you Amber? Because of the color of your hair?"

"Not exactly." She laughed, sounding happier than she'd appeared to be the entire evening. "Amber is short for Ambrosia."

"Ambrosia?" Leo chuckled. "Hippies?"

"No. My father's a chef."

They shared a laugh.

"That's the best reason I've ever heard of for a name." Leo looked at her, really looked at her. With ivory skin, those aqua eyes, and soft red hair, she was striking. Although Amber wasn't runway material, when standing she was the right height. He had a feeling, if he backed her up against his chest and slung an arm around her, shoulder to shoulder, he could rest his chin on the top of her head. . . *Just like, Gina. Damn, stop thinking about her!* The night of the carnival, the old green Volvo, pulling Gina onto his lap, which now, he wished he'd have done instead of sending her into her house with a peck on the cheek because her parents flashed the porch light.

"You knew I left my phone in your office?" Surprise broadened into a grin.

"I watched every move you made." She traced his jaw with a fingertip, then her finger slipped between his lips, edged around his tongue.

"C'mere, you." Leo pulled her into his arms and closed his eyes. With a deep breath he inhaled her perfume; sensual woods, strong enough to overpower the odor of formaldehyde that could have clung to her hair. But her hair had a scent of its own: creamy frosting, like icing on a cake, sweet and mouthwatering.

The next thing he knew they were on their feet, standing in front of the tall living room windows, tearing each other's clothes off, baring themselves before the eyes of every passerby on Fifth Street.

Leo wasn't an exhibitionist, but it felt good, kind of wild and different from the back seat of a car, hotel room, or variety of other random places where he'd unleashed the heat beneath his fly. It was spontaneous, animalistic — and the thought of performing before an audience was turning him on, like her body was. Even with a system full of scotch, his dick was harder than hell.

The expression on Amber's face was enough to make him come. Her eyes were glazed, her stare dark and dangerous. The tip of her tongue slid across her parted lips. She looked like a mama cat ready to lick clean her young. And after seeing Gina's body today, God, did Leo need to be cleansed.

The sight of Amber was driving him crazy. Her breasts were not perky and firm, but rather soft and abundant, settling in an incredibly feminine way. They were x-rated huge, covering her entire chest, and because of the high placement of pink, quarter-size areolas, would always defy gravity. Even if they turned flat as pancakes with years on them, they would never point south — that would be anatomically impossible.

Leo had never been with a woman with breasts like Amber's.

Squeezable and snuggly, like gracious pillows a man could sink his face into. And that's exactly what Leo did; he tossed Amber onto the sofa and buried his face into her breasts. The next thing he knew, it was morning.

Amber cuddled beside him, naked on the couch. "When do you have to leave?" With a yawning stretch, she asked.

Leo's eyes bulged as he watched her body lift, flow, then slide into shape. She was luscious. The other part of him that bulged said, *stay you fool*, but Leo replied, "I should be shoving off right now."

"You think you'll ever get down this way again?" Amber grabbed an afghan and wrapped herself like an island nymph. Her hair cascaded over her shoulders. She stared deeply into his eyes.

Leo shifted his glance across the room, settling on sunshine streaming through the window. Reaching down, he snatched his trousers from a heap on the floor and pulled them on. "Never know. Strange things happen." After zipping, he turned to face her with the same cocked head and blunt expression as when they'd first met. "But if I do, I hope it's for a better reason than to visit a morgue." His lips swept hers, then with an inquisitive look, he drew back. "Last night. . . Did we?"

Amber shushed him with a finger over his lips. "I'll leave you with that thought. It'll give you something to wonder about on the flight home." Before her lips crashed into his, she whispered, "Here's something else for you to think about." Her hand ran up the inside of his thighs, abruptly halting in a clutch.

"Oh, God," he moaned.

While Leo and Amber said their good-byes, another murder was in progress. The killer was getting bolder; this murder was taking place during daylight hours, and would be the second in Atlanta in the same week.

ATLANTA † NEXT VICTIM

The cold rain in the bloated sky promised Atlanta an early frost. Fallen leaves mixed with runoff gathered in gutters, in some areas flooding the pavement where congested storm drains regurgitated heavy downpours. There was no morning wind to freshen the dampness, so the air around town was burdened with a mixture of traffic exhaust and decomposing leaves. Lawns were soggy with puddles, and bordering sidewalks reeked like the damp fur of scraggly dogs.

On the way to work the evening before, the girl's wipers wore out and quit just as she had entered the parking lot. Her night shift finally ended at seven a.m., but the rain did not. Stubborn torrents continued to fall in periodic intervals. She couldn't drive without wipers; she'd have to put in some involuntary overtime while she waited for the weather to clear. Her boss wasn't happy about it, but since he wasn't about to drive her home, and neither would spring for a cab, the cranky man approved the OT.

The girl, Tonya Miller, worked the graveyard shift at an industrial medical complex not far from her home on the outskirts of the city. Quality control shared the ground floor of the factory where humans and machines manufactured everything from bedpans to heating pads, sick room needs, even some heavy duty hospital equipment.

Tonya was part of the quality control team. After a long night on the assembly line, inspecting every tenth item, she was tired but her hands kept moving as her eyes darted repeatedly across the enormous warehouse to the windowed walls, checking for a break in the weather. After the storm subsided she'd go home, catch a few hours sleep, then take her sedan over to the shop where her brother worked. He'd fix her wipers for free.

✝

The vehicle was tucked into a space near the exit of the employee parking lot. Rain was the only thing ever to wash grime off the dark paint, but it did nothing to remove muddy boot prints and candy wrappers that were stuck to the interior floors. Alert, sitting on the high front seat, a figure was dressed in a black trench coat with matching hat, and an intense stare alternating between the driving rain and the dashboard clock that moved as slow as the driver's bowels.

This was a mission that required concentration and strength, fundamentals that had been depleted during the four hundred mile journey to this new and interesting place. The place where the driver had hunted. Hunted and watched. Watched for the perfect one. And she was here. Inside the building. The building with concrete walls, dark paned windows. Steel doors that opened and closed for others, but not for her. She remained within the safety of the building, where rain doused the six story roof, coursed through furrows and drain pipes, cascading to the ground like dozens of waterfalls, cleansing the parking lot. Elevating tension.

Damn rain made it difficult to peer through windblown sheaths, dropping like daggers, pelting the windshield. Agitation crept in, dissolving anticipation as quickly as the grime off the vehicle. If it lasted much longer, nothing could happen today. *Fuck.* Routine could not be broken. Errors could then occur, which in turn would ruin the plan. Serious errors that could disrupt the inevitable flow. Like the casual flow of bodily fluids, such as saliva, vaginal secretions, semen, blood, and the inevitable death of many.

Pointless to wait any longer. There will be another time. Maybe not this particular one, but another would have to do. The engine sputtered then composed, peaceful but for the tap of a sticking lifter that would never be repaired; the rhythmic sound was company, and matched the beat of anxious fingers poised on the wheel. The front tires aimed for the exit, and the vehicle began to ease toward the driveway. The wipers clunked and sloshed, disappointment and depression.

Like mankind, unexpected rain could be a bitch — or a bastard.

As the vehicle crept, a cloud moved aside. A stream of dull light cut surprisingly through the windshield. Eyes that had studied the dash clock shifted to analyze the building's exit door. Hopefully, the vehicle halted. Sure enough, there she was, wrapped in a green windbreaker, tan shoulder bag swinging with hurrying footsteps across the parking lot.

Her dark hair looked coarse and seemed to repel a lingering drizzle that shimmered like a beaded crown encircling her head. In movements swift and deliberate, as a hand shifting gears, she unlocked the door, threw in her bag, slipped behind the wheel, and started her car. For a moment she sat, checking her reflection in the rearview mirror. She rubbed a lash from her eye, sighed, then tuned the radio to the daily news.

"No, Mr. Weatherman," she groaned. "I already know what's gonna happen today. From the look of those storm clouds, today's gonna be as bad as my night."

After flipping to another station, she tugged down her lower lids, "Wake up. Wake up. Wake up," then rocked to the beat of music. "Get your ass in gear, girl. Dumb ass wipers. . ."

Oblivious to morning traffic, she drove along the main road, down a few side streets. Tonya had no idea she was being followed. She parked her car in the driveway separating her tract house from her neighbor's, entered through the front door, grabbed a quick glass of orange juice to drink down her vitamins, then headed off to the shower where she'd shed her damp clothing.

"Oh, yeah, baby. Waited all night for this." She lifted her face to the refreshing spray, opening and closing her mouth, gargling on the stream of water. Lyrics from the ride home stuck in her head, she belted out the song:

"things can't get much worse,
no one called you to rehearse,
what does the world expect,
from everyday people like us. . .
doors to adversity swing in your face,
who wipes the blood from the human race,
oh they rip tears from your eyes,
set the rules without compromise
hopeless helpless endless shame,
pluck the buck pass the blame
anger feeds the monster's fame,
people like us die in this game."

Her small house was at the dead end of a residential street that held an even row of houses exactly the same as hers. The only difference was the shade of door and trim paint, and her house sat on a wooded lot, protected by trees and wetland where other tract houses would never be built.

Privacy. Rarely did traffic, or people, or animals, pass by. That was why Tonya had bought the house, just six months ago, when she realized her factory job was secure, and learned the bank trusted her with a seventy-five thousand dollar mortgage.

It was a nice area with friendly people, some cats — no barking dogs, just a few kids at the opposite end of the modest community. Nothing to disturb her. She could prance around the backyard in her bikini and there were no gawking glances, thanks to a shroud of trident maples with flaring leaves, hickory trees, and cedars surrounding her yard. She was fortunate. The other houses had the next street, and another row of tract houses, almost in their backyards.

Tonya had her own urban forest, congested with noisy birds, furious birds flitting and hopping; flying boomerangs soaring from grove to grass and back, a flocking wall, screeching in native tongues.

She could leave her windows open, but then all she would hear were the birds. That's what she hated most about the night shift; trying to sleep during daylight, subjected to the chaos of overcharged, multilingual birds. The birds were insane — she was insane for working the night shift.

Only a lunatic would drive into a wetland, park inside the shelter of willow oaks, beech and longleaf pines, slop through a muddy morning toward the back of someone's house. Only a bull of a four wheel drive would have tires wide and beefy enough to drag a heavy vehicle out again. And the underground watershed would swallow any tire tracks like quicksand ingested prehistoric creatures. *Genius.* Working with Mother Nature made things easy. But Mother Nature could also be a bitch.

Dressed as a phantom, the figure with the trench coat and matching hat made its way toward the rear porch. Even though the boots deposited prints, it wouldn't matter, because the oversized boots were worn over bulky socks and filthy tennis shoes that bundled narrow feet. And the hardy pockets of the coat carried ankle weights, so investigators would be looking for a suspect at least four inches taller, over forty pounds heavier. An amusing thought as gloved hands tested the back windows. No crowbar needed. One was unlocked, open an attractive inch. The killer's glance swept the outside area clean, slowly slid the window until it met the stop, hoisted and climbed inside. Green florist tape sticking to the boot detached, sank into a print.

The bathroom door was closed, so the young woman didn't

see a shadow slide across her bedroom wall. And with the gushing shower, she didn't hear the fiberboard sheathing creak beneath boots treading on lightweight carpet.

Emerging in a towel, Tonya left the bathroom door ajar. Plumes of steam licked the space, drifted with a breeze blowing through the window she had neglected to secure. First mistake. Her second was to drop into bed, pull a sheet over her naked body and immediately fall asleep. In exhausted slumber, she had no sense of the lurking figure, the stale breath, or the gloved hand clutching the serrated knife that dug a trench across her neck. Instantly, her lids snapped open registering shock, agony. Her throat filled with blood, blocking air — stifling screams.

What felt like an eternity was a glimpse into the brutal eyes of a killer, the distorted face of a madman claiming the final moments she would take to her grave.

Before rupturing internal organs, the knife hammered furiously into the soft tissue of her neck, pulverizing bone, then the blade plunged through her eye. By then she was just another victim, lying in a bed soaked with her own Type O negative blood. Before the killer left, the elegant stem of a red rose was planted in the orbit, and a note was placed on the blood soaked pillow: *Stick a needle in your eye. You'll never make anybody else cry. Sweet Dreams Darlin'.*

BALTIMORE JUSTICE

When Leo's flight landed in Baltimore, he went straight to the airport cafe for breakfast. He was starved. The plane ride home had been exactly as Amber intended — Leo was certain, because during the flight, all he could think about was her face, her body, the way her hand had gripped his crotch before he left her apartment. Oh, and those breasts. . . He got hard on the plane just reliving their encounter. Too bad he didn't remember all the details. Would they ever meet again? Leo had no idea, but other than viewing Gina's corpse, Atlanta had been a hoot.

After cramming down scrambled egg and cheese on a bagel, he drove home, took a shower, dressed in clean clothes, and sped along the thirty minute route from the Bay Area into the city, directly to his office. Even though there was ample underground parking, Leo left his late model Shelby Mustang at the curb so he could use the front entrance of the courthouse. He'd reach his destination faster that way. Judge Antonio Diviniello had left him a voice message. "Get your ass over here, pronto." And there were a few other associates in that part of the building he needed to see before taking the stairs up to his office. Leo avoided elevators.

Maria Chavez, Diviniello's secretary, was away from her desk when Leo arrived, so he tapped a signal of four rapid beats on the judge's chamber door.

"Enter." The voice growled like a watchdog.

When Leo strode inside, the judge scowled. "So you finally decided to join us."

"Sorry, Judge, I had urgent business."

"Atlanta?"

Leo couldn't hide his surprise. How did Diviniello know? No one other than Cassidy knew Leo had flown to Atlanta. "Yes, Judge. Atlanta. An old friend needed my help."

"That so." The look in Diviniello's steel gray eyes warned. "You *do* know I'm about to throw my hat into the ring."

Leo nodded. He and Ben Cassidy, and a few others, had taken bets on whether or not Diviniello had a chance against the incumbent. And if he managed to get himself elected as a Maryland Senator, would it be a good thing, or a bad thing? The verdict was still out on that one.

"I'm aware of that, Judge. And you know you have my vote."

"I don't want any shit hitting the fan in this or any other office in this building. You got that? And about Atlanta. Any news on that maniac? If he *is* heading up the coast, Baltimore could be a target." Diviniello rubbed a manicured hand through his thinning hair. "Christ, that's all we need."

"No other news that I know of. Just the one murder in Atlanta."

"Two."

Leo looked confused and stuffed his hands deeper into the pockets of his JC Penney trousers. "Hmm. . . Really. . ."

"Yes really." Diviniello said with sarcasm. "There was a second Atlanta murder early this morning."

"Oh, shit," Leo grumbled.

"I just want to remind you, Leo, about the food chain."

"Food chain?" Was this some new restaurant the higher crowd was invading?

"If and when I leave this position, someone needs to replace me. Someone has to replace them. So on and so forth. Get me?"

"I get you, Judge."

40

"So stay clean. . . make sure everything runs smooth as your mother's teat, and that there's no bull crap going on behind my back. Oh, and one more thing."

"What's that, Judge?"

"Close the door on your way out."

"Sure, Judge Divine."

"What did you call me?" Diviniello shot him a menacing look.

Leo figured the judge was either incredibly angry or ridiculously frustrated, because his throat and cheeks were the same scarlet as the gold framed spines of law journals lining the shelves of bookcases recessed into the wall behind his massive mahogany desk. Red, white and blue elephant buttons were scattered on the protective glass topper. Leo instinctively swung his eyes across the room, noticing cartons of additional campaign material stacked in the corner of the otherwise pristine office.

"Sorry. . . Judge Diviniello," Leo said absentmindedly. As he headed to the door, his brain was already in high gear, wondering about the second Atlanta murder. If he had Amber's number, he'd call her — get the info from her. He'd also advise her to be careful, and make sure she locked all doors and windows. And to sleep with one eye open, and a .45 in her hand.

"Leo," Diviniello called him back. "Will you be seeing Gloria?"

Leo faced the judge, a smirk creasing his face. "You better not let her catch you calling her that."

"Oh, right. The name her mother and I gave her apparently isn't good enough," Diviniello scoffed. "But then she *did* inherit Bernadette's imagination, and her hot temper." At the mention of his wife and daughter, Diviniello's face softened.

"What can I say? You raised her." Leo grinned as he left the judge's chamber.

As the door snapped shut, Leo heard him mumble, "Glory Divine? What the hell's wrong with Gloria Diviniello?"

Leo strode down several corridors, passing open doors and unoccupied desks, realizing the colleagues he wanted to see were at lunch. He shrugged, huffed a breath of annoyance and mumbled, "Call them later, I guess."

Taking the stairs two at a time, Leo reached the third floor then jogged to the other side of the building. It was a hike. Next time, he'd use the parking garage and let Diviniello wait.

When Leo arrived at his office, there was a stack of messages bundled under the base of his telephone, so the instrument sat on an obvious slant, teetering at the corner of his crowded desk. *Jesus, Ginger. . .How many times have I told you to use the freaking message box sitting right on top of the damn desk?* Then he looked at the still wrapped, three-year-old bar of soap she'd glued to his desktop, threatening to wash his mouth out with it if he didn't stop taking the Lord's name in vain. He shook his head, then dropped into his leather chair, pulled it close to the desk and reached for the stack of files Ginger, his secretary, had left for him.

Ginger's name sounded hot. So did her husky voice on the phone. But Ginger wasn't the least bit hot. She was a matronly mom of three straight arrow daughters, the youngest a knockout, but Ginger wouldn't let that daughter within ten feet of Leo. The two older daughters were settled in careers, and securely married.

Ginger was a good secretary — in her own right, although it was usually Leo carrying in his morning coffee, along with her vanilla soy latte. And even though Ginger wasn't hot, she was one of the most important women in his life; she kept him organized. Besides, Leo could never have a hot secretary. He needed to be able to concentrate on his job. Hot equaled distraction.

Thirty-one year old Leo Gibraldi remained the same fickle guy he'd been as a Connecticut teen. Over the years, all that had changed was his build. He was lanky as a kid. Matured Leo worked out and filled out. Teen Leo had messy cropped hair. The current Leo wore a slick men's cut, clipped and styled every other week at an upscale unisex salon.

Leo pushed the folders aside and flipped through the messages. "Hmm," he grunted when he saw Ben Cassidy's.

He picked up his phone that connected to Ginger's, and hit the call button. No answer.

"Jesus." Leo was becoming tense. He checked his watch. After two p.m. and Ginger was nowhere to be found. So he dialed Cassidy himself.

"Hey Ben. I got your message. Let's get together tonight over drinks."

Ben Cassidy's South Bronx accent and attitude weren't on the other end of the line. The pre-recorded greeting was more civil, anyway.

can i tune your sound
turn your world upside down
shoot you to the moon
wear your insides out

Glory Divine

Main Street was lined with offices and municipal buildings, one of which was the District Courthouse. The surrounding area resembled a fifty grand per semester college campus: manicured and treed, composed of modern structures with clean, white lines, faced with limestone veneers and sweeping smoked glass.

Exiting the building, Leo pushed through one of the front doors and halted on the walkway beneath the courthouse steps. A mid-afternoon sky, tufted with clouds, wept soft drizzle. He'd wait for her beneath the portico.

Leo was impatient. He looked down the street, up the street, across the street. She was nowhere in sight. He shifted from one foot to the other, yielding for visitors entering and departing the courthouse, all the while checking his watch. *Damn her.*

He had wanted to grab a quick bite to eat and get back to the office. There was an overwhelming amount of work he needed to dive into, ASAP. But it didn't look like that was going to happen, unless he stood Glory up. And he knew better than to do that.

Gloria Diviniello legally changed her name to Glory Divine when she turned eighteen. That was ten years ago when she decided to pursue an acting career. That and the fact that in junior high, when she was tall and lanky with a washboard chest, she had earned the nickname, Vinnie. And after playing Tom Sawyer in a school play, she knew acting was her forte. She never reached Hollywood, but attended drama classes, and soon began landing roles in local theatre. No one would ever think about calling her a boy now. Not after a top-notch cosmetic surgeon gave her a beautiful set of stripper boobs for a cost of ten thousand of her father's dollars.

Leo was preparing for a trial. He was nowhere near ready to prosecute the two-time felon charged with armed robbery. He still had files to rifle through. Research to complete. Arguments to draft. Even after he was finished with Cassidy and drinks, he had a long night of work ahead of him.

"Jesus, Glory. Later than usual," he grumbled as he shook his head, growing more annoyed by the minute. He should have been used to her arrogance and lack of consideration by now.

As a diversion, Leo let his thoughts drift . . . for a moment, savoring Amber. Since Atlanta, she'd been screwing with his mind, even in absence. He thought again about phoning the coroner's office to see how she was doing, but his life was too complicated right now to get involved with anyone, especially someone like Amber Hawke. And long distance relationships never worked, anyway.

In a moment of imagining both of his palms sliding across Amber's plush breasts, Leo felt fingernails grip, then pull the hair at the nape of his neck. As if his mind had just been invaded, he turned with a start, and there she stood — five-foot-eight inches of blonde fury… and great frustration to Leo. A strong fragrance of Paris overwhelmed him as his eyes swept Glory Divine from head to toe. She was stunning, with sharp features, sapphire blue eyes, thick caramel mane. *The body of a goddess with the soul of a devil.*

Glory knew the effect she had on men and used it to her advantage. Still, Leo was not an average man. He could handle her.

"About time, Glory. I don't have all day. Some of us have

schedules to keep." Although she'd pissed him off, his voice was resigned. "I'm on a quick break. What was so important?"

She pressed her hips against his, running a hand up the lapel of his jacket, the fingers of her other hand flicking stray bangs off his forehead. "Are you coming to Daddy's fundraiser tonight?" Her voice was warm, her expression unable to be.

"Can't make it. I have other plans." Leo looked straight into her eyes. With four inch heels she was almost his height.

"How about when you're finished with your plans?"

"I'm meeting Cassidy. Not sure when I'll be free."

"Forget Cassidy. He can't do for you what I can. . ."

"Glory. . ." Leo wanted to tell her he was no longer a pawn in her little game of greed and lust, but decided against it. Glory had a powerful influence over him right now. But the time would come. It was a waiting game, and he just had to be patient.

Glory, Glory. A royal pain in the ass, but she did give one hell of a supreme blow job.

The sky cleared, so they walked down the brief courthouse steps to stand on the twelve foot wide sidewalk, barricaded with decorative cement abutments.

"Do you at least have time for a latte?" She flashed a smile.

"Sure. Come on." Leo hooked her arm with his and began to head in the direction of the downtown cafe.

"Wait," Glory tugged his arm, "I have a cab —"

"You've had a cab waiting this entire time?" Leo was stunned.

"Yeah. . .?" She tossed him a blank expression.

They settled into the cab, with Glory pressed to Leo's side, her hand resting on his thigh.

"Daddy's campaign paraphernalia was delivered to his office by mistake. I have to get it over to campaign headquarters, so I'll be coming back to the courthouse with you." Her fingers edged higher up his thigh and squeezed.

"You mean your uncle's bakery." Leo never questioned Glory. He stated.

"Rome wasn't built in a day, Leo," she snapped, then quickly controlled her voice. "It's not only a bakery. It's an exclusive catering hall. And I've gone all out with the arrangements. You should come tonight. It'll be fun. You won't be sorry — I promise." She slid her hand to the top of his thigh, bordering his crotch, and applied pressure.

Leo tried to ignore her, but his body reacted to her touch, and the sight of her long legs, bared by a clinging emerald green dress.

"I'll try."

"It's black tie — and commando," she said, her stare boring into him so he'd have to turn his head and look at her.

Leo gave her face a once-over. *Commando. . .* Her sultry expression said she wasn't kidding. "Hmm. Interesting."

"Why do you keep saying that?" she asked as her eyes left his to watch the city unfold beyond the window.

"What?"

"Hmm." Her voice didn't quite sound like his.

"Just something I picked up at the office —" He leaned close, dropped a kiss on the side of her neck, then twisted a lock of her hair around his finger, tugging on it to turn her around to face him again. "Along with other habits some might consider annoying." His eyes focused on hers. Against the green of her dress, and sun filtering through the window of the cab, her blue eyes looked like gemstones.

"You know. Daddy being a senator will be good for you too, Leo."

"Too? What else is good for me. . ."

"Come tonight and I'll show you." She tilted her head and lifted a brow.

They rode six blocks to the bistro of Glory's choice — classy. Anything connected with Glory Divine was classy. After being seated in a nook facing a window, they were served.

"I'll be right back," Leo said.

"Men's room?"

"I'll be right back."

Glory gave Leo five minutes to relieve himself and wash his hands.

As he was about to reach for a paper towel, the door opened, and she stepped inside as if she owned the place.

"The ladies' is next door, ma'am." Knowing what she had in mind, he grinned, dried his hands and tossed the balled up towel into the trash.

"Very funny," she said as she backed him into a stall and kicked the door closed with the heel of her shoe. She reached for his fly.

"Hold on," Leo said as he shrugged off his jacket and hung it over a hook on the back of the door, then shoved Glory roughly against the cool wall of the metal enclosure. With one hand he braced her arm above her head, reached the other down to her knees, then ran his palm up the smooth inside of her thighs until he hit home.

"Commando," he breathed against her neck. "In some ways, you make life so easy." He swiped her throat with his tongue, ran a hand across her breasts, then mouthed one D cup through the thin fabric of her dress. The nipple immediately hardened.

Glory moaned, and wrapped a leg around his hip. While Leo clutched her buttocks, she unzipped his fly. He kept his moan low.

Before Leo could reach into his pocket, she nipped the side of his neck with her teeth and whispered, "I've got it covered." Then dressed him with a condom before they fused.

After slamming around inside the stall for the same length of time it would have taken to finish their lattes, Leo flushed the used condom down the toilet, and handed Glory a wad of tissue.

As they emerged from the stall, a well-dressed, middle-aged man faced them, enjoyment — and envy — spreading across his face. Slipping past him, they nodded, washed their hands, then Leo pushed open the door, following Glory's long legs out of the men's room. He fell into step a few paces behind her, watching her hydraulic butt cheeks work like wrecking balls, as they strolled back to their nook, and two cold lattes. Before the cab ride back to the courthouse, Leo's cell phone rang.

"Leo." Ben Cassidy's voice shot through the line. "Got your

message. Terry says to come to dinner tonight."

"Nice. What time?"

"Seven."

DETECTIVE BENJAMIN CASSIDY

Benjamin and Teresa Cassidy were high school sweethearts, together for over twenty-five years. They lived in a nice colonial in suburban Baltimore. Cassidy had been on the force since the day they were married, working his way up the ladder, finally making detective. On the rungs of another ladder, they had four kids in steps skipping two years each. The perfect family. First a boy, then twin girls, then another boy. They joked about the kids being their birthday cake; precious layers of beautiful love, and the icing was, Mom and Dad had a terrific relationship, money in the bank, two updated cars, good jobs. They had their cake and were enjoying, what they hoped to be, endless years of the good life.

"Benny! The bell!" Terry called from the kitchen.

Leo heard Terry's voice through the paneled oak door, and through frosted sidelights watched the flossy approach of Ben's husky outline.

"Hey buddy," Ben greeted as he opened the door to a grinning Leo.

When Leo entered the house, the aroma of lasagna snaked its way from the kitchen, around a corner and down the hallway, past the straight flight of stairs leading to the upper level four bedrooms, two baths, and four rowdy kids.

"Hey Ben. Thanks for having me." Leo held out a pink box tied with red and white striped cord. "Good to see you outside the office."

"You too, buddy. What's this?"

"Best cheesecake you'll ever eat. From my secret source."

The cake was from Glory's uncle's bakery, where Leo had stopped on the way to Ben's house. Leo wanted to tell Glory, ahead of time, he wouldn't be coming tonight. Glory wasn't at the bakery, but Leo witnessed last-minute chaos when he snooped inside the catering hall that was being decorated by volunteers trying to figure out how and where to hang streamers. Diviniello's posed face was on a bloated poster, set on an easel in front of a stage that normally hosted DJs or wedding bands, but now held a centered podium. Glory would be disappointed. Leo had let her down — but that was life.

"Cheesecake. Aw. You didn't have to do that." Ben lifted the box out of Leo's outstretched hands. "It's heavy."

"Heavy and rich."

"Ah, just how I like my women," Ben joked.

Leo laughed. "I'm sure Terry would love to know that."

"Yeah. Imagine if she knew about my fetishes?"

"You're a bad boy, Benny." Leo shook his head and clicked his tongue.

"You should talk, Gibraldi. I don't know how you keep up that lifestyle of yours."

"I guess we all have our own fantasies and vices, huh? Hey, I have to warn you though. This cake can put the weight on you, fast. Well worth it though."

"If that's a dig, I lost five pounds last month, Leo. Look how flat the gut is."

"I'm busting chops. You're looking good, Ben. Now that you're losing weight, you have to come to the gym more often."

"Twice a week is enough for me."

As they sparred, Leo peeled off his jacket and hung it on the oak newel post at the bottom of the staircase, then slipped out of his casual shoes and kicked them into a tiled corner of the entrance foyer. His socks matched his brown khaki trousers.

"Place looks good, Ben. You've painted since I was here last."

Leo noticed the living room to the left was now pale celery, and looked brighter than the old creamy white with three foot high handprint stains.

The kids had finished homework and were in Ben's upstairs den, watching television and arguing over who'd pick the next show. They were loud.

Ben noticed the look on Leo's face as the ceiling drummed with footsteps, sounding like it would cave at any moment. "The animals stampeding the jungle." Ben laughed. "The joys of parenthood, huh?"

"Heh." Leo acknowledged with half a chuckle. "I wouldn't know, but you've got a great family. Dinner smells good. I haven't eaten since this morning."

"Hear that Teresa? Leo says dinner smells terrific — and he's starved," Ben yelled, then said discreetly, "she tries to cook Italian," he made a sour face, "but Italian's not her thing. I told her to make corned beef and cabbage, but when she heard it was you coming, she wanted to make a nice home-cooked Italian meal."

"That's sweet." For a moment, Leo's eyes went soft.

"Yeah, cooking Italian isn't her best talent." Ben took a step back, clearing the archway connecting the foyer to the living room so that Leo could pass.

Leo grinned. "Kids are though."

"Yeah." Ben smiled. "Terry's a wonderful mother. And wife. So, what's up? You sounded stressed on the phone message. Glory again?"

"Nah."

"The judge? Look at me making you stand in the entrance. Come on in. Grab a seat on the couch. Terry'll call us when dinner's on the table." Ben still held the cake, cradling it in one arm that pressed the box against his wide chest.

"No, things are cool downtown. It's this psycho. Four murders and he's got himself a name." Frowning, Leo shook his head. "And you were the one who called me, remember?"

"Oh yeah. Atlanta . . . Gina . . . Geeze, I'm sorry, Leo. I wanted to know how you made out. Let me get you a drink. What's your poison? Beer, or a cocktail maybe?"

"Got any scotch?"

"Sure. Go and sit. We'll have a drink and talk."

"Four victims that we know of, " Ben spoke on the way out of the living room and finished when he walked back in carrying two Old Fashioned glasses filled with scotch, "If you're taking bets, he's hacked up others, and he's gonna hit Maryland before the end of the month."

Stunned by Ben's blunt assessment, Leo recoiled. "Catch me up with what you know, Ben."

"Nothing I know. I just have the feeling."

"Why the end of the month?"

"Well — judging from the mileage he's been covering. And regardless of how many he does in one place. If he *is* really moving up the coast, like everybody seems to think he is. Do the math. It's the beginning of October."

"Yeah, but —"

Four sets of feet pounded the stairs, the kids flying into the living room, screaming as tweens do. "Hello. Hi. Hehe." A combination of the boys wondering who was in their house, and the girls acting coy around a tall, handsome man.

"You remember Mr. Gibraldi, kids. Say hello." Ben coached them proudly.

"Hello, Mr. Braldy."

"Let them call me Leo. It's easier." Leo returned a grin to the boys, then mugged at the girls who made silly faces behind their hands, showing off bubblegum pink painted fingernails. When Leo stared them down, they wriggled their noses vigorously, and giggled louder.

"Come on in here kids." On her way from the kitchen, Terry yelled. "And you guys take a seat in the dining room."

When Terry appeared beneath the archway, Leo immediately stood and met her with a hug in the middle of the room.

"Leo. It's been a long time."

"Too long, Terry." He stepped back to give her a respectful once-over. "You look as great as ever."

Terry was an average woman in her early forties, standing five-foot-five, her one hundred fifteen pound figure giving her a taller stance. She wore her brown hair in a blunt bob, and tucked behind one ear where an emerald stud glistened with the light, dazzling against her fair skin. But it was her eyes that made her outstanding. They were violet, faceted with navy streaks. Leo had never seen eyes like hers on anyone before. You could get lost in Terry's vibrant, but delicate, flower eyes. Terry always made Leo think of spring, and Terry was every bit as sweet as her springtime eyes.

"The lasagna smells delicious, Terry. Thanks for having me."

"Taste it first, Leo. Then you can tell me how great it is." She smirked. "Come in and be seated." Her slender arm gestured through the archway of the living room, to the dining room stretched out just beyond where they stood.

They took seats around a walnut table for six, protected by a festive linen tablecloth so colorful that it looked like the fabric could hide just about any kind of splattered food. But it was clean and pressed. The entire house was immaculate.

Over dinner, while Ben and Terry reminisced old times, Leo started to wonder if never having had a serious relationship of his own was any kind of loss. He was busy as hell, but was his life full?

digging for truth
never find answers
digging so deep
you might never resurface

KEEP THE FAITH — AND KEEP IT LIGHT

The dinner conversation was like a holiday reunion, where people dredged up memories that had been buried for years: laughing, joking, sharing. Even if you weren't part of their memories, you were still drawn into the vivid collection of cerebral snapshots of someone else's life. It was like watching a movie, but you knew and truly cared for the cast. For a while, Leo didn't think about Glory, or Amber, or even the Sweet Dreams Psycho, until Terry ruined the peaceful moment.

"So how's Glory? Or is it someone else this month?" After a sip of cranberry colored wine, Terry asked.

"Nah. There's no one." Leo dug his fork into a second helping of lasagna. Ricotta cheese, mixed with homemade sauce oozed around the fork. "This is really good, Terry. Your cooking could put a few extra pounds on me."

"Aw, thanks. So why didn't you bring Glory to dinner?"

"She's doing this fundraiser tonight for her father."

Terry cocked a brow. "Fundraiser? That family's got money pouring out of their ears. What the hell do they need a fundraiser for?"

"Diviniello's running for the Senate. I told you that," Ben said. "You don't listen."

"I listen. Senate, huh?" She shot Ben a snarky look. "I know the man. I don't like him as a judge. Why should I like him as a senator?"

Dismissing Ben, she honed in on Leo.

"So when're you going to settle down with Glory? You seem to spend a lot of time with her, and her family's influential, which doesn't hurt if you're looking to further your career."

Leo coughed, slugged his wine, then said, "If Glory's my only option, I'll remain a bachelor."

Thick red sauce dotting the corners of his mouth, Ben guffawed, then covered his amusement with a napkin.

"And why is that?" Terry asked, throwing a piece of Italian bread at her husband.

"Benny got the last good woman." With a cloth napkin, Leo wiped sauce and wine from the corner of his mouth and chin, then grinned at her.

"You slipped out of that one, Leo." Ben laughed. "Real smooth."

"Shut up over there before I send your arse into the kitchen to start cleaning up." Terry didn't face Ben as she addressed his comment. Her stare fixed on Leo. "You're a real charmer, Gibraldi. I bet you could charm your way through a chastity belt." With a salty look, she nodded, but her eyes laughed.

Leo and Ben chuckled, then Leo thought about the x-rated acts he and Glory performed together, especially in public restrooms. There was something about sex in public places that put a thrill into Leo's life. Nothing much else did. And he had very much enjoyed baring it all to anyone on Fifth Street when he and Amber stood naked in front of her living room windows. He'd better turn off his mind, right now. . . At the concept of Terry reading his thoughts, he almost blushed. "Where're the kids?" he asked.

"In the kitchen. I thought you wanted to talk." Terry replied.

Leo and Ben exchanged amused looks. Ben shrugged his

shoulders, while his hands shot up in a helpless gesture.

"So how's the hospital, Terry?" Leo asked.

"We'll, I'm off the night shift for a month, thank God. Ben and I rotate so someone's always home for the kids. He's on nights this month."

Leo shot Ben a worried glance. Ben sighed and passed on a nod, then said, "It's too quiet in the kitchen, babe. Either they're eating us out of house and home, or redecorating."

"I'll check on them. They should be heading off to bed, anyway."

"Into their cages you mean."

"You're terrible, you big goon," Terry clicked her tongue and shook her head, then planted a kiss on the top of Ben's head.

"You guys talk. I'll be back in a while."

After Terry rounded the kids up for bed, she cleared the table, popping in and out of Ben and Leo's conversation. Each time she entered the room, they changed the subject to sports, then back to the tension that built in both of their minds the moment she left again.

"Every victim was in her early twenties." Ben pondered aloud. "Shared the same blood type. O negative."

"So does half of America," Leo said.

"Right, but my point is, it's a common denominator."

"True. But what else besides long, dark hair ties them together? More than half the country is brunette. Think Benny. Not prostitutes. Skin color doesn't seem to be a preference. Body type doesn't seem to be a factor. It's too random. Or is he making it look random? We're missing something." Leo sloshed a last inch of wine around the bottom of his glass.

"So, tell me, Leo," Terry said as she entered the room and buzzed around the table, removing the platter of lasagna scraps, and salt and pepper shakers, then replacing soiled linen napkins with paper. "How are you doing? *Really* doing." Leaning close, she stared into his eyes, almost making him uncomfortable. Her hand rested on the back of his chair. She touched a trapezius trigger point on the slope of his neck, then rubbed a circle between his shoulder blades to release some tension.

"I'm fine, Terry. But you can keep doing that. It feels good." Leo chuckled softly, but he felt odd. Her touch felt intimate. Leo wasn't used to friendly intimacy.

"Ya sure you're fine? Because I have a locked cabinet of stuff upstairs, if you need —" Terry removed her hand from his back, but stood close to the side of his chair.

"I'm fine. Thanks for asking." Leo drained the last of his wine and handed her the glass.

"If you need anything, anything at all, you let me know, you hear?"

"I will. Thanks again, Terry." He slid his hand lightly down the side of her arm, thinking of the expired bottle of Xanax in his jacket pocket. The Xanax she had given him months ago. And then there was Glory. What a contrast. Leo wasn't sure if Glory relaxed him or agitated him even more than prosecuting criminals.

The crystal chandelier, suspended above the table, lit Ben's face and smile. Ben obviously appreciated Terry's warmth, not only with him, but with others as well. She was an impressive lady.

Leo couldn't help but notice the love in Ben's deep brown eyes when he looked at his wife. They watered with tenderness and compassion, emotions rare for Ben who was usually all hardcore cop.

Everyone said Ben had nice eyes, but his nose was too prominent, overshadowing his lips that should have been broader to fit in better with the rest of his bold features. Still, he wasn't a bad looking guy. A bit overweight, but teddy bear attractive to women.

Terry moved to Ben's chair, where she stood behind him, ruffling his hair with her fingertips.

She directed her question to Leo. "Do you know the odds of being the victim of a serial killer?"

Leo's brows shot up.

"Can't keep anything from this woman," Ben said as he placed his palm over Terry's hand that rested on his shoulder. "Years of being a cop's wife." He grinned, angled his head to snuggle her hand, then kissed the top of it. "What are the odds, hon?" From across the table, Ben tossed a wink to Leo.

"Infinitesimal. Like hitting Lotto or being struck by lightning. So stop worrying about protecting me from the conversation. I'm a nurse remember? Who used to work in a mental ward. I've seen it all. Taken self–defense courses. And was taught by the best, like this guy over here." She swiped the back of Ben's head with the back of her hand.

Leo smiled. "When I said Ben got the last good woman, I should have added, he got the *perfect* woman."

"You're a schmoozer, Gibraldi." Terry laughed, then dropped an empty tray onto the table. "If you guys are all finished here, I'll get rid of the rest of this stuff. Then bring in that delicious cheesecake Leo so thoughtfully brought."

"No dessert for me, Terry. I'm stuffed," Leo said as he patted his well-defined six-pack.

"Me either, Ter, but bring the scotch in with you on your next trip, will you?" Ben tapped her backside affectionately.

"Leo," Ben said after Terry cleared the last of the dinner dishes off the table and set down a bottle of scotch and two clean glasses. "How long have we known each other? Four years?"

"Yeah, something like that. Where are you going with this?"

"Take my word for it. The guy's coming here. I can feel it in my bones."

At the thought, Leo's stomach churned — then butterflies turned acidic. He poured and slugged some scotch. "You know I want this guy caught before he slices up anyone else. But if anybody's gonna nail him —"

"And prosecute him — ah, the glory. In our backyard, huh?"

Leo inhaled, then emptied his lungs with a restless burst of air. "That would move us both up the ladder for sure. But more than that, it would be one for Gina."

Ben appeared to be stuck inside his own head, not paying much attention to what Leo was saying. "He's got no pattern. He's self-centered. He's angry. He was molested as a kid, he was jilted. Somebody cut him off the road. Who the hell knows what's inside the mind of a homicidal maniac? Other than he either likes, or wants to kill for his own twisted reasons." Ben ran a hand through his cropped dark hair, then drained his glass of scotch.

"He doesn't fit any profile. Doesn't rape them, or intentionally mutilate, although the way he slices them up could be considered mutilation. Seems he just wants them dead," Leo said dryly.

"Yeah, but that doesn't mean he's not driven by sexual urges, or issues. He's got to have some kind of motive. Something that drives him to it." Ben's voice was guarded.

"Sure something's driving him to it, Ben. But I really don't think it's sexual. So far, there haven't been any signs of molestation when the bodies were examined. No fluids. No hair, no fibers. He just stabs them and plants his roses. The sonofabitch must wear a fucking decontamination suit. Doesn't leave a goddam trace."

"Come on, Leo. Walk down the street. What isn't connected to sex?"

"Trying to figure what's driving *him*, is driving *me* nuts. Maybe he's just an all around lunatic, with no purpose at all. Just likes to kill any—" Leo stopped mid sentence and fell into thought.

"Any what?"

"I was going to say, kill anything. But so far, his victims have been only women. So much for the, *I'm just a misunderstood head-case*, theory of your average killer. You know. We deal with murder all the time, Ben. Not that it ever makes sense, but there's usually a reason. Passion, insurance money, armed robbery. Eradication of anyone who gets in their way. But this serial bullshit is —"

"Sexual. Everything's sexual. Look around you. Look around in backyards. Perverts. Everywhere — sneaking looks in strollers, sex in their eyes — sickos. The world's full of them and breeding new ones every day. Mothafuckin' sickos — they're everywhere." Ben shook his head, then lifted his glass. "A toast to eradication of all sickos."

"Whoa." Wide-eyed, Leo recoiled. "That was some spiel. You make a convincing argument. I'm gonna have to put you on the stand next time I prosecute a perv." Leo raised his own glass. "To health, and keeping the home fires burning. Figuratively, only."

"Amen. It's all twisted. And what isn't connected to sex, Leo?" Ben seemed to be stuck on the subject.

"Not much," Leo said, then thought of some of the things that made his mouth water. *Commando* was the first to pop into his head. "Right, twisted," for a moment he thought about Glory, "so how do you peg a twisted mind?"

"Fantasy. Serial killers live in fantasy. Murdering fulfills their illusions."

"Hell of a way to get fulfillment." Leo shook his head. "And after each one, they grow more balls, like the last Atlanta murder in broad daylight. Grow balls, and then they want more."

"Exactly, Leo. Reinforcing my backyard sicko theory. It's only a matter of time and he'll be here."

"With luck he'll get sloppy. That's our only chance. He's got to make mistakes."

"If I catch the bastard, I'll shoot him on the spot. Take no prisoners in this case."

Leo looked annoyed. "He's got to be brought to trial — prosecuted. Then you can hang him in the public square for all I care. As long as he's prosecuted and the victims and families get some kind of retribution. We —" Leo stumbled over the word, "they need closure."

"Okay, so I'll shoot him in the kneecaps. But first, we have to be in the right place at the right time when he fucks up." Ben sounded as if he were a gambler who'd soon be cashing in his chips, but the problem was, he wasn't anywhere near the poker table, yet.

"They don't stop on their own, Ben. It's an addiction. They just keep on killing." Leo's mind was a jumble of the past few days. Nothing made sense anymore. He needed sleep. And he needed to stop drinking.

"Right, and how many are never caught? Years later picked up for something unrelated, and we find hundreds of bodies under some loon's house." Ben refilled his glass, then scowled. "Jesus

Christ. What the fuck's the matter with this world that it's shittin' out this waste?"

"He's not sadistic, doesn't try to control with rape — he leaves notes and roses. Which makes me think — it's not some kind of fantasy. He just wants them dead. Why do I think he's actually got a motive? In his own crazy mind anyway." Leo sounded as if he questioned his hunch. "What the hell am I trying to say — What if it's not an addiction, or a compulsion, but rather, he's proving a point — like revenge."

Ben cocked his head and stared Leo in the eye, his own eyes slowly disappearing beneath drooping lids. "You may be on to something. But if it's revenge, why the roses? To me, roses are a sign of love, or sympathy."

"You're talking to a guy who doesn't give *live* women roses. So, I have no clue as to why someone would leave a *dead* woman a rose. Or stick one into them."

"You stick stuff into women, Leo, but not roses." Ben guffawed and slapped a palm on the table. His scotch was showing, and he was getting loud.

"I'm not even touching that one." Leo shook his head and frowned, then emptied his glass. "Women, all in their twenties. All in bed, more than likely sound asleep."

"Geeze, Leo. It's sounding more and more like your love life." Ben guffawed even harder, then slammed his glass onto the table so the scotch sloshed over the lip, soaking the tablecloth.

"I think it's your bedtime, Benny." Leo got up from the table and stretched his arms over his head. He checked his watch. "I'm gonna hit the road, pal. I have a long day tomorrow. Tell Terry thank you for the delicious lasagna."

"I didn't insult you, did I, Leo? No harm intended." Ben stood and crossed the room with a worried look on his face.

"I know, buddy. Keep the faith — and keep it light. Just like the sign over your desk. Got to keep a sense of humor or we'll all go insane." Leo made a fist and took a swipe at his friend's bicep. "Talk to you soon."

CHARLOTTE † NORTH CAROLINA

The distance from Atlanta to Charlotte: two hundred and forty-five miles. About a four and a half hour drive. The dark colored vehicle, now free of grime because of heavy rain, moved at or below the speed limit. The tires were beefy and any wetland mud had dried and caked, and was blowing off with momentum the tires created as the wheels spun away from murder. Spinning almost like a laboratory centrifuge, but rather than separating blood, the tires separated dirt from rubber and metal, and then spit it off to the side of the road, like a centrifuge without a cover. Blood could be purified, sometimes, but dirt was dirt, and would always be nothing but dirt, lying atop more dirt, layer upon layer, and that was the heart of the inevitable.

There was a plan. There were layers. And there was a buildup of layers. When the layers became too thick and heavy, they had to be shed, like dead skin on a decomposing body. In time, the separated layers eventually came together, as dirt. Dirt that mixed with rain, coated tires, dried, caked, and with momentum spun, over and over again until all dirt had been purified.

Although already contemplating and anxious for the next encounter, speeding was not an option. On this mission, there could be no mistakes. That would lead to the *killer's* inevitable. It wasn't yet time. The skin would decide if it was time. Muscles. The eyes, the brain. They were all part of the inevitable. Interstate 75 would also lead to the inevitable.

Moving faster than the speed limit would attract attention and questions, such as, "Driver's license and registration . . . What might you be running from? In what direction are you going? What is your plan?" The plan could never be discussed or revealed. That would lead to the inescapable, the inevitable.

Remove the hat that covers your hellish eyes. Remove the scarf concealing your wretched mouth. You are good at concealing, but they might think you're a terrorist, leading to false arrest. Wouldn't that be something? To be detained, possibly locked in a cell for crime, when you were innocent — innocent of that particular offense.

The rear seat was bundled with bedding and clothing. A cooler held food, but as the vehicle required a refill of gasoline, the cooler would need to be restocked. You're too hungry. You eat too much, too fast. You restock at night, when most markets are closed but gasoline can be found twenty-four hours a day, so that's not a problem. You swipe a card, fill the tank, and no one ever asks your name. Most importantly, they don't see your face, or your hands beneath the gloves that have a mind of their own. They do things you sometimes resist, but they're strong. They can remain stoic. Your hands tremble. Gloves are superior. You stock your cooler late at night in discount stores where no one cares if you look unsightly, if you wear a hat, even a mask. And gloves, no one cares. You sometimes find the inevitable late at night in discount stores. You follow it home.

Charlotte was planned. Charlotte, North Carolina is where the vehicle happened to require a refill of gasoline.

It was late when it arrived, cruising almost-empty neighborhoods, careful not to loiter on the same street too long, and never be there twice. Just a slow and steady pace on two-lane roads, roads with reflective white divider lines. Lines that were mesmerizing until they stopped, just short of the entrance to the park.

The voice was delightful, but the strides of the loose-hipped young woman were irresistible.

"Come back, teddy bear. I was only joking."

"Go fuck yourself."

"Get back in the car, silly girl."

"I'd rather walk than be anywhere near you."

"Suit yourself."

Josie Delaney walked two blocks, from what she thought was a deserted park, to the bus stop.

As it passed her, the vehicle wanted to stop, to offer a ride, but once the door was opened and the interior lights flicked on, the young woman would never enter. The sight behind the wheel, along with the staggering odor of old food and urine, would make her run screaming. That would be impossible. The killer stopped the vehicle a safe distance from where the girl stood, and in a fit of rage, shattered the light with a gloved fist.

There were no buses after ten at night, so she called for a cab that delivered her safely home. Home to the apartment she shared with a friend. A friend named Roxie. Roxie who would be away until tomorrow. They lived on the ground floor of a house. A house with two apartments above them, on the second and third floors.

Josie hated living on the ground floor. Her roommate liked it. Easier to carry musical instruments in and out of a flat, as Roxie referred to the ground floor apartment. But Josie had nothing to carry in and out other than herself, and a bag of groceries now and then. Most of her meals were eaten at the little cafe around the corner. That's where she met him, two months prior, on the patio of that cafe. The one that had plump bagels and cream cheese for breakfast. Chicken salad for lunch. Filet of sole as a dinner special every Friday night.

Josie worked in an office as a receptionist, and brought nothing home from work that couldn't be carried into a second or third floor apartment. Nothing but gossip, sometimes a head cold, an occasional doggie bag from a luncheon, even a kitten. But the landlord didn't allow pets. Although a grown cat would be independent and wasn't exactly classified as a pet if it just ate from a bowl on the floor of the small kitchen, used a litter box now and then, when it wasn't outside roaming the neighborhood as the adorable kitten was the day Josie found it. The day she brought home the little ball of fur stray. When the landlord said she couldn't keep it, she cuddled it for an hour, kissed it good bye, then brought it to a local shelter, hoping it would find a good home, and not be euthanized like many animals were. She had left in tears.

Humans were euthanized too. Josie remembered her grandfather, the man with Alzheimer's. She remembered his face of confusion, the one that rarely recognized her during later years, when *he* was not easily recognizable, either. The gathered mouth that said off the wall things, stumbling with convoluted memories and random nonsense, repeating meaningless words to her, to the air, to himself. Sad. It made Josie cry. Cry for the kitten. Cry for her grandfather, because after less than a week in the nursing home, he had been euthanized. Euthanized with morphine. High doses of morphine. She would never forget the way he looked when she entered the room, just missing his last moment of life. The skin on his face was smooth marble gray, chin to crown of his head bound by gauze, safety-pinned, pinned to hold shut a mouth left agape by a final gasp for breath. The sight was horrifying. Josie would never forget. She would never forget the odor of death in that room so small, six relatives stood cramped around the old man's body.

Did bad things happen to loved ones in every family? What about pets?

Josie opened the side door that led her into the kitchen. It was worn, but spotless. A drainboard held clean dishes, and Josie had scoured the sink before she left. She had also cleaned the bathroom, all the floors and carpets, and changed the sheets on her bed, just in case. In case he accompanied her home. But he was acting like an asshole.

Josie wondered if he was seeing someone else. Someone

besides her. Because he hadn't acted like this when they first met. He was sweet, he was warm, he complimented her. He had even brought her flowers. Flowers which, before they completely wilted, she had pressed between the pages of her favorite book. The one that always rested on her nightstand. Tonight he was an ass. He called her something that troubled her. Insulted her. Angered her. Brought back memories of the past. Almost made her cry.

Before disappearing into her bedroom, Josie opened a kitchen cabinet, the long shelf lined with rubber matting and so many glasses, logo faced glasses, promotional offers she'd bought from every fast food place she'd ever eaten at, or swiped from every bar she had ever consumed draft beer in. She plucked off the shelf a fairytale glass, filled it from the tap, then popped into her mouth two aspirins, which she flushed down with tasteless warm water.

January Valentine

maybe you don't know it yet
but this wolf can only cry
just so many tears
till reality drops by
and dumb turns wise
so open up those eyes

THE STALKING UNKNOWN

After following Josie, and then the cab, the vehicle with dark paint and beefy tires parked on a side road, a block away from Josie's apartment, which was not all that far from the deserted park, although too far for Josie to walk alone at night.

The streets were empty. It was after midnight. The sky was slate with a slice of inadequate moon failing to light a footpath to Josie's door. Tonight it would rain. Rain was in the air. The air smelled of impending rain. Sweet, cleansing rain.

Josie loved rainy nights. She opened her bedroom window to let in sweet air of the autumn night. A refreshing stream rushed into her room, ruffling the blue curtains that didn't quite cover her window, making her room smell almost as fresh as the outdoors. She closed her eyes, lifted her chin, and inhaled. She loved the smell of fresh air. Fresh air and rain.

It was dark outside. Especially dark in the alley that flowed along the side of the house, all the way around the back, where Josie's bedroom window was halfway open, open to invite inside, sweet autumn air.

That's all Josie invited inside; just the air. Not him. And definitely not the thing standing outside her open bedroom window, a glove resting on peeling white molding, a second glove following, dislocating a fat spotted spider webbing its way across splintering wood.

Captivated eyes peered through the screen, into the lighted bedroom where the pretty thing began to undress. For her date, she had worn a yellow angora sweater that went great with her long chestnut hair and slim navy pants.

She had unzipped and kicked off her high heeled boots when she first came in, then picked them up, but left them standing at the doorway, so the only things on her feet were two soft white socks, one covering each pedicured foot. Socks that could be clearly seen, after she unzipped her navy pants, pulled them past her rounded hips and thighs, and let them drop to the rug, where with the toes of her right foot she sent them flying into a corner. Angry. Josie was angry. He was the pair of pants she kicked across the floor. How could he call her that? They had kissed, made out actually, in his car in the park. He had almost slid inside her. Then he said that to her.

Josie padded around her bedroom, removing earrings, brushing her hair, pulling it up to fasten it with a clip into a knot so she could take a shower without wetting it. She'd washed it before she left for the date. It didn't need another washing tonight. And she was so tired. All she wanted to do was to flop into bed and fall fast asleep. Then she wouldn't have to think about him. Or what he had said to her.

She'd probably never speak to him again. If he apologized, maybe she would.

The eyes outside the window watched every move she made, every breath she took. Watched her remove her earrings, brush her hair, pin it up, yank the sweater over her head which undid the knot in her hair. Her hair spilled over her bare shoulders. She was beautiful. Beautiful in bikini underpants and matching pushup bra. Her undergarments were yellow, yellow like her sweater. In fact, they almost perfectly matched the angora sweater she pulled over her head.

"Like canary. Maybe lemon. Only a shade deeper, richer,

satin but velvety looking, if that makes sense," Josie had told her roommate, Roxie, when she described on the phone what she would be wearing on the date.

During their earlier call, Josie heard chaos in the background. Music and voices, excitement bellowing from over fifty miles away. Then the static on Roxie's cell grew stronger as she hurried into the Echo Logic, the club where her band would be performing until closing time. Closing time was three a.m. They would stay the night, and after a hearty breakfast, they would drive fifty miles home. Home to the apartment. Home to Josie.

Roxie was the lead guitarist of the struggling rock band, *The Next Life*. This was a big break for the group who'd been together for over five years, entertaining at local clubs and high school concerts. This booking was their first *real* gig, actually their only gig in several months.

Record moguls had been known to send scouts to the popular club, unexpectedly. The band was freaking out. Tonight could be their night. This could be their ticket, shooting them straight into the world of rock music and fame.

But Josie had chosen to miss it, so she could keep her dream date with him, a last minute decision for which she was now sorry. She should have gone to watch *The Next Life* perform. Cheer them on as any good friend should have. Had she gone, things wouldn't have turned out this way.

Josie disappeared into the bathroom across the narrow hall, turned on the shower and let the water run while she pulled her hair back into a knot. With bulging eyes, the killer outside the window strained to see her, but the bathroom door, across the lighted hallway, was halfway closed. *Damn.* The others had all been asleep. They had made it easy. But this one made it enticing. She was lively, and she was lovely. As lovely as a rose. A white rose, not maroon like the one shoved into the pocket of the coat, the coat that also held the note.

The inevitable would love her, as the killer was beginning to. But that was impossible. The gloves wouldn't permit that. And the gloves had a mind of their own. No matter how the killer resisted, the gloves always had their way.

When she streaked past the bedroom doorway, naked, naked on her way to snatch a towel from the linen closet next to the bathroom, her movements caused a sensation, a sensation difficult to resist. Even more difficult to resist than the gloves. The gloves that were strong.

The others never caused a sensation. Perhaps because they slept quietly. Peacefully. And they were covered by clothing, or covered with sheets. But this one, this one was special. This one was beautiful, and she was enticing. The sensation grew strong. This had never before happened. It was puzzling. It was disturbing. It was agitating. It caused a tug of war that raged between the sensation and the gloves.

There she was! Walking back into the bedroom. Beautiful in a white towel fastened around her waist. Her breasts had been dried, and they were beautiful. But her shoulders still glistened with shower. And the ends of her hair curled, curled from steam and overspray of fine mist and time, time that had taken a painful ten minutes to the second. The clock on the wrist said so. And the clock was never wrong. Ten painful minutes of waiting were calming, in a way, yet triggered increasing apprehension. The gloves gripped the molding of the window more tightly, almost desperately, while the eyes bulged so hard they hurt.

Josie undid her hair, let it spill down her back, tossed her head forward so her hair fell almost to the floor as she brushed it. She brushed it until it hung like a shimmering curtain. Her breasts fell along with her hair, but not to the floor. They fell like teardrops, teardrops that crossed her chest, but they held their shape, held their beautiful shape.

Josie heard the phone ring. The phone on her bedside table. Dropping the hairbrush onto her vanity, she walked quickly, but didn't pick up the receiver. She waited. Waited for the fourth ring. She couldn't answer on the first or second, that would make her look anxious, like she was sitting on the bed, phone in hand, waiting for his call.

"Hello." Her sweet voice traveled across the room and out

the window.

The killer watched. The killer listened. Then swallowed hard, hard because of the knot, the knot in the throat, the knot growing deep inside.

"No. I wasn't sleeping. I just got out of the shower."

Long moments of silence.

"Yes. It *was* wrong. I was upset."

Silence.

"No. You shouldn't have."

More silence, then a soft laugh.

"Really? Ooh."

Josie had been sitting on the bed, but when the conversation became extended, she lay back, propped on a pillow, and held the phone with her shoulder. Her breasts were still teardrops, teardrops pointing to the ceiling. The towel loosened, then fell from her waist. She pulled up her knees, then let her legs fall to the side, along with her hips. Comfortable. A comfortable position. With one hand, she grasped the phone, the other played with her hair, twirling a lock around her finger as she smiled and laughed, then spoke softly into the phone. Whispers. Then a yawn. A smiling yawn. A contented yawn.

Josie hung up the phone, slipped between the sheets, then reached to the nightstand to snap off the lamp.

What now? The room fell into shadows. The show was over. But she was not asleep. As the eyes adjusted to the dimness, the killer watched her turn, settle into the mattress, then finally, silence. Stillness. Soft breathing. It had been worth the wait. Now was the time. Time for the inevitable — carefully remove the barrier, the window screen, the loose window screen — carefully, quietly. Done. The gloves were ready, as was the knife, and the rose, and the note. One glove pulled up, then the other, up onto the sill. One, two, three, hoist. One leg up, over, inside, then the other. Boots be quiet!

January Valentine

forever searching for a place to feel
what exists for others yet for some unreal
have i been nurtured in a house so full of lies?
for there is no peace inside a restless mind

JUST WHAT THE DOCKHOUSE ORDERED

Leo couldn't get comfortable. He tossed and turned. Kept looking at the clock. He hated being a clock watcher. But it was his nature, since this job, anyway. He remembered the days when time had no meaning. Days, nights, weeks, months, nothing mattered. Not like too many things mattered to him now, other than thoughts of dinner at Ben Cassidy's house. His mind revolved around the conversation they'd had. Even though days had passed, the dialogue lingered. Lingered like a morning-after hangover even painkillers couldn't erase. Not until it wore itself out hours later, after a shower, no breakfast. Leo couldn't eat with a hangover. He needed a cool shower and iced tea. For some reason, iced tea soothed the lining of his gut. Then within a few hours he'd begin to feel better, and hungry. He'd eat lunch, then be ready to do it all over again.

But nothing could stop his mind, or the conversation. There hadn't been any news since the word of the last murder in Atlanta. The one following Gina's. Still, his mind would not rest. Not until the murders stopped. Fat chance of that. He knew serial killers didn't just decide to stop killing. They may drop out of sight for a while. But they always returned. More than likely bolder, more experienced, as he and Ben had discussed. Their killer had already become bolder, and frequency would follow, so the psycho could fill that evil thing inside him, whatever it was that motivated him to be so brutal, so vicious. Even animals were kinder. What was it about the human mind that it could become so distorted a person could commit such heinous acts? But this guy was a monster, so maybe calling him human gave him too much credit.

Sleep was impossible. Leo checked the clock again. Eleven p.m.

"What's the point," he grumbled as his legs slid over the side of the bed and his feet hit the floor.

Leo decided to throw on faded jeans and a soft blue v-neck sweater. He'd drive to the club. Like Glory, he'd go commando. Maybe there was something to it. The inside of his jeans did feel good against his bare skin without the cling of boxer briefs. There was a freedom. And it felt good. Leave it to Glory. She knew every good thing imaginable — and then some.

After Leo dressed, he ran a comb through his hair, slid his wallet into a pocket of his jeans, then grabbed his cell from the nightstand. For a moment he held the BlackBerry in his palm, staring at it, contemplating. After checking the clock yet again, he pulled a paper from the nightstand drawer, unfolded it, then punched a phone number into the BlackBerry's worn face. Leo had a finger on the disconnect button. After four rings he almost pressed, then a raspy voice said, "This better be good."

"Doc," Leo said. "Did I wake you?"

"Of course you did. Who the hell is this?"

"Leo Gibraldi."

"Baltimore? How'd you get my number? It's unlisted."

"Acquaintances in high places."

"I never said I was a doctor. Pathologist in training."

"There was a murder the day I left."

"Yeah. You missed the body by a few hours. Could've seen it."

"That's okay. Any details?"

Pause

"Sure. Come on down. I'll show you what I have."

Pause

"I like what you have. Any details though?"

"Meet me for breakfast, Baltimore. I'll bring the coroner's report — and a copy of the killer's note."

"Hmm."

"Hmm, what?"

"Thinking. Damn, Amber, I'm drowning in work up here. I have to be in court —"

"Whatever you want, Leo."

"You're making it hard for me."

Raspy chuckle. "That's my intention. So, you coming?"

Amber's voice was hoarse and muffled. Leo imagined her warm body in bed, stark naked beneath the sheets.

"Maybe."

"Hey, Baltimore. I thought we had chemistry."

"I flunked chemistry. That's how I ended up in law school."

"Christ, Leo. You never give a straight answer. Are you always this evasive?"

"Not evasive. Non-committal."

"I've got an early morning."

Click.

Although the realtor had described Leo's rowhouse as waterfront, when he stood on his deck, the view was more city than ocean. The only waterfront semblance was the pungent scent of decaying fish when the sea breeze blew hard in the right direction. Still, Leo found comfort in the place he called home. His unit shared the long street with a charismatic line of others, the only original homes left standing in the Bay Area. Two streets away, throttling the Atlantic, identical structures had been demoed three years prior, where upscale condos had taken their beachfront place. But the developer's wife liked the urban-flavored homes so much, she talked her husband into redressing this block of houses, even moving her in-laws into a corner unit.

Built in the forties, the brick structures withstood hurricanes and families with scores of kids. There was something about older homes that exuded warmth and charm, with white painted porches that shouted tales of family and neighbor gatherings on summertime stoops, all unity and community.

When the agent first showed Leo the ill-described residence, his groan told her he wasn't enthralled.

"Don't judge a book by its cover." The menopausal woman squawked with a shake of her honey-streaked head of razored hair. "Remember what I told you about face value?" Her brown, hyperthyroid eyes protruded. "If the outside of this house looked anything like the ones two streets south of here, you'd be paying at the very least, a hundred grand more. Reserve judgment, kiddo. Wait'll you see the rooms."

"Hmm," had been Leo's only reply until he set foot inside. Then he fell in love. The woman hadn't been kidding when she called the structures *mismatched dwellings*. The exteriors remained rejuvenated forties, but the dramatically renovated interiors were space-age ultra modern, with nine-foot ceilings, bright white walls, iron banisters, track lighting, all handsomely floored with natural beech wood, angled and gleaming.

Leo left his bedroom, jogged down the stairs, stopped in the snazzy kitchen to slug some juice, then exited through the kitchen door leading to the cement covered driveway, and his convertible.

The air was still. No neighbors, no pets, no ocean breeze. After pulling onto the road, Leo cranked the radio. Music and night blasted across his face, cool and invigorating. He didn't feel tired at all. It should have been afternoon. He had so much energy, he felt like he could put in a day's work.

Half of a bright moon flashed across arched windows, while the Mustang's headlights ricocheted off white painted columns bracing terraces of noble mansions. The Mustang sped down Davis Drive, with Leo on his way to the Dockhouse, a local club that longed to be upscale, like the neighborhood. The club he inhabited on rare occasions hosted an influx of roaming execs and social snobs looking for a good time. Leo wasn't looking for a good time, but he needed a change of scene. He wasn't in the mood for one of the dives he usually hung out in, littered with transients. The kind of place where locals called guys like Leo and Ben Cassidy, migrants, eyeing them as if they were from another planet, planning an invasion. But, the area *was* becoming overpopulated with aliens, such as Leo, northern transplants seeking mild weather and soothing tides.

When Leo parked, the lot was only half full and the bay looked rich, velvet, and inviting. Inviting enough for him to consider hopping onto one of the dozen or more august yachts moored in style, and in starlight. He inhaled a salted breath. Fresh. Revitalizing.

The scene reminded him of the autumn night when he was a teen, cruising the Atlantic with Michael and Sienna. Sienna's birthday cruise. Leo smiled with memories of old friends, of Connecticut, when his life was uneventful, calm. Still, he had felt like a caged animal in that suburban existence, even when he flew like the wind on the worn seat of his Honda, daring fate and his skill to handle the bike on treacherous paths. Dark paths that cut through forests so dense, on foot or wheel, a wanderer would be lost without a ravenous light that could eat though midnight skies. The headlight of his Honda was that paralyzing. He missed the bike. Maybe he'd have it brought down to Maryland, ride it on the beach. Be adventurous again. Adventurous in different ways: inventive, adult stimulation, not teen thrills.

His late night Connecticut rides had been dangerous. He realized that now, when at the thought, his stomach could lurch if he let rekindle the feelings of innocent temptation, so simple yet insanely dangerous. But that's how Leo let off steam. Confronting danger.

Stepping through the door of the Dockhouse was even better than entering Connecticut's River Station Lounge. Dress was casual, and on weeknights the place wasn't mobbed. The interior, comprised mainly of an L-shaped bar and sweeping, ocean-view windows, wasn't as spacious, but it was an easy place to get lost in. Lose yourself. Lose your thoughts. Lose your virginity. Leo laughed at the thought. Virginity wasn't something he could even recall.

A modest dining room, nestled beyond an archway cutting through the far left wall, held a horseshoe design of tables that curled around stained timber siding. *Like the ski lodge in Whistler*, but without the fireplace, without the girl in the Eskimo jacket trimmed with fluffy white fur that flattered her face, and her body, when Leo stretched her out on it.

The Dockhouse was charming and adequate, as most patrons came for booze, not to dine. Leo paused at the entrance, then moved closer to the bar. Relaxed by the atmosphere, and memory-taste of the scotch he'd soon be swallowing, his stare drifted serenely as he looked for a vacant seat. Shadows obscured part of his face and soft knit shirt. The feature most visible was his broad neck, driving into the top of an even broader chest. He stood tall, and in a halo of mellow light from globes suspended above the bar, he looked even sexier than Glory proclaimed him to be, especially when they screwed in a stall, or pretzeled against a pier in moonlight, gasping ocean air, exhaling moans and obscenities that some people mumbled while having sex that almost drove a mind, and a body, wildly over the edge.

As Leo scanned faces, his hazel eyes stopped dead in their sockets when they wandered into a gauzy corner of the barroom. At an intimate table, beneath a shower of light from a brass chandelier, a woman sat alone. She poised in her chair, like a porcelain figurine in a specialty shop window, perched demurely with crossed legs as she nursed a goblet of rich, red wine. Along with the visualization of the body beneath the classy clothing, there was something else about the woman that attracted Leo's attention. She was stunning in a quiet way, much quieter than Glory, and appeared much more sedate. Not that Glory was the least bit sedate.

Her silk ruby blouse buttoned to her collarbone, and her peasant skirt covered every inch of her thighs. Most impressive, she didn't raise an arm and slug down a shot like most of the women Leo encountered in dives. She sipped her drink like a lady. He'd like to know more. Maybe someone like her could ease his mind, permanently. *Ouch*, he shut off the thought faster than he gulped the scotch the bartender set down before him.

January Valentine

erase me
misplace me
forsake me
come take me
i want you to make me
make me into something fine

SCARLETT MONTGOMERY

From across the dimly lit room, she immediately noticed Leo, impressed by his unintentional swagger, and broad shoulders he squared when he caught her stare.

Intrigued, she assessed his face, his hard body, her attention drawn to the masculine form that obviously satisfied the jeans he wore so well.

When she realized he was heading in her direction, her senses jolted. She focused on his face, intent on his eyes that seemed to search, then shift, right before hers dove and clung to the swell of his lips.

A cascade of auburn hair fell softly to her shoulders, hiding all but one diamond studded ear that twinkled through wispy tendrils, while the top was bunched beneath a clip at the back of her head. She continued to watch him with curiosity. He was young. He looked hot. She never thought she'd be a cougar . . .

*

Leo figured the woman's age to be around forty-five, give or take, but then again, from a distance, and with artfully applied makeup, it was difficult to gauge. The years had been kind, preserving her flawless complexion that glowed with soft blue light filtering from the dining room. With an elegant upstroke of a delicate hand, she raised the goblet of wine, almost level with her cinnamon eyes, then slowly brought it to her lips, still observing him. Was she lifting her glass in a toast? Was it a snare? Did she nod?

When Leo realized her stare was locked with his, shooting off the same kind of signals he felt inside his jeans, his mind began to wander, and his pace quickened from *perhaps* to a *definite yes*, as he approached.

*

She had never done this before — and her sanctuary in the corner of the room was about to be invaded. Invaded by someone who could rock her world. His expression told her. A blinking shift of her eyes led into a deep breath that hesitated in her throat before she exhaled. He *had* noticed her, even through the dimness. Distraction warmed her cheeks as she waited for the stranger who was about to pause beside her chair.

"Hello," Leo said smoothly, eyes baring his thoughts. "Alone tonight?"

She tilted her head, squinting with questioning brows, then nodded.

"Would you like to be alone?" At the concept of appearing an unwelcomed guest, his lips curled irresistibly. "Or invite me in."

With a careless gesture of her hand, she motioned to an opposite chair, droning a hint of *south* as she said, "Have a seat."

Lowered lashes couldn't hide the rise of interest. Leo watched her eyes wash him from head to toe. Before sitting, he offered a brief smile, and his hand.

"Leo Gibraldi."

She brushed his palm lightly while her body remained inflexible. "Scarlett Montgomery." Her cagey stare melted into his.

Leo eased into a chair across from Scarlett. His body moved smoothly, like an undulating python.

When Scarlett smiled, Leo almost tasted her full red lips. Strange . . . Even stranger, were the colorful names of other women in his life: Ginger, Amber, and now Scarlett, he mused. Although this woman wasn't part of his life — yet.

"I've never seen you around here," Leo said, then motioned for a waiter with the same confidence and fluid movements he'd entered the club with.

"I'm from out of town." The words dripped from her lips with deepening *south.*

"Where do you call home?"

"Tennessee."

"Vacationing?"

"Working."

"What kind of work?"

"I'm a psychologist." Suddenly, she lifted her chin, as if remembering who she was, and eased into the placid flow of her own husky voice.

"Private practice?" Leo was relentless.

"I occasionally see patients in my office. But I'm actually a criminologist working with law enforcement, nationwide."

Leo didn't know if that was good or bad. He dealt with enough criminal issues at his job. He didn't need more of the same in his private life, even if she was beginning to turn him on with her tone and demeanor.

"How long will you be in Baltimore?"

"Just a few weeks." Her voice chilled with annoyance. "What is this, an interview?"

"Sorry. Force of habit." Leo's eyes danced across her face and chest, then sank to her hands that were folded on the table.

Obviously interrogating her, he was impressed. A beautiful, intelligent woman, and someone who might be able to understand him and his atypical habits. The fact that she was independent, and a *drifter*, made the woman all the more appealing.

"My turn." She repositioned in her chair. With an elbow on

the table, bracing her chin with a finger, her face settled into an analytical frown. "Where do you live and what do *you* do?" she shot back.

"Assistant Prosecutor for the city of Baltimore, which is where I reside." He deliberately mimicked her articulation, then at the significance of sharing something in common, his eyes narrowed, but quickly calmed.

Without expression, Scarlett stared, as if trying to visualize this rugged looking young man dressed in a suit, arguing cases before a judge. Although cocky, he seemed charmingly boyish, with the physique of an athlete. But then again, with the way he bombarded her with questions, she should have known he was part of the judicial system.

"Then I guess we both have the pleasure of being involved with the uncanny," she said, her voice still crisp.

"Hmph." Leo nodded in agreement. "Never a dull moment, either. So what do you do for entertainment?" His lips spread into a slow grin. Slow and suggestive, calling for a truce.

Her arms crossed her chest, while her head lifted dominantly. He was coming on to her, his behavior as obvious as the difference in their ages. The air needed to be cleared.

"You look about twenty-five." She leaned back into her chair.

"I was still in law school when I was twenty-five." Leo cocked a brow, and his chin. As he studied her, his grin faded. He would never ask a woman her age. Not unless she was part of a case he was working on. He'd have to continue to wonder. "You didn't answer my question." Without expression, his eyes glinted.

"I don't do much socializing. I'm a workaholic." A throaty chuckle before she sipped her wine.

"I fell into the same trap." Leo's head rocked, but his eyes remained steady with hers, then lowered, focusing on his empty glass. "Seems our waiter called it a night. I'll grab a couple of drinks from the bar. Wine?" He offered.

"Sure." Scarlett's lips parted with a brief smile. Her teeth were stunningly white and extraordinarily straight.

With riveted eyes, she watched Leo's commanding gait,

intentional and lazy as his arms swayed with his body language, then he blended with the shadows engulfing the bar.

When Leo returned with their drinks, her seat was empty. His gilded eyes searched the room; no sophisticated fox in sight. He stared at both glasses resting on the table, hers smooth crimson, his crisp and dark, wondering if she'd decided to leave. If that were the case, he'd slug his scotch and vacate the premises. *I should be hitting the road anyway,* crossed his mind as he savored the smoky flavor, then let the alcohol heat a path down his throat.

A few moments later, the click of her heels and storm of perfume signaled Scarlett's return from the ladies room.

Leo spun around to greet her. "Hey," he said, pushing her wine closer to her reach.

She paused beside his chair, almost as if her next words would be, "Good bye," but after studying him for a moment, she breezed onto her seat, her musky scent leaving an appetizing trail, then clasped the goblet with her palms.

"Thank you," she said, then raised her wine in a toast that looked identical to the first, the one that said, *I've got you in my sights. . .* "Za vashe zdorovye." Her voice was provocative in a foreign tongue.

"Russian?" Leo's brows furrowed. This woman could be full of surprises.

"Uh huh." Languid. Oozing sensuality that seemed to come naturally.

"Fluent?"

Scarlett smiled. "My housekeeper's fluent."

Leo grinned, then raised his glass. "To health — and to speaking Russian with a southern drawl. Catchy." *Alluring. . .*

"Is this what you do for entertainment?" Now Scarlett's brow lifted.

"After some of the cases I've been thrown lately, there's not much time for a social life."

"Difficult assignments?" She appeared compassionate, as if to say, *Sorry you had a rough day in the office, dear.* Then her expression turned coy, and she glanced at her bracelet-banded wristwatch. "Isn't it past a working boy's bedtime?" Her facial expression didn't budge, but her playful eyes said she was trying her damndest to get a rise out of him.

With a mild recoil, Leo shot her a sour look. If she wanted to spar, she found the right partner. "Is that an invitation?" He sounded surly. Two could play the same game.

She drank more wine, smiled shrewdly, but didn't reply.

"So I take that as a no?"

"Correct."

Leo checked his own watch strapped with a leather band. "I'm going to need a wake up call. It's almost one."

"Someone else who sleeps through the alarm." Another throaty chuckle. "Insomnia?"

"You too, huh? Should be part of the job description."

"I'm used to it by now."

"So, what brings you to Baltimore?"

"I'm working on a homicide investigation, and also completing a study on seasonal influence on crime."

"Crime and seasons. Fascinating. Sounds like a documentary."

"It *is* quite fascinating, and more than likely, *will* be a documentary." She restrained a smirk.

"So what's your theory on crime and seasons?" Posturing, he rolled his shoulders, then sank back in his chair, the spread of his legs masculine.

"I haven't even come close to formulating one."

Silence. Deep stares.

Leo grinned. "So are you going to fill me in on the concept of crime and seasons?"

Scarlett's hands rested on the tabletop, her index finger twisting an oval amethyst pinky ring. For a moment she looked thoughtful, then leaned forward, sliding her palms as far across the gleaming wood as her arms could reach. Her eyes were as lively as her words as she explained. "I select a year. As an illustration, we'll use 2011. Then analyze the months when most homicides have occurred, trying to pinpoint any correlation between seasons and biological mechanisms. Why do some months have a higher incidence of crime than others? What's the pattern? Why?" Frustration was apparent. "So far this year, April has had the highest activity, and this month's showing the lowest of all — thus far. What I'm trying to determine is, are there cyclic connections? Is climate a factor? Is there an astrological component that generates — perpetuates abhorrent behavior?" With a toss of her hands, she gestured disappointment. "I just don't know —"

"Mind boggling." Leo shook his head, as if shivering off a cold rain. "Sounds like a brain teaser. I've got to give you credit."

Scarlett shrugged. "Psychology is more than a profession to me. It *is* me. I've always been inquisitive. I psychoanalyzed my kindergarten classmates. It seemed natural."

Leo laughed.

"I'm serious." Her cool eyes widened defensively, the *south* in her voice unleashed.

"I believe you." Leo appreciated her enthusiasm, but questioned *her* emotional balance. Was she truly so dedicated? Or just odd. "Why all the way from Tennessee to Baltimore? We have criminologists here."

She sighed and tossed her head. "Guess I have a reputation." Although Scarlett's goal might have been humor, her actions bordered arrogant.

"I bet you do." Leo eyed her cautiously. The woman was flying on a rollercoaster with more emotional turbulence than he'd ever seen before. She was obviously affected by her work, and the world around her. Was this psychologist OCD? Or a voracious individual, unable to let her hair down long enough to discover fulfillment in life, rather than just in her profession. Leo's mind wandered. Was she even interested in sex? Would he ever have the chance to find out?

"You weren't kidding when you said you're a workaholic." *More like a junkie.* She was incredibly passionate about her work. Just thinking about how wild she might be in the bedroom began to tighten his jeans. And without boxers, Christ, would it show.

Her spirited eyes darkened. "I've also been profiling the killer they call the Sweet Dreams Psycho."

Leo stiffened, brought his legs together, sat up straight. "He hasn't hit Baltimore —"

"No, but I find the case intriguing. I've been putting a file together, on my own time"

Now she was talking Leo's language. "That's why I'm here tonight."

Scarlett looked puzzled.

"Trying to figure this guy. Like you, on my own time. What are his motives? Where will he turn up next?"

She eyed him curiously. "Personal interest?"

Leo nodded and emptied his glass of scotch. The thought of Gina in the Atlanta morgue elevated his pulse, even more than the woman sitting across from him with parted lips and sultry attitude.

"Don't waste your time. Not easy to figure out, if at all."

"So how do *you* do it?"

"Years of insomnia, and experience."

Did she just time stamp herself? He watched her lashes flutter above her high set cheekbones.

"So what do you think about this guy?"

"Unofficially —"

"I'll never tell."

"I have a hypothesis." As she spoke, her expression slipped from chaste to sardonic.

"This has been driving me nuts. Mind sharing?" Eager to hear her theory, Leo switched in his chair. He angled his body, stretched his legs into the walk space, and rested a forearm on the table, fingertips tapping his glass. He watched intently as Scarlett transformed from woman in lamplight to professor on podium.

"How much do you know about serial killers?" she asked.

"Just what I've read. I've never come into contact with one."

"This is just my personal opinion," she cautioned.

Leo nodded.

"He's not in this for sexual gratification. He doesn't mutilate.

He doesn't sodomize. He doesn't rape. Being privy to some gruesome pictorials, I've seen what some of these sadistic killers do to their victims." She scowled, then added, "This one doesn't fit the profile. Not yet, anyway."

"Not yet?" Leo's voice was edgy.

"Just a figure of speech. But at this point, he's not displaying the characteristics."

"So what do you think — getting even with his mother? Girlfriend?"

"I'm not sure yet. But you could almost say, he kills quietly. Striking when the victim is asleep — he's a coward. An introvert. He wants the person dead, but can't handle the confrontation of meeting his victim head-on, or partake in the act of kidnapping. He carries out his fantasies in *their* environment — not the safety of his, and doesn't attempt to hide the bodies. This is what throws me. Is he sloppy? Or trying to prove a point."

"Maybe he just doesn't give a shit. Excuse my French. Because he's on the move. He thinks he's infallible, super human." Leo slugged his drink, removing his stare from Scarlett's long enough to search the room for a waiter. "On the move," he repeated quietly, "maybe in this direction."

"I know he's on the move, which is unusual. Most serial killers remain within their own comfort zone. This one's a nomad, which makes him even more difficult to find."

"Road, rail, sea and air." Leo shook his head. "Itinerant psychos. Jesus. . . The most dangerous is the one who kills for pleasure."

Scarlett nodded. "You've been studying case histories."

"Still doesn't tell us why. So how are they apprehended then? Most of the murderers I put away have a motive. Something to trace them to. Let me rephrase that. In their own minds, they think they have a motive."

Scarlett drained her glass of wine. "There are murderers with motives I'm sure you're familiar with. Then there are serial killers, classified by the number of victims. Usually antisocial, with low or no self esteem at all. They can also appear normal and outgoing.

But usually share something in common; a past of cruelty and abuse. They themselves may have been controlled, and find the need to control others. In every case I've studied, their actions have always been sexually motivated."

"I thought you said he wasn't —"

"I don't believe he is."

"Hold that thought," Leo said. "I need another drink. You?" Scarlett nodded.

"I'll be right back. Don't disappear." His cheek puckered with a half grin.

"Wouldn't think of it."

By the look on her face, Scarlett seemed to be collecting her thoughts while she watched Leo's movements, and form-fitting jeans, as he retreated, then emerged from the darkened bar, carrying their drinks. His leisurely gait was now rigid.

"Thanks." She took her wine from his hand. "With the subject matter we're discussing, this is an absolute necessity." She took a lingering sip.

"A girl after my own heart." Leo's eyes warmed as he watched her. She was different from anyone he'd ever known, socially or professionally, but she was also magnetic.

This time Scarlett *did* smirk, although she seemed to be getting off on the conversation. Leo noticed she also seemed anxious to share whatever was on her mind.

"There are categories of serial killers. Thrill seekers, who want attention. They send messages, keep records. Mission oriented, doing society a favor by eliminating whom they consider unworthy. Visionary psychotics directed by voices or a god. Then there are lust killers who need to be turned on. The amount of pleasure they derive depends on how much they torture their victims. The more heinous the torture, the more aroused they become. This type is in touch with reality." She paused, as if to appraise Leo's expression.

"I'm with you. Go on," he said, although he was drowning in facts, and this woman's spicy eyes.

"He's not any of the above. What we're dealing with is

definitely a signature killer, hiding from society, from himself. He's even hiding from his victims. He's not in touch with reality. He has no life. He lives in darkness. He's a killing machine on a mission."

"Christ. You make him sound worse than the others."

"Not really. The end result is the same. Makes no difference why or how, they're all pure evil."

"I agree. Evil lives. We see it every day."

"Physiological." Scarlett pursed her lips and bobbed her head.

"What?"

"Brain chemistry."

"So that's your theory? A brain damaged signature psycho?"

"Looks like it. That's what they do. Leave psychological markers. Some like posing a body in a certain way, or inserting objects after death. They possess a sick unique preference."

As if Scarlett were teaching a class, words spilled from her lips, flowing faster than Leo's mind could process.

"So this guy prefers sleeping young women, which makes sense, if you can call it that. I'm just speaking figuratively, here."

"Right. His MO is slitting their throats. And his signature is planting a rose into the victim's body. This sets him apart from others."

"I've heard of rocks, sticks, even glass, but never flowers."

"The human mind is capable of strange behavior."

"Why roses? This may sound weird, but why not, uh, a candy bar? A cigar. A stick of gum?"

"Roses symbolize love."

"Yeah. And death. I'm starting to catch on."

"Trophy killers for instance, take a victim's personal items, which helps them remember the enjoyment they experienced during the kill."

"Pleasant memories of murder. Christ, how sick is that? So his sig is slicing and planting roses —"

"Right." She appeared impressed. "Confusing signature with MO can be a common mistake. MO is the series of actions required to locate, capture and slay a victim, then escape back into his own life without detection. And this guy's signature, for additional gratification or whatever sick reason, is leaving the rose. Controlling them. Claiming them for his own. Like a cowboy brands cattle, this killer's branding his victims. And until he's caught, we won't know why."

"So this is your method of profiling. Interesting. I hate to repeat, but Christ, it's mind boggling."

Scarlett nodded. "And by the way, inserting objects into a body after death is rare."

"So we're dealing with a rare psychopath. Maybe he doesn't rape because he's really a woman parading as a man. Ever think of that?"

"It's actually a possibility, but without a witness, we really don't know. I still believe it's biological —"

"I like the way you think, Scarlett. Can we continue this conversation another night? Say Saturday? It's almost time for work." Leo stifled a yawn, remembering how Glory had roped him into taking her to the opera on Saturday night. "Actually — how does Sunday sound? Brunch?"

Scarlett hesitated and eyed him slyly. "Against my better judgment. . . Sure. Why not."

"Great. Let me walk you to your car."

By the time they left the Dockhouse, it was almost three a.m. The air was damp, fragrant, relaxing.

"I could talk to you all night about this subject," Leo said, thinking, I could talk to you all night about anything.

Scarlett unlocked the door of her Jag, and Leo pulled it partially open, standing in front of it.

"Nice car. Rental?

She nodded. "Almost like the one sitting in my garage." In moonlight, her eyes sparkled. "Although I can think of a variety of palatable topics that would have been more enjoyable, it's been an intriguing discussion," Scarlett said airily.

"Yes it has — and how about we shoot for normal conversation on Sunday?" Leo sounded genuine, but knew damn well their future conversations would either begin or end with the

Sweet Dreams Psycho.

Even at the late hour, and alcohol consumption, Scarlett was alert and radiant. Leo's head was also crystal clear. So clear, that he was able to resist the urge to lean in and drop a kiss on her cheek.

"So, I take it you're not married." The words rolled easily off his tongue.

"No, I'm not. And I take it you're not either."

"Never even been close." Leo leaned against the door, blocking her entry into the Jag. "For the record, I got your signal back there." He shot her one of his provocative half-grins.

"And you took the bait." Her voice held no humor. Neither did her expression.

Leo usually wore the poker face. While she was more than likely psyching him out, he couldn't figure her out. "Guess so." His eyes narrowed.

"When you bite, is it for more than just one night?"

"Hmph." She kept catching him off guard. Leo's chuckle failed as he stepped away from the car door.

Scarlett slid behind the wheel, started the engine, then stuck her arm through the open window. She shoved a parchment business card at him.

"If you ever need a psychologist —"

"What about Sunday?"

"I changed my mind."

January Valentine

make you in good time
fore the nite turns white
when wrong feels right
be such a pretty sight

Eyes Deadlier Than A Shark

Falling asleep with his apologetic voice lingering in her ear, Josie drifted immediately into dream. Her slight movements created rasping sounds as her skin brushed the freshly laundered sheets. The sheets she had hoped to bring him home to. But she was alone. Or so she thought as her mind tumbled into a place where she was held captive. Kissed and caressed. A magical place where he began to whisper enchanting phrases.

The killer was inside. Inside the bedroom where Josie slept peacefully, breathing gentle sounds like the purr of the kitten she'd deserted at the shelter.

Frozen like a marble statue before the open window, for a moment the killer waited, plotting the next move as he stood a few steps from her bed. Stood on the carpet. The carpet that would buffer the sound of boots. Anxious boots. Curious boots. Cautious boots.

Quiet: boots, gloves, brain. . . must be quiet. Logic echoed inside the killer's head, bouncing across his brain like a rubber ball on a warped playground. The sleeping creature could startle. Could awaken. Asleep was best. Asleep deceived the inevitable. Inevitable was eternal. Sleep was not.

With prudent steps, in heavy boots he tried not to plod to her side, as he had through the mud. But, rather to move smoothly, graceful as her legs, remaining as motionless as she now appeared.

In less than three beats of his heart, the killer stood at her side, hovering over the sleeping goddess. The goddess who slumbered between fragrant sheets. The sheets meant for the voice on the phone. Not for the maniac with the glove that reached into the pocket of the coat. Her breathing was effortless, as effortless as the arm with the knife in the glove that moved closer and closer to her neck. Her creamy, pulsing neck.

It could have been the putrid odor that jarred Josie from dream. Or an internal alarm that sensed a presence in her bedroom, sharing the air just above her. Whatever it was, it caused her eyes to snap wide open. In a moment they adjusted, and instead of emptiness, the first sight her eyes transferred to her brain was the ominous thing. The black hovering thing. The thing with the putrid breath that had awakened her from a dream of her prince. The first physical thing Josie did was to gasp in horror.

The killer watched the tip of the knife reach her neck, just as Josie's lids sprang up like a window shade, snapping into a petrified stare.

Caught in the act. Caught off guard. Thoughts of confusion. Thoughts of surprise.

The rate of her heart raced the bubbling scream in her throat. "Oh — My — God!" Josie belted out so loudly, her ears reverberated with terror.

Soulless eyes stared down at her. Lifeless eyes. Eyes without passion, eyes without pain. Eyes deader than a shark's during a bloody, fatal attack.

As Josie's body jerked away, the knife plunged like a bomber jet crashing from the sky, sinking deep into her pillow. The pillow where here head had just rested. The knife plunged so deep, the long blade penetrated beyond the fiberfill, slashing through the mattress where it lodged, the glove still holding the metal handle.

"Josie?" Her name rang out as the bedroom light flashed on and glorious illumination flooded the room. "Josie!" Her roommate screeched when she saw what was leaning over the bed. About to plunge what looked like a butcher knife into her friend's soft flesh.

Startled, the killer's attention focused on the girl operating the light switch. The blonde haired girl who filled the room with so much brightness his eyes pained. His body held fast, but his head spun. Spun in the girl's direction. The killer was furious. Furious because of the interruption. The inevitable had been interrupted! He almost made a move toward her, then swung back to Josie.

One glove freed the knife as the other reached for Josie's neck. But Josie was already leaping up and out of bed, bare feet hitting the floor, running toward the doorway where her roommate stood with one hand over her mouth while the other had a death grip on the neck of her electric guitar.

Knife in glove, he straightened his stance, eyes shifting from one trembling woman to the other. Thoughts flashed. Thoughts whirled. Thoughts of power. Thoughts of pleasure. Thoughts of impending satisfaction. Thoughts of escaping. . . for now there were two. That had never occurred. Still, he watched. He calculated. Calculated the inevitable.

Josie stumbled toward the door, arms flailing, tripping over her own feet, reaching out for Roxie to catch her. The guitar dropped to the floor with a thud as Roxie struggled with the weight of Josie's body that slammed against her like a hundred pound punching bag. Roxie groped for the doorframe, but Josie's arms were in the way. Both girls tumbled to the floor.

"What the hell is happening? What IS that thing?" Roxie screamed.

"I have no fucking idea." Josie panted.

Thoughts burst. Thoughts of opportunity. With the weight of confusion, the killer's boots rocked on the floor as he deliberated.

Like a flash he was beside them, knife in glove, poised for attack. The girls sat on the floor, shaking uncontrollably, shrinking away as he converged upon them.

One glove began slashing prematurely as the other glove

caught Josie's ankle, pulling her to the center of the room where he dropped her unexpectedly, spun, then vaulted toward Roxie who was stunned on the floor. He bent, took her arm, pulled it like a weed from a neglected garden, then raised the knife and took aim.

Josie screamed loud enough to wake the dead. The dead in his eyes. Angered by the scream, the killer whipped around to face her, and for the first time, Josie had a chance to take a good look at what was inside the bedroom. Inside the bedroom with Josie and Roxie whose bodies twitched as their minds stammered with panic.

Her raw throat tightened. She'd be incapable of further screams. Josie focused on the hollows that should have held eyes, but saw nothing but two black beads surrounded by gray skin, loose skin, gray loose skin that covered the entire face. The face that looked ancient. Like some ancient, mummified dead thing. Mummy! Zombie! Walking dead?

Their eyes locked. Josie's eyes and the killer's. There was something magnetizing about the dread Josie felt. Something that prevented her from tearing her eyes away from his. She knew she should scramble to her feet, run screaming from the room, but she was paralyzed. The killer reacted to her stare by releasing Roxie. As he approached, Josie's mind raced.

Is this it? Is this how I'm going to die? At the hands of a dead thing? I'm going to die! She managed to slide her body across the rug, for the first time realizing she was naked.

Once more the glove locked onto her ankle, dragging her back toward the bed. The friction of rug fibers against tender skin burned.

"I'm not dying!" She cried as tears blurred her vision. So Josie started kicking, kicking harder than she'd ever kicked in her life. Stretching her legs as far as they could reach, elbows on carpet bracing her hips, she kicked like her life depended on it. Because her life did depend upon how hard she could kick.

The more Josie kicked, the harder he pulled, jerking her vigorously, jerking her violently, until it felt like her leg would dislocate from her hip. Swiftly, the gloves gripped both of Josie's ankles, lifted her into the air so that she dangled, then tossed her onto the bed. Tossed Josie like a ragdoll that was about to be savagely torn apart.

After Josie's body had been thrown onto the crumbled bed, the slashed bed, barricaded by a leg and a boot — the killer hovered above her splayed body. With heart-stopping eye contact, Josie almost fainted, but fought to stay awake so she could continue to fight for her life.

Thoughts insisted. Sleep! Sleep into the inevitable. The killer yearned for Josie to sleep, so the inevitable could be finalized.

Sobbing, Josie tried to roll into a ball, but the leg with the boot held her in place like a vice. The pressure on her chest took her breath away. Josie was terrified, but struggle slowly dissipated into resignation. "Oh God," she moaned. "God help me."

Having been rousted from sleep, dragged back and forth across the floor, hung by her legs like a butchered calf as she battled for her life, Josie felt weak, but continued to kick. Fluttering kicks that deteriorated each time the glove deflected a meager attempt by her bare feet.

Miraculously, the leg and the boot lifted their weight and Josie could breathe more easily, but the glove quickly replaced the grip of the *leg-vice* and held her to the bed. Like an instant replay, Josie watched the knife rise to the ceiling then plunge.

"No," she cried as the blade lowered, slowly now, but every bit as determined. Josie closed her eyes and prayed darkness would be fast, death would arrive quickly, painlessly, faster than the plunge of a blade sharp and long. She wanted to faint. Faint it all away. But now she couldn't faint. Adrenaline surged. Revitalizing her limbs. Keeping her wide awake. Awake and lucid so she could easily focus on the gleaming blade that was about to end her life. The twisted mouth leaking saliva.

The sound was like a crack of thunder as Roxie slammed the back of the killer's head with her guitar. The impact arrested the knife mid-stroke, but the glove didn't drop it. Knife in glove, he turned to face Roxie. Furious. He was furious. Thoughts.

Frustrated thoughts. Frenzied thoughts.

"Roxie!" Josie yelled as she scrambled off the bed.

"Josie, get out —" was all Roxie had a chance to say before he reached out and grabbed her by the neck. Fingers, long boney fingers, like fishbone, covered by a glove, tightened around her throat. The partner glove slashed at Roxie with strikes sharper than lightning. As it ripped through the air, the blade of the knife glinted beneath overhead light.

Josie watched in horror as the blade slashed at Roxie's neck. But Roxie didn't feel the blade, or the fatal gash, because right after Josie felt something shove her body aside, Chris made a flying tackle, a split second before the blade made direct contact with his girlfriend's sweet throat.

Freed from his clutch, Roxie ran to Josie, and the two girls huddled together with hope, because Chris was there. Chris was fighting with the killer. They were rolling on the floor, hugging like lovers in heat.

Chris rolled over and over, tangling with the tails of the trench coat, with the gloves, with the boots, trying to gain control. But it was impossible to pin the killer down. Each time Chris appeared to gain the upper hand, the killer flipped his two hundred twenty pound frame as if he were a baby, a baby tossed into the air at playtime. Each time the knife charged him, Chris's swift maneuvers averted the blade that seemed glued to the glove that kept slashing the air. Slashing at his face. Slashing at his throat. Violent stabbing motions nearing his chest, still covered by his jacket, which constricted his movements.

"Call the cops — " Chris managed to choke out as his air was cut off. Because a glove clumsily lost hold of the knife, Chris was now being strangled. Strangled by the other glove as they fought for control: Rage, strangle, or slice?

"In a minute —" Roxie's fear shouted. No time! She grabbed Josie's wooden vanity chair, lifted it high as her arms could stretch, and smashed it as hard as she could against the killer's head. With the impact, the wide brimmed hat flew across the room with the broken leg of the chair, then dropped to the floor.

The sharp pain in his head stifled the killer's wrath. Stop! Recoil. Stare at Roxie. Turn back to Chris. Thoughts beat the overtaxed brain. The killer sprang to his feet, ready to snatch Chris by the collar of his jacket, throw him against the wall as if he were a toy.

Josie held the phone in her hand. Trembling, she dialed 911, then covered herself with a robe. The only other thing she did was to try to explain to the operator on the other end of the line, that a horror flick monster was attacking her and her friends. She questioned her eyes. She questioned her sanity. She thanked God Roxie and Chris had returned earlier than expected.

Roxie gasped when she saw the head without the hat, small, too small to be so powerful. "Oh my God," she gasped a second time. "What the hell?"

The scalp was bare, but for patches of spindly hair encircling festering blisters. Roxie almost vomited. Shaking, she broke into sobs.

Without warning, the killer lunged for the hat, slapped it over his head, shoved the knife into a pocket, and the next moment he stood before the window where sirens could be heard. Before leaping out, he surveyed the room. The trashed room. The battered bed. The bed where the inevitable should have occurred, but did not. Staring from one terrified face to the other, the eyes narrowed a warning, then in a moment he was gone. Out the window faster than he had entered.

Landing upright, he disappeared into the night. Disappeared into the vehicle. The vehicle with beefy tires that gripped the road at a moderate speed as it vanished before the sirens arrived at the place where he had just lost power. Disheartened. Infuriated. Depressed. The spirit waned. The eyes were dead. But the ego remained. The ego raged.

January Valentine

inside this coma i hide your lies
lies and hurt that i despise
you're not the peace i thought i'd find
trapped inside my mind
my mind's not mine . . .
i sacrificed my sanity
just before you abandoned me

WHITETAIL

Fleeing the city, he would slowly recover. Contemplate, contrive the next. He would also commit abominable acts. Imaginative, satiating acts.

Hours elapsed, miles, and just before dawn the vehicle halted in a resting place, dense and silent: a refuge for wildlife, playground for hunters.

Powerless, he was restless. Disappointed, he sought release. Last night there had been no inevitable. The rose had been destroyed, along with his ego. From the bowels of hell a frantic refusal choked the air. The hunt was on.

The cavern of trees ignited the brain, triggering memory. A stream rushed alongside the path, just like Louisiana. But this stream was on its way to a waterfall, not a creek. He foraged, he roamed.

A perfect leg stretched across the path, tripping a boot. A whitetail's partially denuded carcass, half buried in the overgrowth. The boot swung a few times, clearing the area. A nudge, then a kick. No movement. Dreadful silence. Eerie silence. Although he craved human interaction, an animal would have to do.

Knife extracted from pocket, gripped by glove, the arm drew an arc. Dropping to his knees, as if in prayer, he inhaled the remains. With the butt of the knife he prodded the swollen belly, then flipped handle to blade. Head cocked, his eyes narrowed, then the blade sliced through the firm underside of the animal.

With each thrust power surged until a malnourished young was bared. A defective fawn, shriveled, hide stained with mother's berry colored blood.

The killer inspected the underdeveloped fawn, lifting paper thin lids, exposing lifeless orbs without pupils: a creature akin. Bared and torn from the mangled pouch, the fawn was laid to rest beside the path. The path that led to the inevitable.

The killer leapt to his boots. Governed by a hell-raising howl, the gloves pounded the front of the coat, wiped the knife on the decaying doe's hide, then stuffed the key to the inevitable into the darkness of a pocket.

Dominating whitetail, the gloves undid the coat, rummaged inside, and within moments a stream of pulsing fluid varnished the mutilated carcass. The carcass he had conquered.

The killer was potent. The killer was released. Killer attained redemption.

Whitetail was not a *sleeping pretty*, but if the knife divided flesh, there would be power. Revival. Defeat had been defeated, and he was stronger than before. The killer was becoming the inevitable. Killer was god.

The moon began to falter, and a brilliant sun would eventually sail the sky. The sky streaked with pink and blue heaven. Pink and blue heaven sprinkling beauty upon the glittering river. The rushing river. Rushing with life. Rushing with secrets. Rushing with reverie.

The gloves tumbled to the ground, followed by the coat, and finally the hat which landed like a weary bird.

The gloves knew the boy who'd bathed in a river — with fish, squirming fish without heads. There were pockets knives and sharpened rocks, and fishbone fingers plucking barbels from catfish families. For a fleeting moment, the heart was light. Simple pleasures of a life long gone. He floated, then slumbered. A deep, dreamless sleep. A black sleep. When he awakened he was rested, he was eager. The past was dead. The vehicle found the highway.

January Valentine

tearing down walls
drop into your soul
with distinct impression
of tripping into hell

It Didn't Look Human

The flight from Baltimore to Charlotte took less than an hour. An hour from their hectic workday. But this matter was urgent. If they were to understand, and prepare, this was something that absolutely had to be done.

When Ben and Leo arrived at Josie's apartment, Ben knocked on the plain white painted door. No response. He knocked again, louder this time.

"Hold your horses," the voice yelled. "I'll be right there."

Wearing a bathrobe that reached her ankles, her hair wrapped in a towel, Josie answered the door, a perturbed look on her face.

"Yes?"

A safety chain clinked against wood, then strained as Josie eased the six panel door into the kitchen, but didn't unhook the latch. She peeked through the two-inch crack, then studied the hand that gripped a photo ID in its palm.

"Detective Benjamin Cassidy. I'd like to ask you some questions about the break-in." Ben would go easy on her, wouldn't utter the word *attack* until he was safely inside where he'd grill the hell out of the girl. Although he was compassionate, witnesses, especially surviving eye witnesses, needed to be straight with him, sharing everything they could recall, dismissing not one single detail. Give it all to him. He'd be the one to sort it out. Decide what was pertinent, and what, if anything, was not. Rarely was a detail not important. Witnesses didn't realize this. It took a cop to know this. That it was extremely important for him to capture and comb through every single shred of evidence. Devour every last syllable emitted from the drawn lips of the annoyed witness.

Josie hesitated, but after Ben shoved his shield through the door, and his sausage fingers closer to her face, she relented. The safety lock clicked as she unlatched the chain, then swung open the door for Ben and Leo to enter.

As they walked into the kitchen, Ben said, "This is Leo Gibraldi. We're working on this case together."

"Oh," Josie said as her chilly eyes skipped over Ben, then warmed as they breezed over Leo.

Josie motioned to the round pine table, covered with a blue plastic tablecloth. "You can sit down."

They each grabbed a chair and for a moment stared.

"Why are Baltimore detectives investigating in Charlotte?" Josie looked confused.

"We have a vested interest in this case." Ben cleared his throat, shoved his ID deep into a pocket. His voice dropped an octave. "It's not uncommon to cross state lines."

Josie, sleepy, sullen, "Oh," sounded skeptical, but would comply. The young guy was hot.

As Ben pulled out his note pad, Leo's eyes wandered the kitchen. It was spotless. A kettle on the white range leaked a trickle of steam, and a mug rested on the counter, a ghostly plume of steam rising.

Ben did all the talking. "Can I call you Josie?"

She nodded.

"Are you feeling okay, Josie?"

"Somewhat better now." One hand tightened around the collar of her robe, while her other supported the terrycloth turban. "Excuse me. I'm going to put some clothes on," she said, before disappearing down the hallway. While towel drying her hair, she poked her head out the door and yelled, "You can help yourself to tea, on the counter, or look in the fridge. There's soda and bottled water. I'll be out in a second."

"Not uncommon to cross state lines," Leo said with a smirk. "Fast thinking." Would be true if the killer had hit Baltimore. At the thought, Leo's heart tripped.

"We better make this fast. If anyone finds out we're doing our own investigation, in another state no less, without cause, we'll be tarred and feathered."

"Add more stress, why don't you." Leo patted his pocket, feeling for his Xanax, but didn't take any.

"Eh. Don't worry. I'm just thinking out loud. We'll be back in Baltimore in time to head out to lunch." Ben stifled a yawn.

When Josie returned, her robe had been replaced by a patterned knit shirt and indigo jeans. She still wore pink fuzzy slippers. Her damp hair, like burnished shanks of rope, curled at the ends, enlivening with a stream of daylight filtering though the locked window.

"More comfortable now?" Ben asked.

"I'm fine. Would you like anything to drink?" She directed her question to Leo.

"A water would be good."

The refrigerator was a five foot high apartment model, just a bit shorter than Josie. She grabbed a bottle for Leo and asked Ben again, "Can I get you anything, detective?"

"Sure. Water for me too, and call me Ben."

A brief smile passed from her lips to Leo's face as she set the water onto the table in front of him.

"Thanks." Leo smiled back.

Josie set Ben's bottle down while still admiring Leo.

From then on, when Ben asked a question, Josie replied to Leo, who snapped open the cap and slugged down half a bottle of ice cold water. Ben pushed his bottle to the side without opening it.

"What can you tell me about the other night?" Ben got right

into his line of questioning.

"I've already told the other investigators everything that happened."

"If you don't mind. Tell me — tell us again." He readied the pen and pad he removed from his jacket pocket.

"It was about midnight. I got home and went straight to bed. Well not straight to bed. I talked on the phone first."

"To who?" Ben asked.

"A friend."

"A good friend?"

"It wasn't him if that's what you're getting at, detective."

"Did you get a look at his face?" Leo asked.

She looked directly into Leo's eyes and replied. "I couldn't exactly call it he or she."

Leo recoiled. "What?"

"The face. The body. It was weird. It didn't look human — well maybe human, but." She took a bolstering gulp of air. "You'll never believe me. I have a feeling the FBI agents thought I was crazy, or in shock."

"Try me," Leo said in a persuasive voice he rarely needed to use.

"It's so hard to describe. Everything happened so fast. I went to bed, fell right to sleep. I was in a dead sleep. Dreaming. Then I felt a presence beside me — standing over me." The look on her face told Ben and Leo the girl was beginning to relive the horrifying night. The last thing they wanted to do was to drive her back into the nightmare.

"Take it slow," Leo said as he softly tapped the top of her hand with his fingers. "One step at a time, okay? And I'll ask the questions. Just give me the answers." His fingers slid over hers then came to rest on the tabletop beside his bottle of water.

Josie looked relieved, relieved she didn't have to explain every last detail of the night she almost died, the night that would haunt her until the day she *did* die — a natural death.

Ben shot Leo an odd glance, as if to say he didn't mind Leo muscling in as long as he got all the facts. He snapped his water open and nursed it while Leo and Josie conversed.

"When you woke up, what was the first thing you saw?"

"It."

"Okay. Let's try it this way. Your room was dark, correct?"

"Yes. Just a bit of light from the hallway. But pretty dark."

"Did a noise wake you?" Leo wondered how the guy got into the window that was at least eight feet off the ground, and through the modest opening without making a sound loud enough to wake her.

"No. The smell woke me. The strong feeling of a presence, and the smell."

"What smell?" Ben had to ask. The conversation was beginning to sound bizarre.

"I guess I felt breath on my face. And a smell like —" She paused to find the right words. "Sick. A sick smell. Like when someone hasn't eaten all day, and you can almost smell the inside of their stomach. Or the inside of a dirty refrigerator with rotten food. Raunchy."

"Phew." Leo said. "Sounds gross. What else do you remember?"

"Let's call it *he*, even though it didn't really look like a man, or a woman. It — he had a small build. Not much taller than me, but strong as hell. He picked Chris up and threw him across the room like he was a ragdoll. And Chris is over two hundred pounds." Josie's eyes were wide with awe, but she appeared calmer as she drew Leo into her thoughts.

"He was relentless. All he wanted to do was stab me. I was naked." Josie's voice fell low and she looked uneasy. "I mean. I was naked on the bed, and he didn't touch me, other than pull me by my legs, hold me down, stuff like that. He didn't try to rape me — which he could have easily done. He was so frigging strong."

Ben and Leo exchanged glances. Reinforcing Leo's theory, revenge for what someone might have done to him, rather than lust or sexual retribution.

While Josie spoke, Ben took notes in his own special

shorthand not another soul could decipher.

"Sounds like it was a hell of a night," Leo said.

"So he wasn't tall, but he was strong. Was he built like me?" Ben asked. "Or Leo?"

"Nah ah," she replied to Ben while watching Leo. "Not like you, either." She passed him a sugary grin.

"He had a bulky coat on but I got the feeling he was skinny. Like when I kicked and hit a leg or arm, it was like I was kicking his bones. He felt hard, and I kicked him with bare feet, so I could feel —" She shuddered. "Oh, God. The face was the worst. His eyes looked like marbles inside cavities. Ick. Like how could the guy even see without pupils? And stringy hair. It was like a zombie. Like the walking dead. That's what I kept thinking the entire time. It was one of those walking zombies that was going to start eating me alive."

"Hmm. Interesting." Leo was beginning to wonder if this girl was still suffering shock, or maybe she was high. "You've been through a hell of a lot. We won't keep you much longer."

"Thank God for Roxie and Chris. If it wasn't for them, I'd be dead. They weren't supposed to come home that night." She shivered. "But their concert was a bust, so they left early. Struggling rock band. . ." She grinned weakly.

"So the three of you fought him off?" Leo asked.

"Not really. I kept trying to get away from him. Roxie's the one who slammed him with her guitar, and my chair, thankfully." Her eyes were so large they strained. "The funny thing was, he didn't seem to want Roxie. She hit him, but he kept coming back to me." Her voice cracked.

Again, Leo reached for her hand. "Try to relax. It's over and you're safe."

"I was never so happy to see Chris. He parked the car, then when he came inside, heard us screaming. He tackled the guy. It's kind of a blur, but somehow I called 911, and I think he may have heard the sirens, because he got up suddenly and jumped out the window. He could have killed us all. Thank God they came home and chased him —"

"Well, we're all thankful for that," said Ben. "And for your help."

"Oh, one more thing," Josie said. "After it was all over, we found purple flower petals on the floor. Like roses, but almost black." She wrinkled her nose. "I've never seen black roses. They must have fallen out of a pocket or something when Chris was rolling around on the floor with him. Why would he have roses in his pocket?"

"Hmm," Leo said. "You're sure they weren't red?"

"Absolutely positive. They were black. Well, purplish black."

"Thanks for speaking with us, Josie," Leo said as he and Ben stood. Ben carried his water bottle outside with him.

The door snapped shut, but in a minute flew open, with Josie springing onto the porch as if she'd forgotten something urgent. In one hand she held her cell phone, in the other a folded piece of paper that she handed to Leo, with a smile. "If there's anything you need, detective. Let me know. I'll do whatever I can to help."

The men exchanged glances, both assuming her phone number had been pressed into Leo's palm. Ben just shook his head.

When the door closed behind them, for a moment Leo and Ben stood on the sidewalk, facing each other, then separated, each completing their own survey of the grounds. Before leaving, they rejoined to complete a final inspection of the exterior bedroom window and surrounding area. As they walked around the house, Ben said, "What kind of aftershave do you wear, Leo?"

"Offensive?" Leo faced him with furrowed brows.

"Just the opposite." Ben kept shaking his head in disbelief. "Put you within ten feet of a broad and she wants you to screw her brains out."

"It can be a curse." Leo's response was flat and humorless.

"Glory?" Cassidy chuckled.

Leo laughed. "Now those are some potent pheromones."

"Some curse. I'm considering Viagra, and you whore around this city like an overheated rabbit. Like one of those guys in those romance novels Terry reads. Magnetic stare. Heated gaze. Exuding charm. You know, all that crap."

Leo laughed. "Are you sure those are Terry's romance novels?"

Ben shot him a smirk. "Whatever it is you do — just keep it away from Terry. I don't want her getting anymore ideas, or sudden bursts of energy like she did the other night after you left. I'm getting to be a tired old man."

"You know what we all need, Ben?"

"What —"

"A weekend at the retreat."

"Huh?"

"My cottage in the Connecticut woods."

"I didn't know you owned a place in Connecticut?"

"I don't exactly own it. It belongs to a friend. Any of us can use it, whenever. It's a sweet crash pad."

"Hmm. Interesting."

Leo laughed. "You're starting to sound like me." Then he turned serious. "Black roses? The others were all red."

"I caught that. Our guy's changing his signature."

"Spur of the moment? Maybe that's all he could get his hands on."

WHAT ABOUT GRAPHOLOGY?

"Good morning, Ginger." Leo handed her a tall, lidded cup. "Here's your latte."

"Thanks, Leo. How are you —"

Ginger had been arranging files on her desk, but when she lifted her gaze, the dark circles forming beneath Leo's normally bright eyes stopped her. "What happened to you?"

"Insomnia."

"You're starting to worry me."

"I'm fine. Late night."

"Glory? I told you she's not good for you, Leo." Ginger began another round of trying to run his life. "When are you going to settle down with a nice girl?"

"Do you have someone in mind for me?" Leo's grin teased.

"Don't look at me like that." Ginger sipped foam off her latte, holding the cup to her lower lip as her breath cooled the hot lid. "How are you doing with the Connolly case? Court's in three days. Do you have everything ready? Need me to do anything?"

"Everything's under control." Leo winked. Ginger was easily charmed — by Leo.

Before he could reach his office, the phone rang. Ginger

answered it, then put her hand over the receiver. "It's Ben Cassidy." Her coral mouth bared all of her teeth, her fat bottom lip rolling under as she discreetly over-enunciated *Ben Cassidy.*

"I'll pick up in my office."

Leo dropped his briefcase on his desk, then set down his coffee and plucked the receiver off its base. "Hey Ben."

"Meet me for coffee."

"I've got a cup right here on my desk."

"I got my hands on some reports. Sitting right in front of me. Impressive."

Leo checked his watch. Only twenty minutes had passed since he'd walked through the door. His boss would shit a brick if he looked for him and found him gone, yet again.

"Where and when?"

"Right now. I'm across the street at the deli, having breakfast. Join me." A tinge of excitement radiated through Cassidy's voice, revving his Bronx.

When Leo walked from his office to where Ginger sat at her desk, she immediately said, "No way. You're not leaving again —" Her petite filigree earrings shook with disapproval.

"I'll be back in a half hour or so. Just going across the street." Leo slipped into his charcoal jacket.

"Leo." Ginger sounded like a mother chastising her child. "You're already on thin ice with Appolito, because of what you did for that weasel Sam Landes. Albert hasn't gotten over that yet. If he finds out you're doing detective work while you're supposed to be putting a mugger away he's going to —"

"Fire me. I know." Leo strode to the door. "If anyone asks, I've got a hangover. I'm running across the street to buy some aspirin." He smirked. "Cover for me."

As Leo stepped into the corridor, Ginger's voice followed him out the door. "You're a prosecutor, Leo. Not a detective."

Without waiting for the traffic light to change, Leo darted across four lanes, dodging commuter traffic. When he entered the deli, Ben was at a rear table, eating an egg salad sandwich on rye. A bottle of diet Coke, within arm's reach, perspired beside a Styrofoam cup of coffee.

"I thought it was breakfast."

"It is. I'm eating eggs. Pull up a chair." Cassidy shoved a steaming cup across the table to Leo.

"I don't have a lot of time, Ben. I'm getting in over my head. Appolito's already up my ass for burying the case against Landes."

One glance told Ben this wasn't the usual cavalier Leonardi Gibraldi. He seemed subdued and looked *really* stressed.

"Those rose petals that were collected from Delaney's apartment," Cassidy spoke between bites, "were rare roses — called Nigrette. None of the shops in Charlotte had anything close. They had to be ordered and overnighted from another state."

"So you're saying the killer special ordered roses to stick into a corpse?"

"No. A florist in Charlotte ordered two dozen, three days before the Delaney attack."

"Who was the customer?"

"The *owner* of the flower shop . . . in Charlotte."

"You're not telling me much, Ben."

"For a funeral. The roses were ordered for a funeral. The florist doesn't stock them. The roses went from his shop, to the funeral home, to the cemetery."

"So he got the flowers from the funeral home, or the cemetery." Leo shook his head. "How the fuck did he pull that off? This gets more interesting by the day. What about the notes? Anything on the paper, or handwriting?"

"Nope. No prints. Everything's garden variety. The paper could've come from the victims themselves. I'm not saying it did. But it's plain note paper. Some torn. Nothing specific. Nothing uniform. And he wears gloves. Delaney confirmed that. Said he was almost completely covered during the attack. The only thing to fall off was his hat."

Ben slid a sheet of computer paper across the table, inches from Leo's hands.

"Here. Look at this." His smile reached his eyes.

"How the hell did you get your hands on a forensic report?"

"I've got my avenues."

"Hair sample?"

"Yep. Recovered at Delaney's."

"Damn. She didn't say."

"Probably didn't know. She seemed hung up on the roses."

"Pigment loss. Male Caucasian. So he's an old white man? Doesn't make sense."

"Maybe he's albino. That would account for lack of pigment. Ever think of that?"

"You're a step ahead of me, Cassidy. What's your gut tell you?"

"My gut says egg salad and pickles don't mix at ten a.m." Ben pushed the sandwich he had been eating aside, washing down the final bite with black coffee.

"What about graphology?" Since his visit to Atlanta, Leo's brows furrowed almost constantly. He was beginning to form a permanent line where the bridge of his nose met his forehead.

"Inadmissible in court," Ben fired back.

"Personality assessment isn't admissible. But how about a profile? Behavior profile. We don't have much now. At this point, I'm willing to consider anything. Maybe the killer's some rejuvenated senior with super human strength. Who the fuck knows."

"I saw one of the notes." Ben smiled slyly. "He scribbles like a first grader."

"You bastard. You saw a note and never told me? Where is it?" Leo sprang fully awake, his widening eyes erasing every trace of lids.

"It was never in my possession. I got into a classified file. If I could've fived it, you'd have had it after the first murder."

"I need to get my hands on one of those notes." Leo's stare questioned.

"Don't look at me, Leo. I can snoop, but can't physically remove anything —"

"If I had a copy. . . I know someone who could probably

profile him for us." Leo's eyes narrowed. "I also know someone who might be persuaded to get me a copy of one of those love notes."

*

"Anyone looking for me?" Leo huffed as he jogged into the office.

Ginger stood at the wall of filing cabinets, slim-figured and chic in a dark pants suit and red heels. At the sound of Leo's voice, she checked the wall clock. It was after ten.

"There must be Irish under that Italian skin of yours, Leo. You slipped by, yet again. But I wouldn't push my luck if I were you." Ginger's gray eyes, usually dove-like, were eagle sharp, as were her words.

"I'll be working late tonight." Leo brushed by with a trail of cologne, pausing to lean a forearm playfully on her shoulder. "Leave everything you have on the Connolly case on my desk before you leave today. I have to wrap things up before the weekend."

His face was so close, Ginger inhaled a mix of coffee and peppermint gum.

Black frames pushing back her coiled bangs, Ginger slid her eyeglasses up to rest on top of her nutmeg hair. In her often confrontational pose, she asked, "What's going on this weekend?"

"I'm flying to Atlanta."

January Valentine

i'm clawing those walls
nothing sweet to find
my mind is wired
and ready to blow

INDEPENDENCE † VIRGINIA

The vehicle moved along US-21 at a moderate speed. The hat rode low across the forehead, the brim a plunging wave ensconcing the face. From beneath the brim, calculating eyes peered through the dusty windshield. Eyes without prominent pupils. Eyes wrapped with membrane, like the skin of a grape, yellow sclera grainy with veins, rarely blinked. The broad collar of the coat climbed the back of the neck, leaving uncovered remnants of fragile shafts of hair, separated by blisters foraging the otherwise naked scalp. The first crop of boils had months ago healed, producing irregularly shaped keloids. A recent eruption ravaged remaining roots; like an acid bath, pustules melted hair.

The gloves on the wheel grew weary. Anxious. Plagued with thought. Plagued with need. And as the exit sign read, Independence, the mind grappled with images.

Ego. Independence. God–self. Independence. The inevitable. Independence.

The vehicle made a thoughtful right onto Main Street, where the beefy tires slowly cruised the area. The town was small. The town was peaceful. The cemetery was gated.

Instinct told the mind to find a resting place. A place near the cemetery. A place to rest and settle. Settle to plot the inevitable. Excitement festered with blisters.

Beefy tires ground the road, a road not far from town, a side road, a private road, protected by trees, tall trees. Many trees. Streams. Bubbling rivers.

Memory of the southern shack fluttered, like wilting leaves on October trees. The shack where he had lived. The shack near the swamp. The swamp filled with gators. The grave by the river, not far from the shack. The grave with no headstone.

A rambling fence engulfed the farmhouse beyond the field. A comfortable farmhouse. An endless field. An easy fence to cross. And a barn. A big barn. A barn without animals.

Peace. Rest. Plot.

He abandoned the vehicle in a forested nook beside the river. Hidden by massive pines: hemlocks, cypress, cedar and oak, a conservationist's haven. With fallen limbs and branches, scrub and brush, he disguised the vehicle until it appeared as a sleepy knoll at the foot of the great mountain's ascent. An autumn-trimmed knoll at the foot of a mighty mountain.

He sat beside his knoll, immersed in color, until a bright sun fell from the sky, staining blue and white, scrubbing white and blue with orange and red.

He sat against the knoll, immersed beneath a shimmering dome, a black dome, black as his eyes, where a full moon grew the spiny tips of ghostly peaks. Long and boney. Boney, like fishbone fingers. Peaks of pines straining toward the dome.

The night was calm. Quiet, before forest creatures awakened. Nature in abundance.

Crickets. Noise. Loud noise. Disturbing noise. Clenched gloves, stop the night!

When he approached, two windows on the lowest floor of the farmhouse were aflame. Aflame with a steady glow of table lamps. The undraped window of the kitchen, where a man and a woman feasted on a meal, invited. His mouth watered, but there were two. And they were not asleep. They moved. They spoke.

They smiled.

Twenty yards away, a barn. An unlocked barn with a floor of hay, and a loft of hay. Sharp utensils hanging on a wall. Appealing. He felt his pocket for the knife and pondered the objects on the wall. Large objects. Sharp objects.

Inside the farmhouse, Travis and Marla Booth shared a meal of beef stew, homemade biscuits, and coffee with cream. After dinner, dessert. Always dessert.

"This is great pie, Marla," Travis complimented, digging his fork into a quarter of the pie. Cinnamon sauce swarmed perfectly sliced apples, washed and peeled.

"I got the apples fresh from town, after I left work," Marla replied with a smile. "Mr. Barnes was selling them outside the market. Fresh. Plump and juicy. Reminded me of Halloween dunking."

"Halloween dunking." He laughed. "We should do that, Marla."

"I used them all in the pie you're about to finish all by yourself." Lovingly, she rubbed the top of his head.

Her broad smile lit up Travis's heart. On evenings like this, he was happy he'd finally surrendered his sworn state of bachelorhood to take the hand of the sweetest girl in town.

"We have our anniversary coming up soon," Travis said.

"Two years." Marla's eyes joined a heartbreaking frown.

"You'll have those kids someday, Marla. Just not now."

For Travis, the leap from freedom to married life had been a difficult one. He couldn't face the thought of children, not yet.

With a growling stomach, growling with hunger, the killer settled into the loft, the second floor loft padded with hay. Lighted by the moon until after the inviting meal, the man from the table closed the door on him. Darkness. Darkness and the smell of hay. The smell of long gone manure from empty stalls. Mouthwatering aroma of dinner resting on the man's shoulders as beef stew hung in stillness of air.

As he waited for the sun to fall, the killer listened. Listened to the faint sound of bovine lowing. Cows. Interesting cows. Thoughts. He thought about alternatives. Slaughter. Hunger.

Exhaust from the tractor the man drove into the barn before he closed the door rose, along with fumes from a gasoline can. Invisible plumes. Nauseating. Fumes now rose, along with the husky handle of a pitchfork stabbed enticingly into a bale of hay resting on the floor. Thoughts of tools. Sharp tools. Slaughter. Then sleep. Sleep without dream.

†

The creak of the opening barn door was stunning. He started. Noise. Quiet boots! For a moment, the man stopped at the wide mouth opening, stopped moving toward the tractor, halted, listened. Listened to the sounds of shuffling hay.

Travis's heavy boots stopped as he listened. "Imagination," he mumbled, then moved on. Moved onto the seat of his tractor.

Eyes scanning. Scanning eyes piercing through morning sun. Morning glare. Hunger. His stomach growled so loud, he curled into a ball. A ball in the hay. Into a dark, quiet corner, until the man and the tractor departed, the machine growling across the field. The endless field.

With careful steps he descended the loft. The wooden ladder creaked louder than the barn door. Onto the old wood floor the boots landed.

When he was certain the man on the tractor had gone, the killer moved quickly, pitchfork in hand, to the house. To the lowest floor windows. He watched. He waited. Like he had done last night, last night with a foaming mouth and grinding stomach.

Inside, the woman cleared breakfast dishes, scraping, feeding uneaten food to a barrel in the corner of the room. A white plastic barrel. The killer watched. Anxiously. Hungrily.

After finishing her chores, the woman left the kitchen. As she moved around inside the house, he moved around outside of the house. The boots . . . the boots outside the farmhouse, outside the windows, from room to room the boots followed as she walked, humming a song.

Memory: A voice, a woman's voice humming a song. Deep in the memory a name: Troy. Troy the destroyer of sin. Troy the destroyer. Sensation. The head tilted to the sun. In thought. In memory. Troy.

The woman disappeared up a long flight of stairs, to the bedrooms above. Pitchfork in glove, into the farmhouse. Instinctively, silent. Silent boots. Silent gloves. Into the kitchen. To the white plastic barrel. Scraps. The scraps fed the growl. Filled the stomach.

Stairs! Footsteps! Humming!

"Travis?" Marla called out. "Is that you?"

Pitchfork aimed like a dagger, he waited. He thought. His mind thought. At the sound of the woman's voice, a boot jumped. The plastic barrel tumbled. Tumbled over and scraps spilled across the floor.

As the glove readied, what remained of the mind alerted. Not now! Out the door, the kitchen door, the boots plodded, then plodded faster. To the knoll. Quiet boots! Pitchfork in glove, the killer skulked across the yard, slipped through the fence, crossed the narrow road, through the forest, to the niche, to the knoll.

After relieving himself, he sat. Sat against the knoll, immersed in color. The killer sat, eyes scanning the place the inevitable had led him to. Unsure. Uncertain. Strange. . . Disturbed. The need for power escalated, pumping through the pulse, filling his body, his fishbone body with imagination. With need.

Windswept clouds forced the noon sun aside. Thunder rumbled in the distance as Travis made a final pass across the fields, clearing, in early preparation for winter's blanket of snow. There was nothing worse than fields congested with soggy weeds after spring frost. He had learned that lesson well. Two years ago, when he took possession of the family farm.

He had broken the cycle by attaining a college degree and an office job. Travis knew next to nothing about farming when he and Marla happily accepted their unexpected wedding gift, along with the unhappy, unexpected death of his father and mother, the original owners, who died in a car crash not long after the Nuptials. The next service in that little church was their funeral service. Then they were buried in the town cemetery. The gated cemetery. The cemetery where graves were sprinkled with roses, waning roses as the weather turned cooler.

"Marla?" Travis called while he unlaced his boots outside the kitchen door. "Honey. You upstairs?"

Of course she was upstairs. His pickup was in the driveway. And before he came in from the field, he had seen her small white car, parked where the pebbled driveway wrapped the side of the house.

For a moment, when the house was so quiet, he wondered why he'd called his wife. She'd be at work at the bank in town. Travis then remembered it was Saturday. Marla would be out hanging wash. But not today. Today the forecast called for thunderstorms. Thunderstorms with heavy rain. Possibly hail.

"There you are," Marla said on her way down the stairs. "Why'd you do that?"

"Do what?"

"Knock over the kitchen garbage and leave it layin' all over the floor for me to clean up."

A puzzled look washed over Travis's face. "What are you talking about? I was plowing all morning. This is the first time I've been in this house since breakfast."

Marla looked uncomfortable. "I cleaned up the kitchen. Went upstairs to make the bed and gather laundry, and I heard something down here."

Her eyes widened and Travis swore it was fear that pushed her mouth into that kind of a pucker. It wasn't the same pucker her lips formed when they kissed with passion.

"Then I called you, but you didn't answer."

"I didn't answer cuz I wasn't here." He huffed annoyance.

"So who or what made noise down here and knocked over the garbage?" After shrugging the air, her hands landed palms down on her hips, fisting as she glared at him.

"How am I supposed to know, Marla? I'm out working the field. It must have been an animal."

"The door was closed, Travis." She was indignant. "What kind of an animal opens a doorknob?"

"It's got to be a coon. It's fall. They're getting ready for the winter. The Almanac says it's gonna be brutal. It's nesting —" Travis's reasoning sounded dumb, even to himself until he remembered, "You know. I thought I heard something out in the barn early this morning. It's got to be an animal. I flushed it out, so it ran into the house. That's got to be it."

"Great. So now we have an animal, smart enough to turn doorknobs, that wants to live in our house."

January Valentine

i never knew it could be this way
i never knew i could love so much
rainbows on your fingertips
burn when they brush my lips

EAT ME IN ATLANTA

Amber met Leo at the airport, in the rain, in jeans and a plunging purple sweater, the vibrant color a striking contrast against her cherry hued hair.

"Hey there, beautiful." Leo brushed her cheek with his. "Thanks for the ride."

"Anytime." Amber drew in his spicy cologne. "Mmm. You smell good enough to lick. And you can thank me later for the — ride." Her eyes, like a morning forest, glittered under terminal lighting.

Leo leveled his brows and shook his head. It wasn't even noon, he'd been with her for five minutes, and she was already starting. Not that he minded. At least her approach was straightforward. "Did I ever tell you my *thank yous* qualify for *thank yous*?"

"No. But we can thank the hell out of each other at my place."

His lips formed a half grin, dimpling a cheek. "By the way, you look good enough to eat. I like your sweater."

She laughed. "Who do you think you're kidding? You like what's *under* my sweater."

He nodded. "Hmm. I can't argue with that."

Her tongue rounded her mouth. "So, eat me." Her stare locked on his.

A cocky smile lifted his jaw while a brow shot up. "Right here?"

Chuckling, she hooked his arm with hers and they moved toward the exit doors. "If only . . . How was the flight?"

"Not bad. I brought reading material." He carried a briefcase with the Connolly files, so he'd be prepared for day one of the trial he hoped would be won by day three.

"You don't plan on reading while you're here, I hope."

After glancing at Amber's drowsy eyes, he corrected, "In-flight reading. I doubt there'd ever be much time for reading when you're around."

Leo held Amber's thoughtful umbrella as they walked to her car. She beeped the door lock open, but before entering asked, "Déjà vu on the flight?" She tilted her head.

Leo knew what she meant. "Like I told you. I wish I remembered more of our first meeting."

"Maybe this will refresh your memory." Amber tossed the umbrella into the back of the car, turned, wrapped her arms around Leo's neck, and planted her lips on his for a kiss lasting a full minute. A minute in the rain.

"That was a hell of a welcome, Amber. Nice shower too." Leo brushed the cool rain from the shoulders and arms of his jacket. His wet hair hung beyond his ears, rain dripping down the sides of his face.

"We'll dry you off at my place." A light chuckle. Amber was obviously affected by the kiss, and his presence.

When they stepped into her apartment, as promised, Amber handed Leo a thirsty bath towel in exchange for his jacket, shirt, and trousers, which she threw into the dryer on gentle setting. Feeling silly parading around in black mid-calf socks, blue boxer briefs and towel, Leo took a seat in a recliner beside the living room picture window and elevated his legs.

"Coffee or a drink?" Amber called from the kitchen.

"Your call. I'm good with anything."

Amber returned in a few minutes with a bottle of ruby red wine and two goblets. "It's after twelve." She smiled.

Leo watched her set the things onto an occasional table, admiring her silk robe that matched the rich wine. As Amber moved, so did her bare assets. Leo admired them too.

"I'm glad you phoned." She poured, then handed him a full goblet.

"I have to be honest." Leo was always honest. "I had ulterior motives." He took a long drink, then let a sip fill his mouth, flooding his tongue with flavor before swallowing. "Mmm. I don't usually drink wine. This isn't bad."

"I told you, whatever, whenever. And I meant it." Amber stood before the chair, took the goblet from his hand and set it on the table. When she turned to face him, without warning, she stripped off the robe and let it drop to the floor.

Leo did a double take, then decided, with this woman, anything less would have been a disappointment.

Before straddling him, Amber tugged off his boxers. "I have the information you wanted," she said, then threw the towel and boxers onto the floor. Before mounting him, she slid a condom on his ripened appreciation of her, and her actions.

"Full service, huh." He couldn't conceal even more appreciation as he sank deeper in the chair and eased her onto him.

Ambers lips were moister than her rain soaked hair that curled and draped over Leo's shoulders. She arched her spine and gyrated, then stilled, allowing her muscles to do their thing, contracting and easing rhythmically until Leo's slackened expression said he was about to keel over with pleasure.

Leo heaved a series of moans. In the grasp of a Boa Constrictor, he was wrapped, choked, swallowed alive. Glory had educated him on Kegel exercise, but *this* girl had the maneuver down to a science. What an edge women had over men.

Finally, Amber leaned in close, pulling Leo's face into the breasts she knew he couldn't resist.

When all was said and done, Amber's climax united with

cries and moans, while Leo ground to a grudging, groaning halt.

"You feel so good," he whispered against her neck, his breath warm and fast, hands locking her in place, guiding the movement of her hips as they wound down from a final surge of bliss.

"Yes I do," she gasped into his ear before collapsing onto him.

Afterward, Amber grabbed the towel, relieved Leo of the condom, then snuggled against him. Together they polished off half a bottle of wine as Leo grilled her about the second Atlanta murder.

"I'm probably going to repeat everything you already know from the papers, and your detective friend."

"That's fine. Repeat everything I already know."

She smirked at his sarcasm, tweaked one of his nipples, then planted a wet kiss where the tight bud began to swell.

"From A to Z then. You left. I got a call from Andy a few hours later, and met him at the office." She referred to the morgue as the office. "The body arrived about an hour later. A mess, Leo. Words can't describe." She slid off the chair, and his thigh, to pour more wine into both goblets, then nestled back against him.

"Same MO?"

"Yeah, but worse."

"What could be worse?"

"Per Andy, preliminary cause of death, suffocation —"

"He strangled her first?"

"No. She choked on her own blood, the loss of which probably killed her before the knife even hit a vital organ."

"He slit her throat . . ."

"You got it. Almost beheaded her."

"Jesus."

"I guess we should all be praying this guy gets caught, and fast."

"Do you have the note?"

"I made you a copy." She nuzzled his neck.

"You're a good friend." He swept her ear with his tongue. "Can I see it?"

"In a little while." Amber reached for a second condom.

"You're insatiable." Leo chuckled, then pulled her close.

"It's all your fault. . ."

It wasn't until almost four p.m. that Leo actually came into physical contact with something other than Amber Hawke.

"Here you go." She handed him the eight by twelve piece of copy paper. "I didn't fold it, just in case."

"In case what?"

"Whatever. Habit, maybe. I'm used to being cautious I guess, since we have to look for stuff CSI can't find. Like things inside the body. . . I try not to touch too much." She grazed the back of his neck with her fingertips, whispering, "That doesn't apply to you. . ." as she sat beside him at the kitchen table.

"Can you make any sense of this?" Scrutinizing the note, Leo ran a hand through his hair.

Amber rested her hand on his, smoothing his bangs to the side. "Your hair's longer."

"I haven't had time for a cut."

"I like it."

Leo sank into her stare, then his gaze touched every part of her face. Amber's features were ordinary, but remarkable because of her drastic coloring, and permanently inked makeup. Pale skin, vibrant Caribbean irises, shocking hair, and lush lips that were tattooed crimson. A perfect outline of chestnut eyeliner, also indelibly inked, kept her sleepy eyes wide.

From his expression, Leo seemed about to say something passionate, something unrelated to murder, something a woman would like to hear.

As his eyes searched her face, Leo did contemplate, but his roaming thoughts were not of Amber. In a moment his attention shifted to the note burning his fingers, then he repeated the scrawling rhyme: "Stick a needle in your eye. You'll never make anybody else cry. Sweet Dreams Darlin'." He let out a troubled breath. "Darlin' . . . All I can picture is a tall Texan leaning against a bar with a drink in his hand. Stupid, huh?"

"Well, he probably is from the south —"

"I know. I'm just saying. . . Mind games. He's playing mind games, and *my* mind's playing games with me. It's all too obvious. As if he's trying to trick us into believing he's something he's not — or something he *is*, and isn't trying to conceal it. Stick a needle in your eye. The rose stuck into the eye socket. That's pretty obvious."

"Never make anybody else cry. Lovesick." Amber tugged his earlobe with her teeth.

"That's what I've been thinking all along. Revenge. The guy hates women because he was jilted. Plain and simple."

"Makes sense. But being jilted doesn't make a killer, otherwise there'd be mass murder all around us."

"Something else I've been trying to figure."

"What?" She sucked the side of his neck, bringing blood to the surface.

"His size. We have three eyewitnesses in Charlotte who claim he's not big, maybe five six or seven, painfully thin, yet he overpowered a twenty-three year old college football player. Was slammed in the head with a guitar, by the guy's musician girlfriend, and didn't seem to flinch."

"I didn't know that." She grew serious.

"After that, she smashed a chair against his skull and he got up, shook it off, picked his hat up off the floor and hopped out the window. And of course, disappeared into thin air."

"Ugh. Sounds supernatural."

BALTIMORE & GINGER

Leo arrived at the office early on Monday morning. Surprisingly, he was fully rested, and the dark circles beneath his eyes had faded. With slicked back hair, he looked like he just stepped out of a shower, or a courtroom.

"Jitters?" Ginger asked when he breezed through the door, a hand in his jacket pocket. Leo always did a pat down for his Xanax bottle before going to trial.

"Nah. I'm fine. As a matter of fact, I had a relaxing weekend for a change. I'm still feeling the effects." He brushed past her on his way into his office, continuing to speak as he dropped his briefcase onto his desk and snapped it open. "Got a lot of work done."

Ginger followed him, but stopped inside the doorway and crossed her arms. "It's about time." She shot him her evil eye, but as he rummaged through a drawer, he didn't notice. She walked to his desk and tapped her knuckles on the oak finish. "Don't bother looking. The files, and anything else you should need, are already on the table inside the courtroom." She lifted her eyeglasses, her gray eyes squinting from the bright light on the wall behind where Leo stood. "Good luck today."

"Thanks." On his way out the door, Leo paused. "New glasses?"

"You noticed." She struck a sultry pose and grinned. "Foster's had a special on variety packs."

"Damn, Ginger." Leo shook his head. "Why do you have to be married." Suit jacket slung over a shoulder, he disappeared down the hallway, adjusting his gray striped tie.

"Like it would matter to you." Ginger laughed, fingering the sides of her new hairdo.

The phone on her desk rang.

"Leo Gibraldi's office." Her words sang.

"Hi, Ginger." It was Glory's voice, smooth as silk and just as slippery. "Can you buzz Mr. Gibraldi for me?"

"He's already left for court, Miss Diviniello." Ginger's voice neutralized, but a mischievous smile spread across her face. Everyone knew Glory hated to be called by her birth name. "Is there anything I can do for you?"

"No thanks. Just leave a note for him. Tell him the poll numbers just came in. Daddy's taken the lead," said Glory, her tone triumphant. "And remind Leo about the play. I'll be out all day, but he can reach me on my cell."

"I'm writing this all down, Miss Diviniello." Second stab. Ginger's shoulders vibrated with silent laughter.

"Make sure he knows it's black tie." Glory sounded exasperated. "He's got a bad habit of showing up *vanilla*, and that can't happen tonight."

"I'll tell him, Miss Diviniello."

Click.

Ginger chuckled as she dropped the receiver onto its base. A half-dozen gold bracelets wrapped her wrist with the sound of delicate chimes as she snatched up a pen and scribbled out a note. She sauntered into Leo's office, bypassed the note holder on his desk, and stuck the paper, ink side up, beneath his phone.

"Old habits die hard," she sang on her way out his door, then moseyed back to her own desk with a look of satisfaction on her pleasant face.

Leo left court at four. Before heading home, he stopped into his office. When he found Glory's note beneath the phone, he shook his head and rubbed his temples. Ginger watched him through the doorway. She angled her head, possibly deciding if the gesture was because of the placement of her note, or the message it contained.

"Got any aspirin, Ginger?"

"Here." She handed him a foil wrapped package, and an extra bottle of spring water she always kept in the bottom drawer of her desk. For Leo.

"Was it that bad?" she asked, watching him throw back his head, gulping the tablets and water.

"Court went fine. We have a strong case. Not much to object to." He shrugged. "Because his attorney didn't have much to say. The guy's guilty as hell. The defense has to know he's going down. They're just playing the game first."

"Well that's good. Oh, don't forget your tux tonight." Ginger smirked. "That's an order — from your girlfriend."

Leo grinned. "You're my girl." Then left for home.

hook me up   hook me up
throw me some of that heat
hook me up strap me in
yeah i'm lovin every zap

Opera House — Bathroom Stalls

Glory was electric in sapphire blue crepe. Her champagne highlights and olive complexion gleamed with light drizzling from the crystal chandelier in the theatre lobby. With Sicilian amenities, she was a striking blonde with a natural tan glowing all year long.

As she waited for Leo to arrive, she flirted and laughed, the focal point of two male sparring partners who were decked out in tuxedos and lust. Regardless of her whereabouts, Glory was in political rhetoric mode, campaigning for the Senate seat she wanted for her father, and for herself.

Glory stood out in a crowd like a flowering hibiscus advertising its worth in the middle of a field of nothing but goldenrod. When Leo walked through the door, he immediately zeroed in on her. She stood sandwiched between her ex, Steven Harris, and Sam Landes, a relentless admirer. Leo knew Landes had been trying to hook up with her since the day they met. The day she walked into Leo'soffice, introducing herself as the big boss's daughter. The day she claimed Leo as her own.

Neither of Glory's male companions appealed to Leo. Harris wore green dollar signs in his shit brown eyes, and Landes was a prematurely graying, fortyish swindler and would-be politician who yearned to be part of the Diviniello brotherhood, as soon as he could ditch his wife, which he wasn't about to do without having Glory as a backup.

"You're late," Glory called out as Leo approached.

Earlier, on the phone, she had promised not to nag him about anything, especially about the JC Penney suit he'd decided to wear instead of picking up a tux on the way home from the office. The tux Glory had ordered for him a week ago.

"Traffic was a bitch," Leo replied.

"That's okay. I forgive you." With moist, possessive lips, she kissed him.

A top-heavy brunette in a sexy lavender gown swooped from the staircase, locking eyes, and bodies, with Landes who swung his right arm around her waist. On his left hand, he openly displayed his glittering diamond wedding band.

The brunette broke free for a moment to reach up to Glory, dropping an air kiss alongside her face. "Hi darling. So happy to see you. And you." She turned to Leo and extended a hand. "I've heard all about you." Her false lashes fluttered.

Glory rolled her eyes behind the brunette's back. "Leo, this is Andrea Lopez. Andrea," she pulled Leo to her side, "this is the Leo you've been dying to meet."

"Nice to meet you," Leo said with his now, more than ever, poker face. He offered a brief slide of his palm, which seemed to be the *in* thing to do at Glory's social gatherings, for women *and* for men.

"Working on the campaign with Glory is an incredible experience. The judge has the support of so many people. We're all rooting for him," with full, berry lips, Andrea gushed.

Leo had no idea why she was telling him this, other than to advise him of where she could be found during the forthcoming months. Leo wasn't being presumptuous: Andrea presented her luscious backside, then smoothed an alerting palm across his when Glory's head was turned toward Sam Landes.

The final seating announcement shot through the PA system, and they filed into the auditorium along with a crowd of other guests, including a few celebrities and politicians.

"Big turnout for a weekday," Leo said to Glory as they walked arm in arm.

"It's a big deal event, Leo. And opening night gets the most press. I want to be seen."

Leo furrowed his left brow, raised his right. "Hmm."

"There are a lot of important people here. I'd love to get some good coverage for Daddy's campaign. Imagine the support we could gain here?"

Leo held Glory's arm with one hand. His other hand was shoved into his trouser pocket, casually lifting the hem of his black pinstriped suit jacket as they found their balcony seats.

Leo noticed Andrea and Landes paired off, but Harris sat with them, so Andrea had a man on either side of her. From across the aisle, Leo saw the placement of their hands. Harris had one resting on Andrea's, while Landes's hand groped her thigh.

The director took the mic, greeted the audience, gave a well rehearsed description of what everyone was about to see, why and how it came to be, then left the stage to the players. But not before receiving a standing ovation.

"What were you doing with Landes?" Leo asked.

"Are your hazel eyes a little greener tonight?" Glory's lips curled into a smirk.

"I want to let you both know, I'm not getting him out of another coke bust. I'm not losing my job over him, or you."

"He's over that."

"He's scum."

The orchestra introduced the opera with the sweep of a harp, leading into a melody that definitely sounded oriental. Then the soprano began.

The Japanese musical shifted into high gear, flowing with nature and a brilliantly costumed Maiko and Geisha cast.

"Now I see why you didn't get a part," Leo whispered to Glory. His voice held humor.

"Shush," Glory said, then pulled his hand onto her lap, where she pressed his fingers against the triangle between her legs. That was her signal.

Leo's fingers played for a bit, moved to her thigh uncovered by the slash on the side of her gown, then slowly crept higher until his tips reached the right spot. Glory flinched, pressed back into the seat, and tried to act as inconspicuous as possible as her pulse quickened faster than Leo's fingers. Leo heard her stifled moan. That was *his* signal.

"I have to use the men's room," he whispered, intentionally blowing the words into her ear.

Releasing a breath, Glory said, "Five minutes." Then pulled her legs together and aside so Leo could skim by.

Leo used a urinal, then washed his hands. Five minutes were up. When he swung the door open, Glory about to push inside, grabbed his arm and pulled.

"What are you doing? I thought —"

"Oh, God. Please, Leo, not the men's room."

"What?" His eyes burned into hers.

"I know too many of them."

"I bet you do."

"You know what I mean." Her tongue clicked.

The lobby was deserted. Glory shoved Leo toward the ladies room. Inside the spacious restroom lounge, the plush love seat looked inviting. Leo thought about dropping his trousers and dragging Glory with him onto the soft cushions.

"What do you think?" He gestured to the cozy sofa that presented an erotic fit.

"Uh uh. No privacy." Her eyes flickered with desire.

"Damn, Glory. You look like pure evil."

"Leo . . . Get into the stall."

"Yes, ma'am." He laughed.

Inside the stall, Glory immediately threw her arms, and a leg around him.

"Hold on." Leo took a cramped step back, shrugged off his jacket and hung it over the hook on the back of the door, then rolled up the sleeves of his white dress shirt. His precise movements made him look like he was about to whip up a quick dinner for two, or deliver an unexpected baby at his office.

With hungry eyes he turned to Glory, backed her into the wall, pulled down the top of her gown and French kissed her perky breasts. He then withdrew to watch ecstasy control her expression. Her eyes were glassy. Her sex-slack mouth bared ultra white teeth, and the tip of her tongue.

Leo's gaze dropped to her breasts that reminded him of balloons he blew up as a kid: tight, smooth and firm. He couldn't bury his face in them, but his plump lips and wet tongue loved to tease Glory's taut, dark nipples.

They kissed with fury, their tongues coiling long enough to over-lubricate Glory and completely harden Leo. Even with a dry condom, he slipped easily inside, and finished before intermission.

"Now that we've fucked in just about every public restroom in this city, one of these nights we're gonna have to try a bed," said Leo as he discarded the condom and handed Glory a wad of tissue.

She feigned lowered lashes, then cocked a brow and asked, "Is that a proposal?"

why should i care
how much you plead
the dead don't care
the dead don't bleed

HEAVENLY HILLS CEMETERY

Until dusk, the killer sat beside the knoll. During the long afternoon: ragged thoughts, delusions, ricocheting whispers. Whispering thoughts. Whispering memories. Memories of the shack. Memories of the grave. Memories of a Louisiana swamp. Faces flashed, vanishing as quickly as they attacked.

Agitation. With agitation, he jumped to his boots, thrashed, ripped branches, brush from the vehicle. Clear the vehicle. Drive the vehicle, slowly, but drive.

The vehicle ignited when dusk turned eerily dark. The beefy tires crunched gravel as it crawled down the road. The road on which it had arrived the night before. The night he hid in the barn. Slept in the barn. The barn with the tractor, sharp tools, and the man. The barn with odors. Odors like his. Not half as putrid as his.

His brain was twisting, wringing out thoughts like water from a soaked sponge. Too many things were happening too fast. Difficult to comprehend.

Zombie, flashed in his mind. He angered. The boot angered. The boot pressed harder, pushing the vehicle closer to town. The town that was tucked in for the night. Dark shops. Dark diner.

The small town with no houses at the center. Only one diner, one market, one bank, and four churches. Four churches and a cemetery. A cemetery with a sign on the gate that read:

HEAVENLY HILLS CEMETERY
VISITING HOURS ARE FROM SUNRISE TO SUNSET
TRESPASSERS WILL BE PROSECUTED

A cemetery outside a small town with a sign that read:

INDEPENDENCE   POPULATION 961

The sun had set hours ago as the vehicle cruised past: passed the cemetery, found a lonely road protected by trees, tall trees, many trees, where it stopped dead in its tracks. The engine ceased.

Open the door. Boots, stand on caked mud.

Mud from a rainstorm earlier that day, when the man came in from the field. Came into the barn where the pitchfork no longer stabbed the bale of hay on the floor. A rusty old scythe no longer hung on the wall.

The husky handled, sharp iron tools were strong. Stronger than the killer. Stronger than the knife. The knife was in the pocket. The sharp tools rested across the back seat of the vehicle.

With boots on sodden ground, the gloves quietly closed the door.

The iron fence stretched the length of the cemetery, across the front of the neatly groomed grounds, but on the sides and in the back, the only barrier was a wall of trees. Trees and some bushes. And leaves on the ground. Autumn leaves. Crunching leaves. Leaves that crunched when the boots trudged.

The cemetery, pleasant in silent night. Comfortable. Trees, bushes, and grave markers inscribed with names, dates. Decorated with flowers, plants and flags. The killer paused. The grave his fragmented mind recalled was barren. Barren without a marker. There was no headstone on that barren grave. No name. No date.

But there was memory just the same. A mound of dirt. A second victim. With memory, the brain was jarred. Sparked by images: Violence. Roses.

Beneath less than half of a brilliant moon, through the thickly treed barrier, the killer entered the cemetery. Quiet. Deathly still. Perfect rows of headstones shone beneath moonlight. Moonlight and starlight. Like her eyes. Screaming eyes. Angry eyes. Bulging eyes. Callous eyes: his. The heart raced faster than thoughts. Hunger. Graves. Roses.

Up and down the rows he wandered in moonlight, finally pausing beside a fresh grave. A fresh grave mounded with soft earth. Like hers. Soft earth covered the fresh grave sprinkled with flowers. Roses. Red with long green stems. The glove selected only one. Plucked it from the pile, then the boots began to plod. *Stop!* The brain reminded the boots: *Stop!* Return to the grave. Seize a second.

The brain recalled the farmhouse, the kitchen with the food. The kitchen with the woman. The woman who sang. Who spoke. Who hummed. Who screamed, *Travis!* But Travis was in the field. The woman screamed to no one, but there had been no plan, so the killer ran. Ran from the screaming woman. All things planned. Plan. Plot. While the moon smiles. Tonight, an unfortunate soul would meet the inevitable. Not the woman in the farmhouse, screaming for Travis. Tomorrow he would think of that one. The glove gripped the two roses tighter, almost crushing the delicate buds.

The killer returned to the vehicle, placed the roses onto the seat. The seat beside him as he drove away. Away down the road. The dark road. To an isolated place that captured his interest.

Visions. Exciting visions. New visions. Bolder.

The vehicle halted on the dark road. No street lights. Only moon. Glaring moon. Glittering moon, surrounded by stars. Starlight, like eyes. Laughing eyes. Seductive eyes. Eyes that grew dark with anger. Eyes that bulged.

The house was dark, but for a light beckoning from a window on the second floor. The killer paused. Observed. No voices. No faces. No disturbance. Silence. No interruptions. Not like the last that failed. That would never happen again.

As he approached the quiet clapboard home, the killer carried with him the knife, blade facing up, handle down, shoved deep inside the pocket of his coat. Over a shoulder hung a scythe, one of the barn's finest attractions.

His fishbone fingers moved the glove. The glove that strangled the husky handle of the pitchfork. The alluring pitchfork. Iron spikes. Like teeth. Strong teeth. Not like his, with swollen gums the teeth had begun to loosen. Loosen and bleed. His teeth were weak. But the pitchfork was strong. And tonight he would gain power that had been lost. Lost in the first floor bedroom of the sleeping pretty. The brain churned.

A white fence trimmed by vegetation surrounded the house. It was an old house. More than likely as old as the town, but pleasant and well cared for. Cared for as the owners. The Johnsons. Lester and Sara Johnson. Lester and Sara Johnson and their daughter, Meredith. Twenty year old Meredith, or Merri, as her friends called her, slept peacefully inside her bedroom. Her bedroom on the second floor where the faint light beckoned. Slept in her bed framed by wrought iron. Peacefully sleeping in her painted white wrought iron bed.

The boots circled the entire perimeter of the house, the glove pausing to test windows, a back door, a front door. Locked. Thoughts. Thoughts of entry. The killer wore gloves. Strong gloves. Gloves strong enough to think, think in step with plodding boots. Gloves strong enough to crack the bone of a human neck. Strong enough to crack the glass of a window.

The windowpane cracked, separated, fell to the floor. A glove reached inside, twisted the latch, lifted the window, quietly. Without a sound, gloves on ledge, one boot up, then the next: one, two, three, hoist. Up and over. Over and inside. Inside the old house with the sleeping family. Into the dark downstairs.

The old floor creaked when the boots moved, then stopped when they halted. Quiet boots! Don't stumble through darkness.

In darkness, the killer surveyed the entire downstairs. The

parlor, the kitchen. A closed door leading to the basement. *Interesting*. The glove reached for the knob on the basement door, but the brain said: *Stop!*

The light in the hallway at the top of the stairs attracted his attention. The killer climbed, carefully, quietly, pausing on each tread, each almost creaking tread. To the top. The top floor of the house where the family slept. Breath quickened. Quickened with excitement. Impending power. Thrilling.

On the top step the boots paused, eyes scanned, brain calculated. Wondering. Wondering who lived here. Who was asleep? Wondering if a sleeping pretty was hidden in an upstairs room.

He turned to the left where the light was not so bright. Quietly, carefully the boots moved down the hall, passing a room. A dark room. An empty room. Lifeless. A desk. Cardboard cartons. Television on a stand. Easy chair in a corner.

He continued down the hall. To the Johnsons' bedroom. Where Lester and Sara slept. Lester soundly. Sara lightly.

The room was dim, outlines barely detectable. But the eyes suddenly viewed things well. Viewed through the night like a cat. A cat who found his way through darkness. A cat with a purpose.

From the doorway, his stare fixed. Across the room. To the bed. The bed where the man slept upon his back, the woman on her side, facing the window. The slightly open window with a gently fluttering curtain. Fluttering with a breeze. Fluttering like her lids. Like her breath. Gentle breath. The window where the breeze entered beside the bed in which she slept.

Thoughts. Coherent thoughts. Sharp. Pitchfork for the man. Knife for the woman. The older woman. The woman older than the swamp. Old like the grave. The barren grave in Louisiana, near the hungry swamp. Hungry like his stomach. Empty stomach. Empty eyes.

Louisiana. The brain formed images. Thoughts flickered. Repetitive. The boots almost stumbled, but the glove held the pitchfork tightly, gripped the husky handle with strength. Strength of something tall. Something big. Something powerful. Something he was, but only when he killed.

The man snored. Let out a loud, choking snort. Gagged, then coughed. The woman stirred.

"Lester," her groggy voice groaned. "Turn over. You're keeping me awake with your snoring."

Snort. "Sorry, dear."

Lester rolled onto his side. Sara snuggled against his back. In a moment, breathing. Peaceful breathing. Dreams. Dreams of tomorrow. Of Sunday. Of church. Of dinner with the family. Possibly friends.

Dreams of Meredith in college. Meredith missing this semester because of money. The lack of money. The man worked hard. Two jobs. The mother worked in town. They saved money. Enough money so Meredith could catch the spring semester of college. College in the big city in Virginia. She would be a nurse. Maybe a doctor, Lester hoped. Sara wrung her hands at the thought. A doctor in the family. Even a nurse. Respectable living. Meet a nice doctor. . . Grandchildren. Sara counted heads inside her family dream.

If they had money, Meredith would have been in college this fall. Not sleeping in her bed. Working in town. Saving money for spring.

"Don't worry," Merri consoled her parents. "There's time." Her sparkling eyes danced.

"I'll catch the next semester." Her skip around the room, her playful skip, matched her dancing eyes. Dancing brown eyes. Soft brown eyes.

"We'll have more time together now. Think of today. Don't worry about tomorrow." She wrapped her arms around them. "Come on. No worried faces. Group hug!" Meredith's voice sang merrily.

Together they watched summer end. A long, hot, lovely summer. And in fall they planned for Halloween. A party. Thanksgiving with family. A real old fashioned dinner, where all the family joined together. Joined together and reminisced the past — planned the future.

"To our future nurse," Sara rehearsed the toast.

"Or doctor," Lester would chime in. And everyone would cheer.

Together they thought about future. Together they would feel life come to a close. Close into the inevitable. Tonight would be their inevitable.

must be some mistake
the mirror's telling lies
a pale unshaven face
there's a stranger in your place

CRIMINOLOGIST SCARLETT

"Things seem pretty quiet," Cassidy commented on the phone while sitting at his desk. As he conversed with Leo, he stared at the sign that hung on his office wall. The sign Leo had quoted over dinner. KEEP THE FAITH — AND KEEP IT LIGHT

He wished there was a *light* to keep. A light at the end of the tunnel. This god-awful tunnel he felt he was groping his way through. A tunnel filled with murders and murderers. Rapists. Thieves. Wife beaters. Molesters. Pervs. He hated them all, but the grisly murders were getting to him, because too many murderers were going free. Free to murder again and again. Like the nut who wasn't even in their jurisdiction, and they were already hunting him. Risking their careers by flying down to question witnesses in other states, as if they were already part of the investigation.

He was beginning to hate his job. Robbery-Homicide Detective Benjamin Cassidy. He could take the robberies, junkies, whores. But not the homicides. The grisly scenes were wearing. Battered bodies lying in gutters was something he'd never get used to. He worried about Terry. He worried about the kids. He worried about his parents, his sister. He'd worry about his grandmother had she been alive. And then there was the next victim. He ran a hand across his temples.

"Quiet? I guess you could say that," on the other end of the line Leo replied with a voice lacking emotion. He was thinking. Thinking about court. Thinking about the murders. Thinking about the note in his hand. The note Amber had given him, unofficially, off the record. Illegally. They could both lose their jobs if anyone found out she'd taken files. Copied files and worse, passed them on to a third party. A prosecutor in another state, no less. A prosecutor who had no business sticking his nose where it didn't belong. No business holding evidence in his hand. Evidence that didn't belong in his office. As Ben spoke, Leo barely listened. He scrutinized the note. The childlike handwriting that scrawled meaningless words, silly rhymes, across the page with what seemed to be a blunt pencil.

"So what do you think?" Ben said.

"Think about what?" Leo was distant.

"About what I just told you."

"I'm sorry, Benny. I'm all screwed up right now. Inside my head. So much shit going on. I can't think straight."

"Yeah. I know the feeling. All too well."

"I saw Amber this past weekend."

Ben laughed. "How many fucks and blow jobs?"

Visions of her softened Leo's words. "More than you could handle." He laughed.

Why was the thought of Amber enough to make him laugh? Or was it what Ben just said about getting laid and blown. She was a woman in heat. He was a dog. A dog who never went out of heat. Sometimes he disgusted even himself. Why couldn't he settle down with just one woman?

Why couldn't he just settle down — period? Was he heading down a dead end street? He opened his desk drawer. As it slid out, the bottle of expired Xanax rolled to the front. He slammed the drawer shut.

"You want to get together for a drink? I'd like to go over some things with you."

"When?"

"Right now."

Ben checked the wall clock. The afternoon had flown. Where had it gone? He had no idea it was suddenly eight thirty. Terry should have called by now. "Where the hell are you? Dinner's been ready for hours. Now it's ruined. Nothing new. . ."

The kids would be screaming in the background. He'd say, "I'm sorry, honey. I had to tie up some loose ends." Yeah. Loose ends my ass, he'd think. Loose ends of cases that would never be solved. Murder cases. With ends that would always flap in the wind, circle his mind, bits and pieces, threads that tied his gut into knots. "I'll be home in ten," he'd say. Terry would smack a kiss through the phone line. "Drive slow. See you in ten." God, he loved his wife. He loved his family. He loved humanity. Why couldn't everyone love humanity? He'd be out of a job then. Ben laughed aloud.

"What's so funny?" Leo asked.

"Nothing. Hey, I gotta pass on the drink, Leo. I need to get home to the family. It's three hours past dinnertime."

After hanging up with Ben, Leo rifled through the stack of files Ginger had plopped on his desk before she left for the day. It had been a long week. But the armed robbery case was over, and Leo had put another creep behind bars. For only eighteen months. Better than nothing. Unfortunately, there were plenty more like him, and worse, roaming loose.

He rose from his desk and strode to the window. His back was stiff and his legs ached. He thought about going to the gym, hopping into the hot tub, then thought of Scarlett and chuckled that the concept of turbulent, ninety-nine degree water temperature brought on memories of a woman he'd met only once, briefly at that.

He stared out the window. Occasional, slow-moving traffic in dusk made it feel like midnight. But he couldn't go home. He'd never sleep. He needed to relax. To cut loose. Unwind from the trial. He often celebrated a win with fellow prosecutors, but in this case, Leo had been the only attorney for the state. He'd like to celebrate with Scarlett. He could use her company. Seeing her would serve two purposes: business and pleasure. He pulled out the parchment card she'd shoved at him and dialed the number, hoping to hear her pleasant voice and not be confronted by an answering machine.

"Hey." Leo's voice was smooth. Being an attorney helped him conceal a wide range of emotions. Helped him attain and maintain his poker face; putting on a good show was easy. So was hiding his feelings.

"Scarlett. It's Leo Gibraldi." He turned from the window and moved back to his desk where he parked himself on the corner. "We met a couple of weeks ago at the Dockhouse."

"I remember you." The allure of the south. The warm south. . .

"Are you still in Baltimore?"

"I'm leaving tomorrow."

"I'd like to see you before you leave. How about a late dinner?"

"I've already eaten. I'm in the middle of packing."

"A farewell drink then."

"What's on your mind, Leo?" It had been more than two weeks. Her voice was frigid.

"I thought it would be nice to get together —"

"Cut to the chase."

"I have a copy of one of the killer's notes."

"How did you manage that?" The pitch of her voice instantly changed.

"It's on loan from a friend. Let's get together over a drink and I'll share."

"I *would* like to see it." Thoughtful pause. "Where would you like to meet?"

"We should do this in privacy. Where are you staying?"

"Do what in privacy?" Scarlett sounded amused.

"No." Leo chuckled. "Not that I wouldn't love to. . . I was hoping you'd do a handwriting analysis. Give us some insight into what makes this guy tick."

"I see."

Did Leo detect a tinge of disappointment in the voice on the other end of the line?

"My place or yours?"

Her tone elevated his smooth and cocky attitude, the one women couldn't seem to resist.

"I'm at the Beaumont on Fair Street."

"I'll be there in fifteen minutes. What room?"

"Three-forty-five. Take the east elevator."

"Be there in a few."

Click.

There wasn't much traffic, so Leo arrived at the Beaumont in less than his projected fifteen minutes, took the east elevator, as the sweet southern voice had instructed, and began tapping lightly on the door of three-forty-five just as Scarlett zipped her jeans over her flat tummy.

When she opened the door, her expression was pleasant. Leo had almost forgotten how attractive she was, in that subtle, mature way. Her smooth skin, and the way her hair was pulled up into a high ponytail, took ten years off her appearance.

"Come on in," she drawled.

"I didn't have time to stop off for —" He looked absent, then apologetic.

"Don't worry. Room service." She snapped the door shut behind him and stood with her back against it.

"Great. Order me a —"

"Scotch, neat." She motioned to a table beside her.

When he realized she'd already had their drinks delivered to the room, Leo's lips broke into an easy grin. He stood directly in front of her, close enough to inhale her apple-scented hair.

"How've you been, Scarlett?"

"Good. And yourself?" She tugged the hem of her cherry knit top that almost reached the waist of her jeans, and side-stepped him.

"Overworked. Underpaid. You know, same old story. But who wants to listen to a complainer?" He followed her to the center of the room.

"I learned long ago, no one likes a complainer." Her smiling eyes glistened, matching the scotch in the bottle she held. "Have a seat." She motioned to a tawny sectional sofa dividing the spacious suite into separate sitting and dining areas. Through a doorway, a king sized bed was neatly tucked and covered by cranberry polished cotton.

"Were you ever married?" The question dropped from Leo's mouth like an unexpected bomb from a placid sky.

Scarlett shot him a surprised, *invasion of privacy* glance, but replied. "Yes." Then handed him a glass of scotch she poured as they spoke.

Leo watched her gracefully cross the room to perch on the upholstered arm of an easy chair set alongside the draped picture window. Her movements were agile and deliberate, like a prowling jungle cat, bare feet grazing the blueberry colored carpet, enticingly feline. Although his mind had been on the folded note in his trouser pocket, Leo found it difficult to concentrate on anything other than the slim fit of Scarlett's jeans, and her eyes that gripped his from across the room. He wondered why she had chosen a distant seat, rather than one beside him on the sofa. Then her wary expression told him something he was certain she would never admit. "How did your case resolve?" Leo asked.

"It was touch and go for a while, but thank goodness for an intelligent jury who was well instructed on forensics."

"How's your crime and season theory going?"

"I haven't had time to even think about it. Where's the note?"

Leo leaned forward and slipped the paper from his pocket. "You should come over here so you can see it in brighter light," he motioned to an ornate lamp on a provincial end table, "and explain to me." He patted the cushion beside him.

With an air of superiority, Scarlett slid off the chair arm like a lithe creature, but without the lazy stretch. She sauntered toward him, snatched the note from his fingers, then settled elegantly at the other end of the sofa. She turned up the lamp on the table beside her, and picked up a pair of reading glasses.

"Let's see what we have here." Now she had the upper hand. "Definitely a physiological disturbance with his mental process. The stroke pressure skips, indicating degenerative exhaustion." She reached for a glass of wine she had earlier set onto the coffee table, sipped and set it back down. "This isn't the original." She sounded annoyed, borderline hostile. "If I had the original, I could be more precise. Copies lose. . ."

"Christ. You know this just from glancing at his handwriting — or should I say scribble?"

"I have a good memory." She remained perturbed.

"Huh?"

"Personality charts." Relaxing, she smiled. "I memorize them."

"Photographic or practice?"

"Eidetic imagery is a fallacy. If humans remembered every single image, it would be difficult to make it through the day. Years of methodology. Years of practice. Here, look." She patted the cushion for Leo to move to *her* side. "The writing isn't smooth or clear. It's sketchy. His hand is trembling, more than likely with his thoughts."

"Fascinating."

"Yes. Absolutely fascinating."

"Degenerative exhaustion. So he's sick as in physically ill? Or stressed? Or what?"

"I don't know. Possibly both. As well as excited. See the erratic stokes? Chaotic. It appears he was frenzied when he wrote this. There's no harmony in this writing. No sense. No reasoning."

"Terrific. A confused, frenzied serial killer who could be physically sick."

"It's like this note was written by more than one individual."

"Split personality? Or are you saying there's more than one guy doing this?"

"No. It's all the same handwriting, with different patterns. Momentary mood swings like his mind is flashing signals faster than he can process."

"Great." Leo got up and refilled his glass. This time, scotch licked the brim.

"Dangerously unpredictable. To me, these four words — *never make another cry* — translate his demand for obedience, for domination. He's king. He's god. Typical for a serial killer. Look at this line; *needle in your eye*, the style of this stroke is indicative of unrealistic mentality — fantasy."

"In your opinion, does this guy ever have a sane moment? Or does he exist entirely in a world of death and fantasy."

"I don't know, Leo. Some of these deranged individuals lead what might be considered, normal lives. Double lives." She shrugged her shoulders. "In some cases, even those closest to a killer haven't a clue as to what he may do in his private life."

"Crazy."

"Yes they are. And cunning. Our guy's DNA went through ViCap."

"The hair from Delaney's?"

"Yes."

"Come up with anything?"

"Nothing. So either he's new at this, or —"

"We have nothing else to compare it to because he's never left DNA before — or he's too damn smart — maybe lucky."

"Or he's left it, but we've just never found it — or his other victims."

"True. Who the hell knows how long he's been at this, or how many. . ."

"Well, he's now part of our national database for next time."

"You're that positive, huh?"

"This guy's got a savage appetite, Mr. Prosecutor."

"I thought this would help, but you're not making me feel any better, Scarlett." Leo drained his glass of scotch. He studied her wire rimmed eyeglasses that made her look librarian sexy.

Sitting inches apart on the sofa, their breath was the only thing to touch as they continued their conversation.

Pitchfork, Knife, or Scythe?

The killer stopped. Stopped peering through shadows. Two shared the bed. Disturbing. Retreating boots slowly led the killer down the hall to where a small light glowed. Glowed like a dim moon. A moon that was dim because it now hid behind clouds in a starless sky. Hid like the face beneath the brim of the hat, the face with the starless eyes.

Closer. Brighter. Pause in the doorway. He paused in the doorway, where a table lamp sprinkled irresistible light across a sleeping pretty. Thrilling. The boots aimed straight for the bed.

Merri slept peacefully, especially on weekends. After seeing a movie in town, she and some friends had stopped at the diner for ice cream sundaes. Vanilla with hot fudge. Hot fudge and sweet whipped cream. They dined inside the modest eatery, which was now a gloomy shadow on a deserted square.

As they enjoyed ice cream, the diner had been bright and lively, with juke box music, laughing patrons. Accommodating staff. Meredith's friends and neighbors. All had gone home, safe and sound tucked into beds, enjoying a peaceful night's sleep. Tomorrow they would assemble at church, share reverence then brunch which would include omelets and fruit, small talk and later, perhaps a dinner of pot roast. Sunday was pot roast night at the Johnson home. Merri just might invite Paul. Paul worked at the bank. The bank where Merri met him when she deposited paychecks into her college fund.

Merri slept on her side, facing a moonless window. The window facing the rear of the home. The home surrounded by picket fences and forestland. She always faced the window where the two-faced moon rarely smiled, which is why Meredith's table lamp glowed most nights. Merri hated suffocating darkness, and open closet doors.

She made certain her closet door was tightly closed before retiring to bed. Tightly closing her closet door was a lingering ritual since she was a little girl. A little girl frightened by nightmares, boogeymen, and clowns. Clowns in the closet, which Sara had to rescue from trash bags and store in the attic, or donate to charity.

Everyone knew Merri feared the night, and clowns, but without fail, a birthday or Christmas rarely passed without Merri being gifted with something resembling a clown, be it a doll, or a dress, stuffed animal, even slippers! Clown slippers with ruffles and dots and big red rubber nose toes. For a while the clown slippers were stashed under her bed. Then out they went to the summer flea market the morning after Meredith's dreadful night terror that could've, "Raised the dead," Sara said the next morning, when over breakfast, she recounted the night.

The killer stood beside the bed where the boots had taken him. Taken him silently across the floor. Through the doorway into Merri's bedroom. Across the braided carpet, stopping dead in his boots, at her side.

Sensing an eerie presence, Merri's mind alerted of danger. Or was it just one of those stupid old night terrors? She whimpered.

Leave! If she stirred, she'd awaken. She would scream, same as the last one. *Damn shit! The other two!* For sure they would awaken, run to the room of the screaming pretty. Run to her side. *Just like the others! Damn shit!*

Retreat. From Meredith's room, boots retreated, pausing at the doorway. Soft breathing. Close-lipped, rhythmic breathing. Through nostrils. Not at all like the gurgling panting from a tightening throat, drooling mouth. Sensation. Throbbing genitals. Dry eyes watched her. Hungry eyes inciting gloves that could barely wait. Gloves that caressed, then stashed the scythe in a darkened corner of the hallway, just outside her room.

She *would* enter the inevitable, but first *the two*. The two who slept down the hall. In the bedroom at the other end of the hall. *Boots. Move.*

The boots aimed for the Johnsons' bedroom, where the couple slept side by side. Lester and Sara Johnson, in peace that would be eternal.

Eternal peace. The inevitable. Thoughts churned. *Two. Quickly. Knife be faster than ever!* The brain flashed the message to the glove. The glove that remembered the tool, the tool from the barn, the tool the glove dragged alongside the boot. The pitchfork with long sharp tines. Ten tines.

Down the hall. Follow the boots down the hall. Doorway. Pause. Peer through shadows. Snoring. Slumber. *Creep to the bed. Don't drag the pitchfork!* Knife in pocket. Two gloves, *hold the pitchfork. Cradle the knife!* Toward the bed. Beside the bed. Standing beside the bed.

The killer stood beside the bed. The sleeping figures curled together as one. Curved like a spoon. A spoon tucked beneath a lace-trimmed sheet and handmade quilt passed down from a generation ago.

Sara was the first to awaken when she heard the old wood floor creak. Creak beside Lester's side of the bed, where her husband slept soundly, snoring loudly. Snoring and gagging on saliva.

The pitchfork lifted high. Sara's eyes were alert, but she didn't move. She didn't move because the pitchfork fell instantly, precisely, pinning Sara and Lester together, shoulder to shoulder, rib to rib. Forever together, in marriage, in life, and in death.

Lester gagged a few more times, not on saliva, but on blood

gurgling up from punctured lungs. His eyes never opened. Sara's never closed.

The killer left the pitchfork where it was, handle aimed at the ceiling, tines embedded in Sara and Lester. Embedded so deeply, the tines vanished into flesh and bone.

Adrenaline surged. Power fed the brain. Fed the body. Fed compulsion. So powerfully, delightfully, the killer craved more. Craved the sleeping pretty. The boots knew the killer's brain. Knew it well. Brain and boots moved together as one: Down the hall. To the doorway. Her doorway. Pause. Silence.

The boots led the way, quietly down the hall, to the light. To the light at the end of the hall. To the bedroom. The bedroom where Meredith Johnson was unaware. Unaware that her family had been massacred. And that she would soon meet the inevitable. If she awakened, what would she do? Scream? Flee? Human ears were closed. *Scream, pretty.* The boots and the brain wouldn't care. It might even sound nice. Feed a new craving.

Slumber made it easy. But screams were a challenge. A challenge to be met head-on. From failure, a lesson had been learned. Interest had been sparked. Permanent memory. Thrilling memory, revolving again and again through the brain. A constant reminder of fulfillment long after the act.

To the side of the bed the killer crept. Crept silently to stand beside Merri who slept with a smile. A small smile on her pretty face. He halted. He stared. Then the glove did something it had never before done. It reached. It reached for her without the knife. The knife that remained undisturbed in the pocket.

Visions of the last one. The screaming one. The one who escaped the inevitable. Although the inevitable lost its prey, the screams lingered. Heightened desire. Excitement. *Glove. Reach the pretty. Gently. Gently touch her hair.* Her long, dark hair. *The same as the other!* Roll back the days. Defeat the defeat. Rectify failure. Redemption. Frustration. Reenact!

Glove, cover the mouth. The breathing mouth. The smiling mouth. Plump lips cherry red with warmth. Warm blood. Warmed by a fluffy comforter and life.

It was more than a presence. Merri didn't need her mind to alert her. The glove clamped down over her mouth. Disgusting. A disgusting smell, then realization. Her mouth was held shut. *By what? Why? Scream!* Merri began to scream through sealed lips as she bolted awake. In lamplight she saw him. Standing over her bed. Most of his face was covered by the large brimmed hat. The floppy hat that shielded him from Merri, and thankfully, Merri from him. What would Merri do if she saw the face?

Terrified, Merri bit down on the glove that restrained her. Held her fast to the bed. Her heart pounded. Her teeth raked the leather. Old, dirty leather. She tasted leather, dirt, and she tasted blood. The blood of her parents, and the others.

Head cocked, he watched the awake girl. The screaming girl. The struggling girl. Glove remain. Until there is silence.

Merri, in a prone position, prone and at a grave disadvantage, shocked awake, glove over mouth, pulled her hands from beneath the comforter. She grasped the glove and pulled as hard as she could. The second glove swatted her hands away. She grabbed the wrist. The wrist bone. Tightly, frantically, she pulled, wishing for a nightmare, night terror, clown in the closet, mother at her side. Merri kicked her legs. Her feet. Flailed her arms to be free.

Her lips struggled to move beneath the glove's pressure. "Mom! Dad!" But the words weren't formed. They were moans. Pitiful moans. And then she gagged. She gagged her hours earlier dinner. The ice cream sundae flooded her mouth. She choked. Her eyes bulged.

Traci! Bulging eyes. Choking breath. Lifeless Traci. Fragments of the first drilled the brain. *Traci, you're so darn pretty.*

Merri was dying. Gagging. Turning red, then blue. As suddenly as it clamped down, the glove released the hold. The boots stepped back, but only one half of a step.

Screams. Loud screams. Petrified screams.

"Help! Help me!" Merri shrieked and coughed. Coughed her lungs out. Then shrieked until her throat was so raw, the only appeals were gasps and gulps for air.

Merri was free to attempt an escape. She lurched from bed,

but the glove shoved her down. When she scrambled to the other side of the bed, so did the killer. In desperation, Merri huddled into a corner. She pulled her legs up to her chest and hugged them with her arms. Her trembling arms. She buried her face against her knees and sobbed.

SHOULD HE TELL HER ABOUT THE BARN?

"Travis."

"What?"

"I can't sleep."

"I can."

"Travis!"

"What is it now, Marla?"

"I been thinking about the kitchen garbage — and the barn. Did you lock it?"

Travis's sigh sounded more like a gasp of irritation. "Marla. We both need to get up early tomorrow. Now roll yourself over and try to go to sleep."

"You didn't answer me."

"Yes."

"Yes what?"

"For cryin' out loud, Marla. I locked the darned barn, okay?"

"That still doesn't explain what happened in the kitchen. It's still bugging me. I don't feel comfortable in this house anymore. Let's sell it. Move into town where it's safer."

"Honey." Travis softened. The last thing he needed was to stake a FOR SALE sign in front of the house. Pack their belongings.

Search for a new residence . . . higher prices. More painting. Carting around furniture. Hanging pictures exactly where Marla saw fit. "We're safe here, but, how about we have one of those alarm systems installed? Like they advertise on TV. With a panic button." He chuckled. "You sure seem to do enough of that."

She elbowed him in the back.

"Would *that* make you feel better?"

"Why? Do you think we need one?" Marla sounded startled. "That's a lot of money, Travis. You wouldn't spend extra money unless you thought. . ."

"Marla, I'm bone tired. Will you please shut up?"

"Did your mother like me, Travis?"

"What?"

"Did she *like* me? Was she happy you married me? You know, with your college degree and all, well, maybe she would have liked you to marry a doctor or — "

"You're educated enough, Marla. The bank wouldn't have hired you if you were dumb. Why the sudden concern about my mother?" He said before letting himself doze off again.

"Do you believe in ghosts?"

"No."

Should he tell her about the barn? Warn her that it seemed like something strange and smelly had set up camp? Alert her, so she could be cautious? Or would it just cause her to stampede into a motel in town? What about the missing pitchfork, and rearranged tools hanging on the wall? Some were missing. . . Like a scythe.

Thinking aloud and still half asleep, Travis whispered, "Maybe I misplaced them."

"What?" Marla clung to his back. "What did you misplace, Travis?"

"Dad's old rifle. You want it for protection?"

"Protection against what?" Her body stiffened.

"I'm just asking."

"That cannon would probably blow up in my face if I pulled

the trigger, which I'm not sure I could do."

"How about I get you one of those Taser things? You could carry it around with you."

there's a big sky for everyone
but mine's getting smaller
eagles soar cuz they're peaceful
i can't it's too painful

DESTROY DEFEAT REENACT!

The sky was sculpted with placid clouds. As the moon floated time passed, but the sun was yet to rise. Had the light filtering into the room been fingers of day, Merri might have clung to hope. But for Meredith, the night in itself was eerie with creepy shadows crawling across the ceiling, rising and falling on her bedroom walls. Night often gave birth to monsters, but this one was human, and more terrifying and brutal than any imagination could spawn, and it was staring at her.

Merri was trapped. Trapped on the bed he pushed against the wall where he trapped her. She was trapped between the wall and something worse than a nightmare. Like a cat stalking a mouse, he taunted. Each time she tried to jump off the side of the bed, before her feet could reach the floor the glove shoved her back, foiling her attempts to escape.

Barricaded. Backed against the wall, she hugged her drawn up legs, burying endless sobs into her knees. A caged animal, and *he* had control.

The killer lorded over her, watching, listening. Elated. Excited. Powerful.

Merri ran out of sobs. Ran out of breath. She quieted. *Control.*

The killer had taken control. The lovely warm body cowering on the bed was Merri. And Merri was his.

"Who are you?" She asked, her voice ragged. "What do you want?"

The killer had been mute for so long, he didn't know the sound of his own voice. He hadn't spoken a word since Louisiana. Since Traci. Did he have a voice? If he had a voice, how would it sound? What would it say? The boots and the gloves had been the teachers, the sole communication for so long. Head cocked. Agitation. *Stop the words!* the glove said. But the glove failed to move. Failed to stop the words that poured from Merri's pale lips. The lips that had been plump and red with slumber, but were now pale and stricken with fear.

"Where are my parents? If you've hurt them —"

Threats? Head straight. Boots step forward. Glove rise.

Merri cowered.

Control!

"What do you want?"

Thoughts revolved. Recapture the night. The glove pointed to the open doorway, leading from her bedroom into the bathroom. Merri didn't move. Merri didn't understand. Once more, the glove pointed. When Merri remained on the bed, the glove grabbed her arm, wrenched her to her feet, and pushed her against her dresser where she faced herself in the mirror. She faced herself and the killer who stood behind her. Shock dissipated into sickening horror as she stared, eye to eye with him through their reflections in the mirror. Covered in black, head to boot, all that was visible were dead eyes, eyes without remorse. Eyes that motioned toward a hairbrush resting on her dresser.

The glove shoved the silver scrolled brush into her hand, guiding her to use it. Pushed her head down forcefully, so that her hair tumbled toward the floor. Brush harder. Remove the earrings. Remove the clothing. Twirl around the room.

While Merri stood in the middle of the floor, brushing hair and tears, he slammed the bedroom door shut. There was no lock. He pushed the dresser across the doorway, sealing her into a tomb.

Merri looked more petrified than when she first awakened. Not only was he horrifying to look at, but he was even more horrifying as he approached, spun her around, tugged at her nightgown, then stood before the locked bedroom window watching her stumble into a corner.

"God," Merri cried out, hands protecting her face. "What do you want from me?"

The glove pointed to the shower adjoining her room.

"Oh, God. No."

The glove pointed again.

"I'm not taking a shower!"

The glove continued to point.

Merri flew into her bathroom. Snapped the lock on the door. Cranked the shower full blast. Then rushed to the window. Twisted the lock. Raised the sash. Higher. Raise the window higher — but it was so small.

The door exploded with a scream of rage. A deafening scream as the killer splintered the aging wood, rushed through the doorway, dragged her from the window. From her escape. Shoved her, nightgown and all, into the shower.

As she trembled beneath the pelting stream, arms locked around her body, Merri's tears flushed with the shower, flushed down the drain — along with any hope of escaping.

From the doorway, the killer watched with enjoyment. Conquering defeat.

Inside the stall, Merri was drowning. Drowning in water. Drowning in tears. Drowning in terror. The shower ran full force as Merri stepped from the stall, snatched her robe from a wall hook and wrapped it around her dripping nightgown weighted with water.

Indignant. Merri was indignant. Gathering strength, gathering courage, she reached for the only thing available, the only thing that could possibly become a weapon. Her razor on the shelf above the sink. Numb fingers plucked the blade from the head, squeezing it in a death grip. With shaking hands, Merri lunged for his throat. The throat beneath the coat. The hidden throat protected by the glove. The glove that smashed her arm against the wall. Followed by her shoulder, then her head. The razor fell to the floor. Fell to the floor a moment before Merri fell onto the tiled floor. Blood trickled from her nose.

He was furious. This was not the way it should happen. The brain scrambled to reason. To reason what had gone wrong. Why this one did not behave as the other had. The one who had escaped. A blood curdling bellow filled the room. Filled Merri's ears with terror. Wave upon wave of terror as the killer howled his head off. Howled so loud she covered her ears with her hands. Closed her eyes and waited for rescue. To be rescued by death.

He grabbed her foot, dragged her to the bed and tossed her. Tossed her onto the mattress. Then shoved her beneath the covers, pulling the comforter up to her neck. The glove then covered her mouth. Covered her mouth with such force, the roots of her front teeth loosened. Loosened in the sockets of her upper gum tissue. Pain. In her mouth, blood and pain. Smothering. Merri was being smothered by the glove. The other glove held the handle of a favorite tool. Held it over the bed. Over her face. Over her neck it lifted, then swung. Splat. Better than the others. Beneath the power of the glove, her throat severed with ease.

The clock read three a.m.

He dragged the scythe across the bed, wiping it clean on Merri's sheets. Picked up the knife from the floor, from where it had been cast aside without care, because something else had taken its place. After inspecting the knife, the glove buried it, blade up, deep into the pocket of the coat. Dropped the coat on the floor. Then the boots were shaken off, kicked across the room. The hat followed. Followed by any clothing he wore. Then he stepped beneath the powerful stream of water. Water in the shower where Merri had stood, not five minutes before. Naked. He was naked. Naked and wet as he used the toilet, then walked back to the bed. Crawled beneath the sheets on the bed that cradled Merri's bloody body. The body he rolled against. Curled against. Like the man and the woman. Curved like a spoon.

LIKE A HURRICANE BARRELING UP THE COAST

By Sunday evening, along with rambling roses, yellow crime scene tape climbed the white picket fence. The fence that surrounded the silent clapboard house. The tape screamed of death and destruction that had taken place sometime during the night. Destruction of an entire family.

The rural area was turned upside down. Turned into a media camp, with news cameras, anchors, neighbors, family and friends converging on the normally tranquil street. Local law enforcement was not even permitted to enter the home while Crime Scene Investigators scoured the structure, collecting DNA from the shower, bathroom sink, Meredith's bed, and from the kitchen where the killer had helped himself to breakfast before leaving at dawn.

"Are you a family friend?" An anchorwoman shoved her mic toward Paul's trembling lips as her cameraman captured his frenzied face.

"I know. . . I knew Merri." Paul's voice broke into a sob.

"Are you the one who found the family?" The anchor moved closer.

"When Merri didn't show up for church this morning, I called her. When there was no answer, I figured she was on her way to brunch, but she never showed up at the diner."

"So you had plans for today?"

The mic brushed the side of Paul's face when he turned his head.

"We do every Sunday. Church and brunch. When she didn't show up, and didn't answer her phone, I drove out here and found the broken window. Saw the cars were still in the driveway, so I called the sheriff." He stifled a sob and began to walk away.

"Did the family have any enemies?"

If the mic had been shoved any closer, it would have picked up the gurgling sounds inside his throat. The pounding of his heart. "No one in this town has enemies. We're all friends, or family."

"Who could have done this? Any idea?" The anchor's eyes widened.

"I can't talk anymore." Paul turned his back to the camera.

"Sheriff," the anchor directed her attention to Leroy Floyd. "What can you tell us about this tragedy? Is this the work of a serial killer? Are there similarities to the murders that recently took place in Atlanta? What about in Alabama where a body was found last month? Is this the same killer?" Questions flew faster than squawking crows scattering from tree to tree.

"In thirty years I've never seen anything like this," said Floyd, then pushed the mic from his face. "I don't know anything about Alabama — or Atlanta. You've got to move, ma'am. We have work to do here."

"One more question, sheriff."

"You're in the way, ma'am."

"Put every car we have around the perimeter of the town. I want this guy caught," Floyd instructed a deputy.

"We only have four cars, boss."

"Then call over to Bluefield. Get them to send some help over here."

"What kind of a monster is this guy?" The anchor insisted,

pushing herself into the center of the circle of local law enforcement. "Sheriff Floyd. Is this the work of the Sweet Dreams Psycho?"

"I have no information at this time," Floyd replied. "Move before we have to remove you."

"You have to understand. This is big news. We have thousands of frightened residents calling the station. They want details."

"When we get them. You'll get them."

"Word is, it *may* be the same one hitting up the coast." Floyd ushered a young uniformed officer into the foyer of the Johnson home. "So don't go shooting off your mouth." Standing with a hand on the revolver holstered around his hip, the sheriff shook his head. "Like a blasted hurricane barreling up the coast. Only this one's not in the least predictable."

"Yeah, we can figure hurricanes, huh, sheriff? Track 'em," said the deputy, striking a similar pose. " I guess you can compare 'em too. Mother Nature at her worst, ya think?"

"What do we have?" Floyd asked the one remaining investigator as he came down the stairs and halted beside him in the foyer.

"A hell of a lot more here than any of the other scenes. Enough where we might eventually be able to link them." He lifted two sealed paper bags. "Hair in a shower drain. A bicuspid in the sink in the same bathroom. An electric toothbrush with remnants of gum tissue and blood. That was also in the sink."

"Bizarre."

"Sure is."

"So he slept with the Johnson girl after she was killed?"

"Appears that way. My thoughts — either showered with her, or after he killed her. Then slept with the corpse. Got up and rummaged around the kitchen. Had to be out of here before dawn. No one saw anything. No suspicious vehicles."

"Any tire tracks around the house?"

"We're scanning the area. But with all of these," the agent motioned to the street beyond the open doorway and the wall of onlookers and media. "The area's already been compromised."

inside your head the panic starts
but you've seen the streets before
toy soldiers cut across your mind
yet there's no turning back in time

Faces In The News

In his Baltimore rowhouse, Leo sealed leftover pasta in a Tupperware container and stowed it in the refrigerator, for another night's dinner. Tired of eating fast food and microwave meals, Leo had taken seriously Glory's satirical suggestion of cooking lessons, but instead of attending classes, he picked up a copy of *Cooking For One — Marathon Edition* — on sale from Amazon. He'd become so experienced at whipping up tasty and easy meals, if he wanted to, he could moonlight as a chef.

The local news played on the TV, but not over the sound of running water in the kitchen sink. Lost in thought, Leo was oblivious to the breaking news that indirectly linked the serial killer to a slaughter in Virginia. The FBI had no leads, and DNA found at the Virginia crime scene had not matched anything currently in their database. The maniac was still at large. Leo caught the tail end.

Walking into the living room, he yelled, "Virginia? Fucking Virginia?"

The female anchor of the local station was in the process of telling her audience that the chief profiler had wrapped up her work in Virginia, and would be flying back to Tennessee in the morning, where she would continue her analysis.

"Scarlett?" Leo said aloud, as if she were there to reply.

Pacing the room he considered phoning her, but last they spoke, she had promised to inform him if she uncovered anything new, anything that might help in preventing the spread of the maniac's wrath. She'd been working in Virginia. Why hadn't she phoned?

He thought of calling her, for the hell of it, suggesting she swap her morning flight to Tennessee for a night flight to Baltimore. Leo had been doing a lot of thinking lately, about Scarlett, about Amber, about Glory, but the only materialization of thought was in the form of a hot blonde. The rest of his thoughts just swirled around his head, quickly evaporating, like a swig of spicy scotch that bit, satisfied for a while, then disappeared into thin air, requiring a refill every few hours.

Leo showered, then stretched out on his bed with no intention of drifting to sleep so early. It was only nine. He'd never sleep through the night. Since the murders, Leo's nights were spent tearing his mind apart, trying to block the image of Gina in the morgue, pushing aside crime, hatred, anger. Too much negativity. He needed downtime. He knew where he could find solace, but he also knew it was not the time to escape to Connecticut. Not in the middle of a heavy workload, and maniac murders.

Lying on top of the covers, Leo dozed then fell into a dead sleep, his mind and body exhausted. His body would rest, but his mind would not. Waking thoughts, sleeping thoughts, always the same. Tonight the years rolled back. He was a kid. He was home. He was in Connecticut.

On his own since the age of ten, Leo was learning to rely only on himself, developing characteristics and emotions he'd haul through life. And here he was, more than twenty years later, a grown man and regardless of whom he met, what emotions might fight to surface or boil inside, he still couldn't set himself free. He would never be anything other than a loner.

The Honda was a bully, and Leo needed to cut loose. He slowly wheeled the bike out of the garage, balancing its weight with the strength of his arms, then rested it on the kickstand while he quietly closed the shed door. It felt good to straddle the seat, even though it was worn; the bike was overpowered and could still run with the best of them. He coasted down the driveway, tires crackling grit, knees bent with his boots resting on foot pegs. He wouldn't ignite the bike's fury until he reached the road.

Leo wouldn't disturb the folks he lived with, the ones he referred to as aunt and uncle — the caring couple who had taken him in after irresponsible parents abandoned him when he was ten. Leo would never use drugs like they did. He'd have a beer or two, but never hardcore drugs.

Leo's thoughts were upon Gina. He liked this new girl at school. She was different from others, and he respected her. She was the kind of girl a guy could think about settling down with. But Leo couldn't settle down. He had to release smoldering tension. The best place to accomplish this would be on a wild ride through isolated woodlands. While his friends off-roaded in Jeeps, Leo cut loose on his Honda.

He almost tasted Gina's lips. The bike was loud. Gina's lips were sewn together with wire. A rose dangled. He sped past farmland, flying past Gina. Why didn't he stop? Put her on the back of his bike, as he'd done other nights.

When Leo saw the weirdo following her, he dumped the bike to rush to her aid. Gina disappeared before he could help her, and his soul wouldn't rest until the maniac who mutilated the beautiful young girl was dead.

The night had cooled and the overcast sky was drab. The only glow shed upon the road was the blaring headlight of Leo's bike. The light flashed across the killer's face. It was white. He was grotesque. He was pacing Glory as she jogged at dawn. Sunshine replaced the Honda's headlight, and Glory wasn't jogging on the road. She was lying beside him in bed. Her lips were crushing his. Her hands were warm, soft. She stroked him. His palm pressed her breast as he eased in with a groan.

The thought of her touch, even in dream, was enough to set him off. Leo woke up hard, which wasn't at all unusual in the morning, but it wasn't morning. It was only ten p.m. He'd passed out for an hour and felt more anxiety now than when standing in a crowded courtroom facing the enemy, getting creeps off the streets. Court was a mix of apprehension and elation. That's what Leo thrived on. He flicked on the television. Every news station continued to carry breaking news of the Virginia massacre, which is what the news now called the murders. How they loved to sensationalize for ratings. But it *was* sensational. Not in the same sense as a hot woman. It was hideous. He switched channels, watched the weather, wondering if Ben had seen the news. Should he call him? He picked up his cell and dialed Glory's number.

Her phone rang six times. If she didn't answer on the next ring, he'd disconnect. He couldn't leave a message. What would he say? *I'm horny. Come over.* Actually, he *could* say that. Glory would more than likely love it. Even if she didn't come over, they'd have phone sex which excited her almost as much as the physical stimulation offered by his flesh. But he'd have to say it to *her*, not to a recorded voice that barely resembled hers.

"Hey." Glory sounded groggy. Or was she preoccupied? "What's up?"

"Nothing much. What are you up to?"

"Just watching a movie with Daddy. How about you?"

"The weather." He was disturbed and couldn't hide it.

"You're a working boy. Why aren't you in bed?"

"I am."

"Umm."

"Can't sleep."

"Poor baby." Her words grew muffled as she placed her hand over the mouthpiece to keep their conversation private. "You okay?"

"I'm fine. It's early. Why don't you come over."

Glory occasionally called him from one of the nightclubs she favored. But the background noise on her end of the line didn't resemble a club, or movie night at the Diviniellos'. It was more like the rustle of sheets and Glory sounding stranger than usual.

"Where are you?" Leo asked.

"I'm home. . ." She grew defensive.

Sam Landes groaning in the background. "Come back to bed, babe."

"Since when does Landes sleep over? Or are you at his place?"

Muffled whispers, still audible. "It's my father. . ."

"I may be a lot of things, Glory. But not your father."

Leo disconnected and slapped the BlackBerry back onto his nightstand, unsure if Glory would call back to explain. She didn't. He grabbed the TV remote and started flipping stations again. Even though he had grown accustomed to Glory's bitchiness, this was over the line. Leo couldn't have cared less if she had something going with Landes. But he didn't like being lied to, made a fool of. On the sports channel he found highlights of a basketball game he'd missed. The next thing he knew it was three a.m. and he awoke to drag cars running the quarter mile.

fall back to earth
you're nothing sweet to find
blow my mind blow my mind blow my mind...........

did i shock you too much baby?

BACK TO THE BARN

By the brilliant break of day, the beefy tires made a right at the intersection and chewed up the pebbled road leading to the mountain, to the niche where the vehicle was re-draped with pine boughs and scrub brush. Nothing to do but rest. Rest and regurgitate thrilling memories of the bloody night before. The last kill — the things that lead up to it — and the things that happened afterward. The heinous things. Memories branded into the brain. Memories that would play again and again until faded. Then urgency would gnaw. The taste for power was powerful. Powerful as the killer. As the inevitable. Power was god. Satiated, the killer closed his eyes as dawn eased in with the wind.

"Travis!" Marla's nerve-shattering wail filled the second floor air as Travis finished shaving and hurriedly dressed. "Eggs are getting cold and you'll be late for work." Like a litter of yelping puppies, her words chased him to the bathroom. Sometimes just the sound of her voice made his ears ring.

"Darn it, Marla," he yelled back. "Can I have a minute of privacy? I'll be right down!"

Marla scraped her breakfast plate, with a paper towel wiped it clean, then carefully set it into the sink. The gold-rimmed dinnerware had been a treasured wedding gift from her parents who had happily handed their only daughter over and into the trusted hands of Travis Booth.

"You'll make me late too," Marla mumbled to the empty kitchen. "Travis Booth. Get your pants down here," she gave a final yell, then chuckled, "with you in 'em, of course."

"Make me a doggie bag, Marla," Travis said as he rushed into the kitchen with his open suit jacket flapping, fingers swiping a loose lock of hair from his forehead, then straightening his tie.

"Already did. Cold eggs on cold toast. See you tonight." Her lips crushed his freshly shaven cheek. "Umm, you smell too good to leave. I'll have to take that up with you tonight."

Marla grabbed a sweater from the three-legged wooden rack in the corner, her purse from the chair, and was out the door before her husband could admire her autumn floral dress. "See you tonight, Travis," she called into the brisk morning breeze. Her voice carried through the air and fell to the ground like a buzzard diving for a meal, while her pudgy-heeled pumps crunched on leaves that had fallen during the night.

Marla unwittingly awakened the killer. At the sound of her voice screaming *Travis*, his lids shot up like snapping rubber bands, then he bolted upright. Memories of Meredith Johnson had left his central nervous system in high gear. He relived her screams, the sight of her cowering in the shower, the feel of his naked body plastered against hers as he drifted in and out of light sleep. Although he had gouged himself with food from the Johnson kitchen before he left, it had been over twenty-four hours since his last meal and now his stomach growled and clawed. He got to his feet, stretched his limbs, relieved himself on a bush and shuffled toward the road, careful to stay within the cover of pines.

Marla's white sedan sped past, followed a few minutes later by Travis in his shiny black pickup.

The killer's memory was clear. He remembered the farmhouse, the singing woman and the man she called Travis. He would rather remember Merri Johnson, but she was back there, and he was here, and he was hungry as a grizzly waking from hibernation, so he skulked across the road and zeroed in on the back door of the farmhouse. Movement was easier without the coat, without the hat, without the boots. But without the boots, who would tell him what to do? The gloves, of course.

Crossing the dusty road, the killer was dressed in Mr. Johnson's black sweatpants, hooded sweatshirt, and dark sunglasses. Without the boots, he wore his frayed tennis shoes. The tennis shoes that had lived inside the boots through thick and thin. Through every murder and escape. The faithful knife was cradled inside the kangaroo pocket.

The back door was locked, so he crept around the perimeter, checking windows, rattling the knob on the front door. Locked. The little reasoning he retained told him not to break a window. The farmhouse could be his home. He would like that. And if he broke a window, she would notice and Travis would find him. Confront him. The gloves didn't think it would be such a good idea. The killer needed time to rest. Time to eat. Time to think about Meredith Johnson. Excitement boiled in his throat, along with bile from yesterday's one and only meal. Digestion wasn't easy. His stomach churned harder than his brain.

From the porch he picked up the newspaper. On the front cover was a sketch of someone familiar, and a story about murders. Interesting. The sketch no longer resembled him. Coincidence. Power.

At the rear of the house, the part closest to the barn, there was a cellar door. It was painted white, like the house, but it was dirty and half covered with debris. It hadn't been used in many years. And it wasn't locked. Perfect. He raised the door, let himself into the darkness, pulled the door down behind him, and found his way across the dingy cellar, the cluttered cellar, the cobwebbed cellar with the dirt floor. Dragging his feet, he found his way to the stairs, the stairs leading to the kitchen, upstairs and into the kitchen where the interior door was never locked.

The killer had some choices to make. Kill the Booths tonight and quickly leave. Reside in their cellar, or hide in the barn. Difficult decisions to make on an empty stomach. A growling stomach. If the gloves couldn't decide, maybe the killer would execute all three considerations.

In the kitchen he opened cabinets, the breadbox, and the refrigerator. He removed the gloves and balled them up in the sweatshirt pocket. Like his eyes, it bulged. From the cutlery drawer he selected a knife, held it up to the light, and as he watched it glisten he ran a boney finger over the smooth edge. With the butter knife, he slashed the air as if it were a tender throat, then grabbed a loaf of bread from the counter, hacked the plastic package open, pulled out a handful of bread and spread it thickly with peanut butter. He swept the hood from his irritated scalp, sat at the kitchen table and devoured three sandwiches. The stomach was satisfied.

The killer left the bread wrapper torn and untied, put the peanut butter back into the cabinet, but dropped the peanut butter smeared knife in the sink, on top of the plate Marla had wiped clean before leaving for work. Next, he wandered around the house, picking things up, setting them down, not always in the same place. When he made his way up the stairs, the stairs leading to the bedrooms and bath, the old treads creaked.

He walked on hardwood floors. No rugs. He passed the small bedroom, the bedroom that was a den with a television, a desk and a computer, and continued down the hall to the larger bedroom. The one with the king sized bed, clean sheets and neatly tucked yellow floral spread covering the soft mattress. Inviting.

He sat, bounced, rolled around, then rested on a pillow and dozed. Comfortable. The bed was comfortable. He'd never experienced luxuries such as these before. As he lay on his side, he faced a nightstand and focused on the framed wedding picture. While watching Marla and Travis walk down the aisle in church, his lids without lashes fluttered then stuck closed. He breathed heavily as he slept with his mouth agape, saliva trickling onto a pillowcase sweetened by peach blossom shampoo.

The sound of a horn in the driveway startled him. He awoke confused. Disoriented. He leapt from the bed. The neatly made bed that was now crumpled and soiled with drool, scented with the same cologne Travis used. *Something Spicy* was a popular men's cologne in the town of Independence, Virginia. Mr. Johnson had used it too, even when wearing his jogging outfit.

January Valentine

blow meeeeeeeeeeeeeeeeee
blow me off
i'm wearing your bite marks
i'm raw

paint meeeeee
paint me graphic
you bled me once
then you bled me once more

FIREFLIES

Leo and Ben decided to stop into Fireflies, an unrefined hangout for a younger crowd. It was an easy place to talk until dinnertime rolled around. Fireflies had the best burgers and seasoned fries on the coast.

The cozy bar was lighted by milk-white overhead globes, and the bar itself was made of split lumber, cracks filled with peanut shells like the ones lining the floor. Not more than twenty feet behind them, a low stage occupied a quarter of the place. The proprietor, and another man who looked like a carpenter, stood in the middle of the modest dance floor, talking and pointing, as if discussing the floor plan.

Leo and Ben sat shoulder to shoulder on barstools, drinking and talking. Talking about the murders of course, but also about Sam Landes.

"Landes is so full of shit he needs to be pumped," Leo said.

Ben laughed. "Septic. You have a way with words, Gibraldi. He drives a brand new Ferrari. He must be doing something right." He funneled the last of his beer into his mouth. "Business must be good, huh?"

"He's slime. And he's dirty. Sure as hell could never afford his lifestyle on the allowance his wife gives him." Leo pushed his glass toward the tap for a refill. "What some guys do for money."

"What some guys do for free." Ben smirked at Leo.

"You wish you could."

Ben patted a doughy pouch overhanging his belt. "Sometimes I do." His empty beer glass followed the path Leo's took. "One more and I gotta hit the road."

"It's common knowledge Sam Landes is mixed up with drugs." Leo sounded thoughtful.

"Yeah, taking them. Not pushing them." Ben eyed Leo with curiosity. "You know something I don't?"

"Who the fuck knows anything anymore."

"Why does Diviniello protect him?"

"Glory obviously . . . and from what I've heard, big campaign contributions from Landes and his influential crowd." Leo shook his head.

Thoughts of Glory brought on other thoughts. Since the Japanese opera, she had been acting stranger than usual. And distant. Something Leo was unaccustomed to. And then there was the phone call when she'd referred to him as her *father*. She had actually hidden him from Landes. Leo did a slow burn. He would have liked to discuss the situation with Ben, but pride kept any discussion off the table.

"We should go to the Cellar," Leo said with half a smile.

"Are you nuts?" Ben roared. "Besides Terry killing me, I don't think the captain would appreciate me patronizing a joint that encourages prostitution."

"We won't stay long. Just take a look around." Leo was serious.

"What the fuck?"

"Don't even ask, Benny. I've just been getting these guts lately. I know you know what I mean." Leo left three singles on the bar, and shoved the rest of the change into his pocket as he stood. "Come on, old man."

"Yeah, I know what you mean. And guts can get our nuts squashed. Right?" Ben made a quick grab for his sack, then joined

Leo at the door. "I'd like to hold onto mine. So would Terry." He laughed.

"You're turning into a sissy. What happened to the Bronx punk with the tude?"

"He got married," Ben said as they strode across the parking lot.

"We better take separate cars, Leo. I know the hours you like to keep."

Leo shrugged. "I've got a big day tomorrow, but suit yourself." He walked toward his car.

The humor on Ben's face turned sober, and he called after him. "Aw, come on, buddy. Jump into the Caravan."

The minivan hit potholes, even though Ben kept swinging the wheels in an attempt to avoid craters and bumps as they sailed along 244th Street, careening in and out of traffic. The Cellar was in an off the beaten path, seedy part of the city, far from the pristine metropolis. With high rise office buildings falling further behind them, the holes became deeper, but traffic thinner.

"Holy shitballs. This place is worse than I remember," Leo said as he stared out the window, attention drawn to the sides of the road. Small shops and aging automobiles parked at curbs flashed by. With hoods up, some looked stripped, abandoned.

"Yeah, if downhill could go downhill, this area sure as shit has." With an elbow jutting out of the open window, Ben agreed as he maneuvered the sizeable minivan, steering with his right hand, wrist resting on the wheel.

He took a few drags on a cigarette, then scowled and flipped it out the window. "How come you don't smoke, Leo?"

"Sports, I guess." Focused on the scenery, Leo was vague. "I enjoy my health."

"Yeah. You got the right idea. I'm gonna quit."

"That's good, Benny. You should." Leo had a mechanical tone to his voice.

"Your eyes are glued to the hookers on the street corners. I can tell." Ben laughed. "You and women. Is all that sex part of maintaining good health?"

"Good for the prostate." Leo's eyes bypassed Ben's head, staring across the road that narrowed. "Hookers and lamp posts. Kids dealing out of cars. It's sad."

"It's another way of life down here. Then on the flip side, there're guys like you and me. And then there're the millionaires and billionaires who don't have a freaken care in the world." Ben blew out a sigh.

It was then that Leo's eyes shifted from the signs of poverty. "Something wrong, Ben?"

"Not really. I should be happy, I guess. Terry might be pregnant. . ."

"Terrific. Congratulations."

"Maybe it's the changes," Ben said. "Which, in a way, I wish it was. The thought of more responsibility, another mouth to feed, well." Ben's voice dropped off. For a moment he took his eyes off the road and glanced at Leo. "Do you think I'm selfish for feeling this way?"

Concern filled Leo's face. Ben looked worn. He'd never seen him this way. "Hey, things have a way of working out," Leo consoled, although he wasn't sure he believed his own words. "Don't they always?"

TRIPLE HOMICIDE SHOCKS INDEPENDENCE

"The mailman left a package in the driveway," Marla's voice grated through the hissing phone line. She checked her watch. It was five p.m.

"No, I didn't bring it in, Travis." She clicked her tongue. "It's heavy."

She kicked off her shoes, nudging them against the kitchen wall, dropped her handbag onto a chair, then set down a sack of groceries she'd grabbed at the market, before heading home from her job at the small bank in town. Travis would enjoy peach cobbler tonight.

"I have no idea, Travis. It's probably the farming equipment or whatever it was that you ordered to work that stupid field. I just walked through the door. When will you be home? I'm about to start dinner. Dessert's a surprise —"

Marla pressed only half of the receiver to her ear as the ruffled edges of the daily newspaper captured her curiosity. It was the morning paper. And it was splayed out on the kitchen table, tattered and worn as if all seven hundred subscribers had fought over the single copy, or the same litter of puppies that had nipped at Travis's ears that morning had debated whether or not to use it as a toilet.

How had Travis found the time to paw across every page? And why did he leave the paper in this abused, practically unreadable condition? All before heading off to work? *No wonder he has to stay late tonight. . . Make up for being late, yet again.* But Travis was far from a slacker. The beautiful gardens surrounding the farmhouse, and cultivated field, proved it.

Travis worked hard around the house, and even harder as district manager for an insurance company. But what was going on with him lately? Misplacing things. Denying the messes he left for her to clean up. Now this. Along with hunger, agitation clawed at Marla's tummy. Travis knew she pleasured in scouring the paper over dinner, checking for sales at local stores, then challenging the crossword puzzle as soon as the gleaming dinnerware was restacked into the glass breakfront, and the roomy kitchen echoed with unused space and cleanliness.

Travis Booth! How inconsiderate. Perturbed, Marla allowed her husband's voice to grow distant on the other end of the line. From twenty miles away, he was complaining about having to work late because a salesman hadn't met his quota, and as management, any overload was bestowed upon Travis.

But Marla wasn't listening. Her bug-eyed stare fell first on the frontpage headline, TRIPLE HOMICIDE SHOCKS INDEPENDENCE, then darted to the police sketch of the killer, whom the police believed was the maniac who struck while Independence slept in what the townsfolk trusted was a peaceful and secure community. The murders had been committed in a secluded area not too far away. *Probably one of those rickety old places over on Chapel Hill. It's such a desolate area. Vulnerable. So is ours! This could have been us. . .*

Marla shuddered at the chilling reality that one of her neighbors could be gasping over a news item announcing the double homicide of Travis and Marla Booth — at this very moment invading their privacy as the neighbor read about their vicious and grisly demise. Mind stalled in disbelief, stomach tightened like a strapped corset, nerve endings tingling, were all of the alarming sensations devouring Marla as she prepared to read about the worst tragedy to have ever befallen the sleepy town of Independence.

Curiosity is typical of human nature, but curiosity is innocent snooping, such as what fancy store did the new furniture in the neighbor's home come from? Where did she buy that dress? Or how could the people across the street afford a classy car like that? Morbid thrill-seeking is an entirely different level of curiosity, and not of Marla's interest. Still, the victims had been her neighbors, and she couldn't help but envision the terror the family must have endured. Marla was stunned and she was distressed, distressed because the murders had occurred not more than ten miles away, and the victims could have been her and her husband.

After regaining composure, if swallowing without a choking knot inside her throat was considered composed, Marla for the first time realized the paper must have been crumbled into a ball and then smoothed, because there were creases and folds slicing across the killer's face and most of the print. She had to iron out the crinkles with her palms so she could decipher the letters, string them together, then digest every startling word.

The newspaper looked like the victim of anger. Before she could concentrate, Marla had to determine the reason Travis had all but destroyed it. She couldn't. But come to think of it, he seemed to be doing some strange things lately. Or was it her overactive imagination causing concern that her strong and stable husband's mind seemed to be slipping? Marla inwardly cringed at the concept that Travis could end up like her uncle Luke, stricken with the onset of dementia at the age of fifty. He had fifteen years on Travis, and though he'd been a heavy drinker most of his life, it still didn't seem possible that dementia could strike a man barely middle aged.

Marla's eyes then honed in on the artist's rendering of what the maniac could actually look like. At the charcoal ovals filled with nothing but unrepentant eyes. The nose without a tip, and taut mouth, made it look like a skeleton. Gruesome. *This must be a Halloween prank. A sick joke. No living thing could ever look this way. But then again, these are the details from terrified witnesses, people who must have been suffering shock when giving their account of the killer's description. Of course, that made more sense. Nothing human could look like this.*

Marla read while Travis spoke nonstop on the other end of the phone, his voice turning nasal after a stifled sneeze. Consumed by the gory details, she was deaf to his relentless drone. "Don't be late or your dinner will be cold," she said absently, dismissing Travis mid-sentence.

She returned the cordless phone to its dock, then sank onto a chair, swiveled her body to the side and crossed her legs, ready to review the story with a fixed mind to accurately absorb the details of the triple homicide she'd already managed to convince herself was an impossibility, and rather someone's sick joke. And boy, was someone at the paper going to catch hell for this one!

The journalist had been creative. His words painted a graphic image, inside Marla's head, of the slaughter that had occurred while the family slept. She'd sleep with one eye open tonight, if she slept at all. She'd never formally met the victims, but was sure she had seen them at church services.

In a traumatic puff of air, Marla blew out sorrow, but stress idled. This was even worse than the three car pileup on I-95, when she'd been stuck behind a police barricade for hours and forced to watch an entire team of firemen drag mangled victims from the wreckage moments before one of the cars exploded into flames. That was catastrophic, but that was an accident. This was horrific, and this was intentional. Marla shivered as if she were standing in the middle of a January blizzard, dressed in nothing but her first of April birthday suit.

Marla's mind took flight. A horror flight. She wondered if the maniac was a transient, or someone who lived right here in Independence. The agonizing thought that she may have serviced the killer at the bank, brushed his murdering fingertips with hers while handing him cash, made her skin itch with tiny red bumps like the measles she had as a child. The prickly rash spread along her arms and thighs, torturing her already irritated stomach. As she scratched her skin almost raw, she considered the tube of prescription cortisone cream stored in the upstairs bathroom cabinet that hung on the wall above the pedestal sink.

It was the sudden thudding sound that jarred her already frazzled nerves, causing Marla to leap off the kitchen chair and quickly scour the room with an anxious stare. She whipped around and listened intently. There it was again. A thump? No. Squeaking wood. The stairs? Travis?

be the ball of fire guide
race the asteroid's glide
my adrenals all stressed
no time ... no time to rest

TOPLESS AT THE CELLAR

"How the hell did we ever live without GPS?" Ben pushed a button and stopped the robot voice directing him to their location.

"Yeah. Who'd ever find this place without help. Christ, it's buried back here." Leo ran a hand across his chin. "I don't remember it looking like this."

"Well, we haven't been here in years, Leo. Things change."

The Caravan hit a final bump, then turned off 244th and glided down a smooth driveway in the direction of a large parking area. Carefully positioned, upscale vehicles were shielded from the real street by a grove of some of the only trees left standing on the west side of the city. The rest of the ghetto was comprised of crumbling apartment buildings, vacant lots that looked like dumping grounds, and actual junkyards. Other than hookers, junkies and dope dealers, there weren't many other people on the streets.

"Like another fucking world." Leo sounded surprised.

On the exterior, the Cellar was a decrepit industrial warehouse, three floors high; a structure of rusting steel and grimy glass that had weathered years. The inside was a different story. The place looked like it had been wallpapered with money. Except it was stunningly white. Fresh paint, lush red carpeting, brass and glass. The club was money, all the way. Laundered money.

Big hands and inquisitive eyes stopped them at the door. "Invitation only," said a goon with a gruff voice.

Leo said the first thing to pop into his head. "Sam Landes."

The hands were removed and the goon stepped aside.

"That's new," Ben whispered. "Never needed an invite before."

"Hmm. Interesting."

After passing through the foyer, which could have been a barroom on its own, the two men entered the actual club. The place was so spacious, ceilings so high, the music seemed to be drifting down from the sky. Once safely inside, a topless hostess greeted them. Ben couldn't keep his eyes on her face. Leo laughed at him.

"Would you gentlemen like a private room?" she purred, initially motioning toward a row of second floor sealed doors.

When Leo shook his head, she nodded in the direction of a dimmed alcove set with low-slung, overstuffed seating arrangements. "A cozy corner then?"

Ben remained tongue tied and statuesque.

"Just a place at the bar," Leo responded with a grin.

"Follow me, fellas." The girl's attitude immediately changed, along with the tone of her voice. Her obviously well-worked-out bottom shifted back and forth like a pendulum as she led them to the sleek bar, wearing nothing more than a white thong and red heels.

"Drinks are twenty bucks a piece, no matter if it's a beer," she said over a shoulder.

"No problem," Leo said, rolling his eyes at Ben, who, between the girl and the prices, appeared to be choking.

They settled on barstools covered with soft, zebra striped fabric. On the wall behind the bar, sheets of glass sparkled. From where they sat they could watch their reflections, or the other side of the room. Leo chose to watch the other side of the room.

He looked around, and ran a hand through his sandy hair

that still needed a trim. "Your hard earned tax dollars at work, Ben."

The club looked like a coliseum, with archways and columns, and floors stacked in tiers. Wrought iron staircases wound around balconies, disappearing up and into the well guarded unknown.

Leo noticed the place seemed relatively quiet, but for a handful of men in expensive suits who milled around. Several others, in casual dress, were scattered along the bar. Without conversation, they appeared to be strangers.

Within moments, a topless barmaid stood before them. Her face was calm and pretty, but her eyes were incredible.

"What can I get for you boys?" She didn't smile. Her voice was amicable, not at all suggestive as the hostess's had been when they first entered.

"Sam's draft?" Leo angled his head.

The woman nodded.

"I'll take the same." Ben's stare hadn't yet reached her eyes.

"She's got to be wearing contacts," Leo said near Ben's ear. "I've never seen eyes so green. They're like fucking emeralds."

"Whose looking at eyes?"

It wasn't until the barmaid almost poked him in the face with her heaving breasts as she served him his twenty dollar beer, that Amber floated through Leo's mind. His emotions stirred, while Ben appeared to be still in awe, or shock.

"Did you see how she looked at you?" he sounded amazed.

"What are you talking about?"

"Like she wants to take you upstairs and bang you."

"Yeah. For a thousand bucks a throw." With the first sip of Sam's, Leo's lips smacked together. He traced his mouth with his tongue, licking off a thin layer of froth.

"At twenty bucks a pop, drink slow." It was the first time Ben had laughed since they'd entered the club. Watching the expression on his face made Leo feel better. *Things always have a way of working out.*

Clandestine cages, still attention grabbing, were recessed into corners where imprisoned men and women wore nothing more than belts, boots, and shoulder straps. Holding whips and cattle prods, they seemed to be waiting to deliver pleasure. Shadowbox figures moved to a tribal beat, oil and sweat bubbling on their bodies beneath soft light. Some hung on chains.

"This place is so fucking illegal. Broad daylight illegal." Ben seemed almost amused.

"Very well protected," Leo nodded to the suited thugs who now congregated at a table near the back of the club, "by gorillas and then some."

Ben looked puzzled, then his face settled into realization. "Gotcha. Our tax dollars at work."

"Private rooms. Sounds interesting. I'd like to see what goes on behind those doors?"

"Stuff we'll never afford."

"Yep. All sorts of characters." Inconspicuously as possible, Leo took in every aspect of the room. "We can't see them, but bet your sweet ass, they're watching us right now. Black glass and back doors. What a setup."

"Filthy rich patrons. Or just filthy." Ben snorted. "Cops. Politicians, even doctors."

Now Leo appeared puzzled.

"My gut says they've got a hell of an operation going on." Ben's words were guarded by his hand, which he placed near his mouth as he explained. "I heard they have labs upstairs." He shrugged his head toward a long staircase, half hidden in a corner behind the long stretch of bar.

"Why the fuck would a place like this need a lab?" Leo's eyes widened. "Duh. Drugs. Of course." He checked to see if the barmaid was within earshot, but she was serving at the end of the bar.

"Medical? Organs maybe?" Ben raised both brows. "To coin your phrase, Leo, holy shitballs."

Leo shut his eyes in disbelief. "You've got to be fucking kidding."

"Got to be more than legalized prostitution." Ben seemed unaffected by the meaning of his own words.

"A shitload more." Elbow on bar, Leo supported his head with a hand, then ran his palm across his forehead. "I need aspirin more than beer."

"What?"

"Look at that kid over there. The girl in the pleated skirt."

Ben turned to see a creamy skinned girl without a crease on her scrubbed face. Wholesome looking, like she should be riding a bicycle in the suburbs. Unlike most of the *servants*, she was completely clothed, but in the company of an older man who seemed to be leading her around on an invisible leash.

"Looks like he's training a dog. How old do you think she is?" Leo pressed, straining to see into the girls eyes, looking for expression, but there was none.

"Shit, I don't know. She's young. Looks underage and stoned. Holy fuck." Ben's daughters weren't all that much younger. His jaw dropped.

"Exactly."

"Are you thinking what I'm thinking?"

"Playground for the rich, perverted, and not so famous who want to keep it that way."

"Look at your face. You're not envious —"

"Of them? Fuck, no. But you never dreamed of being rich, Benny?"

"Just comfortable. I wouldn't want to be hated by the public, like most of them are."

"We're hated anyway," Leo snickered. "Who loves a guy who enforces the law?"

"All the women you meet." Ben jabbed, then grinned. "Nice and dirty, but in a good way. Right, buddy?"

Leo ignored the pointed remarks. As usual, Ben couldn't handle his alcohol.

"Everybody's dirty. Cops, politicians —"

"Don't forget the manmade gods."

Leo cocked his head.

"The rooms upstairs —" Ben motioned to the cages. "This is just an appetizer."

Leo shook his head. "I dunno. But I'd hate to think shit like this is unstoppable." He looked Ben square in the eye. "Have anything in mind?"

"You really wanna go there?"

Leo shook off the unusual look in Ben's gaze, the cold sound of his words. "Maybe I do." He stared Ben down.

Ben's face cleared, but his voice didn't warm. "I don't know, Leo. Pretty powerful shit here. Can anyone stop the political machine where sex and buyoffs are concerned?" Back to normal, he nudged Leo's arm. "Speaking of sex and buyoffs. Look what's slinking down the stairs."

Leo spun, half expecting to come face to face with Glory. He wouldn't have been surprised if she worked the place. Glory did just about anything for kicks. Leather, whips, cuffs, even chains, were right up her alley. Leo could attest to it.

Although the place was cool, Sam Landes's face was flushed as he sauntered down the stairs, followed closely by a Latina in a dress that hugged her like an elastic band. When they reached the landing, he pulled her to his side, slid an arm around her waist, then dropped his hand onto one of her ass cheeks, where it stayed clutched as he propelled her across the room. They settled into a dimmed corner. A character, who looked like he'd just stepped out of a gangster movie, immediately joined them.

Leo's eyes were glued to the transaction: Landes slipped the man a wad of cash. In turn, the guy shoved an envelope into his hand. After a few moments, the three disappeared into the darkness.

"I've seen enough. Ready to call it a night?" Leo said, then surveyed the room for the young girl with the blank eyes. From as far as he could see, all to remain were Doms and thugs.

"Yeah, I'm ready. Look at the time. I'm gonna get my ass kicked for this. You owe me, Leo."

"I'll make it worth your while."

Ben laughed. "What are you gonna do. Buy me a blow job?"

As the Caravan exited, a white van made a screeching turn into the driveway, disappearing behind the establishment.

Bloody Pounding Eardrums

Shuffling sounds, slow and precise. Something dragging across the floorboards upstairs. And it seemed to be coming closer. Marla froze inside the kitchen, then instinctively her rigor mortis feet broke free of their cemented situation in the middle of the linoleum covered floor. Should she run from the house or pick up a baseball bat and confront the intruder? What intruder? she chided herself as her heart doubled its beats. Armed with a cumbersome push broom from the hall closet, alert, she flew around the entire lower level of the big old house, making sure every window was locked and that the front and back doors were tightly bolted. But she didn't go upstairs. She had made enough noise to scare off a burglar, she was certain. And everything was locked, so how could someone be inside with her? Stop it, Marla. She slapped her cheek.

Back in the kitchen she stood still for a moment listening, but all she heard was the gush of her blood singing in her eardrums. *Of course, the wind was banging on the house!* Marla recalled closing the kitchen door to the blustery day when she'd returned from work earlier. On her way from the car, a frigid wind had plastered her dress to the back of her legs, raking a rasp of leaves across the walk before it blew the door shut. That was it! There was no one in her home. Marla came to the conclusion that it was only Mother Nature clawing at the shingles.

Still, she remained on edge, not only because of the atrocity across town, but because it added to the uneasiness she'd been experiencing since things around her home felt somehow different. It was nothing she could put her finger on, but there were those subtle noises, flickering shadows, odds and ends out of place. And then there was that odor she and Travis had attributed to dead animals.

Marla thought of the incident with the garbage. When she accused Travis of knocking over the can, spilling dinner trash across the floor, he'd straight-faced swore he had nothing to do with it. Did she believe him? She desperately wanted to, because she knew *she* hadn't done it, and if it wasn't Travis, then who was it? What was it?

Why would Travis lie? Marla recalled their *together* past. Had Travis ever lied to her? Well there *was* that *one* incident with the redhead in town, which wasn't exactly a boldfaced lie, but Travis sure as hell seemed to enjoy holding one hundred and twenty pounds of overheated female in his arms. He later wangled out of it by insisting the cheerleader had stumbled in the aisle of the diner.

Marla shrugged off a pang of lingering jealousy. The incident had occurred ages ago. Who would have ever thought she'd be standing in her tidy, spacious kitchen, reading about grisly murders, mulling over her past with Travis? All because of a toppled garbage can and rancid odors in their barn, which were probably the result of an animal seeking shelter — and food. Feeling silly, she shook her head and slapped her cheek once more.

After strolling memory lane, she convinced herself Travis had never lied to her and wasn't lying now. He hadn't knocked over the trash. The vulnerability of being alone in the big house that was suddenly satanic struck like the hand of the parlor clock clanging six strokes. Where the hell was Travis? The kitchen was a tomb and Marla was haunted. The hot stare of the unknown bore down on her. She was suffocating with fear. The presence was so thick, she reeled defensively, expecting to see something from hell looming behind her exposed back each time she turned.

Thank goodness the light of day brightened the walls, but soon the sun would collapse behind clouds folding into dusk, and since the farmhouse was surrounded by monstrous evergreens, the windows shaded at will earlier here than in the house where she'd grown up, the only other house she'd ever lived in.

At a jittery glance, the glass paned top of the kitchen door didn't look secure. Sliding the bolt back and forth a few times, Marla tested its strength. Anyone could put a fist right through the panels, reach in and flip the lock open. Marla's heart thumped. Her darting eyes dared another sweep of the paper. With two fingers she snatched it from the table as if it was infected, then crunched it in half and slapped it down on the counter.

"We'll get rid of you right now," she said as she shoved the daily news into the corner between the breadbox and the wall. She couldn't fling it into the garbage as she instinctively wanted to. She needed the crumbled evidence so she could confront Travis when he got home. Travis! How late did he say was going to be? She should have listened more attentively when he had called. She reached for the phone, then hesitated. He'd get home as soon as he could. No sense in her nagging him. She'd been doing enough of that lately.

January Valentine

i bottomed out
can't get much lower
but the ground keeps shrinking
and i'm closer to nothing

FROM FIREFLIES TO AMBER

Watching the stable motion of the Caravan as it departed Fireflies lot, Leo sank into the Mustang's bucket seat. He was relieved Ben was sober, and he didn't have to drive him home, explain to Terry where her husband had been while he should have been eating dinner with his family. Before he had a chance to turn the key in the ignition, his BlackBerry rang, flashing Amber's name and sexy smile.

"Hey, hot guy."

"Amber —" He didn't hide his surprise. "Everything okay?"

"Does something have to be wrong for me to call?"

"Of course not. It's good to hear your voice. What've you been up to?"

"Same old. You know, just hanging around with the stiffs." She laughed.

Leo had forgotten how her sarcasm could lighten the mood. He returned a laugh.

"And how are they treating you?" He joked.

"They keep giving me the cold shoulder," she feigned annoyance, "but it comes with the territory, I guess." She sighed, then with the same *man-voice* she'd used to summon the waitress at the Corky Screw the first day they met, Amber snorted a throaty sounding "heh" into Leo's ear.

Leo laughed harder. "You should do stand-up, you know that?"

"Standing up is nice. But I like laying even more."

"Now you're starting to sound more like yourself."

"What are you wearing?" She faked a groan.

"I'm fully clothed, sitting in a parking lot."

"Why are you sitting in a parking lot?"

"Long story."

"I won't even ask. So why haven't you called?"

"Work's been a bitch. Dealing with felons whose attorneys want them pampered, and humoring a griping boss —"

"One thing about *my* job. I don't have to listen to complaints."

"Unfortunately, I do." He thought of the three new cases he'd received this week alone, and the pressure coming down from the office of the chief prosecutor who refused to recognize anything other than high profile or capital murder cases.

"Crazy busy, huh?"

"You have no idea. Seems to be the season for muggings, robberies, and assaults. There must be a full moon floating over Maryland every night." Leo's chuckle fell flat. "Or maybe everybody's just going insane." He glanced at the worn briefcase sitting on the seat beside him, stuffed with files. "What ever happened to nine-to-five, Amber?" With his free hand he unlatched the cover and leafed through papers as he spoke.

"You sound tense, Leo."

"My middle name these days. At least you don't have to bring your work home with you." He mocked. His ire wasn't directed at Amber, but rather at his boss who expected him to depose three felons, giving him only three days to familiarize himself with the cases while he held his own with the rest of his workload.

"I've got something for you, Leo. Might cheer you up. In a sick sense, maybe."

Here we go again, Leo thought, ready for one of Amber's provocative innuendos, which at the moment, would accomplish more than this small talk which was rare for Amber Hawke.

"Should I take the next flight down?"

"That would be fantastic."

"If tomorrow was Saturday, I'd already be on the way."

"You're just a damn tease, Gibraldi. If the tables were turned, I'd call you a cockteaser."

"You have a way with words, Amber. What do you have for me? I could use some cheering up."

"It would be much easier doing this in person."

"Sorry. Guess we'll have to settle for phone sex."

"Very funny. Now you're turning me on."

Leo felt his fly tighten. Even from hundreds of miles away, she had that effect on him.

"On a more serious note, Leo."

"Just when I was starting to relax you want to get serious—"

"That triple homicide in Independence."

"What about it?" As Leo's chest tightened, his fly softened.

"Okay. This is gonna throw you. It's got the fellas working on the case going in circles."

"Cut to the chase."

"Independence may be a copycat."

"What are you talking about? I thought the DNA matched—"

"That's the puzzling part. The hair samples and the tooth, they match the Charlotte DNA. But an eye witness description of the suspect doesn't jive with the one from Charlotte."

"You're losing me. I thought there weren't any witnesses in Independence?"

"Remember the tire tracks at the scene?"

"Yeah, the ones that turned out to be from the media."

"Because of all of the activity at the crime scene, they were never a one hundred percent match to the news trucks. Just speculation."

"How do you know this?"

"Friends."

"Gotcha."

"Independence is small. The cops interviewed practically

everyone in town, especially in the surrounding area. They came up with a gas station attendant who remembered seeing a strange looking guy that night."

"When and where?"

"Predawn. Just about the time investigators figured the perp departed the crime scene. It seemed to coincide with the time of death and other stuff, technical things. Not as important as what I'm about to tell you."

Leo's gut rumbled. Along with the fact that he hadn't eaten anything since the bagel and coffee at breakfast, stress filled his empty stomach. "Keep going, Amber. Give it to me faster." Leo knew any information would also be of interest to Ben, and couldn't wait to clue him in.

"You're doing it again, Leo."

"Huh?"

"I'm supposed to be saying that to you. Give it to me faster. Harder, baby."

"Damn, Amber. Is your mind ever *not* on sex?"

"Nope. I eat, sleep and drink sex. Especially with a stud like you."

"Christ. You're worse than a man."

Amber blew a husky chuckle through the phone line, then said, "Ready for what the gas station attendant said?"

"Lay it on me."

"I plan on it. Soon as you come on down here." She was pushing his buttons, and this wasn't the time to play around. Her voice suddenly turned serious and she spoke rapidly. "I have a copy of the Independence Daily right in front of me. I'll read you what it says: Lanny Jacobs' account of the ominous stranger who pulled up to an air pump at his station at approximately 4:30 a.m. doesn't match the description given by the only other eye witnesses in North Carolina who described the attacker as less than average height with a slight build. The Independence suspect was described by Jacobs as tall and broad, with unusually long arms and legs."

"What the fuck? Any description of the vehicle?"

"Nope. Jacobs was so disturbed by the face, he said he never took his eyes off the guy. He was afraid he'd want to come inside and Jacobs wasn't having it. He said he filled one tire with air, looked at him through the station's windowed wall. That's what he was worried about. The window."

"What?"

"That even if he locked the door, the guy looked big enough to punch one of his arms through the glass and walk right through the window."

"But he didn't go inside —"

"Nope. Just glared at the attendant, got into his car, and drove off. When the guy looked at Jacobs, he said he got so nervous that he almost crapped his pants, literally, he really told that to the police. He locked the door and turned on the closed sign. It was still dark out and the air pump is at the corner of the building, out of the reach of the spotlights. So even if he didn't get the face right, I doubt he could've been wrong about the height. He said he looked over six feet tall. Like a basketball player, maybe. But uglier than anyone, or anything he'd ever seen. That's a stretch from a five-foot-five, or whatever the Charlotte witnesses said their guy looked like. But the Delaney girl did say the guy who broke into her apartment was very creepy looking." Amber paused for Leo's comments or questions.

All Leo could say was, "Christ."

"So what do you think, Leo? Copycat or did the leopard change his spots. Or has he grown a foot taller? Which we all know is impossible. So the only other plausible reason is, it's not the same guy."

"And the DNA?"

"Not a hundred percent."

"You're stretching your theory."

"This one seems different, Leo. The other victims were all alone. This guy took down an entire family in one night, which kind of squelches the premise that he's focused and organized."

"He's got the same signature. The knife. Roses —"

"Don't forget the notes. Two of them," Amber added. "Somebody loves him."

"Huh?"

"Either he's got an admirer who wants to be just like him — or. . . Shit this is getting very scary." Amber's voice wasn't as cocky now as it had been when she first called.

"Any idea of what the notes said?"

"I'm trying to get my hands on that information. It's turning into one hell of a tight case."

There's A Killer In The Closet

More than ten minutes had elapsed, and the hair raising sounds had disappeared as suddenly as they'd begun. The house was quiet. She felt certain she was alone.

Marla was queasy, but dinner wouldn't wait. Neither would Travis. He was always ravenous when he got home from work. She would tease him about having a tapeworm. He could eat them out of house and home, but every bite fed the rippling muscles of his chest and arms.

The peanut butter coated knife balanced on the breakfast plate she'd left in the sink. Marla shook her head. Travis must have made himself a sandwich before leaving this morning. She walked to the trash can in the corner. Nope, he hadn't dumped the doggie bag she'd made for him. It was then she noticed the open loaf of bread staling on the counter and shook her head some more. Would Travis ever become domesticated? She sealed up the bread, washed the breakfast dishes, dried and put them away.

Before climbing the creaky stairs to her bedroom, she uncovered the crock pot, took out a container of leftover stew from the refrigerator. Lumpy sauce splattered into the ceramic pot.

"Huh? I hope this is sufficient for dinner. Seemed to be more when I packed it away last night."

Stirring a wooden spoon, she clicked her tongue. Only a few pieces of meat, some carrots and not one potato. "I must be losing it," she mumbled and shrugged. While the stew simmered, she'd make Travis's favorite dessert. That would fill him up. And she'd bake some nice fresh biscuits, which would make up for the stew Travis must have consumed while her back was turned. She'd make an ample dinner. But first, she needed to get out of these clothes.

Her eyes made a clean sweep of the hallway, jittery fingers clicking every light switch along the way. In her bedroom, Marla took some things from a dresser drawer and placed them on the gleaming top. Shrugging out of her dress, she paused in bra and panties, inspecting the anxiety rash she'd developed while reading the paper. Focusing on her reflection in the mirror, she didn't sense the curious eyes studying her underwear-clad torso, widening as she intimately touched her own creamy skin.

The brain had to stop the gloves from immediately reaching out to touch the pretty thing as it struggled to slow the rise and fall of the killer's chest, panting with temptation.

Still a bit prickly, the spots had paled. Deciding she didn't need the rash cream after all, Marla wriggled into black stretch pants, pulled a soft blue shirt over her head. Her hair clip unsnapped. Chestnut satin spilled across her shoulders, down her back in ropes Travis loved to curl around his fingers, even when he and his wife weren't making love.

She swept her hair back, this time using a heavy rubber band to secure a substantial tail at the nape of her neck. It was then that she noticed the tousled bed. Travis strikes again! She smoothed the yellow flowered bedspread, annoyed with Travis for defiling it while dressing. He was always messing something up. Then she smelled the cologne — and something else. Something worse than Travis when he hugged her in dirty work clothes.

"Ugh! Travis Booth. Did you lay in this bed without showering? Strange, I didn't smell it last night, and now I do,"

Marla said only to herself, or so she thought.

She shook her head and began to hum, thinking of her husband who often behaved like a child. Gloom lifted. Marla didn't feel the heat of the charcoal eyes absorbing every move she made.

Marla was a lively, animated woman. Young and full of life. As she danced around the room, the distorted mind, dying inside the head that hid behind the clothing rack, struggled with the gloves, and with agonizing thoughts.

Gloves against brain, enticing thoughts battled clever thoughts. The gloves longed to strangle her, to stop her purring vocal chords. Although the sound was alluring, cutting those chords would launch a tidal wave of ecstasy even greater than the one derived by chopping the other pretty's throat with a long, curved blade. Knife or glove? Tantalizing struggle. There would be time. When confusion struck, never act. The inevitable had all the time in the world. The inevitable *was* the world.

As she glanced around her cozy bedroom, Marla forgot about the garbage and the daily news. From a pile on the floor, she scooped up the dress she'd worn, inspecting it on the way to the closet — and darkness inside. The darkness urged a glove to slip around the door frame. Had Marla lifted her head at that very moment, she'd have seen the bloodstained glove wrap around the clean, white wood, where for a moment, it paused. But before opening the door, the glove moved back inside.

The dress was slightly wrinkled but not actually soiled. It had been a relatively easy day at work. She could sneak in another wearing before dropping it off at Cody's. Marla placed a gentle hand on the knob, about to pull. "Travis, you can't close a door, or a drawer for that matter," she said aloud as she noticed the top drawer of his nightstand several inches open, exasperated by the twisted T-shirt that hung like a rag down the front of carefully polished mahogany.

Groaning, she dropped her dress on the bed, slid the drawer open, shook and folded the shirt and patted it into place. She then shut the drawer and padded back to her closet to hang her dress as she'd intended to do before noticing Travis had struck yet again. Undomesticated Travis. She'd have to have a talk with him when he got home from work. His boyish charm could go only so far.

Once again, Marla went to the closet, dress slung over her arm, hand pressing the doorknob, ready to expose the lurking maniac when she caught a whiff of the underarm of the garment. "Guess it was a busier day than I remembered," she muttered with a shrug.

Instead of hanging the dress, she took it to the wicker basket in the corner of the room, folded it neatly, and placed it on top of a pair of Travis's trousers. She'd take the entire contents of the basket with her tomorrow, tomorrow when she went to work, and drop it all off at Cody's Cleaners.

Marla crossed the room and paused once more before her dresser mirror, its mahogany scrollwork matching the king sized headboard. Peering sharply, she smoothed her hair, then hands on hips, whirled from side to side evaluating her tummy to make sure it was still washboard flat after devouring a turkey club lunch that included potato salad, complimented with a pickle on the side of the white china dish. Convinced she still looked every bit as slim and attractive as she had looked that morning, and that her hair was free of lint and tangles, she headed out the door.

Continuing to hum, Marla skipped down the steps and went straight to the kitchen. A portable radio rested on the windowsill, nesting on a cushion of shimmering cobwebs. She dusted the webs with a napkin, snapped the radio on and tuned it to her favorite country station. As she sang along, she nasalized her choir voice with an exaggerated twang, drowning out the singer's wail as she bopped around the kitchen making dinner.

"Travis? Is that you?" Marla called out, holding back a shriek when she heard the stairs leading to the bedrooms creak even louder now than before — creaking like hurrying footsteps — not climbing up, but coming down.

Is Travis walking down the stairs? Now wait a minute. I was just up there. Alone.

Miffed, Marla walked to the doorway and poked her head

around the corner, then edged her way into the dining room where she'd have a better view of the living room, and sinister staircase that faced the front door. Had he snuck in without her knowing? It wouldn't be the first time Travis came in from work and darted straight to the bathroom. But these feet sounded like they were sneaking down, not running up.

Oh Lord. . .

The sound of her voice edging closer to his sensitive ears cast a spell capable of raising the dead from the grave. As the killer reached the last step, the brain shouted, "Wait." Desiring her *now*, the gloves fought for control. Her essence taunted the inevitable, but the cautious part of the brain signaled *halt*.

The humming stopped but now she was yelling. Loud. Irritating. At the sound of her irritating voice and cagey footsteps moving in his direction, the killer held his foul breath and ducked into the alcove beneath the stairs, flattening his body like a dreary mass against the wall.

He was in dream. He knew the sound of her voice, pleasant or shrieking, the feline brush of her feet on the floor. He recalled the Louisiana fragrance of springtime hair, remembered another body unclothed. Unleashing his senses he shut his eyes, imagined her, inhaled her, and thrilled as contrived images coiled through the sickness of his brain.

"Travis?" Marla called again, the cold toes of one bare foot clinging to the oak tread like coagulating honey clung like glue to a spoon. "You up there?"

No reply. Quickening breath. Difficult to proceed. *You're being ridiculous, Marla*! *This house is old as the hills and just as windy!* She longed to see Travis appear at the head of the stairs. Travis walking through the front door. *Travis answer me!* The sun now slept beneath clouds that disguised a slice of moon, and shadows shivered off daylight, drenching the room with fear. Dancing shadows. Slithering shadows.

Praying for the sound of Travis's voice, Marla forced herself to investigate the sound she *knew* had not been her imagination. Ghosts? Dear Lord, she prayed. Were Travis's folks really that angry with her? Had they come back to haunt her? After all, this had been their home. Maybe they didn't like the way she was taking care of it? Her throat tightened as stinging fear gripped her skin.

Broom in hand, one cautious foot at a time, Marla advanced, nimble and surefooted, her one-hundred-ten pound stance agile as a mountain lion stalking prey. Humoring the wear on the wood, she continued up the stairs that moaned and groaned just above the killer's head. Above his head as he crouched in the alcove inches below Marla, his dry mouth moistening with thickening lust that slid down his throat, saliva mixed with rapture, as he regarded the nearness of one of the most enticing pretties he'd ever encountered.

The gloves were the master. They commanded the brain but not the mind. The killer's scalp was aflame. He swiped the hood from his head, and without hair to absorb it, sweat sluiced and gathered around his neck while the rest of him remained cold.

The sounds she made mere inches away were impossible to resist. She was halfway up and could easily be trapped on the top floor with no place to run. He would approach, and her screams would make him stronger. Not confused, but angry. Anger was power. He would force her into the bedroom and thrill as she gasped. Thrill as her eyes dislocated with fear. He would watch her convulse as her brain starved for air, as he now starved for her. Starved for her death.

The gloves were eager, but at times, the gloves were blind and far too daring. Straining, one crept from beneath the stairs that sheltered the killer, feeling through dusk as it groped for the molding, insisting the body follow. But the body refused to move.

Thoughts raided the brain, thoughts that challenged the gloves. When the killer was organized, his victims had always been asleep. The gloves were a risk, confusing the brain, sending images, signaling the body to react as a picture flashed, recollection of what the knife could do to flesh. A fragile throat. How it could be sliced like an overripe peach seeping with savory juices.

Confrontation was risk, the mind repeated. But the gloves were the strength, so one foot dared a step. A step from behind the alcove. The prey was alone. Irresistible. Accessible.

Marla stood at the top of the stairs and gingerly stepped down the hall, heart pounding as she tiptoed from room to room. With rising anxiety her skin itched so badly, by the time she reached the second doorway she had scratched herself raw. Blood painted the underside of her fingernails.

As she surveyed every room, the killer felt the impact of her movements, gauging precisely the location of his prey. The second foot followed the first and he perched boldly at the bottom of the stairs, head alert, sensitive ears in tune. All that stood between him and his need were a dozen creaky treads.

As he climbed, she would hear but not know her attacker until it was too late. She would meet him at the landing, greet him with a blood curdling scream when she saw his face. Then she would try to flee. But she was upstairs without a means of escape, which meant, she was now his.

"Travis?" Her whisper shivered. "Travis, please be you," she moaned, wanting to be anyplace but here at this moment, alone in this cold dark house, listening to footsteps coming up the stairs. "Who's there?" she managed to croak, then the roar inside her ears drowned out the sounds of his steps. Marla was about to faint from fear. Fear for her life.

you can't close the book
or turn yesterday's pages
you can't catch a break
yet you can't fade away

Two Killers † Same DNA ?

Leo sat in Fireflies' packed parking lot, digesting Amber's phone call. She had him wired. Although informative, the conversation had been unnerving. Unnerving enough for him to consider driving to the Dockhouse, spending a few more hours with a glass of scotch, then calling a cab, because he'd sure as hell need one. Sitting on another barstool wasn't going to do much for his sinking mood, or unscramble the mystery that was becoming his obsession, but he decided to drop in, anyway. There was something about the place . . .

The Dockhouse reminded him of Scarlett. Together they had spent a nice evening that hadn't amounted to anything. Still, it had been enjoyable, and he'd made another valuable contact. *A beautiful woman. A valuable contact. Amusing.* He'd like to get inside her head again. Get inside more than her head.

The thought of the collection of excellence working endless hours on the Psycho case should have calmed his mind, but it didn't. Neither did the shot of scotch he consumed at the Dockhouse bar. The pros weren't getting anywhere and women were dying. He grabbed his phone and speed dialed.

"Ben. What are you doing?"

"I'm driving home. What the hell do you *think* I'm doing. Are you going insane? See too many boobies tonight?" Ben's laugh exploded through the phone.

The Dockhouse shrank then disappeared from Leo's rearview mirror. "Meet me at my house. I'll be home in fifteen minutes."

"What's at your house?"

"Amber called. I have more information. And I want to show you something. I've been tracking him —"

"You're driving yourself nuts, Leo."

"No. This psycho is."

"Terry's gonna love this. I've been out every night this week."

"Bring her with you. But get a sitter for the kids."

"Yeah, right. You're so fucking sarcastic, Gibraldi."

"Benny. I've been mapping this thing out."

The Mustang jerked to a halt in the rowhouse driveway, with Leo entering through the kitchen, jogging down the long flight of stairs into the basement.

Other than an oak roll top desk and triple filing cabinet, Leo's basement was empty. The room was handsomely finished with creamy walls, snow white moldings, Berber carpet, and a high ceiling that housed two rows of recessed fixtures compensating for the natural light four small casement windows throttled.

From a cedar closet, he pulled out a tripod easel and set it up beneath the windows, then taped three eight by ten sheets of paper side by side on the whiteboard. With a magic marker he labeled the first, "Atlanta." The second, "Charlotte." The third, "Independence."

Hanging on the wall beside the easel was a wood-framed four foot corkboard covered by a map of the USA. Before Ben arrived, Leo opened the desktop and sorted a stack of papers, then pulled out a box of multicolored pushpins.

Leo heard the muffled engine of the Caravan choke, then the car door collided with the strength of Ben's heavy hand. In a moment, the kitchen door slammed just as hard.

"Leo?"

"Down here."

The carpeted steps creaked under Ben's weight.

"What are you doing?"

"C'mere. Check this out."

Leo's white shirt spread open at the neck, his blue tie looped like a noose around his collar. His hair was equally disheveled from his fingers running through it with frustration. He was a mad scientist about to reveal his master *mind* to the world.

At each crime scene, a red plastic pin secured a piece of note pad containing a description of the murder and victim along with any available details. Crime scene photos displaying each young woman in various post mortem poses were joined at the corners like a handful of playing cards and splayed out on the desktop. As Leo spoke, he rifled through the photos.

"Is this what you called me over here for?"

"Here's what we have. All victims, including our survivor, have long, dark hair. All single women in their early twenties. The victims all found in bed with their throats slashed. Roses. Notes growing in intensity. Tell you anything?"

"He likes young brunettes? You look like shit."

"He's recapturing. They're not random selections. He's reenacting something."

"Yeah. He was jilted like thousands of other saps. So?"

"Delaney said he was slight in stature. How did he overpower two girls and a football player if he's the size of a woman?"

"Okay?" Ben's eyes mirrored gold from the lights that doused his pullover shirt. As he stared at Leo he stood at attention, like a cop on duty, legs spread, shoulders squared, readied arms straight at his sides.

"The last witness stated he was a big guy dressed like a jogger. The original suspect was almost completely covered, dressed like Jack the Ripper. Amber mentioned a copycat. The murder or murderers are taking the same route. Using the same MO. Identical signature."

"How is Amber, by the way?"

"Since I haven't seen her, I really don't know."

"You just talked to her."

"About the killer. Why are you asking about Amber?"

"When's the last time you were with Glory?"

"I told you. The Japanese play." Leo's green eyes rolled. "Since when are you so interested in my personal life?"

"Maybe if you had an active sex life again, you wouldn't be obsessing over this nutcase and let the Feds do their job."

"I didn't call you over to discuss my sex life."

"So what's up with Glory, anyway? She used to practically shadow you."

"She's been slumming it again."

Ben's eyes narrowed. "What the fuck?"

"I know," Leo shrugged. "She's got to learn on her own."

"What does Diviniello think about her hanging with Landes?"

"I have no idea. We don't discuss his daughter — or his personal life."

"I guess Terry's wearing off on me. I'm not trying to invade your privacy." Ben grinned. "But — hey. A good lay would help get your mind off this shit. Why don't you fly down to Atlanta?"

"Why don't you kiss my ass."

"No thanks. But point taken."

"Great. Now back to the copycat theory. The change of appearance. MO. The signature." Leo motioned to the map, then lifted and tossed the victims' photos so they scattered across the desk.

"Your presentation is very good. I've got the same one in my office." Ben said dryly. "Since we already know all of this, exactly what are you getting at?"

"What's making him look different? Why is he suddenly tall? Why did he ditch his clothes at the Johnsons' and take the old man's?"

"He's a growing boy? He's evolving?"

"Stop being an asswipe. Look at these two police sketches."

"We've been through this. I've seen them."

"Look at them again. Look at the bone structure. It's entirely different. This is what's driving me crazy."

"Yeah. One looks like a skeleton. The other, Cro-Magnon.

Fucking weird shit."

"There *have* been cases of psychos working in tandem. But Christ —"

"Is he changing faces intentionally as a disguise? Or is he really some kind of freak?"

"Sure he's a freak. But remember New York and San Francisco? How many women were murdered? Seven? In six months. All with the same MO and sig. Everyone thought the same guy was traveling back and forth, covering his tracks. The airlines were monitored around the clock —"

"Yeah, till there were simultaneous murders in both cities and the DNA matched."

"Right. And the DNA from these murders match. The descriptions don't."

"You're confusing the hell out of me, Leo. So you think there are two killers with identical DNA?"

"No. There's only one." Leo shook his head. "But it's the damndest —"

January Valentine

now you're walking down the stairs
you're heading out to nowhere
crouching in a corpse disguise
breathing gauze instead of air

LAB RATS HAUNTED BY A MAD SCIENTIST

The gloves gloated as the killer climbed the stairs more aggressively. *I told you this was right. This one will be good. Better than a sleeping pretty.*

The truck's tires crunched leaves and the rocky driveway. As Travis pulled around to the back of the house to park beside Marla's sedan, his headlights flashed across the first floor windows. The killer, halfway up the stairs, froze, reeled, quickly retreated. Marla heard the pickup, from her bedroom window saw the headlights dim, then the post lamp turned on as Travis opened the truck door and stepped out. Travis. Beautiful Travis. She pounded on the window. "Travis!"

From his place beneath the alcove, the killer heard the upstairs fuss, the shrill voice screaming, "Travis!" Saw the front yard engulfed in menacing flames of light. From sheer frustration, on the floor he urinated, then edged from the alcove and carefully sidled past the stairs, down the hall and into the kitchen where a split second decision was essential. Go to the cellar or to the barn? But the house was a home. *His* home. The barn was for animals.

Travis was on the walkway. The killer heard the sound of his heavy footsteps that were dangerously close, nearing the kitchen door. Closer now. Too late to escape the kitchen, and Marla was running down the stairs, so he couldn't flee out the front door.

And then there was that light, the threatening light all around the house, thanks to fucking Travis! He hated that name. Hated the man. The mind alerted the killer that *he* was about to become the victim. That's when the gloves took over the mess the *brain* had gotten them into.

A glove grasped the cellar doorknob, pulled the door open and pushed the killer through the threshold where in their haste, the gloves almost tripped him down the stairs. He wanted to pull off the gloves, the gloves that were the cause of his insanity, his anguish, his pain. But the gloves were strong. And with each passing day, the brain grew more decayed. The killer settled into a corner of the dark and peaceful cellar. For the time being, he was safe.

Bare feet barely touching the floor, Marla flew into the kitchen like a kite about to take flight. "Travis!" She threw herself into his arms.

"Well that's quite a welcome home." Travis's solid frame withstood her attack. He dropped his briefcase, and lifted her like a hundred pound bale of hay he was hoisting from the back of his truck to the barn.

Marla buried her face in his shoulder. He smelled like spice, lingering spice and outdoor freshness. "Thank goodness you're home." She kissed his cheek, clinging to him like a frightened child.

"What's wrong, baby girl?" Setting her onto her feet, he held her at arm's length.

For as happy as Marla was to see her burly husband, she flared, "I told you I hate when you call me baby girl!"

"What's wrong, Marla?" The confused look on his face calmed her.

"I'm sorry. It's been a terrible night. Why are you so late?"

"I told you on the phone I'd be late. Were you listening? Of course not, and why'd you hang up on me?"

Marla dragged out the paper from between the breadbox and

the wall. "Explain this." She shoved it at him.

Travis looked even more befuddled. "What's wrong with you? You're starting to worry me."

"You? How the heck do you think I feel with the way *you've* been acting. Lying and sneaking —"

"Hold on a minute. Before you start accusing *me*, I deserve knowing what in the hell you're talking about."

"While you had to work overtime because you were late because this morning you sat at this kitchen table reading this paper —" She slapped the paper against his chest.

"I wasn't late. I told you I had to cover for Charles. And what's this?" He grabbed the paper.

"You tell me. Why did you do this to the newspaper and leave it open on the table? Since when do you have time to read the paper before work? You're suddenly the man of leisure, instead of the man of the house?"

"I don't know what you're talking about Marla, but you're really starting to piss me off."

Marla stood her ground. "I'm getting to the bottom of this right now. Sit down while I get your supper and then we're going to have a nice talk."

"I'm going to shower first. It's been one crappy day." Travis left the room muttering, "Looks like it's gonna be a damn crappy night, too."

"You think *your* day was crappy?"

Travis, already climbing the stairs, ignored her.

While Marla set the table, the killer, directly beneath the floor on which she tread lightly, listened attentively. His sensitive ears and nostrils gathered the information his eyes were unable to.

When the aroma of biscuits baking in the oven made its way to the cellar, he was stricken with hunger. He inhaled the mouthwatering blend of hot stew and buttermilk biscuits, remembering he'd already eaten most of the stew that morning, cold from the container, before napping on the bed. Like an animal in heat sniffing his mate, he grew hungrier for satisfaction. For food. For the thrill of ending a human life.

By the time Travis returned to the kitchen, Marla had relaxed and was in the process of nibbling a warm biscuit, licking dribbling butter from her fingers. She wiped her hands on a linen towel, then hung it on a hook beside the stove.

"What did you have for lunch today, Travis?" she asked as she shoveled stew onto his plate, circling the modest portion with fluffy homemade biscuits.

"A burger and fries at the diner."

"Did you eat the doggie bag?"

"I sure did."

"Even after the peanut butter sandwiches?"

"What peanut butter sandwiches?"

"The sandwiches you made this morning after I left you right here in this kitchen. Before you read and mangled the newspaper."

Travis shook his head and dug his fork into a chunk of juicy browned beef. "If this tastes as good as it smells, baby girl. . ." He obviously couldn't help himself. She was so cute when she was angry. His mouth spread with a teasing grin.

Marla's face tightened. In the most serious voice Travis had ever witnessed, she said, "This house is haunted."

"What?"

"I'm hearing noises — footsteps. Feeling eyes on me. Things are out of place. Look. . ." she pointed to the newspaper he'd thrown onto the seat of the chair beside him. "If you didn't do that, then who did? Because I sure as hell didn't."

Travis stared in amazement. What was happening to his wife? Would she be hearing voices next?

"I don't know. And by the way," he said. "You better call a plumber."

"What?"

"There's a leak under the alcove. And it stinks, Marla. Are there toilet pipes in that wall? Because it stinks like raw sewerage."

"Great," Marla moaned. "Now we have something else to worry about. I know it belonged to your family, but we should seriously think about putting this old house on the market. I don't think I can live here anymore. I feel like somebody's experimenting on us to see how much stress we can take. Like we're lab rats haunted by a mad scientist."

January Valentine

savage enemies tear into your brain
and the dead can't keep pace
with the whole human race
so you lay paralyzed by misery

INTRUDER ALERT!

Diamond light slavered from a blood moon, slicing a pathway through mammoth clouds, inflaming every portal in the Booth farmhouse. Like disjointed arms, streams of light rumba'd with naked limbs shuddering in autumn wind, disturbing the woman who tossed beneath starched linen sheets.

As Marla slept on her back, moonlight dribbled across her face, smokeless and silver, flames licking her awake from tenuous slumber.

The killer, rested from the afternoon siesta during which time the Booths' bed had been desecrated, was curled up like a homeless Sphynx cat in an isolated corner of the cellar. The brain pained and the mind roared. Trembling with need the gloves hadn't slept a wink, and the stomach grumbled with hunger. He was miserable. Darkness was good, but it magnified depression. The remedy: murder.

As the moon sailed the sky, it slipped across the killer's face. Distraught, he sprang to his feet, crept to the stairs and quietly climbed. The glove turned the knob and the hinged door screeched. Quiet! The gloves screamed, then chastised the fishbone fingers. The killer froze, struggling to balance on the rickety oak saddle.

After a tense moment, the mind permitted the entry of the gloves. He crept around the kitchen, carefully opening cabinets and drawers, shuffling the contents of her recipe box. Although the nose was incomplete, the nostrils were acute. Drawn to a specific aroma, the half-nose sniffed the air, following deliciousness to the plastic bag of leftover biscuits. He tore it open and feasted. With shrinking lips, crumbs sprinkled like powdery snow, covering his sweatshirt, dusting a half circle on the floor around his shoes. Not entirely satiated, he opened the refrigerator and rummaged around the shelves. An inept sleeve caught and knocked a jar of pickles from the door tray. It smashed to the floor. Spooked, he fled to the cellar. Poised, the gloves patted the knife, then waited for the attack of footsteps the mind assured would follow his carelessness.

"Travis." Awakened from light sleep, Marla rasped. "Did you hear that?"

Travis continued to breathe horse-like sounds through his parted lips.

"Travis, wake up!" Her voice was urgent.

"What is it now?" he snorted. "For the sake of the Lord, Marla."

"Didn't you hear that crash? There's someone downstairs." The words she spoke were paralyzing to her, annoying to Travis.

"Oh God, Marla." Travis squinted at the clock. Two a.m. "We have to get up in a few hours." He groaned.

Down in the cellar, after a thoughtful moment, the mind directed the killer to escape through the storm door which was just above a short flight of cement steps leading to the yard and flee, flee into the night where his movements triggered the light sensor behind the house. The glare was dazzling and for a moment captured his breath. The brain fired contradictory signals. Food. Kill. Danger. Run. He couldn't hesitate now. But he'd be sure to return.

As the killer approached the barn he heard the crunch of boots on the path behind him. Watched the beam of a flashlight part the comfort of darkness that draped the yard as he hurried to slide open the door and undetected, slip into the sanctuary . . . the barn.

By the time Travis inspected first the grounds, then the space between his pickup and Marla's sedan, the killer had vanished, climbed the ladder to the loft and settled into mounds of hay. The glove fumbled through darkness, hurling strands of straw into the air above his head, showering the killer. Pitchfork! The gloves were angry because the killer had foolishly left the pitchfork in the vehicle. And the scythe. Forgetful. The mind was becoming forgetful. Forgetful and frazzled. Buried. The gloves buried the killer safely beneath a layer of hay. Sunrise. At sunrise they would recover the weapons. The weapons the gloves claimed for their own. The killer would revisit the farmhouse. He would feast. And he would rage.

While Marla waited in bed, curled into a ball hugging Travis's pillow to her chest, she worried. What the heck was happening? What was causing all of these crazy noises and other freaky occurrences? Suppose it wasn't an animal, or an unwelcomed visitor she could report to the police? Suppose it was something unearthly? At the thought, a violent chill wracked her body. She fought to control her quivering lips and chattering teeth. It should be impossible to feel cold beneath all of the blankets she bundled herself with, yet she shook as if she were standing in a cold shower in the middle of winter in an unheated house.

What if the house *was* really haunted? Haunted like the old place she made the mistake of visiting as a young girl. The southern colonial that had been passed from generation to generation on her mother's side of the family. The one set deep in the desolate woods of Virginia. The last time she visited her grandmother's house, fear drove her out as fast as her limbs now shook, making her skin itch with hives, her hair all but stand on end as it threatened to do now.

She remembered how the blinds that hung on the side door had whipped up into the air then smashed back down as if an invisible force had lifted and dropped them, just for the hell of it. Just like that. There was no answer, so they chalked it up to imagination. That triggered the eerie chain of events that caused

Gran to close down the ancient house and move to town with Marla's family, not long after that night. She thought of Speckles, the Border Collie, who had let out a few yelps before bolting from the room. And when the back door flew open, and slammed shut on its own, she and Gran ran from the house. Who or *what* had slammed that door? And why couldn't anyone see it? Marla tried to shut off her mind, then she heard the footsteps on the stairs. She screamed.

Travis let his jacket drop to the floor beside his boots.

"Stop screaming. It's only me." He looked exhausted, and concerned. "I checked the entire downstairs and we're the only ones in this house."

"Are you sure? Maybe whoever it is ran outside when he heard you coming."

"There's nothing out there, Marla. It was probably a raccoon rooting in the garbage can."

"Well did you check the garbage can?" She held her voice to a low screech.

"No. But I'll check it before I leave for work in —" Travis stared at the clock and said, "Two hours thanks to your vivid imagination."

Travis's red face was hidden in the dim bedroom where he tossed and turned, unable to tumble beyond stage two of the sleep cycle before the alarm blared in his ear.

He groaned. "I'll never make it through this day."

"I'll make you a nice breakfast, Travis. That'll make you feel better."

"What's going to make me feel better is living the calm life I used to live before all of this nonsense started."

Marla lowered her eyes, threw on her robe and hurried down the stairs to cook breakfast. When she stepped through the kitchen door and saw that the refrigerator door had been left open, she slammed a hand against the doorframe and screamed so loud her throat burned. Then she spotted the jar of pickles, crashed and smashed all over the floor.

"Travis!" At the top of her lungs, she yelled. The tendons in her neck strained, her temples throbbed, and her face turned a deeper purple than the hand she'd just slammed into the hardwood molding.

January Valentine

it's run its course
we're over now
we can still be friends
loving you is not for me.
it don't feel right
i'm too unsure
can't give you what you want
can you live with it this way?

Flexible Glory

For an early morning weekday, the gym was exceedingly crowded. Behaving as if she owned the swanky establishment, Glory sauntered around the weight room, shooting daggers at anyone who crossed her path, grimacing annoyance at the world, and two women in line ahead of her who were waiting for the Helix.

Gliding from machine to machine, showing off her sapphire spandex, was almost impossible. Posing in front of a mirrored wall, she tore off her headband and tossed her head a few times. Her hair floated like corn silk then abruptly settled, leaving her to look like she'd been caught in a ten second windstorm.

"This place is a zoo today," she said loud enough for the entire gym to hear as she sauntered toward a gawking man who jogged like mad on a treadmill.

During a leisurely halt, she stretched, aiming her voluptuous assets at him as she twisted, stretched toward the ceiling, bent at the waist.

The morning was against her. Forsaking the perspiring treadmill guy, with an exaggerated sigh she flounced from the room. At the pool, for the thrill of it, she could use her natural tan and mouth watering white bikini to her advantage. She would slink around and find someone to vamp. Glory was bored, so Glory would behave badly. There were still five long hours standing between her and her audition, and exercise — or steamy sexual encounters — had a way of taking her mind off anything.

*

Suspension from Price Holdings wasn't as bad as it sounded. And he was still collecting an executive salary with benefits, along with perks from Glory Divine.

Sam Landes hadn't only been asked to step down as hedge fund manager. He had been ordered to steer clear of the exclusive brokerage house until any pending charges disappeared. Diviniello would have to step in. Glory . . . In turn, Gibraldi would have to scrub his mess clean. Just as he'd done the first time Landes was busted for possession of cocaine. Only this incident was worse. Landes was linked to a deal involving over two hundred pounds of *sparkling sunshine* that had been smuggled over the border. Word of his implication hadn't yet hit the news, and if the judge had his way it never would.

Landes passed the golf course on his way to the club. The plush green extended further than the human eye could see. Here and there a golf buggy crept, but other than that, the course unfurled serenely.

He parked his Ferrari a few spaces from Glory's Porsche. Although the October day was relatively warm, when he exited the car he buttoned his jacket, then stuffed his hands into his pockets and quickly strode inside.

For a clubhouse, the place was posh. Prussian blue carpeting guided guests into a wide foyer, past a cloak room the size of a dress shop, then spread its hospitality inside the glass walled dining arena that overlooked the golf course, which was where the judge waited.

Landes seemed to immediately spot the sizeable man sitting at a table a few feet from the bar. Staring out a window, Diviniello nursed a drink.

As Landes approached, he rose and with a wave of his hand,

led him to a private corner where they settled beside a freshly swept fireplace. The two men had the room to themselves, and like two bucks, they appeared on the verge of a clash.

"Sit down, Sam. What's your drink?" Diviniello nodded and a waiter appeared, took their order and quickly returned with a gin and tonic for Landes, and a second jack and coke for the judge.

Landes shifted in his seat, his words tight. "Is there a problem?"

"No problem. I invited you here to let you know you're leaving town." Diviniello's voice was flat.

"What do you mean leaving town? I'm in the middle of a big —" Landes's round eyes looked huge.

Lifting a hand, Diviniello stopped him. His pinky ring glinted. "You're lucky you're not spending the next twenty years in prison. Pack your bags and be out of Baltimore by the end of the week. And stay away from my daughter."

"What's going on?" Landes acted surprised. "Why are you talking to me like this?"

"Does sparkling sunshine ring a bell?"

Landes slapped a palm to his forehead. "Shit. . ."

"Yeah, shit is right. What the fuck's the matter with you?"

"I haven't done anything, Tony . . . I haven't been arrested."

"Not yet."

Back peddling, Landes changed his strategy. "I'm being framed."

"Stop trying to bullshit me." Diviniello's ice blue eyes narrowed. "We both know you're lying through your teeth. You're getting off easy. Leave like a gentleman."

Landes belted out a sigh. Caught red handed, what could he do but plead.

"We have a history, Tony —"

"It's about to be cut short."

"Does Glory know about this?"

Diviniello set his jaw. His eyes warned. "If you go anywhere near her, you'll spend eternity with the sea life and sludge beneath the Baltimore Bay."

During the entire conversation, the judge's demeanor didn't waver. After he finished speaking he sipped his drink, then turned his head toward the vast glass wall behind their table, indicating Sam Landes had been dismissed.

Landes slugged his drink and without another word left the table. Before exiting the building, he took a farewell cruise around the second floor lounge, stopping at the bar for another drink.

"I'm gonna miss the hell out of the place," he said quietly into his glass of gin. "This place has been better to me than my wife's mansion, or her company." He spoke as if the seat beside him was occupied by a warm body with a comforting ear. He needed to find Glory, the most invigorating part of Baltimore that he would miss most of all. "What will it be like without her? Always a phone call away, ready for anything." Landes looked like he was about to attend his own funeral.

He pulled out his cell, but didn't dial. "I'm leaving town. You're coming with me."

Landes was in uncharted territory. He was out of control. Baltimore had always been his home. He clutched the phone, fingers warming the keypad.

"What the fuck am I going to tell my wife when she sees me packing? What the hell do I say to Glory? I was gonna leave her anyway, babe. You always knew it. Only now, it's going to be without any money. How do you feel about that, Glory? Do you still want me?"

Landes drained his glass, slammed it on the bar. For a moment he stared at his phone, then shoved it back into his pocket. He took another look around, slid off the stool and headed for the stairs leading to the gym. Glory didn't seem to be anywhere around — neither was the judge.

Landes's eyes darted as he walked down the hall, slowing before the glass enclosed pool. Steam from crystal clear eighty degree water, mixed with an overdose of chlorine, filled the air. When he walked through the door, a blast of asphyxiating heat glossed his face. His clothing clung. After a quick walk around the deck, he shrugged off his jacket, loosened his tie. The water looked tempting. "Gonna miss this too," he mumbled to no one in particular, because the pool was unoccupied.

*

After a few laps Glory had departed the pool area, but not before registering her disapproval. When she complained about her routine being broken, the lifeguard had acted apologetic. When she stomped off, his eyes could have burned a hole in her bikini.

She was edgy about her upcoming audition. The part had been written for her. Who was more qualified to play a millionaire rancher's daughter than Glory Divine?

After the twenty-minute timer stopped the whirlpool jets, she simmered in steam. Her cell phone, wrapped inside the thick towel resting on the bench beside her, buzzed. When her eyes flashed across the illuminated screen, her bee-stung lips spread into a smile. She wiped her fingers on the towel, then texted a reply. A few moments later, the warning chime rang as the sauna door was opened.

"Sam?" Glory purred as she slipped off her bikini.

January Valentine

so hook me in lock me up
screeching in a swathe of flame
the next great comet
crashing down full burn

SOMETHING IS WAY OUT OF KILTER

Although the onslaught of disease had abated, in the tertiary stage, without treatment the brain was gradually dissolving. Bacteria had already attacked the body, ravaging the skin, destroying internal organs. He suffered episodes of intense pain and disturbed sensation. Neurons that should have supplied sensory information were degenerating. Thoughts sprang, but died before engaging. The killer was unraveling, physiologically and psychologically. The mind still knew safety from risk, but the gloves were the enemy. Their interference was dangerous. The killer could easily be caught if the gloves overruled the mind, the mind that was losing control.

The transient lifestyle was also wearing. The soul was not affected. The soul had been left behind in Louisiana, where it perished with the first victim. The victim that continued to haunt the killer. The bitch just wouldn't let go!

The sky was a quilt patched with blue, but as she drove to work that morning, Marla's keen sense of smell told her, even though sunshine seeped through the windshield, rain was on the way. Marla was shaken. Shaken from the crazy goings on, and from the early morning argument with Travis. There had been too much arguing lately. They'd never disagreed so much. Travis, although a hulk of a man, had the nature of a lamb. When she confronted him about breaking the jar of pickles, leaving the refrigerator door wide open, he'd angrily denied all the charges, then to appease her he'd shouted, "Fine! I broke the pickle jar, Marla. And I dumped the garbage. And I also tore the paper. Now does that make you happy? Will you put it to rest now?"

No. Marla was not about to put anything to rest. Something was way out of kilter, and her mind was set. Today from work she would call the sheriff's office.

By the time she pulled the sedan down the driveway, a row of cars and occupants waited for the bank to open. Sometimes customers even blockaded the doors, so they'd be first to enter. This angered her. Couldn't they wait for her to get inside?

The day was dreary, and so was Marla's mood as the bank manager buzzed her into the building.

Weather was important because it affected her mood. She wanted it to rain. Watching torrents of rain pour down the windows relaxed her, but the dreariness of the day that only threatened and didn't produce was depressing.

Marla went to the break room, stowed her handbag and lunch in her locker, then hurried behind the counter, not because she was late, but because she hated the idea of the people outside waiting in their cars. She disappeared into the vault, counted out her quota of cash, nodding to the other three employees as she returned to her window.

Being inside the vault made her edgy. She had a phobia of small places and dreaded the thought of being locked in the bank vault, but being assistant manager carried with it the responsibility of tending, filling cash drawers, ushering customers in and out. Travis had joked about it, saying if she got locked in she'd have the keys to the fortunes inside the safety deposit boxes held. Travis had a way of joking his way through everything.

Marla had an idea of what caused her claustrophobia. She swore she remembered floating inside her mother's womb, trying to punch her way out. Her mother often said she had high intelligence, because when she carried Marla she ate lots of fish, milk and calves liver. "All those amino acids swam straight to your developing brain, Marla, making you my little brain child with the highest IQ in this entire family."

Marla thought about the discussion over breakfast, when Travis had tried to lighten the mood with jokes about her acting out because she was feeling neglected. "You don't need to do those things to get my attention, Marla. I always have my eye on you." Then he kissed her like he hadn't in a long time, sweeping her off her feet with one of his bear hugs. Marla responded by wriggling out of his arms, one of the most insulting things she could have done.

"Obsessed," Travis had said on his way out the door. She hoped this wasn't going to affect their marriage the way stress had affected her parents'.

"You haven't been yourself lately," Travis had said when he accused her of sleepwalking.

"Sleepwalking?" she had snapped. "Sure. Blame me."

January Valentine

i'll be judge of the hour
evaluate your power
pick out every flaw
in your lack of character

LEO, BEN & MURDER

Breaking news scrolled across the television screen in the form of a red ticker displaying something about a connection between Atlanta and Baltimore and serial murders. Leo rushed into the room, but didn't have a chance to catch it all. Still, he nearly choked when he turned up the volume and a pageboy blonde recited:

"Channel Nine broke the news this morning. Details after a short break."

Leo hit speed dial and left a message. "Ben, if you're near the TV, turn on nine."

The anchorwoman returned.

"Sources tell us the grizzly slaughter and mutilation of a Virginia family may not be connected to the Atlanta slayings as authorities previously thought. We're not at liberty to release all information, but there seems to be a discrepancy in the DNA collected from the Virginia crime scene and the apartment of a young woman who was recently attacked by, who authorities had originally believed to be the same killer, the one referred to as the Sweet Dreams Psycho.

Adding an additional twist to the case, two members of

Baltimore law enforcement, Detective Benjamin Cassidy of the Baltimore Police Department and Assistant Prosecutor Leonardo Gibraldi, were said to have visited North Carolina and interviewed the surviving victim."

Leo gulped when he stared in horror as the TV flashed a forty-two-inch mug shot of himself and Ben, in candid poses, talking on the walkway in front of Josie Delaney's apartment house. The phone rang instantly.

"That little cunt." Ben was breathless. "She nabbed us on her cell cam. Why would she do that? Do you know what they're gonna do to us now?"

"Yeah, we may be out of jobs. Calm down. Listen to the rest—"

"Charlotte officials refer to the two investigators as the Baltimore cowboys who may have compromised the case they were building," the anchor continued.

"Case? Fucking asses. What the fuck do they know about how to handle a murder case like this?" Ben sounded furious.

"It appears the two are in some way connected to one of the victims, and have vowed to, in their own words, nail the bastard to a cross and burn him. A statement the investigating officers consider a threat, as well as an insult." The anchorwoman disappeared as the station broke for a commercial.

While Leo listened to Ben rant on the other end of the line, all he could say was, "Jesus."

GRAVESIDE ATTRACTION

After the Booths left for work, the killer roamed the farmhouse for hours, touching everything the gloves fancied, switching on the radio then turning it off, doing the same with the television. The mind missed the flutter of Marla's footsteps, and the lure of her voice. He spent the dreary morning rummaging through cabinets, closets and drawers. Since the refrigerator was almost bare of delicious food, he helped himself to a pack of chocolate chip cookies from a shelf, and polished off leftover buttermilk biscuits. Still hungry, he checked the contents of the kitchen trash, but the receptacle contained only a clean plastic liner.

Finding nothing exceptional in the kitchen, he exited through the rear door and out into the yard where he was drawn to the foul odor emanating from the large metal garbage can. The outdoor can contained household garbage, and a potpourri of potently aromatic rotting scraps of food. For a moment he paused, scanning the surrounding area. Nothing but bleak sky and colorful trees, harsh mountains and balmy mist, but rather than scavenging in the yard, he dragged the can into the barn where he dumped the contents on the floor, then sifted through greasy bottles, sticky jars, and cans with caked on food remnants. He settled for licking the fingers of the gloves, and sank his remaining teeth into loose bones with fragments of clinging meat. After consuming every last shred of roasted animal flesh, his belly was finally filled to capacity.

It was a lazy day with a cloud-tumbling ceiling that hung low. Bored. The killer was bored. Exhilaration from the triple murder had occupied the mind, but images were dwindling and he was bottoming out, which wasn't good. Next would come the rage. He was a recoiling spring with moods expanding from dangerous to severely dangerous.

Residing with the Booths had been a unique experience, but he was quickly tiring of the mundane. As with the overconsumption of sugar that nauseated and agitated, boredom caused physical illness, wiring him like a time bomb set to explode the moment the eyes engaged a pretty.

Following the familiar path the scythe had cleaved, with ease the killer found the niche. After unmasking the vehicle, he drove into town, where the tires dragged on roads like a fishing boat trolling a sea. At mid afternoon the town was uninspiring, as was the farmhouse when the Booths weren't at home.

The Independence diner had recovered from lunch, and was leisurely preparing for dinner. A few customers dawdled on the broad, front sidewalk, but they were either workers on break or those who had retired, stealing a coffee and a smoke on a bench. School buses had completed their routes and were tucked into stalls. Pretty things were nowhere in sight. Disheartening.

Like the clang of a lunch bell, memories struck the mind. *Louisiana.* Time passed in the cemetery at the edge of the marsh had been time well spent. Happy-time. Play-time. Sprawling alongside a headstone, lying across a sarcophagus, had a way of easing the mind. Intricacies of chiseled monuments carved with names, dates and phrases, towering statues with haughty chins, folded wings and flowers, beautiful flowers, fragrant flowers trimming unlocked mausoleums with dark interiors—compelling.

The gloves aimed the vehicle in the direction of HEAVENLY HILLS where a long line of cars drew the killer's attention. Three white hearses and automobiles with bedazzling headlights formed a brief but respectable procession into the cemetery. Coincidentally, the killer had the same destination, the cemetery where he had shopped for roses. The procession gripped the circular drive like gloves around soft flesh, then aligned when the pavement straightened.

Curious. He was curious. The vehicle followed at a cautious distance, then vanished into a treed outlet where a broken fork in the road divided the old section from the new. Two beefy tires scraped the crumbling curb edging the caretakers' driveway. The engine quieted. The killer exited the vehicle and scanned the area. His new clothing was a perfect fit. Comfortable. He was comfortable. Anxious to explore, he pulled the hood down to meet the frame of Mr. Johnson's dark sunglasses.

After trudging through a patch of forest, he waded through the prayer garden foliage, the worn soles of his shoes leaving no detectable prints. His toes pinched. His feet ached. Hood gathered close around his thickening neck, he crept behind the treed border and waited.

The dull sky showered privacy and intermittent drizzle. Within moments, one at a time, the cargo from each hearse was unloaded. As the caskets were set onto chrome grave frames, the gravesite buzzed with mourners, sobbing and embracing.

The killer's unemotional eyes filled with intrigue. As the shoes advanced, the gloves parted branches. Caskets were like artwork. He imagined their contents, wondering if one held a sleeping pretty. Could it be his latest? He relished at the thought. If it was so, not only had he had the opportunity to cause her death, but now would share the ceremony, and thrill of watching her lowered into the ground. His stomach growled with excitement, but the shoes held firmly in place. Had the boots been present, the killer might have gone right up there with the pastor and grieving family. But, as they'd been left behind, the boots were no longer an influence.

The dearly beloved wept before the dear dead, with the sole survivor, Bobby Johnson, stretching his arms out in prayer above the caskets containing his family. The killer wouldn't offer condolences to Bobby. Maybe he'd stand with the friends. There were old and young, but most outstanding were the pretties. He imagined how near their homes might be, and wondered if the gloves would decide to direct the vehicle to follow at least one as she left the service.

The sight was nearly unbearable. Six pretties dressed in pleated skirts and fluffy sweaters stood in a tight row, blushed cheeks shedding rose petal tears, slender arms slung across each other's shoulders like a string of beautiful flowers crying out for their stems to be snapped. His mouth watered. Holding the gloves back from impulse was a struggle.

The preacher finished his sermon with the words: *Let us command the Johnson family into the loving arms of Our Father.* A line was formed. Each member of the congregation placed a carnation on top of each casket, mulled for a moment, then single file, went their solemn way.

The service was over. He would finally have the chance to follow a pretty, but no — not yet God-dammit! Not before the caskets were fed into the ground! Decisions were not easy when temptation lurked so near. For as impelling as were the pretties, observing the eternal inevitable was an act he'd never before indulged in, and not to be dismissed lightly. Would he ever have this opportunity again?

JOURNEY OF THE JORDANS

As three disgruntled travelers made their way to the Johnson triple funeral, a bleak procession of spiraling clouds pulled a wool blanket across Independence sorrow.

"Take the first left," Lee Ann Jordan said. "That's what the gas station attendant told me after I used the ladies'. It should be about ten miles north of here."

From the back seat, a clogged nose honked into a tissue. "This is a hell of a ride."

"Pipe down, Billie Jean. Your cousin's dead. Poor Meredith. Such a sweet thing with a bright future. "

"Second cousin." Billie corrected with a wheeze. "Damn allergies. Did you bring any Claritin?"

"You're old enough to keep track of your own medication. What'll you ever do when your father and I die?"

"For heaven's sake, Lee Ann. Why do you have to talk that way to your own daughter? She's only fourteen. Sometimes you need to step up and be a mother."

"And sometimes you need to be her father. Why didn't *you* bring the Claritin?"

"There's just no living with you." Snort.

"I just hope you know I'm missing a big science test to go to a graveyard to visit somebody I never even met. Don't blame me when I bring home another bad report card."

"No respect anymore." Lee Ann shook her head. "Even for the dead. And thanks to you, we missed the church service. Had we been there on time, we'd be on our way home by now. We wouldn't be going to the cemetery at all." Lee Ann grew impatient. "The least we can do is bring them some flowers. I can't believe it: Lester, Sara, Meredith. All three of them gone at one time." Her voice trailed off as she watched the forest pass by the window of their PT Cruiser Woodie.

"That poor family," Will said, as if attempting to sound sympathetic. "Who's handling the estate?"

"Why? Do you want to offer your services? Or just snoop. You know those probate attorneys are expensive. Maybe you could offer to help Bobby handle things. He's the only one left now."

"I guess he'll be selling off the house and property. So young to be coming into what I assume will be a good deal of insurance money —"

"Is that all you think about? Money? And from what I understand, they didn't have a pot to pee in."

"Of course not. I'm just saying. Funerals are so expensive. Cremation is the way of the future, economical and easier on the family. One, two, three and it's over and done with."

"Had Meredith been away at college, like her brother was, she'd be alive today. But they didn't have the money to send her."

"Hear that back there, missy? College is important."

"How'd Bobby get to go to college then?" Will asked.

"Sports scholarships, I guess. The important thing is, he was able to attend and the poor girl wasn't. Now she's —"

"I'm bored." Sniffle and honk.

"Study for your science test."

"I'll get car sick. Change seats with me so I can sit up front."

"We should have left her home," Will mumbled.

"At times like this, families need to stick together," Lee Ann said firmly.

"Do you have any more of those muffins you baked?" Achoo.

"I'm in a morbid mood, Lee Ann. I can't shake it. Maybe Billie Jean's right. Maybe we shouldn't have come all this way to visit people we've never met."

"You can't run away from misery, Willie. It has a way of finding you, no matter where you are. You can't hide either. Hey, how about some ghost stories? A perfect fit for this dismal day."

"Sure. Add insult to injury," Will grumbled.

Lee Ann ignored his sarcasm and spoke in a voice filled with southern drama.

"Now this story originated when my great-great-grandma was just a girl. The year was 1777. And even though I call it a story, it's gospel truth." Lee Ann was reverent. "My mama told me my grandma's house was almost right in the middle of the American Revolution where they lived in the state of New York."

"I'd like to go to New York. A girl in school went there last winter and said there's a huge train station that gets all decorated at Christmastime and they have hot guys playing guitars and violins in the halls. And a lot of shops and food, which reminds me, do you have any more of those muffins or not?"

"Grand Central Station." Will chuckled. "And no. Your mother and I ate the last of them while you were sleeping back there, snoring up a storm like your grandpa."

"Listen now, Billie. You'll find this interesting, and maybe you could write a report for school." Lee Ann's eyes glowed at the thought. "For extra credit in your history class."

"Yeah, right," Billie Jean snickered and rummaged through some packages on the back seat, searching for her allergy relief medication. After digging into the bottom of a shopping bag, her hand came up holding a chocolate covered donut instead.

"There were Native American tribes living on the same land, but before Grandma. At that time, neighbors fought side by side to save their homes, their lives and all their possessions."

"Not like these days," Will interjected. "Dog eat dog —"

"Our relatives lived on reservations?" Billie spoke through munching lips.

"The tribes were long gone before then, and no, there weren't reservations, but it was said that when they died, their bodies were buried wherever they happened to fall. Some in places you wouldn't even believe, like backyards, front yards, side yards. I saw pictures of the area, and it's amazing. There are graves alongside roads! Some small cemeteries are even next to shopping plazas. Imagine? Shopping next door to a graveyard?"

"Yuk. Who'd want to live there."

"Well, it's history, Billie. We'll all be part of history some day."

"Great. I'll be famous then, so people remember my face, and not my gravestone."

"So there was this real lonely road. It ran from the top of a tall mountain. Taller than the ones at home. A local girl decided to take herself a walk down that lonely road one day. Even though it was daylight, the road was dark with trees that bent so far across they met in the middle and formed a tunnel that blocked the sun, making it so dark, you needed a flashlight or car headlights to make your way down or you'd be lost in the woods. With Lord knows what," Lee Ann mumbled the last of her words then turned up the volume when she said, "Just think about how eerie that must have been for the people who needed to travel that road."

"Or ride a horse. Can you hook headlights to a horse, Dad? Hey did they have headlights on their wagons back then?"

"Hush Billie, so I can finish the story before we get to the cemetery."

"They carried lanterns."

"Thanks for that tidbit, Willie," Lee Ann snipped. "Halfway down that road, to this day, there are two gravestones that look like they're sprouting out of the trunk of a gnarled tree, sitting right at the edge."

"They buried people on the road?"

"The roads probably came later."

"Again. I thank you for helping me tell *my* story, Will." Lee Ann's voice was clipped. "Can I finish now?"

"We're waiting," Billie coughed.

"My grandma said that if you dared to walk down that road, which was the eeriest part of that haunted mountain, you could still hear gunshots of war, and screams of the dead, feel the thunder of horse hooves churning up old dirt paths. Paths that are now the road lined with gravestones, like the ones leaning toward the river as if pointing to tell a tale of where people died, how they died. Maybe drowned in the river." Telling the story she hadn't recalled for years stirred emotion that spilled into Lee Ann's words. "But anyway, that's the road that young girl disappeared from, never to be seen again."

"She disappeared?" Billie quacked.

"Yup. All they found were her shoes lying on the ground right beside those two crooked tombstones."

"Blood?"

"Nope. Just her worn out shoes. Like she was running up and down day and night for weeks, trying to find a way out but never did. No one ever heard a word from her again. And that's not the half of it. That place is truly haunted. Some have seen ghosts walking in and out of their own homes. Houses just like ours. They've been said to sneak up on people, stand behind their backs trying to suck the life right out of them."

"Suck their life? Like vampires?" Billie was beside herself.

"Not vampires. Just ghosts feeding off the energy of the living. Trying to remember what it was like to be alive. Missing life as we know it. Touching the living too, in their very own homes. Moving things around —"

"I think we've had enough, Lee Ann. Watch the road. We should be almost there."

"Great story, Ma. Thanks for telling us right when we're about to walk into a cemetery."

INDEPENDENCE POPULATION 961

"Finally," Billie Jean groaned. "The town of Independence. Nine hundred sixty-one people?" She squeaked. "Blink and you passed. I have to pee."

"Why didn't you go in the gas station like I did?" Lee Ann snapped.

"Be-cuz-I-didn't-HAVE-to go when you did!" Billie gritted her teeth."But I have to now!"

"Lord deliver us." Lee Ann calmed. "We'll be in and out, then find you a rest room."

"Here we go. Here's the sign."

THE FUNERAL SERVICE

harsh wind reaches out to touch a smile
a smile that was lost within a child
mourning for the home they'll never find
inside a vacant heart of faded time

Will read the writing on the gate.

HEAVENLY HILLS CEMETERY
VISITING HOURS ARE FROM SUNRISE TO SUNSET
TRESPASSERS WILL BE PROSECUTED

The PT Cruiser's running lights washed across the iron fence that stretched the length of the cemetery. The cemetery bordered on three sides by dense forest.

"Almost sunset," Lee Ann huffed at the sign. "We just about made it."

"It's too creepy here. I'd like to go home, Ma."

"We'll drop the flowers and leave, Billie." Will nosed the Cruiser down the pebbled driveway.

"Reminds me of that *Night of the Living Dead* movie," Billie

Jean was on the verge of tears that made her voice even more nasal. "Scares the crap out of me."

"The sun's still up there Billie Jean. Won't be dark for a while."

"Graveyards still creep me out. If I die before you two, just leave me laying in my bed. I don't want to be inside a coffin — or under the ground."

"Look what you're putting our daughter through, Lee Ann. You and your bright ideas."

The Cruiser followed the barrier of trees down the lonely road until it stopped in the parking lot. Will chose a space beside several other vehicles and cut the engine.

"Watch out for zombies," Billie Jean said as she all but leaped from the car, yawned and stretched her gangling arms and matching legs. Her Converse crunched on gravel as she wandered a few feet ahead of her parents, who were still exiting the vehicle. Reaching up, she tightened the headband that restrained her long, dark hair.

Will's oxford shoes hit the crusty earth. "Some people must still be here, Lee Ann." His ears rang with road noise, so his voice was loud.

"I hope it's Johnson visitors."

"Must be. Who'd be visiting this late?" Lee Ann shot a sour look in Billie Jean's direction.

The three trudged along the path, with Billie reading aloud row and plot numbers from the burnished steel corner posts. "What's their number?" Half of her body swiveled as she turned to ask her mother.

"I believe it's row five hundred, plots two sixty-five, six, and seven." Lee Ann began to feel the full impact of the death of her distant relatives, and her heart hurt.

The cemetery with emerald grass was thickly treed and well maintained, a variety of headstones set in perfect rows. Steepled monuments, more than likely from wealthy originals, towered over modest markers sunken into graves of those less fortunate. Most of the headstones were modern, but the mausoleums the

Jordans scurried past were a ghostly reminder of the powerful residents of the old town of Independence.

As the sky lost its luster, the congregation scattered. All to remain were four men who stood alongside the open graves. Feet shifting, hands randomly clutched in prayer, they appeared to be waiting. Then another three approached, and they were carrying flowers. One was a small pretty. Thoughts crammed the head. Excitement escalated. Within a thicket of trees, the gloves had a difficult time holding the shoes in place.

"Look," Billie Jean pointed out a circle of mourners standing solemnly beside three precisely aligned caskets. Two were constructed of gleaming walnut and the one that was white was Meredith's. Billie had it all figured out.

"That must be Meredith, over there in that one." She pointed. Billie Jean's obnoxious attitude curbed at the sight.

"You must be the Jordans," the young man in the plain dark suit said and extended a hand to Will. "I'm Bobby Johnson. Thank you for coming."

With tears in her eyes, Lee Ann reached for his hand. "Bobby. I'm so sorry. If there's anything at all we can do, you call on us, you hear?"

"Thank you cousin Lee Ann. We've never met but I remember you from pictures. My mother had volumes of photograph albums all lined up on the parlor bookcase." Bobby's shoulders heaved with sobs. "These are friends of mine." He motioned to the other three similarly attired young men who nodded but remained silent. The rows of folding chairs behind them were empty.

"Put the flowers with the others on the caskets," Lee Ann

whispered, nudging Will's arm that held the wrapped bouquets they had picked up at a florist shop while en route. "Make sure you put the red roses on Meredith's." Lee Ann's stare was sharp as she directed Will with her eyes and nod.

While a silent Billie Jean stood close to her mother's side, Will handed Lee Ann two wrapped bouquets to hold. He tore the paper from the first. When unleashed, it exploded into a vibrant collection of wildflowers, filling the crook of his arm.

Green fabric that should have looked like part of the neatly mowed lawn, but just looked like flat green felt, almost covered the three open graves. Beside each hollow was a mound of soft earth that would eternally top off the caskets after the three were laid to rest.

Will stepped forward and placed the flowers on the lid of the walnut casket closest to him, his gaze deliberately avoiding the perfectly chiseled hole in the ground which, before dark, the casket would be lowered into. The hole the green fabric didn't completely cover.

"That's Dad's." Bobby motioned to the casket Will had just adorned. "The flowers are very nice. Mom liked wildflowers. She always kept a vase in the parlor."

Will opened the second, a fragrant package revealing a dozen long-stemmed lilies he carefully placed onto the lid of what had to be Sara's casket.

"That's Mom." Bobby pointed out, although he didn't have to explain because deductive reasoning said it had to be Sara. But he seemed to find comfort in repeating, Mom, as many times as he could before leaving his family behind. "Beautiful lilies. Thank you." His words were genuine and his eyes glistened as he offered a failing smile.

"It's the least we can do," Lee Ann's voice quivered. "I wish we had known them." The darkening of her eyes to slate proved she honestly felt the deep loss words could not express.

Billie Jean shifted from one foot to the other, as if she were standing on hot coals. She tugged at Lee Ann's arm. "I really need to pee."

"In a minute, Billie Jean." Lee Ann's words were clipped.

Will was about to unwrap the last bouquet as the sky turned orange and red.

"They'll be closing soon," Bobby said. "We'll be lowering them before we leave."

"I'm sorry we were late —" Lee Ann began to explain but the compassionate look on Bobby's face silenced her.

"Hurry Will," she told her husband who held an armload of long-stemmed red roses, the last package he tore open.

Bobby's eyes were on Billie Jean's hopping feet, a quizzical look momentarily shrouding his anguish, when Will gently placed the roses onto Meredith's pearl casket. When Bobby turned and saw the velvety red petals, he glared, and with a strong arm reached through the air to instinctively swat the flowers from the top of his sister's casket. But instead of swatting, he gathered and tossed the roses onto a nearby grave that was bare.

"Didn't you know?" Words from a broken heart. "Someone already left her roses," he said bitterly.

Will and Lee Ann simultaneously recoiled, while Billie hopped faster.

"But. What. I don't understand?" Lee Ann was shocked.

"The killer buried a rose inside my sister's throat, hopefully after he. . ."

"We're so sorry, Bobby. We had no idea."

"How would you?" Bobby said as he stared into a dazzling sunset. "Roses were her favorite."

On their return to the parking lot, Will and Lee Ann spoke of their sadness and embarrassment, while Billie Jean broke away from her parents to pause behind a tree that offered the most privacy. She emptied her overfilled bladder. As she pulled up her jeans, a whistling wind wrapped crisp autumn leaves around her legs. The missing sun deepened the sky, and dew accumulated to settle on the ground. In the distance, a stray dog howled like a wolf — as the killer paced the girl.

"Mom!" Billie's voice carried from behind a burning bush in full bloom, all the way to the parking lot where her parents stood with linked arms as they waited in dusk for her to return. "I think I hear footsteps in the leaves!"

"It's just the wind," Lee Ann called out. But her daughter's panic-stricken voice was contagious. "Please hurry, Billie Jean. We need to get going."

Billie Jean made a dash toward the clearing. "I *am* hurrying! I hope they don't lock us in like the sign said. It's sunset. . ."

In the forest, darkness didn't drop gently, it crashed like a satellite pulled out of orbit. With legs like a colt, legs that could kick a soccer ball clean through a net, she stumbled through shrubbery, dodging memorials. Losing her footing, head over heels she tumbled, rolling to a halt at the base of an ornamental bench, a bench where visitors prayed. Head spinning, she looked around. "This isn't the parking lot. . ."

Scraped and speckled with dirt, she stood, brushed off her clothing, then like a wild boar, busted through the line of trees, aiming for a path that *had to be right? Didn't it?* Her bladder felt full again, but this time from stress. "Oh shit . . ." Shrilled through the air.

"Will you listen to her? Yelping like a puppy." Lee Ann shook her head. "She could wake the dead."

"That girl's always running off someplace." Will was obviously disturbed. "Why don't you go and hurry her up. It's getting late. It's a long ride home and I'm tired."

"She'll be fine, and so will you." Distracted by the spotlights surrounding the Johnson gravesite, Lee Ann whispered. "Look . . . They're burying them. . ." A hand flew to her mouth. "Come on."

Rather than climbing into the Cruiser, Will and Lee Ann Jordan stepped back to the path, where they tiptoed over graves to spy on the four men in the distance, with the help of cemetery workers, lowering one casket at a time into the earth.

"I feel terrible," pale-faced, Will's tone was hushed. "What a way to go, huh?"

"Like a nightmare," Lee Ann said soberly, then turned her attention to the patch of forest from where her daughter had screeched. "Gives me a tingle right up my spine."

"Gives me a reason to buy a firearm."

"You know how I feel about guns, Will. Especially with Billie Jean being so curious and all."

"What a horrible way to lose a loved one," Will lamented. "I couldn't imagine dealing with such tragedy."

"Life goes on." Lee Ann's tone changed. "Let's get back to the car. Billie must be there by now, waiting for us."

"Yep. And we'll catch hell for making her miss her favorite TV show."

"Probably bitch and moan all the way home." Lee Ann chuckled. "I don't know where that girl got her spunk from."

"You don't?" Jaw slack, Will raised both brows. Pulled his wife close.

"Wait for me! I'll be right there!" By the time Billie Jean's voice reached her parents, it was little more than a whisper.

"Is she closer or further away?" Will cocked an ear. "Of course we're waiting for you, Billie!" Annoyance turned to amusement. "Like we'd really leave without her."

Billie dropped her pants for another squat. *It'll be a long ride home. Better empty completely this time . . . What's that?* As she reeled, her muscles involuntarily contracted, sealing the flow. More leaves crunched. Her stomach dipped. Springing to her feet, she whipped around in circles.

Trees were no longer trees, but rather giant outlines. Outlines of giant creatures . . . An onslaught of branches restricted each attempt to break free of the forest's hold.

"Mah!" Was lost to a gust of assaulting wind, bombarding her with debris. Hair blown skyward, heart beating in her ears, her mind began to fail. This way. No . . that way. What happened to the sun? Where's the moon? Crunch. Crunch. Crunch.

Creeping up behind her, the glove clamped her mouth shut, cutting short her cries, dislocating her jaw. A gurgling sound erupted in her throat. A small voice inside her head screamed: *Remember what Ma taught you!* Arms and legs flailing, she struggled, but was easily swept off her feet. Gagged. Flung over a shoulder. Lugged through the patch of trees and back to the vehicle.

A door opened, and the girl was thrown onto the back seat. Pounced upon. Hogtied like a steer. Before the Jordans knew their daughter had been abducted, the vehicle was barreling down an isolated road.

"Well. Here's the car . . . and no Billie." Will's words were forced through tight lips.

Lee Ann strained so hard through the veil of dusk, her vision blurred. "I don't see her anywhere. Billie Jean!" she screamed. "Where are you?"

"Don't panic, Lee Ann. She's fine," Will made a feeble attempt to comfort his wife before they both sprinted toward the thicket of trees. "She couldn't have gone far."

WHAT'S IN THE BARN?

The heat of the moment had dissipated into doubt; Marla didn't phone the sheriff as she'd planned. What would she say? I think my house is haunted? I'm hearing noises? Maybe I'm losing my mind?

That old house has one more chance, she had told Travis on the phone during lunch when they discussed the mysterious goings on that were haunting her.

Maybe Travis was right. Maybe it *was* all in her imagination. She *was* high-strung. But for certain, she wasn't going to let this ruin her marriage. She loved Travis deeply and didn't want to ever face life without him.

Dinner was another market-prepared rotisserie turkey she picked up on the way home. Marla hated not being able to cook proper meals for Travis during the week, but she would make up for it this weekend. She'd make him a roast beef dinner. He'd love that. She wouldn't mention strange occurrences again. They would eat, relax and cuddle in front of the television. Their home would once more be a serene haven and there would be no more fighting.

Marla heated the oven and when the temperature reached

three hundred and fifty degrees, she popped the foil wrapped bird onto the wire rack to keep it warm while she bathed. Then she'd have the table set nicely; when Travis got home from work he'd forget about all the arguments.

Marla stepped into the claw-footed porcelain tub. Steamy water flowed full blast from an antique faucet, bubbling and spitting as it fell like a rapid into a sparkling riverbed. The sight of the turbulent current, swirling then pooling, looked most luxuriating to Marla who hurriedly stripped off her clothing and dove in. The bathroom had no shower, but a handheld hose was mounted at the head of the tub and held a delightful showerhead capable of spewing multifunctional streams from fine mist to pulsing.

After a busy day at the bank her calf muscles ached almost as much as her back from standing almost eight hours. Easing into the tub she moaned with pleasure, stretched and sank. Only her head and top of her shoulders were exposed. She laughed at the sounds rising from her throat and out of her mouth. If someone were standing outside the door, they'd swear she was having satisfying sex in the invigorating bath.

She would soak, then dress and before Travis arrived home, she'd heat a can of sweet potatoes, candy them, and boil some beans. The turkey came with dressing, thank goodness. Travis loved potatoes and dressing.

Squishing around in the tub, Marla played mermaid. With two fingers again and again she clamped her nose shut, dunked her head, then surfaced, her raven hair raining down like a shimmering second skin.

While Marla enjoyed her bath, the vehicle returned to the place that had served as its exclusive parking garage for the better part of a week. The gloves guided the vehicle into the forested cubicle the bumper had formed when it first ruptured the overgrowth. This time the gloves remembered to bring with them the pitchfork. The killer disembarked the vehicle and covered it with pine. Cones dropping from trees crunched beneath his shoes.

Dusk strung a pewter film across the cooling air. His eyesight was weakening, so he strained through the static haze of gathering nightfall. Dragging the pitchfork he skulked across the road, creeping toward the house, focusing on the light glaring from the kitchen, then shifted his gaze to the warm glow seeping through the shade of the second floor window. The bathroom window. The rest of the house was dark, with no exterior lights to brighten the yard. Interesting. Of greater interest, Travis's truck wasn't parked in the driveway, only Marla's white sedan, now gray with dusk, casting a lonely shadow behind the house.

All that was missing was, "Hi honey. I'm home!" as he entered like he owned it, but through the cellar door. In a handy corner he rested the pitchfork, as if dropping his lunch pail after a hard day's work, then climbed the stairs to greet his mate and feast on the dinner she'd prepared.

When the killer entered the kitchen, the aroma of roasting turkey immediately hit his nose, entered his mouth. He savored the flavored air oozing down his parched throat. Overcome, a glove tugged open the oven door, trembled then slipped, scorching its hide when the killer reached in to tear off a plump, sizzling leg. The smell of singed leather blended with crisping turkey skin. Wrenching away, the glove shook.

Attracted by the hum of draining water, the killer headed up the stairs in the direction of the bathroom where Marla would laze until the water dropped to a chilling level. She was alone. He was hungry for food, and for her. Beneath the singed glove a finger burned. Tugging off the glove he flexed his hand, airing out the tingling fishbone appendage. The door was ajar, offering a sliver of Marla who was lying in the tub, submersed with bubbles like the frothy ones swarming his mouth. A bare hand reached out. The door creaked.

"Travis. You're early. You caught me being the lady of leisure." She laughed. But when she turned to see the boney fingers clutching the molding, she screamed. The scream pierced his ears. He was not expecting this reception. The hand snapped back, but not before she glimpsed the streaked reflection in the sweating bathroom mirror.

"I know this isn't my imagination," she cried as she leaped from the tub and threw on her robe. "Travis, if this is your idea of a joke."

Travis? Was the man here? After the day he'd had at the cemetery, he couldn't handle an altercation. He fled down the stairs and out to the barn. With the erupting storm, rain pounded the roof. Lighting flashed. Thunder roared.

Marla ran around the house, from room to room, heart pounding. Travis *wasn't* home. Who had it been? Her imagination again? While splashing in the tub, she *had* been lost in thought, dwelling on those stupid ghost stories. "Let it go, Marla. Get yourself dressed, and make your husband's dinner!"

When Travis walked through the door, instead of, "Marla, dinner smells delicious!" He wrinkled his nose. "What's that smell?"

Marla scowled and snapped, "What are you talking about? It's your turkey dinner."

"Huh. I smell the turkey, but I swear there's something else. Like burned rubber. Did you burn a pot or something?"

"No I didn't burn anything, Travis."

Travis shook off rain and hung his coat on the door rack, and with a kitchen towel blotted his hair. "Glad I had the presence of mind to bring my work boots today. Needed them." He sat at the table, unlaced his boots and slid them beside the kitchen door.

Marla snatched the towel from the table and whipped it across the nape of his neck.

"This is for drying dishes, Travis. Not your head."

With all of the hubbub, the bathroom incident retreated to the back of her mind, along with annoyance. Solemn during dinner, Marla lost hope in having a cozy evening. Travis complained about his job, coworkers, the long, hazardous drive home. Marla joined him, complaining about being stuck in the bank vault, forced to close out the day as the manager had left early. Both too tired for recreation, they decided to call it an early night.

Marla cleaned up the kitchen, telling Travis to dispose of the turkey garbage, which was already overpowering the room. When he made no attempt to remove himself from a favorite chair, she threw on a pair of shoes, her jacket over her shoulders, and stomped to the door shooting her husband a sour look.

"Leave it for the morning, Marla. I can't wait to hop into the shower and hit the sack." Eyes closed, his words were thick.

"It'll smell up the whole house. Once that odor takes root in my nose, I won't sleep for sure. Turkey tastes good but the smell of leftovers is horrible, and since you all but picked the bird clean. . .Oh hell. Never mind. I'll do it myself. The darned can's right outside." Hearing the icy mix pelt the windows, she shivered.

Without a word, Travis headed for the shower, while Marla stuck a foot out the door. "Travis, where's the can?" she screeched into the wind, barely able to see through the night. Lugging the overfilled kitchen trash bag, she sprinted to the side of the house, but facing driving rain, couldn't see her hand in front of her face. Back in the kitchen, she huffed as she shook off like a duck, kicked her shoes into a corner, and with a paper towel dried her face and dripping hair. Before heading upstairs, she made sure everything was locked up tight.

When she entered the bedroom, she found Travis burrowed beneath a mound of fluffy blankets. "Thanks for telling me you moved the garbage can. I'll probably have pneumonia in the morning . . ."

Travis sank deeper into the mattress. "Ah. This is heaven."

"I'm glad *you* feel so good." She kicked the side of the bed. "I left the bag on the porch. When you find the can, you can put it in."

"Don't be mad at me, I had a hell of a day."

"So did I, and don't sidestep." Marla stood over him, hands on hips. "I've about had it, Travis."

"That's good, baby girl." Yawning, he buried his face deep into his pillow.

She swatted him. "Well? What about it?"

"I didn't move the can, Marla." His voice was muffled. "It's dark. You probably just didn't see it."

"Like hell, Travis Booth. If you don't believe me, get up and see for yourself."

From the small loft window, the killer watched the lightning, the house lights, the puzzling activity. First the woman — now the man with the flashlight, shooting agitating yellow beams around the yard. He hunkered down in the hay, thankful he was not out in the storm.

MYSTERY SOLVED?

Cursing as he stomped through the door, Travis threw the flashlight onto the counter, wiped rain from his face with a clean kitchen towel.

"Well?" From the doorway, Marla demanded.

"The can's not there."

"And?"

"And what Marla?"

"Call the sheriff."

"Okay. In the middle of one of the worst storms of the season, I'm gonna tell Sheriff Floyd my garbage can's missing. Right?"

"I didn't want to add to anything. But before you got home tonight, I was in the tub and heard noises."

"Not again." Travis turned his back.

"I saw something in the bathroom mirror."

"What did you see this time, Marla?" he patronized.

Marla spoke through gritted teeth. "There were fingers on the door, Travis. Skinny white fingers like sticks of chalk, and a horrible shape in the mirror."

"Probably your own," he mumbled. When he attempted to leave the room, she blocked the doorway.

"What did you say?" She glared.

"The bathroom was filled with steam when I got home. I'm surprised you could see yourself in that haze."

"Either you call him or I will."

Travis looked long and hard at his wife. The determination on her face. She was serious, not hysterical. And things *had* been weird lately. Travis reached for the phone.

Within a half hour, Leroy Floyd arrived with a deputy. Marla fell over backwards to get them inside, but the two men remained on the porch, gripping the collars of their raingear.

"Power lines on the other side of town are down, Mrs. Booth. We'll take a quick look around, but when your husband called, we were about to head out and block some roads. Live wires are dangling."

"So, you've got weird occurrences?" Deputy Tieboe's plastic covered cap caught rain dripping from the awning. He wiped his mouth as he spoke.

"I've checked, but maybe you could. . ." Travis then said something that surprised his wife. "Have you heard of anything going on around town? You know, with those murders and all, we're out here in the boonies. Marla and I are concerned things just aren't right."

Floyd's jaw tightened. "You check the barn," he instructed Tieboe. "I'll cover the perimeter."

Marla brewed coffee as she and Travis waited, and set out a plate of powdered donuts. Five minutes later, she answered the door.

"Come inside and have some coffee," Marla offered, feeling for the officers who looked soaked to the skin, backs to the wind as they stood on the porch.

"There's nothing but footprints," after taking a seat at the kitchen table, Floyd reported, "and with this weather, they're disappearing fast."

"Footprints?"

Marla's mouth dropped.

"Sure enough. Around the back of the house and leading to

284

the barn," while sipping coffee, he confirmed.

Travis looked puzzled. Marla never went into the barn, and he hadn't been in there for days.

"Can I grab a few tissues?" During a sneezing fit, Tieboe covered his mouth with a hand, then reached for a box on the counter.

"Catching cold?" Floyd looked concerned. "We've got a long night ahead of us."

"Allergies from tossing around that hay." He blew into a wad of tissues, then helped himself to a donut. "You've got yourself an animal problem. From the awful smell in that barn, garbage and bones all over the place, for sure something from the woods staked claim to your property." Popping the last bit of donut into his mouth, he held out his cup which Marla filled with steaming coffee. "Spotted your missing garbage can in a back corner."

"Mystery solved." Floyd pushed back his chair. "You can call the animal warden in the morning. They'll come out and set some traps."

Backed against the counter, Marla shot him a dubious look, fear still registering in her eyes.

"They'll catch it. Don't you worry, Mrs. Booth," he assured. "It's coon season, you know?" Floyd swung his head toward Travis.

"But how did the can end up in our barn? That's what I want to know." Marla couldn't let the officers leave without a rational explanation.

Floyd shrugged, repeating, "Call animal control in the morning. We've got to get back out. These roads are a disaster."

The Booths watched through a window as the patrol car's taillights disappeared, then sat at the kitchen table sharing cocoa, and a serious conversation.

"Do you think it's possible for a bear to drag a can that size?" Marla's eyes were wide.

"Maybe." Travis set his mug into the sink, then took her by the arm. "Let's go upstairs."

She didn't budge. "What about the footprints?"

"We'll take care of it tomorrow. I can't go another night without sleep."

"Who's gonna sleep after this, Travis?"

"I'll sit in the arm chair if it makes you feel better, Marla."

"Now you know I'm not insane." With a smug look, she headed upstairs, with Travis trailing, interrogating.

"Have you been out to the barn, Marla?"

"Did you put the garbage can in the barn, Travis?"

"Fair enough."

On The Road Again

After the commotion, even the killer couldn't fall into a peaceful sleep. Between the replay of the cemetery scene, and the young girl's face when he handled her body, the brain bubbled with excitement.

When the uniformed intruder had entered his barn, washing the killer's loft with a bright beam of light, the pitchfork poised for action. The glove had begged to stab and stab again, but the brain said "No." Damn shit. Internal battles were shit! A glove beat the head as the brain stepped in. Too much activity in this place. Stressful. The killer wasn't up to confronting *fucking* Travis. So that left Marla out. Damn shit! She would have been so good. Maybe the best. He tossed in the hay imagining Marla, ejaculated, then regardless of desire, the brain said it was time to leave.

During his excursions to town, the killer had foolishly run his gas tank so low the warning light had flashed. No money. No food. Fuck! Now he was losing the only home he'd known since Louisiana. Damn shit. A sudden thought struck him. The man's truck. Fuck Travis. He had it coming to him.

After a final look around, the killer climbed down from the loft, snatching up his possessions: pitchfork, scythe, the knife he had arrived with.

The hose from the tractor would do well. Clever! Wait till Travis tries to start the damn thing. The prospect was amusing. Serves him right, damn shit. And the can in the corner. Perfect!

In growing discomfort, his stare fell to the damp floor. His canvas shoes were shredding, exposing gnarled toes. His feet were freezing.

Out in the storm, mud sucked at his heels as he crept from the barn, to the house, to the driveway. Between the sedan and the truck he hunkered, siphoning gas until the can was full.

The next order of business, the painful feet. Travis had boots. He'd seen them in a corner. That's the least he could do after depriving him of her. He took his anger out on the shoes, ripping at the canvas, hurling what was left behind a hedge, then hobbled to the house.

Forced to use the cellar, which the fools never locked, a glove creaked open the kitchen door, found the boots and without looking back, departed. When the kitchen door slammed with resentment, Marla flew out of bed.

"Travis! You're supposed to be awake." She shook the chair.

"I was just dozing. What's wrong?"

"I heard a crash downstairs."

Lightning brightened the room, while the backyard rumbled. "It's thunder, Marla."

"No it's not!" she spat. "Someone's in the house!"

"Damn it. This is getting insane." Travis vaulted from bed, threw on his robe, and landed in the downstairs foyer just in time to see a shadow skulk by the kitchen window.

"What the hell?" He grabbed his coat from the rack by the door, went to the corner for his boots. His boots? "Marla? Where are my boots?"

"What's wrong?" Marla came flying down the stairs and launched herself at him.

"I swear I saw something outside. You seen my boots?"

"Oh, God." Marla whimpered. Drawing her robe tighter, she shoved the flashlight at him.

"I'm not going out there in bare feet!"

Fumbling through darkness, the killer crossed the road. Trudging through muck, slapped around by soggy branches, he found the vehicle, fed the tank with Travis's gas. Tools safely stowed, he folded his body almost in two in order to climb inside. By the time he noticed something felt very different, his hood brushed the overhead light casing. Was he outgrowing the vehicle that had fit him like a glove? Like the gloves that were now splitting at the seams. *Fuck . . . Damn shit.* A glove pounded the steering wheel.

Soaking wet, irritated enough to tangle with even a loft intruder, within moments he was on his way, tall in the seat, head cocked so his scalp didn't scrape the roof. Had it not been for Travis's size thirteen boots, he'd have been barefoot.

As Travis and Marla stared from the kitchen window, headlights flashed, taillights glowed then disappeared.

Travis scratched his head. "We're on a dead end road . . . where'd *that* come from?"

While Marla stood frozen, he reacted. "Better get Sheriff Floyd back here."

The Booths spent the rest of the night huddled on the living room sofa. In the morning, the sheriff's office called to apologize.

"The whole town's in an uproar. We're getting more calls than we can respond to. Just don't have the manpower to cope with the aftermath of a triple homicide." The dispatcher's voice was weary. "Someone will be out there today."

"By now he's long gone . . . I hope." Momentary silence as Travis poked his head through the kitchen curtain. Limbs were down, leaves scattered. When he saw roof shingles strewn in the yard, he groaned. "Tell Leroy, don't bother to come. Doesn't much matter since we don't have a description of the vehicle. All we saw were taillights."

Marla and Travis dressed for work, hugging in the driveway, just like old times. But now they were comrades as well as lovers.

"I hate to leave the house alone." Marla brushed his bangs from a brow. "Do you think he's gone for good?"

"I have a strong feeling he's outta dodge." Travis straightened his tie, tossed his lunch bag into the truck. "He got what he wanted from us, Marla, for at least a week. If he wanted to hurt us, he would've." Shifting, his eyes washed over the grounds, then fixed on the barn. "Probably just needed food and shelter. Yeah, he was just a vagabond."

"Or the murderer." The storm was over. The sky was clear and the sun was strong. Still, Marla shivered.

Husband and wife shared stares, then a bear hug, their lips locking until Travis gently pulled away. "We should probably be getting to work."

"I'll take this up with you tonight . . ." Marla blew him a kiss before slipping into her sedan. She waved, calling out the window, "Love you."

With a big hand, Travis caught her kiss. "Love ya back . . . baby girl." He winked, then playfully shielded his face with an arm.

Travis hopped into his pickup, but halfway down the driveway, the engine sputtered and the truck stalled in its tracks. The dashboard fuel gauge read empty.

"Where's the gas can?" Marla asked when Travis returned from the barn without it.

"Don't know." A puzzled look stole his charm.

"What do you mean, you don't know?" Her voice pitched so high, Travis held his ears.

In the white sedan, the Booths rode to the sheriff's office, in dead silence.

Don't Forget The Moose Tracks

"I hate second shifts," Ben complained over the phone.

"Just make sure you get home early," Terry instructed. "Julie can only stay with the kids until six. She has homework."

"What's for dinner?"

"You're cooking. You decide."

"Whatever happened to barefoot in the kitchen," Ben grumbled. "When's my car gonna be ready? I'm tired of bumming rides."

"I didn't get a chance to call the shop. I've gotta run, honey. See you tonight."

"Yeah. Have a good night." Ben paused, thoughts of the killer, and the Cellar, jolting his brain. "Be careful, hon."

Terry kissed the kids, grabbed her purse, then ran back up the stairs to her bedroom dresser to pick up and pin on her name tag that read: Teresa Cassidy.

While most commuters were heading home, Terry fought rush hour traffic to get to work on time. She parked the Caravan on the first floor of the six level garage provided for visitors and staff.

St. Vincent's Hospital, a fair-sized facility, sat on the outskirts of the city. Two additions added needed space, but not aesthetics, as the original structure remained aging block with a lot less glass than the atrium and new wing.

Terry worked in the Emergency Department that was located on the first floor, where wide corridors wove together treatment rooms, ICU, specialty suites and laboratories into one neat honeycomb shape.

Tonight she worked the rooms leading to the broadest section of the corridor, the side of Emergency that faced the underground parking. From the nurse's station, she could see the high roof of the Caravan. She was parked that close. A footpath, trimmed with shrubbery, also rounded the back entrance to the hospital. Terry Cassidy was not the only one who could see the high roof of the Caravan.

Unbeknownst to Terry, she had been followed into the parking garage. The two vehicles, separated by several others, were now parked three rows apart. A hostile stare had her in the crosshairs as she shut the door, beeped on the alarm, and entered the hospital. The dark figure now stood just beyond the inviting plate glass offering a bird's eye view of the waiting room, nurse's station, and of course, the corridor, where Terry walked briskly toward ICU.

With her out of sight, the figure moved through the maze of parked vehicles, halting beside the Caravan. A gloved hand held something electronic, and in a moment the car alarm disengaged, the door opened, and the accessory compartment, crammed full of odds and ends, was methodically examined. Sitting on top, a bank envelope contained $96.84, proceeds from a check Terry had cashed earlier that day.

Sifting, the glove inspected a variety of papers, pushing aside some folded napkins. The vehicle registration and insurance cards fell to the floor. The glove retrieved them, slipping both into a jacket pocket.

A quick sweep of the rest of the interior turned up nothing out of the ordinary: a woman's sweater, a few books, an extra pair of running shoes, some cookie crumbs on the back seat. That was all. The door was closed and the alarm reset.

The nurse station clock read 10:46 p.m.

"Hey. I'm getting ready to leave. How is everything?"

On the other end of the line, Ben hesitated.

"Are the kids okay?"

"Yeah, everything's fine. Just watching the game. I'm glad you called. Can you bring home some moose tracks?"

"For God's sake, Ben."

"I've got a taste for ice cream. Come on. I'd do it for you."

She sighed. "Okay. Be home soon."

Terry slung the strap of her bag over a shoulder and walked out the door, along the way, wishing coworkers a good night. The dark eyes paced her, cautiously observing as her Crocs dragged her burning feet across the lot, to the Caravan. With a sigh, she slid behind the wheel. Each time she moved, the figure moved. The engines of both vehicles ignited almost simultaneously, with the intruder trailing the Caravan by a few car lengths, to the Safe Way twenty-four hour market, three blocks away.

January Valentine

i'm searching my conscience
for answers to rejection
offer them a challenge
to justify inspection

of me of me

the enemies that i've made

let them step inside
where i lock my inhibitions

I Took Your Ear Cuz You Can't Hear

When Leo entered the judge's chamber, the morning paper was spread across the judge's desk. The headline read:

Baltimore. The Killer's Demise

"Baltimore Detective Benjamin Cassidy and Assistant State Prosecutor Leonardo Gibraldi visited a North Carolina woman, interrogating the only victim to survive an encounter with the Sweet Dreams Psycho. Although out of their jurisdiction, as they explained to Ms. Delaney, the interview was to help gather information that would aid in the capture, arrest and prosecution of the murderer. As Gibraldi put it, "We're gonna try him and fry him."

"Shit," Leo mumbled under his breath. "Guess it was only a matter of time, huh?"

"I stepped on a lot of toes to get this job," Diviniello pointed a finger at Leo. "But I never even came close to doing some of the stupid assed things you've been doing lately." His voice threatened to rise, but Maria was outside at her desk. "I had high hopes for you, Leo, but I hate to say it, you're walking yourself right out the door."

Leo stopped staring at the judge, heaved a sigh, and went to the windowed wall. He looked out over the traffic, at the orange sun arcing over the tops of buildings ping-ponging across the city, his eyesight straining through fog banks to reach the bay. He wished he was there now, in one of the yachts, a speedboat, anyplace other than the judge's office.

"I really don't know what to say, Judge, other than I'm sorry." Rather than sincere, he sounded wistful.

"The election is only two weeks away." Diviniello looked like he was about to have a stroke. He held his head, pressed a finger to the pulse in his neck, then with a deliberate look on his face, calmed. "I can't keep covering for you, Leo."

Leo let out a breath, then inhaled slowly. "I know, Judge. I appreciate anything you can do."

"Listen. I have some things to do before lunch. Then I'm meeting with your boss, who's already looking for another assistant." Diviniello shook his head as he pushed his high back chair out from behind his desk. He stood and stretched his back. "Disappearing to chase leads during business hours is one thing. But for Christ sake, what the hell were you thinking?" While his face turned red, Diviniello's neck began to blotch. "Why the hell did you go to North Carolina to interview a witness you're in no way connected to?"

Hands in pockets, Leo faced Diviniello. "Call it a crime of passion. I don't know what else to say." In a few steps, he stood before the desk, leaning in close to the judge. "How would you feel if something happened to Glory?"

Divinello took a deep breath and blew it out hard. "Now you're hitting below the belt. Take the day off. I'll talk to Appolito. Just keep out of sight until this blows over. Minnie Kozlowski's always looking for brownie points. She can cover your files until we clean up your mess."

Leo's shoulders dropped with relief.

"Don't get your hopes up. I'll do what I can." Waving a hand,

Diviniello dismissed him.

When Leo left the building, the morning sun had rolled out of sight, earlier than the weatherman predicted.

He parked in the: POLICE VEHICLES ONLY lot, close to the AUTHORIZED PERSONNEL ONLY side entrance of the green and white building. As he approached the door, he felt the bite of chilling air. Dismal and damp, the foggy day rolled nimbly into the disjointed autumn season.

Inside the vestibule, Leo brushed moisture from his jacket, and ran a cold hand through his hair. He nodded to the uniformed clerk who buzzed him in, habitually scanning the counter and desks to see who was visiting and who was getting booked, then took a flight of stairs to the second floor.

Leo spotted Ben Cassidy, head down, tucked into one of the quieter corners of the squad room. Phone held by a shoulder, Cassidy was huddled over his desk which was positioned beside one of the five windows lining the outside wall. A true claustrophobic, Cassidy had finagled to acquire and maintain his window-side position. His holster was strapped in place, but his Glock wasn't cradled. The handgun was in his top drawer.

The phone receiver was still shoulder to ear when Leo reached his side, but Ben wasn't talking. He was scribbling on a notepad.

For a polite moment, Leo paused, then held his voice low. "I need to talk to you."

"Talk." Cassidy continued scribbling. "I'm just making a shopping list."

"Who are you on the phone with?"

"Nobody. Terry hung up."

Leo took the receiver from Ben's shoulder and set it on its base.

"Did you see this morning's paper?" He slapped the Baltimore News onto the desk, slamming his hand beneath the headline: Heavenly Hills Abduction. Further down the page, was a column that once more outlined the brutal murders, but this report included news of the young girl's abduction and ensuing search. The paper also printed a follow-up artist rendering of the killer.

"I saw that. Christ. Is he evolving or what?" Ben's anger reflected in his eyes.

"So much for public outreach. The artist sketch in Monday's paper is for shit now." Leo shrugged off his jacket, and hung it on the back of the chair he then sank into. "He left his clothes at the Johnson house. I was banking on that weird outfit of his being spotted by someone."

"Yeah. Me too. Either the sonofabitch is walking around naked, carried extra clothes with him, or fived some of Johnson's before he left."

"The house was ransacked." Leo rested an elbow on Ben's desk, knuckles supporting his chin. "I doubt even family members will know if anything's missing. So once more, we know nothing at all about the lunatic, other than along with corpses, he doesn't seem to give a shit about leaving personal items behind."

"What else did he leave, Leo? We should compare notes here."

"A tooth."

"What?"

"A lot of this info is being withheld." Leo stood and moved to the window. He watched the harbor in the distance. "It's too damned bizarre, but from what I understand, he made himself right at home. Even used the victim's toothbrush."

"Jesus. Who told you this?" Ben asked.

"Scarlett's officially on the case."

Ben shot Leo a sly look. "I thought Scarlett left town."

"She called me from Virginia. She knows my interest."

"I figured we'd trip down there ourselves. Nose around." Ben rose to join Leo who stood with his hands stuffed deep into the pockets of his navy trousers.

Leo stopped staring at slow moving barges and focused on Ben's face. "Don't think I haven't considered it. But I'm walking a tightrope. Diviniello's trying to talk Appolito into letting me keep my job. Nothing happened to you?"

"They threatened me with disciplinary action, but were just blowing off steam. This place is a zoo. They've got more to worry about than me and North Carolina." Cassidy ran a hand through his hair. "Too bad we can't get down to Virginia. He left so much crap behind. I'd like to see firsthand. The creep's under my skin."

Leo was thoughtful. "Wouldn't be a good idea anyway. The Feds are all over the place, looking for the girl." He shook his head. "He's throwing us for a loop. I figured it would be bad, but not —"

"Not a kid. I know." Ben pushed away from his desk, stood and stretched.

"Anything we need, I can get from Scarlett. Besides, she said he tore the Johnson place apart. It wouldn't serve any purpose for us to be there." Leo lifted his jacket and slipped his arms through the damp sleeves. "He's not a textbook psycho. He's a rabid animal. I've never heard of a serial killer this destructive. I mean, they leave bodies, but ransacking houses?"

"So now he's killing out of rage."

"It's a hunger he needs to satisfy. When a hungry animal's craving, don't get in its way. And he *is* evolving."

"I worry about Terry, you know. And the kids. You never know where he'll turn up next. And with what you're telling me, Leo. He's beyond psycho, and he's slipping through the cracks. Makes me very uneasy."

"Good reason to be uneasy, Benny. There was more than rage in the Johnson bedrooms. Anger. Hatred. The DNA matched the other murders. Roses and notes. He's our guy."

"Notes? As in two notes at this crime scene?"

Leo nodded. "Yep."

"Fill me in."

"A rose was planted into the Johnson girl's throat. Showed up on x-ray. Stuffed so deep down her windpipe, the coroner had to fish it out with long nose pliers."

"Christ." A seasoned cop, Cassidy still paled.

"And the note. *Screaming in the shower. I'm the only power. Cut off your air. Not all your hair. Sweet Dreams Traci.*"

"Traci? The murdered girl's name was Meredith." Ben's eyes widened. "This gets weirder and weirder. Who the fuck is Traci?"

"You've got me. But now you know as much as I do." Leo

turned to the door but didn't move. "Wait, there's one more thing. He slept with her after he killed her. They found semen on her clothing."

"He raped her?"

"Nope."

"So he jacked off on her clothes —"

"Guess so. And it gets better."

"What could top what I already know?"

"Besides her throat being slashed, the girl's facial bones were crushed — and her sternum, and her ribcage, and her pelvis."

"What did he do? Run her over with a truck?"

"Nope. No evidence of that during the autopsy."

"So what are you saying? She was squeezed to death?" Ben's jaw slackened. "Unless he's a thousand pound pissed off bear . . . I told you it was fuckin' sexual. Always is." Ben looked like a mad scientist who was a step away from concluding the experiment that was about to save the world. "What about the parents? What condition were their bodies in?" His eyes narrowed, then gleamed.

"Looks like he pinned the parents together in their bed before he killed the girl."

"Pinned?"

"Coroner said the murder weapon was a pitchfork. Rows of tine punctures from chest to chest. Pierced their lungs. They died instantly."

"Do they have the pitchfork in evidence?"

"No. It's gone."

"Took the weapons, but left his clothes. And those disgusting boots. Doesn't make sense. Unless he's trying to change his appearance. Maybe the freak's going public." Ben had never been more sarcastic, or serious.

"He jammed the stem of a rose through the mother's eardrum, and also left a note on *her* pillow." Leo waited for a reaction.

"Her ear? Holy fuck." A grim look crossed Ben's face . "What did it say?"

"*I took your ear cuz you can't hear. Sweet Dreams Mama.*"

"Mama? He's doing more than living out fantasy. Sounds

like he's reliving his childhood. Speaking of which . . . the hair they found at Delaney's indicated he could be an old man. Now he loses a tooth? What are we chasing. A geriatric serial killer?" Ben laughed. "Sorry, but this is getting ridiculous. What's he gonna do next, deteriorate and crumble into ashes?"

"You're the cop. You tell me, Benny." Leo turned to leave.

"You know what's next, Leo —"

Before he stepped out the door Leo replied, "Baltimore."

January Valentine

your candles burn on my table
spewing oils of the sea
dolphins dance in crystal circles
hanging from a hook in sunlight fantasy

Deadly Dinner Conversation

"Are there any leads on that Baltimore woman who went missing?" Terry Cassidy implored. Her eyes jumped from Leo's face to Ben's, then landed on Scarlett Montgomery. "Could it be him? Or . . . You know, I heard something on the news about a copycat." Terry looked pale.

As one of the finer establishments in town, the Dockhouse dining room was usually jammed at eight p.m,, even on weeknights, but the two couples enjoyed privacy as they sat around a cozy corner table, playing their own version of "how to catch a killer".

Candlelight flickered from the votive centered on the dinner table. The tendrils of hair settling on the sides of Scarlett's face glittered like copper strands. "We're not seeing the same MO in her case. This woman disappeared during a ten a.m. trip to a supermarket. Not from her home. . ."

"Or a cemetery." Leo's eyes didn't stray from Scarlett's lips, even as he spoke with sarcasm.

"Women go missing all the time," habitually gruff, Ben cut in, "the culprit's usually the old man — or a boyfriend."

Terry fidgeted with a napkin ring, rolling it back and forth on the table. "Something strange happened to me the other night. Maybe coincidence, but scary as hell."

"What happened, Terry?" Leo's voice held an edge.

"I think I'm being followed. Or *was* followed."

"What?" Leo shot Ben an inquisitive look.

"Honey." Ben rested a hand on her shoulder. "Don't let your imagination get the better of you."

"Then how do you explain what's missing from my glove box?"

"You probably misplaced the registration, or it fell on the floor and one of the kids kicked it out of the car."

"What about the things inside that were completely out of order. You know how organized I am. I can tell when something's been touched. Were you messing inside the glove box, Ben?" Terry demanded, looking hopeful.

Letting out a sigh, Ben shook his head. "I don't have any reason to go in there, Terry." For a moment, he looked thoughtful. "Yeah. You're so organized, the cans in our kitchen cabinets are alphabetized." He laughed with affection and tweaked her nose. "And I can think of better things to mess with."

Terry ignored Ben's stab at humor. "Why would someone take my registration and leave an envelope of cash? Doesn't make sense."

"No, it doesn't." Leo's palm came down on the table; the scotch in his glass shuddered. "Why didn't you ever mention this?"

Ben's mouth tightened. "Because I had other things on my mind. Like my face being plastered on some news station."

"Oh, my God," Terry cut in. "You don't think someone's trying to—"

"Payback for meddling in their jurisdiction? The thought just occurred to me." Leo's head seesawed as he watched Ben scowl.

"So a few pissed off cops are trying to get info on us? What, to muscle us? Just because you two visited the Delaney girl?" Terry's face reddened. "They wouldn't actually *do* anything. . ." She searched her husband's face for a sign of reinforcement.

Ben covered her hand with his. "If it was a warning, we got

the message, now forget it. You've got a .38 in your purse. Stop worrying."

Leo had been sipping his drink, glancing from Ben to Terry, while catching peripheral glimpses of Scarlett's elegance as her finger traced the rim of her wine glass. "What do you think makes a murderer tick?" His gaze roamed her face, the plunging neckline of her cognac dress that matched her eyes.

"Serial killers are difficult to define."

"And apprehend." Ben slugged tap beer from a pint glass.

"And now he could be in Baltimore." Terry shot a sour look in Leo's direction, then focused on Ben. "What if he saw you two clowns on the news and wants to retaliate?"

"That's ridiculous. He's not gonna fuck with the authorities." Taking a swipe at the air, Ben dismissed her.

Leo's arm hung across the back of Scarlett's chair. He leaned in and whispered. "It's good to see you."

Her fingers lightly brushed his thigh. "I have a flight back tomorrow — right after the Behavioral Science Conference."

"Then we should make the most of tonight —" Leo's eyes were soft, his words firm.

"So you follow this killer around?" Terry asked.

"I visit the crime scene — try to pick up vibes." Scarlett's voice gained strength.

Leo had been enjoying their intimacy. He slid a hand over her knee, nudging her leg closer to his. "Fascinating work." His grip tightened, fingers roaming higher.

Mid thigh, Scarlett blocked his advance. "I sort through police files, Terry, crime scene and autopsy photographs. I analyze the information and try to determine what occurred. Is there a motive? Was it staged? Who did this and why? Is it the work of a serial killer?"

"My head's spinning just listening to you." Terry slugged her drink.

"I look for things that give me an idea of behavior, so I can get a better fix on what type of individual to look for." Scarlett swept a hand across the side of her hair, then drew in a long breath.

"My head sometimes spins, too."

"Sounds good in theory, but I don't see how it's helped, in this case anyway." Terry frowned. "This guy's still killing."

"And could continue." Scarlett shrugged. "We do our best, but most serial homicides go unsolved."

"Terrific. So this could go on indefinitely."

"Maybe not. Serial killers aren't always the geniuses they're portrayed to be."

"Is ours a genius? Or lucky. . ." Ben drained his pint glass of draft beer.

"Jury's still out on that one. We're piecing his notes together like a puzzle. He's telling us he does have some kind of emotion — warped reasoning."

"Is it a vendetta we're dealing with? Or just plain old insanity?"

"It's anyone's guess," Scarlett responded to Ben. "The roses he left at the Johnson crime scene came from the same cemetery the victims were buried in, which tells us something." Her eyes grew dark.

"Yeah, the creep shops in cemeteries," said Ben.

"How morbid is that?" Terry shivered.

"They always come back to the scene of the crime, huh, babe?" Ben ruffled the edges of his wife's hair.

"What makes your skin crawl, turns him on." Leo drained his glass of scotch. "Pathetic."

"And now he might have his hands on a young girl. Poor kid. I hope they find her alive." Terry was obviously shaken. "Can we get another round over here?" she called to the waiter. "It's bizarre. If it *was* him, he kidnapped her right from under her parents' noses, and at the funeral of three of his victims, no less. I can't seem to wrap my mind around this." Elbows on table, her hands cradled her temples as her head rocked back and forth.

"I hate to break the news to you, babe. But you're gonna hear sooner or later." Ben was blunt. He looked at Scarlett whose expression froze in a frown.

Eyes widening, Terry stared. "What news?"

Sighing, Ben shook his head. "They found her this morning, strapped to a tree alongside the road. The sonofabitch strung her up with jumper cables."

"Dead?" Terry's voice broke.

"Of course she'd dead."

"Did they release a cause of death?" Leo blew out a breath. "Other than the obvious."

"Pending autopsy results. But from what I understand, any one of the things he did to her could have killed her. They can't rule out a heart attack, either." Ben scrubbed his face with a palm. "Parts of her were scattered around the immediate area."

"This doesn't sound like our guy." Leo's eyes narrowed as he turned to Scarlett. "We're sure?"

"We're testing. . ."

Ben cut Scarlett's reply short. "It was him. The mother fucker was at the funeral. Either he wanted to throw us a curveball, or he couldn't resist temptation."

Terry gasped. "Dear God. That poor child." Her fingers tapped the sign of the cross on her forehead, chest and shoulders.

Leo drove the conversation away from the young victim. "I believe his notes could be his way of venting."

"This guy's out there, Leo. I've worked with emotionally disturbed patients in the psych ward. They vent, but nothing like this. We medicate them — send them home to hopefully live normal lives." Waving her arm frantically, Terry flagged the waiter. "I don't think they turn into murderers."

"Psychopaths are born, not created. I doubt you could create one if you tried. And not all are violent. Four percent of the population are sociopaths or psychopaths. That's higher than the rate of colon cancer, which is considered alarmingly high." Scarlett sounded as if she were teaching a class.

"Can we get another round over here?" Leo's voice carried across the room, beckoning the waiter who seemed to be ignoring Terry, then he turned to Scarlett. "What else do you have?"

"Lab analysis from Virginia gave us more than you could imagine." She leaned into him, as if to offer a kiss. Their lips inches apart, she whispered. "We collected a lot from the Johnson crime scene. Are you sure you want to discuss this over dinner?"

"Please." Terry strained to hear.

"DNA taken from the scene was unusual, exhibiting abnormal cells."

"He's a deformity? He's sick? Which is it, Scarlett?"

"Calm down, Terry. You're causing a scene." Ben reached for her hand, dismissing curious stares from patrons at nearby tables.

"Don't shush me, Benny. We should know! He could hit Baltimore next." Her eyes rounded. "Or maybe he's already here . . ." She watched her husband's mouth drop.

KIDNAPPED IN BROAD DAYLIGHT

if i saw those eyes
staring in my direction
it would be just like
the first time

When Leo answered his cell, he had no idea of what he'd be facing. He'd never heard Diviniello's voice shudder before, and the judge never privately summoned him in the middle of a busy work day. Leo sprinted across the building and jogged down the stairs to Diviniello's office.

"Hi, Maria. The judge wants to see me?" Leo panted.

The secretary's mahogany eyes shot Leo a sympathetic look. "He's waiting for you. Just knock."

"That bad, huh?" Leo said, catching his breath before tapping on the chamber door.

"Enter." Diviniello's growl wasn't vicious.

The judge sat behind his desk, head in hands, his hair sticking out like strands of straw from the constant stroking of his manicured fingertips. His cheeks were flushed and his red neck indicated he may need a double dose of blood pressure medication.

"Judge. Are you okay?"

"Not really." The sockets of Divinello's eyes were tinted a pale shade of plum, the lids lined red. Leo had never seen him this way before.

"Can I do something for you?"

"Sit down, Leo."

Leo dropped into a leather chair directly across from the judge. He balanced an ankle over a knee, leaned forward attentively, and stared.

Diviniello sighed deeply. He reminded Leo of a criminal about to unload a heavy confession onto the prosecutorial staff, regardless of the charges awaiting him. Sometimes a man just needed to cleanse his soul, regardless of consequences.

"I'm not sure if you can help. But you should know." With slumped shoulders, Diviniello gulped water from a plastic bottle, then set it on his desk, and with a pained expression looked Leo square in the eye. "Glory and Landes are at it again."

"I know."

"Landes might be in over his head this time. I can't risk my family's involvement. I told him to leave town," Diviniello's palm slammed his desk, "the bastard obviously doesn't listen."

"Hmm. Busted for coke again . . . why am I not surprised?" Leo didn't hide his distaste.

"He's in deeper than using. He hasn't been arrested — yet —but it's only a matter of time before he hangs himself. With the campaign, and my dear daughter fucking around with him —"

"Christ." Leo shook his head. How dumb could she be? "So you want me to take care of anything that might come up?"

"Anything you can do would help." Diviniello looked like he was about to vomit.

Leo inhaled deeply and blew out a loose-lipped bellow of air. "I can understand doing this for Glory. But Landes. I hate the thought of him reaping the benefits . . ."

"Leo. My campaign. If this gets out, I'm ruined. And I need you to take care of Glory. I don't want her associating with him." He buried his face in his hands, then surfaced. "He's a fucking liability. She doesn't listen to me. Maybe you'll have better luck."

"Glory's a free spirit, Judge. She doesn't take kindly to advice from anyone." The chime from Leo's cell phone interrupted. He checked the ID. "Speak of the devil."

Diviniello looked apprehensive. "Glory?"

"Sure is." Leo mouthed. " What's up?"

"Leo," Glory sounded rushed. "I need to talk to you."

"Yeah. I'm up here in your father's office." Leo's voice was guarded.

"Shit. I'm right outside. Can you come down?"

Leo shot out of the chair and went to the window, almost forgetting Diviniello was in the room. "What the hell's going on, Glory?" From the window Leo saw her standing on the walkway below, staring up at him, a smirk on her face. She wore a long dark wig topped off with a beaded cowgirl hat, short tight skirt, and tan boots that made her legs look hotter than usual. "Why are you dressed like that? What's the rope for?"

"I don't have time to explain. Come on down, cowboy, and I'll show you," with a stiff grin, she taunted. "I'm commando. Take a look." She turned her back to the building and leaned forward at the waist, a hand ready to tug the back of her skirt higher.

"I'm in your father's office," Leo repeated in a stronger voice.

"I've got an audition in ten minutes." Her tone flurried as she straightened and whirled around. "Just come down! I have to talk to you. Not on a fucking cell phone, Leo. Face to face."

As Leo debated, he noticed the drab green vehicle troll by the courthouse, slowing almost to a stop behind Glory, then catching up with traffic. Just before the red light, the driver pulled a u-turn, doubled back to the courthouse, then crawled to a dead stop beside the curb. When the dark-clothed figure flung his door open and stepped into traffic, leaving the vehicle idling, Leo didn't think much of it. People did it all the time. But when the odd looking figure seemed to be targeting Glory, an alarm sounded in Leo's mind. Something was off. . .

"What the hell's going on? Who's that, Glory?"

"What are you talking about, Leo?"

"The guy walking up behind you. Turn around!"

From his desk, the judge heard the conversation and rushed to Leo's side. "Glory's on the phone? She's outside? What's going on, Leo?"

Diviniello arrived just in time to see the skulking figure close in on Glory as she pitched a hand toward her father, who stared through the window. His mouth hung open.

The judge couldn't open the window, but at the sight of the degenerate wearing black pants and hooded sweatshirt, obviously stalking his daughter, Diviniello began flagging his arms. "Glory!" He yelled through the plate glass window.

"What did you say to Daddy?" Glory demanded." Why does he look so agitated —" Glory wasn't able to finish her sentence, because the killer slammed into her like an evil force seeking entry into her body, punching the air from her lungs.

Glory turned with a start, but didn't have a chance to say *what the fuck?* Because in less time than it took a human heart to beat twice, he zapped her with the Taser he'd taken from Marla's kitchen. One glove then slipped the Taser back into the sweatshirt pocket and in an efficient move, the other swiped Glory off her feet. Catching her tumbling body in his arms, the killer lifted her like a baby and cradled her, then clamped his vile mouth over hers. One of her arms dangled over his shoulder. He slung the other around his neck so it appeared they were embracing in the center of the walk.

"What the fuck?" Leo's voice hammered the window with the same rapid beat of his fist.

"Call 911," he yelled at Diviniello.

Diviniello's flushed face was a combination of confusion and fury as he ran back to his desk to snatch his phone. His hand shook as he lifted, then accidentally dropped the receiver while screaming, "Who the fuck is that? What's happening to Glory?"

Diviniello's panicked voice carried into the reception area. Without knocking, Maria charged into his chamber looking horrified. Her earthy eyes stared into Diviniello's, then ripped across the room trapping Leo. "What's going on?" she said while moving toward the judge.

"Here!" Diviniello shoved the phone at her. "Dial 911. Tell them to get their asses over here now! Glory's downstairs. She's in trouble," he sputtered, spittle dotting his chin, then ran back to the window to watch his daughter whisked off her feet. "Sonofabitch. Kidnapped? Jesus Christ. Right in front of our eyes . . . Why would someone want to . . ."

"Glory!" Leo screamed, but Glory's phone had already clattered to the sidewalk where it was kicked to the curb.

Passersby with quizzical expressions yielded to the inconsiderate couple who looked like they were dressed for Halloween, obviously annoyed that the two were blocking a stream of hurrying feet while locked in passion. All the while the old green vehicle idled at the curb, tailpipe filling the air with a stream of fumes.

With Diviniello following at a slower pace, Leo raced out the door. He sprinted down the stairs, breaking his connection with Glory's phone to punch 911 into his dialer. He made a mad dash from the building and down the courthouse steps, followed by two security guards. Taking the stairs two at a time, the three men landed on the walk just in time to watch the killer toss Glory onto the front seat, climb in over her, slam the door shut and accelerate. The engine roared and the tires spun.

"Holy shit," Leo yelled. "Glory!" Although moving as fast as he possibly could, the world around him moved incredibly slow. Leo was a few feet from the vehicle, reaching out with both arms, yet he was helpless. He leapt from the curb, collided with the fender, and skimmed the dusty green paint with both palms as the vehicle sped off, leaving him hunched over on the side of the road, inhaling a burst of exhaust that burned his throat and eyes.

By the time Diviniello reached the scene he was wheezing and coughing, calling out Glory's name. Tears gathered in his lashes. Perspiration beaded his face and neck. "Dear God. Right under my nose. What the hell am I going to say to Bernadette?"

"911. What's your emergency?" Through Leo's cell phone, the operator asked.

"Listen carefully." Leo fought to control his thoughts, his breathing, and the pace of his words as he spoke as rationally as possible. "I'm calling from outside the Baltimore courthouse.

There's been a kidnapping. Take down this plate number and then make this the fastest call you've ever dispatched. . ."

✝

The killer reached across the seat. *Traci. . . You're so darned pretty.*

But the glove ignored the killer and snatched Glory's hand. *Bitch. Damn bitch.* The glove squeezed her hand so hard, the killer felt the crackle of bone. Then the struggle erupted inside the brain. A glove slammed her head against the passenger window. Unconscious, Glory slumped against the door.

The vehicle drove swiftly away from the heart of the city. At the time, no sirens could be heard. The gloves knew exactly where the vehicle should turn, and obediently it headed for the suburbs, bumping along back roads until it reached the cemetery, and the garage carved from the earth beneath a hill.

The vehicle slowed, then crunched down the cracked cement driveway and inched into the cavern that had years before been used by caretakers. Rusted lawn tools still clung to clips hanging on the studded walls.

After the killer exited the vehicle, the gloves lowered the overhead door. The only light came from slivers of day licking through gaps in the decrepit door.

When the killer reentered the vehicle, the interior light flushed Glory's face with a buffered glow. Her eyes were shut tight, lashes curled with thick mascara pointing to the roof. She sucked air from flaring nostrils. Other obvious signs of stress were furrows between her brows and her drawn mouth that twitched from time to time. Flung onto the seat, jostled by the erratic motion of the vehicle, her wig had loosened and the elastic strapping crept up her head, exposing blonde hair.

The killer climbed onto the seat beside her and sat. Sat beside Glory and stared at the receding wig. *Traci?* The killer was unpredictable, but the gloves were deadly. They ripped the wig from Glory's head. One held it, then twirled the fake hair like a lasso until it propelled through the air and onto the back seat while the killer shrieked his disapproval of the detachable hair.

Traci. Traci. What did you do to Traci? He took hold of Glory's limp body and shook her, like an animal tenderizing his kill. Agitation escalated to frenzy. One glove seized a handful of Glory's blonde hair, tugging so violently, her head rolled side to side each time her thick locks were snatched and released.

The gloves were unrelenting. *Bitch. Bitch. Bitch.* They lifted Glory's upper torso, shoved her forward at the waist, then using her own rope, tied her hands behind her. When the gloves were finished, they angrily flung her back into the seat.

They removed her boots and bound her ankles, then stuffed her twitching mouth with a rag, methodically sealing her lips with silver duct tape. As the gloves secured her restraints, from the cargo area, a coil of wire stared. The killer stared back: perfect for sewing lips, decorating eyelids, nipples . . .

He reached for the buttons of her blouse, then stopped. Rocking in the seat, he cradled the cowgirl boots, the brain calling, *Traci* . . . until Glory awoke with a start.

January Valentine

i stopped breathing for a while
and let the fear take over
i knew i'd lose sooner
or later anyway

THE KILLER UNVEILED

Glory's eyes opened slowly. She was dazed. The last thing she remembered was standing on the sidewalk in front of the courthouse, talking to Leo, attempting to ask him if he could ever forgive her. Forgive her for ditching him for Sam Landes. Sam was a greedy pig. Not only was he still involved with drugs and the underworld, but now he was dealing. Sooner or later he'd end up behind bars. He'd pay for the mess he'd dragged her into. Sooner was better. It hadn't been that long since she and Leo had been on good terms. Could he help her now? Leo! Her mind screamed.

She risked a peek at the lunatic beside her. About to lose her stomach, she recoiled. Now she understood why Leo had stared down at her with a petrified look on his face, pounding on the window of her father's office, obviously signaling for her to run. Not only had she been Tasered and kidnapped, but her kidnapper was an abomination.

She gagged on the rag that soaked up every ounce of saliva in her throat. She didn't taste the blood. Her mouth was stuffed so full, she couldn't taste anything. Her lips were numb. Her throat felt scorched. From fear and frustration, she wanted to cry, but knew better. If she cried, her nose would plug up and she'd suffocate.

Despair rose to an intolerable level. No one did this to Glory Divine . . . Frantic, she grasped at fleeting thoughts of freedom, a means to escape who she realized might very well be the Sweet Dreams Psycho. Glory shuddered. Her mind raced. She had a hard time believing she was being held captive, and a harder time acknowledging she was about to be a victim. But why?

Glory had no way of knowing, in costume, she resembled his first, and what had attracted him was the long, licorice hair, the cowgirl hat, and of course, the shapely legs and boots.

The killer squirmed in his seat, attempting a move onto hers. A haunch balanced on the console. The console filled with decaying food and human teeth. His teeth. Dingy teeth with blood-streaked roots, like the others that continued to dislodge and fall from inflamed gums faster than he could think. Faster than the skin peeled from his ulcerated scalp.

The smell inside the vehicle was nauseating, but his face. His face was something out of a nightmare. Or a horror movie. And the glove made her face him head-on.

Her eyes pleaded thoughts her mouth was incapable of delivering. She tried to twist toward the door, but her tethered arms pained. The ropes cut into her wrists. She tried to move her legs, but her bound ankles locked her lower extremities. Through the rag, she groaned. She couldn't help herself. If her lips were free, she would have cursed him out, which could have led to instantaneous extinction. But for his own reasons, the killer wanted her alive, although the gloves disagreed.

As he watched her struggle, the killer cocked his head and scrutinized her face, her hair, her restricted limbs. His jaw bone quivered. *Traci. You came back to me. You screamed. You choked. Sweet Dreams Traci.*

The gloves reached for Glory. Reached for her throat. Her eyes bulged with terror. She shook her head as if to scream, "No!" While her mind cried, "Escape!" There had to be a way out of this. She was not going to die today. Not at the hands of this monster.

When the killer pulled off his hood, a scream lodged in

Glory's throat, along with her Cobb Salad lunch. When she began to choke, one of the gloves did a surprising thing. It ripped off the tape, pulled the gag from her mouth. Freed, Glory's mouth could drop.

Most of the hair had been illness-stripped from his scalp. Irritated, it glistened. His head, flat on one side, resembled the art of a mad sculptor. Bashed Frontal bone to Temporal bone to cheek, it appeared as if a chunk of skull had been surgically removed, and all that remained was a loose skein of skin encircling an enormous eye cavity. The remaining facial structure was Cro-Magnon.

The mind and the brain were at odds, but both registered the look on the victim's face. Uncertain, the killer studied her until a glove prodded her side.

January Valentine

losing me lost me can't face me erase me misplace me
forsake me come take me i want you to make me
make me into something fine

THE SHIT HITS THE FAN

"Ben!"

"Leo, what's wrong? You sound like shit."

"He's here."

"What?"

"Listen to me. I'm on my way over there. Meet me outside. I saw the killer. He has Glory. We have to find them, Ben."

"I'm on my way out the door."

Sunshine from a window blind striped Ben's face as he struggled to fathom the connection between Glory and the killer. Since the first murder, following this gruesome case was like watching a B horror flick: impossible, illogical, unrealistic. The only problem was, what was now happening was *real*, and it wasn't a movie Ben would ever want to watch.

He tried to figure how Glory had managed to turn herself into a victim. One would think, with a justice for a father, and Leo as an ex, she'd be able to fight off the devil himself. And apparently, a devil was exactly what they were dealing with. Had she been snatched from her bed? The generous side of Ben felt sadness that Glory was in danger, but indomitable cop was elated to finally be in a position to track and capture the madman. Capture or kill. He pulled open his desk drawer and grabbed his Glock. After checking the clip, he shoved the gun into his holster, grabbed an additional clip and slid it into his pocket, then ran out the door with the ease of a cheetah, considering his size.

The silver Shelby was an aggressive jet claiming the road, running red lights and stop signs. Leo heard sirens in the distance. He knew they were headed in the direction of the courthouse where not ten minutes earlier, he had left the judge in the capable hands of Maria who, while waiting for police to arrive, compassionately listened to stories of how the judge had protected Glory from harm as she grew into a woman, and how the hell had he failed her now?

The easy stream of mid-afternoon traffic was erupting into rush hour congestion. By the time Leo arrived at the 10th precinct, Ben was impatiently pacing up and down the shoulder of the road, his large fists tense in the pockets of his American Eagle khaki jacket, his rigorous expression adding to his soldier of fortune appearance.

The minute the Mustang swooped to the curb, Ben jumped in and the bull-nosed car bullied its way back into what was turning into usual Baltimore five p.m. gridlock.

"Christ. This isn't working." Leo swerved back onto the shoulder and drove with one wheel on the curb to the intersection where the tires screeched a right.

"Where are we going?" Ben reached for the passenger grab handle to keep his body from wobbling. "Slow down, Leo. We're not on a race track."

Bypassing Main, they headed down a side street that paralleled, but with much lighter traffic.

"I watched him, Ben. I almost made it before they pulled away. My hands slid over the side of the SUV. I saw her — slumped in the seat." Leo's voice choked.

"Jesus, Leo. I'm sorry. So what are we looking for?"

"Dark green Bronco. Peeling paint. Here's the plate number." Leo handed Ben a slip of paper containing the numbers and letters he'd jotted down as the vehicle sped off. "I called it in to 911.

Run it, Ben."

Ben immediately got on his phone and contacted the precinct to have them run the tag through the Law Enforcement Information Network. Almost instantly, he had the information.

"The vehicle is registered in Louisiana to a Lysette Norton."

"Louisiana, huh?"

"You don't sound convinced he's our guy."

"I don't have any doubts. Where would he go now? Think, Benny."

"Shit. I don't know."

News and police helicopters flew at treetop level. Sirens could be heard above the noise of rush hour traffic.

"It'll be dark soon. We have to do this. If anybody's gonna find them —"

"Yeah, I know, buddy. We will. Hang tight." Ben steadied his voice.

"Where does he go before he makes his selection?" Leo's tone switched from concerned to sarcastic.

"Roses." Ben looked over at Leo. His face was strained and pale. He had a stranglehold on the steering wheel.

"Cemeteries." Leo smacked the wheel with his palm. "Where he picks his roses. That's where he's got to be."

He snatched his BlackBerry from the console and speed dialed. Ginger picked up on the third ring, but as she answered he abruptly cut her off.

"Ginger." Although Leo sat behind the wheel, smoothly running the Mustang like a demon, his breathing was erratic. "You're still there."

"Leo —"

"I need you to do something for me, Ginger."

"Anything —"

"Compile a list of every Baltimore cemetery starting with the ones nearest the courthouse and call me back — like yesterday."

"You've got it. Should only take me a few minutes. I'm already on Google. Anything else?" Along with gentle breathing,

Ginger's keyboard clicked into Leo's ear.

"Have you seen Diviniello?"

"No, but the entire building's buzzing about what happened. What did happen anyway? There are some unbelievable stories floating around." More keyboard clicking.

"I'll let Ben tell you, but first, I need that list."

"Call you right back, Leo." Click and disconnect.

"Just in case," Ben's voice was guarded as he watched Leo fight off frenzy. "Were does he go afterward —"

"He's got to be living in that car. So fuck knows. They — or he, could be on Ninety-Five, leaving Baltimore right now."

"So we're about to check every cemetery in Baltimore. Am I correct?"

"Yep," Leo said as his BlackBerry chimed. He checked the caller ID and tossed the battered phone onto Ben's lap. "Get your pad out and use your shorthand."

Leo patted his jacket pocket. The Xanax was there. This was the first time he'd ever been so close to popping one of those little white tablets under his tongue, but he needed to be clear headed. Just touching the plastic bottle had a calming effect.

"BEN. THOSE MAUSOLEUMS."

Glory was a bitch who never took guff from anyone. Why should she start now? Just because her hands and feet were bound? And she was seated beside a monster?

As the killer studied Glory, she began conducting her own mental analysis of him — the vehicle — the tomb she was trapped in — and the wheels inside her head were turning: *how the fuck am I gonna get out of this one? How do I loosen these fucking ropes?*

She should never have let him get her from point A to point B, point B being a dank garage tomb. She should have known better, but being zapped with fifty thousand volts of electricity at the base of the skull would have knocked out King Kong. Glory was tough, but she wasn't Superwoman.

Several years prior, a mugger had tried to rip her handbag off her shoulder. She held tight to the strap — screamed at the top of her lungs, "I'm gonna kill you!" Kneed the guy in the groin and when he hunched over, she knocked him cold with an upper cut she'd learned at boxing class. She straddled him until police arrived. Then the State took over. She was called as a witness at his trial. The prosecutor had been Leo.

The thing sitting beside her with the threatening glove looked like something from another dimension. The thought of his touch made her cringe. Shrinking in the seat, she flattened against the door. But she had to do something to distract him. She considered befriending him, but since he didn't look very friendly, decided conversation wouldn't do. She needed to fight him as an equal if she was going to walk away from this one.

Avoiding his face, Glory's eyes swept his wide frame, then focused out the window behind him. She strained, trying to determine if what she spotted was the outline of a rack of gardening tools hanging on the wall.

"The nearest is Rosary Park Cemetery over on Chestnut." Ben said as he studied his note pad. His bulky back and shoulders filled the Mustang's seat.

"That's east," Leo said as he jammed on the brakes. "We're heading west." He pulled a broken U turn on the narrow street and gunned the car in the direction of the first cemetery on their list. To avoid traffic lights and jams, they drove through residential neighborhoods.

Rosary Park Cemetery was located right off a main highway. It was one of Baltimore's largest. As they neared the gaping wrought iron entry gates, Leo looked doubtful.

"This place is too big and accessible, Ben. There's too much activity going on."

The Mustang cruised up and down blacktop lanes edged by orderly rows of graves. Like a gated community, each corner was posted with a metal pole and sign displaying plot numbers, sections and rows, instead of house numbers in communities of the living. As they drove deeper into the cemetery, they passed thousand dollar mausoleums. A small Caterpillar was in the process of digging a foundation, while two men with rakes tidied the area torn apart by the machine's destructive tires.

"Talk about leaving a legacy," Ben grunted. "They call these garden crypts, if you want to get technical, lawn crypts. A waste of cash if you ask me. I told Terry, when I'm dead, just burn me. She can sprinkle me on the garden."

"We're not sightseeing. Keep your mind on what we're doing, Ben."

"Just thinking out loud. Did you know they don't really bury you six feet under anymore?"

"Haven't given it much thought."

"Yeah. Now they only dig about four feet deep because they put your casket into one of those cement containers and seal it with this sticky tar —"

"Christ, Ben. I'm not planning on a funeral anytime soon."

The cemetery was impeccably manicured by workers who also hand shoveled granulated earth into every new grave, then topped off the final layer of soil with squares of emerald green sod.

As they passed a flock of mourners, milling beside a freshly covered burial site, Leo shook his head. "Why do I think we're not gonna find them here. It's too fucking busy. He's a night crawler, not our average citizen."

"I have the same feeling. But you never know, he could be trying to blend in rather than hide out where he could easily stand out."

"That bomb would stand out anyplace. Now that we know he's driving that beat up piece of shit, it won't be hard finding him if he's still in the area. What's the next on the list?"

When the crime scene photos of Billie Jean Jordan flashed across his mind, Leo's gut tightened. It didn't take much imagination to figure out what hell the young victim had gone through. Hopefully, she'd died from the first blow to her head. It had taken eight photographs, pieced together like a puzzle, to view the entire scene. The sliver of scalp hanging from a branch had to be the worst, or was it the face that looked like it had been fed through a meat grinder?

"Saint Michael's on Elmhurst. Do you really think he grabbed Glory and will risk flower shopping in a cemetery in broad daylight?"

"We have nothing else to go on, Ben. We know the creep likes or needs to pick his roses from cemeteries. It's either this or go home and pace."

"Okay. I'm with you." Ben stared out the window. "I'm waiting for my phone to ring any minute now. Hear Terry's voice. You know, at times like this I miss my wife and kids. They're probably sitting around the dinner table, talking about their day, enjoying Terry's delicious cooking without me." He sounded distant. "I'm a lucky bastard."

"I'm going to call the judge to see if there have been any developments on his end. Meantime, can you get a couple of patrol cars over here? I'd feel a lot better if they canvassed this entire place. We just don't have the time."

"Good call."

While Ben called for assistance, Leo speed dialed Judge Diviniello who answered his phone on the first ring. The judge sounded nasal.

"It's Leo. How's it going?"

"I've got my hands full with Bernadette."

"I can imagine. Who showed up at the courthouse? Anyone we know?"

"DeGarmo and Ritchie. They looked around, took witness statements from anyone on the street who saw it happen," Diviniello's voice cracked. "Yours truly being one of them. God Leo, I can't get that picture out of my mind. That creep holding her that way, his mouth on hers, violating her like that, throwing her into his car. I can't stop thinking about what could be happening to my daughter at this very moment, as we speak."

"Ben and I are out now, Judge. We're doing all we can." Leo knew his words offered little comfort. He'd worked with enough survivors to understand and identify with the horror of trying to cope when a loved one was missing, or worse yet, found murdered. It was like closing your eyes to visual images of the victim's torture, closing your ears to their terrified screams while you waited for the phone to ring. And when it didn't ring within twenty-four hours, forty-eight hours, seventy-two hours, then your hope evaporated faster than a hundred degree summer day's unanticipated shower.

"I know you're doing all you can. And I appreciate your efforts. Keep me posted and I'll do the same. Oh, the FBI is on the case. The same guys from Virginia. . ." His voice stalled like an engine that was running out of gas. The possibility that Glory could become the next butchered fatality hung in the air, draining Diviniello's already weakened tone.

"FBI," Leo echoed, his hands gripping the wheel tighter. "That's good." His anticipation spiked. He'd like to be part of their investigation, but knew it wasn't plausible. Hunters and counselors didn't work together on the streets. "Try to take it easy, Judge. Everything's going to be alright."

"Yeah. We'll see, Leo. I have to go deal with Bernadette." Click.

"Ben. Those mausoleums." Leo was a warrior. His mind hadn't stopped strategizing since Glory was snatched off the street.

"Huh?" Ben replied vaguely as he stared out the window. The setting sun began to cool the day, but his window remained almost all the way open. Although the air he inhaled was fresh and floral scented, in his imagination, the atmosphere surrounding the cemetery was tainted with decay. Instinctively, he rolled up his window and turned to face Leo.

"What are the odds of getting inside one?" Leo said as the Mustang looped around several more lanes, making one final pass before exiting through the gates that would soon be closed and locked to visitors.

Ben's brown eyes looked brighter than the streetlights snapping on automatically as they headed for cemetery number two. "The cemeteries are gonna be on lockdown pretty soon. The sun's setting."

"Yeah, and now we hope the ghouls come out." Accelerating, Leo lit up the tires.

January Valentine

don't try to change me
rearrange me to you
no recycling damaged parts
when you can't control your anger
i'm the one who wears the marks

TRACI, I'M GONNA KILL YOU

Glory forced herself to remain calm, permitting a glove to prod her side. His body reeked. Vomit bubbled in her throat. His breath, foul like road kill, made its way to her nose. She knew it was wrong to stare an angry bear in the eye, and although the thing beside her looked like an animal, she knew it was some sort of man. As she stared, she thought the expression on his face changed. She wouldn't show fear. She'd stare him down. Maybe intimidate him.

"What's your name?" she asked, her voice firm.

The glove quickly withdrew. No one had ever asked his name before. And there was no screaming. At the sound of Glory's voice, his head cocked to the side, but his eyes remained fixed on hers.

Her brunette wig lay on the back seat, but now her blonde hair appeared dark — as dark as the interior of the vehicle. Even more interesting; the woman sitting beside him seemed strong. *Traci?*

His eyes shifted side to side, and Glory thought he shuddered when she spoke.

"Nice car," she said with a pasted on smile. "So are you from around here?"

The eyes focused on her face, her flowing hair. The glove rested on her shoulder, then firmly on her arm, sliding to her waist where it dropped, clamping onto her hipbone.

"Hold on big fella. Untie me and we can get to know one another." Her voice was powerful. Her intention — turn predator into prey. And it seemed to be working. He twitched, then did something she wasn't expecting.

"Immortal Rest Cemetery," Ben said. "That's the last one in this area. The next is more than thirty miles away. It's getting dark. They could be long gone by now. If we don't find them at this place. I hate to say. . ."

"Then don't. We're gonna find them."

"Take Claudia Way. It'll be faster. Then turn down Foley to Jamaica. I'm gonna make a call." Ben speed dialed his cell.

"Brady. Get in touch with the caretaker over at Immortal Rest and tell him to make sure those gates are open. We'll be there in ten."

Ben's words offered encouragement. Leo pushed the Mustang harder than he'd ever pushed the old Honda on late night rides. He wasn't thinking — just reacting like a programmed machine. There was no room for mistakes. No time for human error. Leo was detached. Along with Glory, Gina had been at the killer's mercy. Adrenaline overflowed. The muscles in Leo's legs tightened. Accelerator flattened to the floorboard, the engine was maxed out. So was Leo.

The glove slammed into the side of Glory's head.

He was strong. He was powerful. He was about to take charge.

Glory was stunned. Her vision blurred and her head began to pound. She couldn't lose consciousness now. Focus! She had to focus! Change her strategy.

"You're so big and strong," she said in the most seductive voice possible as her head began to clear. "Untie me and we'll have some fun."

With barely no lips, mouth slack, drool easily trickled. *Traci* was a dark outline beside him. A glove snapped on an interior light.

When the image hit her brain, instinct told her to scream at the top of her lungs. But, sucking in a breath, Glory held it together. At the sight of the tongue snaking its way toward her, her stomach lurched. She stiffened. Did the mouth just try to smile?

A glove found her breast. Squeezed. Caressing in the most clumsy effort she'd ever experienced. Cruder than any virgin's first attempt. The glove pressed harder. The face moved closer: the wretched tongue hung limp, then without warning swept the length of her neck, the side of her face. Licked in a straight line as if she were something so sweet it couldn't resist another long, lingering taste.

About to be sick, Glory gathered a ball of sticky saliva, pursed her lips and aimed for his face, screaming, "Get off me!"

The glove sprang from her breast, grabbed her cheeks and squeezed. His mouth opened wider. More drool ran to his chin. Was he about to kiss her? *God, this can't be happening.* To avoid the odor she held her breath for as long as she could. The smell was an unfathomable blend of perspiration and rotting flesh. So much for playing it cool. Instinct took over. "Get off me you sick fuck."

Ignoring her pleas, while the tongue swiped, a glove explored the length of her inner thigh, forced her legs apart, zeroed in on her crotch. Searching, it scraped her delicate skin. Her commando. The caressing glove now circled her neck, pinning her to the seat while the repulsive head dropped toward her knees, slobbering tongue following the path of the abrasive glove. Like glue, saliva coated her thighs, the glove forcing them to open wider.

He had been silent, but now his breath was heavy, noisy, a rattle drawn from struggling lungs filling her ears. His hips began to writhe.

The pressure of the head, working between her legs, strained the binding on her ankles, the rope stretching, burning, slicing her skin. "Fucking freak," Glory screamed. "Untie me and we'll have a fair fight, you fucking weirdo."

The sound she emitted was guttural as her thighs snapped together. His head was caught in the vice. Harder she clenched until she heard a gasp for air. The glove tightened around her throat. Was it her gasp? With her last ounce of strength, she pulled up her knees in an attempt to snap his neck.

Springing up, he growled. Stared with a look surpassing hatred. Once more she tightened her legs, drew up her knees, shifted her body and slammed him, dislocating what she felt was his stomach. He groaned and loosened his hold, brought a glove to his midsection.

Traci. You fuckin' bitch! I'm gonna kill you!

For a moment the killer glared, then a glove reached for the door handle.

Glory sank into the seat, thankful for a momentary reprieve. *But what now?*

"Where are you going?" Without thought, the words escaped her lips that longed to tremble.

The killer ignored her, lowered his head to clear the door frame and clumsily exited. When a glove lifted the overhead door, twilight rushed inside. He shot a quick look at the vehicle, at her face through the windshield, then disappeared behind headstones and falling darkness.

The moon was on the rise with clouds parting for its radiance. The cemetery was serene, and filled with fresh flowers. Roses. He needed a rose before he could proceed.

It took seconds for Glory's eyes to focus on a piece of lumber that had been nailed to an inside wall of the garage. A heartbeat later, her eyes confirmed the assortment of gardening tools. Since her hands were bound they were useless. *Think fast! This is probably your only chance. . .*

Her door was locked, but she knew his was open. *Fuck me . . .*

No way I'm staying in here.

Sliding across the seat, she hurtled over the console. With bare toes she hooked the handle, lifted the cold metal, managed to push open the driver's door. Time was definitely not on her side. She'd have to hurry if she was going to free herself and kick his mother fucking ass.

Her maneuvering space was so tight, it felt as though the garage had consumed the vehicle. Glory could barely open the door, and with bound hands and feet, as she rolled herself out, balance was difficult. With a hop she backed into the rack, stretched as high as she could, and sawed her restraints against the sharp edge of a garden clipper.

Heart about to burst, her chest heaved. The wrist ropes fell to the floor in pieces.

Thank you, God. I won't forget you for this.

Fingers trembling, she unbound her ankles, scrambled back into the vehicle, found her boots and pulled them on. Before leaving the garage, she grabbed what appeared to be the best weapon, one that was strong and something that would keep her a safe distance away — while she fought him. She knew exactly how she would use the tool.

January Valentine

i'm your sick creation
you can share the blame

led me thru the flames
now you're walking in the ashes

others wait to catch me
but i'm scattered in the wind

don't you leave me !
don't you leave me !
don't you leave me !

HEADSTONES & CRYPTS

When Leo and Ben arrived, the gates stood wide open. The Mustang shot into the cemetery, methodically cruising interior roads.

"See if you can spot anything that might look out of place, Ben. Off road tracks — dirt trails — anything."

The headlights washed at least five feet on either side of the car as they parted the darkness like a freighter forging a sea. Their eyes searched narrow paths between rows of headstones and crypts. Nothing moved but the car.

"Christ. This is worse than looking for a needle in a haystack. Think. Think." Leo slammed a fist on the steering wheel.

The killer found a grave blanketed with roses. The glove selected the perfect red with the longest, sturdiest stem. A stem that could easily be shoved down her throat — after he strangled her. Or maybe he would strangle her with the rose? This one would be different. The knife was in the pocket, the tools were in the trunk, but he wouldn't need them tonight. The gloves were the almighty power. He'd snuff the life from her just as he'd snuffed Traci's before feeding her to the alligators. Perspiration gathered beneath the cumbersome hood. He swept it from his head. His stark white head that in moonlight gleamed like a rain-soaked boulder.

Glory stood at the doorway, eyes adjusting to changing light, carefully scanning to get a fix on where he had taken her. She knew this place. She'd been here before. For funerals. This wasn't going to be hers. She tightened her grip on the handle of the spade she held close to her side, and stepped into the night. Her boots crunched in gravel; she tiptoed. The garage was at the end of a long road. A lonely road. She spotted lights in the distance, but at the moment, the distance felt like a thousand miles. Flashlights? Caretakers? Were the lights coming from the Bay Area?

Slowly, cautiously, she stepped, listening for something other than her own breathing. The grounds were damp and free of leaves. A twig cracked, but before she could turn, a glove clamped her jaw shut while an arm locked around her throat, limiting her air. She gasped, choked. The partner glove gripped the rose, stem raking her cheek. Her immediate instinct was to struggle; she flailed. The spade slipped through her palms, scraping her knee as it fell to the ground with a thud. This wasn't getting her anywhere.

Glory was tall, she was strong, she lifted weights for Godssake! But the killer had six inches over her, and he was powerful. Still, she wasn't going down, not without a fight. *Focus. Remember the moves, Glory.* She grabbed his arm, shrugged her shoulders, and sank her chin into the crook of his elbow, all within seconds. Bending, she hooked her leg around the back of his, quickly turned, and effortlessly flipped him onto his back. Lying on the ground, he seemed stunned, then moved faster than Tequila down her throat during a night out on the town.

Once more he was upon her. Twisted in his arms she was suffocating, and this time her move had no effect. Like an angry mare, she rear kicked, connecting with his shin bone. He grunted, the first human sound she'd ever heard escape his twisted mouth. Managing to shift, she brought a knee to his groin. He seemed to buckle before her eyes. *The spade. Find the spade.* As Glory hunched, he recovered, shooting her a bone chilling stare. She stumbled, regained her balance, then swung the spade like a batter swinging for the fences. Instantly, it connected with the side of his head. Metal hitting skull; the beautiful sound of freedom. She swung again, then delivered a second blow to his groin. The rose he had managed to hold onto was launched, falling to the ground seconds before his legs buckled.

Raising the spade above her head, Glory brought it down forcefully, but a glove deflected it, stole the tool and dragged her to the ground beside the killer. Before she could wiggle free, he was straddling her, pinning her arms while he reached for the rose. The next thing she knew her mouth was pried open. The stem bit into her tongue, drawing blood as he shoved the rose down her throat.

Glory gagged and turned her head, twisted her body, freeing an arm. Blindly, she groped for the spade. Her fingers stretched, dug, nails scratching at the handle. She felt it roll into her palm. Her hand closed around it. Hard wood never felt so good. Jabbing at the back of his head, again and again she hammered until he stiffened. Then his body fell heavily onto hers. Scrambling free she jumped to her feet and took a gratuitous swing at something that looked like it had been dead for months.

The tips of Glory's boots formed a sharp point. "Bastard," she said as she kicked his head like a soccer ball. Satisfied he would never ever rise again, she snatched the trampled rose and stuffed it into his mouth, with the tip of her boot shoving it deep. "Here's what you can do with your rose, you freak."

Glory took a moment to pull herself together, catch her breath, then sprinted down the road in the direction of the lights. The lights that grew closer.

†

The Mustang continued to cruise up and down the interior roads.

"This is our last bet. I'm getting out," said Leo. "You keep driving. If you find anything, blow the horn." He jammed on the brakes, grabbed a flashlight from the floor at Ben's feet.

He flung the door open to see a figure jogging toward him. He aimed the light. The beam flooded Glory's tangled hair, anxious face, then illuminated her entire body that looked like a jittery gazelle.

When the light hit her, she squinted, threw an arm across her eyes and ran faster.

"Thank God it's you," she said, slamming her full weight against the fender before throwing herself at Leo.

He held her at arm's length. "Where is he?"

"Let me catch my breath." Bending at the waist, she took cleansing breaths, then faced him. "I left him back there, lying on the ground." She held the spade in the air like a trophy, then it slid from her grasp and clattered to the road. She let out a burst of air. "What a shit experience. For a crazy while, I didn't think I'd ever see you again." Back to normal, hands on hips, she appeared annoyed.

"Did you kill him?" Ben asked.

"I don't know."

"What do you mean you don't know?" Ben was gruff. "You stay 'til the job's done. Haven't you learned anything?"

"Fuck you, Cassidy," she quipped.

"Thank Christ you're okay." Leo cut in.

"How did you know —" Glory started to ask.

"Not now." He turned to Ben. "Call for backup."

"Already did."

From out of nowhere, headlights glared. The vehicle closed in, aiming straight for the Mustang.

"What the hell?" Ben yelled.

"It's him. It's his truck —" Glory was breathless again. "Get out of the way!"

Leo snagged the spade, then flattened against the fender.

The vehicle appeared to slow; a hair away from sideswiping the Mustang, it paused long enough for the killer to show his face. He shot Leo a chilling look, then as fast as it had appeared, the vehicle lunged forward with a screech of bald tires.

"Get out of the car. I'm going after him."

"Take my gun." Ben dropped the Glock onto the seat.

Ben and Glory made a mad dash for the entrance gate. By the time they arrived, both sets of taillights had disappeared.

"Here come the troops," said Ben as choppers closed in, beams of light flooding the area. The persistent whoop of sirens increased. "Let's hope they stay on his ass."

Unsure of which route to take, Leo drove like the madman he chased. Racing down side streets, he headed toward the bay and I-95, the most logical route the killer would take if he wanted to flee the city.

Leo's thoughts spun. The moment had finally come. This was his chance to stand face to face with Gina's killer. Retribution would feel better than an animalistic fuck.

He floored the Mustang. The Bronco's worn engine was no match. Within minutes, Leo found his taillights and dropped into his shadow. Ready for the big showdown, his stomach knotted. Glancing at the 9mm on the seat beside him, his chest heaved.

As if the killer sensed he was about to lose the biggest battle of his life, the vehicle slowed.

The Mustang followed closely as they crossed the city. Other than accumulating police cars, traffic was almost nonexistent. Electing to disregard the sirens, Leo wondered how things would play out. What developed, however, was nothing like he imagined.

The bay lights glittered a welcome. After a quarter mile of cruising, the vehicle suddenly increased its speed, ran red lights and stop signs. The Mustang was like a magnet in its tracks. Nose to bumper, they crossed the bridge leading to the marina, where they would soon run out of road. Leo had to think fast. Would he face him? Would he ask him "Why?" How would he overpower him? Forget about trying to reason. Maybe just use the 9mm. Suppose he ditched the vehicle and took off on foot? Not a problem. Leo was faster than lightning on a basketball court. He'd be even faster with adrenaline pumping through his system as he chased the bastard down.

A split second decision was made. To hell with the gun. Leo wanted to stare into the eyes of the devil. Wanted to wrap his hands around his neck. Feel life drain from his body.

Dock lights shimmered. The road quickly shrank. Leo was certain the vehicle had to stop at any moment. Instead it sped down the ramp in the direction of moored crafts.

To avoid a guardrail, Leo braked hard, coming to a skidding halt. The Bronco did not. It went airborne like a bulky rocket unable to make liftoff, then smashed headlong into what had been a tranquil bay.

Two tons of steel made a belly-wop landing. A thud. Enormous splash. Within moments, the vehicle was surrounded by a collar of disturbed water that expanded then burst. The vehicle bobbed then nosedived, sinking with its own weight. The lights were swallowed, fenders, roof, then the bay gulped bundles of air and calmed.

While the Mustang's headlights searched, Leo sat in the driver's seat, stunned, eyes tracking the vehicle's flight. He hadn't seen a door open. What had happened so quickly, was difficult to comprehend. Leo was out of his body again. "Fuck!" This always happened when the level of stress was too much to bear. Safety mechanism for an overburdened mind: de-realization made it feel like a dream.

Leo held his head and shook it side to side, as if the movement would clear his thoughts. Screaming, "Son of a bitch," he slammed his fists on the steering wheel. At the same moment his mind flashed Glock, his palm clutched the black polymer grip. He flung the door open and leapt from the car. Gun in hand, he dashed across the dock to where, moments earlier, the vehicle had launched. Standing in the beam of headlights, his eyes strained for any sign of movement. Had the creep survived the impact? Should he dive in to search for the body?

January Valentine

i'm brittle i'm snapping
they're working on me
stretching me out on a stretcher
working me over

It's Now Or Never

Behind him, lamp posts poured an eerie blush, their arms reaching out to nothing. Across the way, an explosion of brilliance haloed upscale condos that claimed the horizon like a futuristic empire. In afterglow, the old neighborhood, an aging toad, clung to the border, too bummed to hop the fence between them.

Looming before Leo, the epicenter, a sinister mass of midnight, separating heaven from hell. *What a time for reality to strike,* crossed his mind. Would the madman surface? Or had the bay claimed him, drained the life from his pathetic body as he'd done to so many?

In the distance, Leo heard the sirens and the whir of helicopters. The pulse in his neck paced his hammering heart. His right arm hung loosely at his side, the Glock dangling from his fingers. He took two steps forward to the edge of the dock, the tips of his shoes teetering, at the mercy of the weathered wood.

His eyes roamed the bleak surface like a trawler, the only ripple of life his shifting shadow as he paced, breath mixing with rising mist.

A cluster of bubbles appeared, gathered and popped. A second later a glistening head broke the calm. The gaping mouth gulped for air. The eyes darted, found Leo, then stared.

Not more than ten feet apart, they were locked in place by their eyes — the hunter and the hunted — while the current dragged the killer closer, his morphing form bobbing, floating like tide ravaged debris. Then the long arms began to flail.

It's now or never. Leo drew a quick breath, and with both hands leveled the Glock. His finger stroked the trigger, tightened, then suddenly released. With a thud, the pistol dropped.

The face-off endured. Balancing on planks, Leo's feet rocked. His body turned rigid, nerves firing off signals: irrepressible urges tumbled through bitter memories . . . Gina.

He wavered as a tree in a storm with roots about to be torn from the earth, its downfall unpredictable. Mind faltering, his legs took control. Jaw clenched tighter than his fists, with a labored breath, he took a step.

"What am I doing?" His fingers uncoiled. Lifting his hands, he studied his palms, then his eyes found the Glock. Inches away lay the justice he sought. The end of a long and bloody road.

Like a freight train, eight by ten glossies slammed his mind: the innocent victims, the story of their deaths, the pain the killer had caused. The little girl who had to be pieced together, in photos as well as her casket, would permanently brand his brain.

His eyes swung back to his adversary, thrashing in the bay. Did the face have expression? Was it fear? Leo hoped it was.

"This is ending . . . now."

†

Cruisers flooded the marina, rollers flashing, sirens still blaring. Police and news helicopters hovered, spotlights intersecting. Chaos erupted as the area filled with law enforcement and medical teams.

Ben and Glory emerged from a patrol car.

"What happened?" Ben asked, eyes scanning every direction.

"Nothing." Hands stuffed in his trouser pockets, Leo's stance appeared casual. But his face gave it all away. "He just drove into the bay like it was nothing."

"I thought he got away." Glory inched toward Leo.

"Fuck me." Ben appeared annoyed. "I missed it." He shuffled a few feet away, staring into the murky water, then spotted his gun on the dock. Miffed, he snatched up the weapon, holstered it, then shot Leo a questioning stare. Cell in hand, he walked back. "The wrecker's on the way."

Glory had managed to wind herself around Leo, oblivious to the water pooling at his feet. She stroked his damp hair. "Baby, you don't look good."

"What the fuck?" Ben recoiled. "Did you? You didn't really. . ."

Leo's face was blank. "This dock needs repair."

Ben's eyes narrowed. "I'd never hold it against you, bud."

"Go see for yourself," Leo snapped. "On second thought. Maybe you better not or they'll be pulling you out, too."

Ben shook his head, grumbled, then turned to watch uniformed officers take command of a raucous crowd of curious onlookers.

Lips on Leo's cheek, Glory whispered, "Do you forgive me?"

"Forget it." His voice sounded disturbingly stiff as he set her aside.

An anchorwoman stepped through a congestion of vehicles. Holding a mic close to her face, she smiled into the lens of the camera her assistant held on his shoulder.

"This is Judy Bennett reporting for Channel Nine news. We're at the downtown marina, covering a breaking story, where shocking events are unfolding. It is here, in this usually tranquil body of water, that the gruesome reign of a serial killer comes to a close, right before our eyes. It looks like Baltimore has made good on its promise. Thanks to a lead from a detective and state prosecutor who chased him down, the Sweet Dreams Psycho has been stopped, dead in his tracks. A police rig is pulling an SUV from the bay as we speak."

Stepping clear of the camera, she held up a hand. "Get them lifting it." Motioning to the wrecker, she sounded frantic. "Make sure you get great shots, Dave. Dear Lord." She brought a hand to her mouth. A look of disbelief filled her face as a stretcher rushed by, supporting an unzipped body bag, its grisly contents exposed. "I've never seen anything like it," she remarked in an odd voice that wouldn't be captured on tape.

A reporter is trained to face her audience expression free. Nothing should be so disturbing that it halts her words. The woman took a deep breath, signaled her cameraman with a nod, then resumed her report.

"Calling what I've just glimpsed *a man* is stretching it. What's been carted away on the gurney that was just wheeled by doesn't look human." She paused dramatically. "What divers hauled from the depths of the bay looks more like sea life. A beast from the ocean floor. The color. The texture of the skin. Like . . . squid-like, with arms instead of tentacles. How is this possible?" She sounded more like a fascinated onlooker than a seasoned reporter.

A bulky shoulder slammed into her, while a large hand covered the lens of the camera. "No reporters."

"I'm just doing my job." Obviously annoyed at being manhandled, she shot him a nasty look, then moved close to her assistant whose jaw appeared to be sealed shut.

"I'm just doing mine," said the man with a southern beat, low and menacing.

The cameraman seemed to awaken, stepped between the anchor and the plain clothes officer. "You're not from around here. . ."

Crime scene tape cordoned off the area. Uniformed police secured the perimeter, while a dedicated task force took charge.

With Leo the only witness, once the remains were removed, and the vehicle towed away, the incident was a quick wrap, with the scene clearing in a matter of hours.

Apart from the others, Glory leaned against the fender of a patrol car, now and then sparring with a young officer, but mostly sulking.

"What's up with her?" Ben jerked his head toward the vehicle they'd arrived in.

"She's just being herself." Leo laughed. "So I guess it's over, partner." He exchanged fist bumps with Ben. "Gonna miss riding with you."

"Yeah, right." Ben laughed. "You love that cushy desk job of yours."

"I don't know. This has been pretty wild. Kinda gets in your blood." Leo felt his pants pocket for his wallet. "Hey, how about a drink?"

"Drop that one off first. Christ, what a pain in the ass. The whole ride over here she didn't stop bitching once. I don't know how you stand it."

"Hmph. You have to acquire a taste for a woman like Glory."

"Yeah, I'd spit that one out fast." Ben angled his head. "Although . . . look at her over there in that cowgirl outfit. You oughta nail her in the back of the squad car."

"Christ. You never stop."

Ben guffawed. "What's wrong with me? You already have." He openly stared at the tight fit of Glory's skirt, the amount of breasts her vest revealed. "I'd need to grow another penis to service something like that."

"If your wife heard you talking this shit, she'd kick your ass, and rightly so. You're a dirty old man." Leo shook his head.

"Hey, after living with Terry all these years . . . her reading all those romance novels and the way she likes to roleplay. Hell, I'm a *tired* old man. But looking can't hurt."

Leo laughed. "Listen, I'm gonna shoot home and change. Catch up with you at the Dockhouse."

Ben eyed Leo's sagging pants and shirt. "Sounds good. And then you've got some explaining to do."

Leo's face tightened. "I can't wait to get my hands on a scotch."

"I can't wait to get my hands on the coroner's report." Eyes shifting to the bay, Ben fell silent.

January Valentine

it could hurt
it could hurt so bad
it could hurt so bad but I'm numb

Closure?

Leo took a quick survey of his room, zipped his duffle bag, then reached for his cell. "Hey . . . Yeah, I'm okay. Did you get the autopsy results?"

Ben's voice was low, secretive. "Inconclusive. The body was in and out in a matter of hours. What does that tell you?"

"Why would someone want to cover it up?" Leo did a pat down for his Xanax bottle. "Any idea who claimed the remains?"

"No clue, man. But shit, what a mess. Gross. Really gross. And in my line of work, I rarely use that word." Ben laughed.

"Huh?"

"Contusions. Broken bones. All fucked up."

"Really?" Leo jogged down the stairs, stopping in the living room to snap off the TV, then headed to the kitchen.

"Maybe part of his weird deformity. Maybe his joyride into the bay. Fuck knows." Ben took a breath, his voice testing, "Maybe you kicked his ass when you dove into the bay after him, huh?"

After a long pause, during which Leo didn't reply, Ben chuckled. "Yeah. Fuck knows. Fuck gives a shit. But, I can tell you this much for sure. The guy was a walking laboratory. Full of chemicals."

"Street drugs?" Leo checked his watch.

"Nah. Other stuff your average freak couldn't get his hands on."

"What kind of stuff?" Bag strapped over a shoulder, a hand clutching his phone, Leo snapped off the kitchen light and left his condo.

"Steroids. HGH, stuff like that. And some rare compounds, crap even the pros haven't heard of. They're doing further analysis on tissue samples."

"So it's still not over."

"What do you mean?"

Leo breathed heavily into the phone. "Never mind. Listen, I've got to get going."

"Hold on, Leo. There's something else." Ben chuckled. "The freak was really fucked."

Duffle thrown onto the passenger seat, Leo slid behind the wheel of the Mustang. "No shit." He snorted. "Tell me something I don't know."

"You're not hearing me, bro. He was on the way out. So even if we hadn't nabbed him that night, he would've bought it soon, anyway."

"You're confusing the hell out of me, Ben."

"Coroner said he was in the latent stage of syphilis."

"You've got to be kidding." Leo shook his head and ignited the Mustang. "Gets more fucked up by the minute. Listen, I've got a flight to catch. Keep me posted."

"Where you going?"

"I'm heading down to Louisiana."

"Why?"

"I need closure."

"I hear you, bro. How long will you be gone?"

"As long as it takes."

"Need company?"

Leo's laugh was more of a comical grunt. "I'm making a couple of stops along the way."

"Let me guess. Atlanta and Tennessee. In which order?"

"That remains to be seen."

HAVE WE ONLY JUST BEGUN?

On the flight to Baton Rouge, Leo wore ear buds, half listening to soft rock on his iPod, half dozing . . . dreaming. He pictured Amber, wondering if their next meeting would be as explosive as their last. Would she slip eagerly, hungrily into his arms? His level of heat took a nosedive when Scarlett gained control of his senses. When subjected to her elements, his body reacted accordingly. She could be like the weather. An apple scented spring morning, warm and inviting. An evening in the dead of winter, where she could be as brisk as the ocean breeze and every bit as breathtaking. Sleek, elegant, Scarlett wasn't a plaything.

Direct opposites, he was equally drawn to both women. With Amber he could cut loose. They were like two teens drifting in and out of infatuation. But, Scarlett lived up to her name: like rich red blood flowing through arteries, she could be the cleansing source of life for a man.

He'd have to stop his brain from dicking around, visualizing Amber spread out on the sofa, Scarlett nestled in his arms. He had to remind himself: business first. Then pleasure. Yeah . . . the pleasure he'd enjoy after his work in Louisiana was finished.

His mind swung back to the scene at the dock, the sight of

the madman who had held Glory's life in his hands. Glory . . . Why hadn't she turned up in his sexy in-flight reverie? The jet landed before he could decide. After disembarking, he hopped into a rental and by early afternoon reached his destination.

Leo had called ahead to alert the sheriff he'd be arriving, and wanted to speak with him regarding an urgent matter: Who...Why?

When he pulled up in front of the office, he noted the group of men congregating on the sidewalk facing the redwood building. In casual dress, they appeared enrapt in conversation. Leo and his rental stuck out like a creampuff Cadillac in a junkyard. No sooner did he cut the engine, a tall man broke free and strode to the car, poking his head through the passenger window, displaying a blend of confusion and annoyance.

Over sweating bottles of soda dispensed from an outdoor vending machine, the sheriff introduced himself as Boulard, quizzed Leo about his flight, then abruptly altered his attitude. "What's your business in Lutcher?"

Leo's reply was as blunt. "What do you know about the Norton's?"

Back to the sun, Boulard squinted. "Not much. People 'round here keep a mind on their own affairs." He lifted his bulky frame from the bench they shared, pulled at the neck of his navy T-shirt, then raised the brim of the All Stars baseball cap that had been hiding his brows. "All I can tell you is . . . they don't live here anymore."

Leo shot up from the bench and caught up to the man who walked toward one of the aging structures that helped shape the town. "Someone must know something. People don't just drop out of sight." On the seventy-eight degree autumn day, perspiration clung to Leo's face, mixing with aftershave, dripping like slime to coat his neck."Christ. I feel like I'm wrapped in plastic," he grunted, swiping a hand across his forehead as he confronted the sheriff.

Boulard's eyes swept Leo from head to toe. It was the first time the man showed a full set of buff colored teeth. "A T-shirt would've worked better than the jacket and tie you're wearing."

Leo smirked. "Guess I expected an official meeting."

With his big hands stuffed into the pockets of baggy jeans, Boulard frowned. "This is bayou country. Folks disappear all the time." A burgeoning smile didn't seem to fit his demeanor. When Leo didn't return it, Boulard's voice deepened. "The woman stopped seeing doc. He figured her heart condition finally took her. Other than that — well, that kid of hers was always kind of an oddball. So nobody bothered, I guess."

"I'd like to see their house." Leo removed his jacked, slung it over a shoulder and loosened his tie.

"I can bring you out there, but I've got a full schedule this afternoon. I can't hang around."

Leo nodded, wondering what kind of business a sheriff would be conducting while dressed for a baseball game.

The rental car followed the plume of dust trailing Boulard's pickup as they sailed over gravel and dirt. Boulard drove with his left arm hanging out of the truck's window, rhythmically tapping the door with his palm, occasionally making hand signals as they traveled, drawing Leo's attention to various landmarks. Then the pickup slowed and his arm extended, flagging to a dead end road where they parked their vehicles and disembarked.

"The house burned down. So there's not much to see but a foundation and some charred timber," Boulard explained as they hiked through a forested area to where trees and shrubs had been cleared, but now encroached upon the ruins.

"When?" Leo swatted at gnats.

"Few months ago." Boulard shrugged.

"How'd that happen if no one was living there?" Leo attempted to pin Boulard's wandering gaze.

"Gas leak maybe." Boulard ground the cigarette he'd been smoking into the dirt, then slid his boot aside and aimed a mouthful of frothy saliva at the ash.

Leo's lips tightened. "More like arson, wouldn't you think?"

Boulard's broad shoulders and capped head synchronized another shrug.

Before leaving Baltimore, Leo had done an Internet search

of the area which proved to be close to what he expected. So was Boulard. Leo knew extracting information from him would be as likely as a gust of arctic air finding its way across his overheated body.

"The mother's grave's by the backswamp."

Leo stared.

"Over there . . . by the creek." Boulard pointed, leaning heavily against the flaking trunk of a cypress.

"Not in the local cemetery?" Leo's eyes crawled over the pile of charred logs the sheriff had referred to as a foundation. A rancid odor still hung in the air. Angling his head, Leo squinted through dense foliage, focusing on a shallow bed of water in the distance.

Boulard barked out, "I wouldn't. . ." He shook his head slowly, his demeanor jerking Leo off the path. "You may run into a Cottomouth, or the likes. Probably nothing left out there but pounded dirt, anyway. Never was a headstone."

Boulard's warning caught Leo mid stride. He challenged with a stare more aggressive than the sheriff's, about to ask why someone would be buried near a swamp . . .without even so much as a grave marker. Deciding Boulard's answer would have been as generic as his attitude, he let it go. If there was nothing to view but a mound of dirt, what would be the point? Boulard more than likely knew a hell of a lot more than he was letting on. Things Leo would have to guess at. Maybe make his hair curl.

In silence, the two men made their way back to their vehicles, with Leo taking in every inch of the place where the killer had been born, had lived, had murdered. At the thought of sharing the same path Norton must have taken thousands of times, a chill swept the sweat on Leo's back. He wondered if Norton had brought any of his victims to this place. Had he played here as a child? Was he ever human? Was Leo stepping on someone's grave? Boulard's voice shattered the images crowding Leo's overactive mind.

"That lab is where it all started." The words sprang from the sheriff's lips. When his eyes widened, his mouth clamped shut.

Leo cocked his head. "Where *what* all started?"

Boulard hesitated, raised his palms then swatted moss from the rear of his jeans. "The first woman gone missing."

"And you withheld this information . . .why?" Leo crossed his arms, sank back against the fender of his rental car, refusing to release Boulard's eyes. "Come on, man. You've got to give me more than this." Leo wondered why no one had clued him in on these explosive facts. "The federal investigators . . . Do they . . ."

Shaking his head, Boulard drew a breath. "You're the first one to even come out here. We're like the town the law forgot. Most murders around these parts are investigated from inside an office. Know what I mean?"

Leo nodded. "This meeting never happened . . . Go on."

"A look of relief gripped Boulard's face. "Traci Bell worked at the lab. Went missin' bout a year ago. Never did find her. Or a body. But we figure she could be linked to the other two across town. The ones that turned up around the same time she dropped outta sight."

"There were more than the two reported in Shreveport?" His story was getting better and better. Or worse, depending upon how you digested it. And Leo was not digesting it well. He ran a hand over the back of his neck, rubbing off humidity, and the deepening of concern. He'd come here for closure, not to unearth more pieces obviously missing from the puzzle he thought he'd solved on a moonlit Baltimore dock.

"Yep. Far as I know, there were three down here. We recovered the remains of two. Figured Ms. Bell as a third, even though we never found her. No leads either." Eyes narrowing, Boulard lit another cigarette and took a long drag. "We figured it to be a drifter, you know? What's gone stays gone. Like I said, this is bayou country."

"The two victims . . . Did you see the bodies?"

"Yep. Throats slit — clean through with the same razor sharp . . . whatever. And before you even ask, roses and notes."

Leo shook his head, sucked in a breath, blew out exasperation. "Where's the lab?"

"Not far from where we're standing. They're still running experiments and treating folks."

"What sort of experiments?" Laboratory. Freaky looking serial killer. Chemical soaked body tissue. A bizarre picture began to develop. Leo dragged a hand over his head. His hair was soaked. The stagnant air had the effects of a sauna, and this new information only added to his discomfort. He massaged a temple. He needed scotch, but would settle for aspirin.

"Don't know exactly. But what comes outta that place just don't seem normal. Some in town want it closed down. This guy included." The sheriff thumbed his chest. "Multiple, unsolved homicides in a town this size ain't exactly what I'm after. Upcoming retirement's a better option." His laugh was forced. "But when you're dealing with a medical community with fat backing coming from the good Lord knows where, well, you know what I mean?"

"Tell me about it." Leo fished the car keys from his pocket. "Should I follow you?"

"Nope. I'm heading back to town. But if you take that road over there, leads you to a bridge. Cross it. Stay on the road, don't take the fork. You can't miss the place."

"I appreciate your help, Sheriff. And I'll keep you informed."

Boulard closed the space between them, reaching for Leo's outstretched hand. The meeting had ended. Leo checked his wristwatch. He had a lot to do. More than he'd expected when he arrived. He stripped off his button down shirt, balled it up and threw it on the back seat. Reduced to undershirt and trousers, he slid behind the wheel.

By the time Leo buckled his seatbelt, Boulard's pickup had pulled onto the road. Before driving off, the sheriff tossed him a two finger salute. Through the open window, Leo heard a blast of country music, watched Boulard's moving mouth, his bopping head. He was a sight that lightened the moment, but Leo couldn't laugh.

Following Boulard's directions, Leo easily found the bridge. His rental crossed the solid span of steel construction; relatively new, it definitely didn't fit the area. Traveling the same route the killer's vehicle had traveled not long ago was disturbing, angering.

Leo angled his head toward the window, catching the warm breeze generated only by the car's movement. His lungs burned. His tearless eyes stung. And his imagination soared into overdrive. He was now walking in a killer's footsteps, struggling with the unsettling sensation of passing through the shadow of death. Trying to get inside the head of the dead thing. What had happened to the man? What created the monster? What was the motive for senseless killing? He'd never be able to describe this feeling to anyone. Not even Ben. There was something deep in his gut that gnawed. Pain. Fury. Helplessness? He shook it off.

Although he had never been here before, Leo felt a wave of déjà vu. Surrounded by wetland, trees appearing like their branches had been hacked off with a chainsaw, he questioned why anyone would build *anything,* no less a medical facility, in such a desolate area. There seemed to be water everywhere. Stagnant. Muddy. More roadside marsh. More broken trees. Ruts cut deeply into the road, then suddenly the pavement smoothed. The ride softened, the car now sailing to its destination.

Finally a clearing — and the lab — a structure resembling an asylum. Strange, like something from another era. A soulless institution where people were taken against their will, lobotomized, never heard from again. The only things missing: charcoal skies, claps of thunder, claws of lightning — and goons in white uniforms. Uncertain of what he was about to encounter, the blood drained from Leo's limbs, as it had the night he watched the killer drive himself into the bay.

Ben knew Leo was in Louisiana, but not the exact location. So the fleeting thought of Baltimore was of little comfort to Leo, whose body perspired profusely — not merely from the weather. Could he trust Boulard? Once he opened up, details gushed like a downpour through a storm drain. The sheriff had been generous with information. Maybe too generous. Why? Had he sent him here to disappear? Like the unfortunate lab worker?

Leo parked at the side of the road, locked the car, then

cautiously made his way to the building. There were no concrete walkways. Just pebbled paths and dirt. For as far as he could see, all to meet the human eye was patchy scrub grass, swamps of leafless trees, muddy creeks, and dirt. And he was smothering . . . smothering in Louisiana humidity, and in mind-blowing mystery.

As he climbed the steps leading to the lab's entrance, Leo dialed Ben's cell, but the only reply was his voicemail. "Hey, Ben. I'm down here. Spoke to the sheriff. About to walk into this laboratory, or whatever. Creepy place. Fill you in later." He paused, but did not disconnect. "Ben. I'm in a small town outside of Baton Rouge . . ." The voicemail bleeped. End of message.

The building could have passed for a modest courthouse, with evidence of cinder block construction visible beneath a coat of white paint. The front columns were four-by-four posts that secured a roof overhang to the wooden floor of a wide front porch on which Leo's feet were firmly planted.

For a moment he hesitated, then drew a long breath. His palm closed around the brass handle, fingers about to pull, when a force shoved him aside. The door swung open and two hooded figures emerged. Appearing almost identical, they wore dark sweatshirts and loose fitting pants. Even through the clothing it was obvious they were slight of build.

Their sallow complexions registered next. Unique features protected by dark, large framed sunglasses, they bore a striking resemblance to something all too familiar. Leo's mouth hung open as they brushed past.

"Christ," he mumbled. "It couldn't be. . ." His foot rested just above the threshold when a third figure bounded through the doorway, almost knocking him off his feet. *Slight, but powerful as hell. . .* A trail of interior air carried a strong scent of antiseptic. Leo caught a whiff, and then a closer look as the figure paused beside him.

His hood hung loose around his neck, exposing a glistening scalp, hairless, smooth as a newborn. Black plastic frames wrapped around both ears, but the sunglass lenses rested on the flat of his forehead. His movements were fluid, and before departing, his head snapped a startling ninety degrees.

Inches from Leo, he stared with green, luminous eyes, potent against his pale skin, then flipped down the sunglasses. Taking the steps two at a time, he met the others who waited before the open door of a white van. Before climbing in he spun, smiling sardonically. It was a smile that seemed to come straight from the lips of Satan himself.

January Valentine

you ripped me to shreds
too wicked for hell
some souls stay dead
but others they dwell

EPILOGUE

Leo paced before the laboratory entrance until shadows crossed the columns, fell to the floor. The importance of this trip had never been in question, but now that Leo knew Norton's background, the closure he sought *was*.

Daylight was fading, along with optimism. What the hell are they doing in there? Come on, Gibraldi. Open the fucking door . . .

UNIVERSAL ABNORMALITY

spit into this world
i'm fumbling for theory

hurled into panic
i don't wanna know
who i don't wanna be

eyes of all the moons
attacking on me
i'm battling your stars
slicing scars into my destiny

struggling for oxygen
breathing my own energy
fields of passion barren
i gasp for the last drop of me

paying the price
for your mistakes
what were you thinking
when you brought me to this place?

i'm the worst for them to see
nature never planned on me

Troy Norton

The Beginning

From the day he left his mother's womb, Troy Norton was damned to be different. Underweight and frail, he needed a strong name. Troy was a strong name. Troy, the destroyer of sins. Troy, the destroyer. And if the name, Troy, in any form was good enough to be mentioned in the Good Book, then it was a good enough name to call her one and only son.

"Troy, you're nothin' but a bag of bones," his mother would lament, and force him to eat until his stomach felt it would bust wide open. When she couldn't keep the meat on his bones that way, she decided to pour nutrition into him with concocted tonics, which meant throwing anything she considered healthy into a jar, chopping it, juicing it, and forcing it down her son's throat.

His features were what his mother considered comely, but comely features were useless when a corpse-like frame was the first thing people saw when they set eyes on him.

As a young boy, Troy began terrorizing the woodlands, splashing in streams, hunting in creeks, where any harmless creature fell victim to beheading. And as if pulling wings from insects wasn't enough, he'd rip barbels off squirming catfish.

One day, metamorphosis began. Years of being an outsider came to a head and burst like excruciating blisters beneath his different skin. Troy began growing a set of balls that would soon be so big they'd drag on the ground. That's when his mind stopped developing and his body started, just in time to meet the woman who would change his life forever.

Traci Bell was a Texas cowgirl who migrated to Louisiana to work in a privately funded medical research laboratory. Cutting edge and secretive, the facility was tucked behind a marsh filled with gnarled trees and hungry alligators.

The lab wasn't more than fifteen miles from where Troy and his mother shared a dilapidated shack near a river that coursed into rock congested rapids on its way to merge with the Mississippi. All Troy and his mother needed to do was to climb into their vehicle with beefy tires, cross a wooden bridge, and follow the dusty roads delivering them into the hands of the miracle that was going to cure Troy of his lifelong affliction of *undersized and pasty white.* That's when, instead of skinning rats, Troy decided to became one. A lab rat.

Traci Bell was a tall, buxom brunette who wore tons of makeup and low-cut shirts advertising cleavage, clunky jewelry, and a butterfly tattoo that stretched across her chest, wings fluttering when her breasts bounced. As his case coordinator, she took Troy under her wing. She had a lot of bad habits she liked to share, one in particular, sleeping around with just about any guy, any place, any time.

During his visits to the lab, Troy would watch Traci jiggle and strut, swinging her hips, snapping her gum, disappearing into research rooms with men, emerging later with a smile as she straightened her clothes, finger-fluffed her tresses. He figured her to be part of a test panel like his, where they drew vials of blood, prodded, and charted results that were compiled and fed into a classified database.

Troy couldn't pronounce his diagnosis, but Traci called it "albino-like". She said his eyes soaked up every pigment they shot into his body. "I can't tell if you're looking at me, or through me, Troy Norton," she would say. "You're eyes are getting so black, you're starting to scare me."

But Troy didn't care about his beady black eyes. At least some part of him had color. And besides, now they were actually paying him money. Money he could use to take Traci on a date. His ego expanded. The lab wanted him, and soon Traci would too.

Attempting to make him more presentable, Traci covered his colorless hair with dye. But his lids were still loose and bare, and with midnight hair and brows, he looked like a mannequin that somehow sprang to life.

Traci was not happy with Troy's transformation. She said he looked like the devil himself. "I'm waiting for you to grow horns and a pointed tail." She'd slap a hand over her mouth, infuriating him.

Still, she'd let him peek through the closet door to watch her perform. At first, Troy was shocked. He'd never seen a woman naked before, and his eyes popped when he saw what certain body parts could do. Things like their tongues, lips, hands, and private parts could do a lot more interesting things than he'd ever done with his. He wondered if she'd teach him how to do those things? If it looked so good, would it feel so good?

Traci was most obliging. One night, after everyone else had gone, she led him into a room and hopped onto a table. "Come here, you misfit." Her smile was sly. "Did I ever tell you zombies turn me on?"

"I think I love you, Traci Bell," he said when he touched her breast. "And I got you a present."

"Where's my present?" she asked the minute they finished doing clumsy things that Troy thought were amazing.

He handed her a long-stemmed red rose he'd stolen from a florist van.

Traci looked at the rose and laughed. "You call this a present?" She hopped down from the table, slipping into her short, tight skirt, western shirt and cowgirl boots.

A lump of disappointment clogged Troy's throat. "Someday

I'm gonna get you a diamond. A diamond as pretty as you, Traci Bell." He pulled his shirt over his head and tugged on his pants, covering his cadaverous ribcage and hipbones.

"I doubt that, Troy Norton. You're never gonna be nothing but a freak who'll never afford diamonds." The words had barely sprung from her lips when Traci watched his face begin to twitch. "What's wrong with you?" Her voice lost its courage.

"Maybe it's them shots, or maybe it's what you done to me on that table," Troy said. "But whatever it is, I feel —"

"You feel what?" she asked, backing away.

"I feel like I want you to marry me."

Traci laughed. "That'll never happen. Not in your sweet dreams, darlin'. After tonight, you'll never see me again. I'm done working in this shithole. I've had it with this job, and misfits like you. There ain't nothin gonna help you Troy Norton, so you might as well just walk your floured ass out that door and never come back, the same as I plan on doing right now."

As his eyes began to bulge, Troy's body started jerking. Traci withdrew even further into a corner of the room. Like a heat seeking missile, he zeroed in on her. The strength of his arms had increased tenfold. And when he wrapped her with his fishbone frame, she was locked in a vice.

His body shouting, *get back onto that table with her*, Troy aimed his mouth for Traci's.

Her lips spewing profanity, along with saliva, Traci wiggled and squirmed, trying to escape the invincible misfit, biting his mouth so hard it bled.

Troy's eyes flared. His breathing became uncontrollable, so did the fingers of his strong hands that twined around Traci's neck. The more she screamed, the harder he squeezed until she gagged, and then her eyes bulged as much as his.

Troy choked every ounce of bubbling life out of her, shoved the rose down her gaping throat, then dragged her body to the swamp. To the alligators.

Something inside Troy changed that night. Instead of weak, he felt powerful. Powerful felt good. Before walking away from

Traci's sinking body, he said, "Sweet Dreams Darlin'."

That night, Troy Norton became a man, an evil man. Traci Bell was his first. But other bodies would pile up. That night in the lab, and in a Louisiana swamp, a killer had been born.

On his way to the vehicle, he let out a howl of delight, then pounded his chest like an ape. He had controlled the fate of another. Traci's death was of no consequence. She had made it clear, parting was inevitable. So was death. His papa was dead. Now Traci was dead. Death was inevitable.

Troy was the god he had never believed in. He had controlled the inevitable. He looked at his hands, the hands that ended Traci's life. They looked the same, with long, boney fingers, but they felt different, as different as Troy Norton viewed the world, the world he now held in his hands. He felt no remorse.

Midnight approached as he stumbled home to the shack where his mother stood in the kitchen, looking angrier than he'd ever witnessed.

"Where have you been?" she shrieked, shoving him against the wall so hard his nose began to bleed.

Troy tasted the blood that poured down his throat easier than any tonic his mother had ever brewed. He swiped the warm liquid from his face, studied it, then rubbed a wet glob on his arm. Color. For a moment, he was amazed because his body had actually produced a vibrant shade of red.

"Tell me," his mother screamed. "Were you with that tramp at the lab? What were you doing Troy Norton? Did you sin with her?" She beat his face with her fists. More blood . . .

With a swat of his hand, Troy flung her across the room.

He didn't care much that he'd killed his own mother, and buried her in a place near the river, where people with no money for proper funerals were laid to rest.

Troy stole a rose from the local cemetery, stabbed it into the unsettled soil on top of his mother's shallow grave and chanted, "Sweet Dreams Mama." If he had a pencil and paper, he would have left a note as a marker.

Troy Norton had a tormented soul, until the night he lost it.

For the next six months he remained in that shack, scavenging for food, sleeping away days at a time until he forgot who he was, who he had been, or what he had done, and as an animal, relied upon instinct alone.

There were times he felt sick with nauseating head pain, aching bones, fevers. Rashes patched his chalky skin. He had passed the primary state of syphilis he'd contracted from Traci, and was suffering through the secondary.

Troy fantasized about blood, death, and taking lives. The first two deaths were acts of passion, unplanned passion. The others would be acts of pleasure, plotted pleasure.

Pleasure of a serial killer.

AUTHOR BIO

January Valentine is the pen name of Victoria Valentine, New York writer and Indie Book Publisher.

Sweet Dreams is the second book in her series of Dream Books.

Contemporary erotic romance, *Love Dreams,* is available in print and paperback on Amazon, and other booksellers. Also available in other formats including Kindle, Nook, Apple Ibook,

Bad Dreams, which completes the series, is a thriller/horror, tentatively scheduled for 2013.

Victoria also writes poetry, and has published a collection entitled: Desert Noon. She's published a children's full color story book: The Cutest Little Duckie. A horror anthology of stories accented with poetry, and has a lot of irons on the fire.

She's currently working on a contemporary romance for young adults.

Facebook: http://www.facebook.com/VictoriaValentineBooks
Twitter: https://twitter.com/VictoriaSkyline
Amazon Author pages: amazon.com/author/victoriavalentine
amazon.com/author/januaryvalentine
Websites: www.januaryvalentine.com www.victoriavalentine.net
Books: www.waterforestpressbooks.com

January Valentine

Song lyrics appearing in this book were written by:
Victoria Valentine, *The Next Life (2002) Eyes of Ash CD*

Eyes Of Ash
People Like Us
Make Me Fine
You Said

Unpublished Titles:

Universal Abnormality
Critical Condition
Silent Dreamer
Mess
Blow Me Off
Comatose
Coming Down From You

ACKNOWLEDGEMENTS

As always, I owe so much to my family and friends who support me every step of the way. Thank you isn't enough.

Sil, Phae, Tom: For hours of listening, reading chapters, and for your belief in me as a writer. What can I say?

Mucho grande love and a gazillion thank you's to my beautiful daughter, Phaedra, who catches all of my mistakes. Without her, this book wouldn't have made it to print.

Ditto to my other beautiful daughter, Cindy, who urged me to start writing many years ago. Who could forget *The Last Resort* . . . Thanks, Cin, for everything.

To first readers of *Sweet Dreams*, Jill Lapin-Zell, Kailyn Terlato, Micki Peluso, Susan Sabia, and Lynda Frazier. You bring with you a blessed sense of security and the encouragement every writer needs. I cannot thank you enough.

A special shout out to Lynda, (E.R. Nurse) for your techical assistance and medical description.

Amanda R. Tucker, friend and cover artist for many of my projects. Thank you for the fantastic cover of *Sweet Dreams*.

jacob erin-cilberto (Fog), poet and great friend. You're always here to offer help, support, and an ear. It means a lot to me.

For my parents, Marian and Bill. You guys are with every one of us, every day, in thought, heart, and reminiscence. I know you would be my biggest fans if you were here.

For Polo Pony: wuff wuff.